The Tomorrow Project

Published in 2020 by Lisa Jade via lulu.com
Copyright © Lisa Jade, 2020

All rights reserved
No part of this publication may be reproduced, stored digitally, or transmitted in any form without prior permission of the copyright owner.

This is a work of fiction. All characters, locations and events portrayed in this novel are products of the author's imagination.
www.lisajade.net

∞

One

    Shane's arms are so warm.
    We embrace in a darkened alleyway, hidden from prying eyes. It's raining tonight, making the tarmac looks slick and shiny around us. The puddles reflect the glow of the streetlamps, and the headlights of the ugly yellow pickup I drove here.
    His lips find mine, and my heart flutters happily.
    And then he pulls back, tilting my chin so he can look me in the eye. In the dim light, I see the finer details of his face – the thin scar running across one cheek, the gap shaved in one eyebrow. Even the grey-brown shade of his eyes, matching the stubble on his head. It strikes me as odd, even now, that someone like him might take an interest in me.
    "Why'd you stop?" I ask, ignoring the puff of warm air around my mouth. It's cold. We can't be spotted together, so we meet at night. Usually in some dark, dirty corner of Amare. Shane fires me a small smile.
    "Reya."
    I smile at the sound of my name.
    "Yeah?"
    "We've been together a while, right?"
    "About two months."

"Exactly," he smirks, "I've been thinking... I really like you. I think it's time we take this to the next level."

Heat fills my cheeks and I pull away, but his hand tightens around my waist. His touch is warm and comforting, so I don't push him off. I bite my lip.

"The next level, huh?"

"I was thinking we could, I don't know, make this official."

"Official?"

He lets out a small laugh, and I sink back into his embrace. I spread my fingers across his chest, impressed by the firmness. Shane could pass for a goddamn supermodel. He could be successful if he wanted to – if he could just stay out of jail long enough.

"You know," he says, "we could do more 'couple' stuff. Instead of always having to meet up in an alleyway like this."

My heart leaps.

"You mean like a trip? I don't know how I'd manage it – I'd have to go MIA for a while, but the Project would get over it eventually. Maybe we could go to the beach. I've always wanted to see the ocean!"

Shane presses a finger to my lips.

"Woah, slow down. Let's start smaller."

"Smaller?"

"Yeah. How about tomorrow, you come meet my parents?"

I stare.

"You want me to meet your parents? Are you crazy?"

"Why not?"

"In case you've forgotten, I'm not exactly girlfriend material. Being an artificial human means I have no rights. I'm not legally human. I can't get married. I can't have kids. Not to mention the whole 'freak of nature' aspect. Once they realise who I am..."

"It's none of their business who you are," he growls, "I'm dating you, not them. So?"

I take a deep breath. Meeting the parents - now that's a scary thought. I was made on a computer and raised by scientists, so I never had parents of my own. I'm not sure I would even know how to interact with them. And if they're part of this 'Mortalist' movement that's been targeting us, I could be stepping into a minefield. But then Shane's smile widens, and my chest aches.

"Okay. I'll meet them."

"Fantastic," he says, "and then you can introduce me to your family."

I pause.

"Oh."

"What? Is it my record? I can explain why I didn't deserve to end up in cuffs..."

"No, no. It's not that."

I stare at him for a long moment, enjoying the sensation of his arms around me. It's been fun, these past few weeks – a form of escapism, I suppose. Like playing house. I pull away.

"Reya?"

"I'm not going to introduce you to the Project."

Hurt crosses his face.

"Why not? It's only fair."

"No, it's not. You know me better than most. I can't cross that line."

"I don't get it," he shrugs, "I'm not a Mortalist, you know. I'm not going to attack the Project for creating you. If I wanted to hurt you, I'd have done it weeks ago. Doesn't that stand for anything?"

I step away.

"Look, if the Project Head even knew you existed, I'd be looking at house arrest. I'm not really supposed to leave Lockless House without permission, much less have relationships. If they found out about us, we'd probably never see each other again."

"I could convince them."

"No," I say, "you couldn't. Believe me, I've been barking up that tree for years. They don't care what I say, so they won't listen if we tell them you're not dangerous."

"I'm not just some random person, though. I thought we were getting serious."

"We are! We just can't get involved with the Project. Besides, you know how I feel about them. They barely put up with me as it is. I don't want to stir the pot."

Shane runs a hand over his head.

"This isn't fair. You know that, right?"

"Why would you want to meet them, anyway?" I snap, "they're just a bunch of bio-geneticists, doctors, psychologists... half of the time I don't understand what they're talking about, and I live with them. You won't like them."

"What about your sister? What about Alya?"

My heart sinks.

5

"What about her?"

"Isn't she supposed to be amazing?"

Shane's eyes light up with intrigue as he speaks, shifting towards me. I back off as quickly as I can, suddenly on edge. He doesn't notice my discomfort.

"Is it true that she can heal from any injury?" he asks, "and even survive without food, water, and air? I heard a theory that she could live forever."

"I don't know about all that."

"But you're her prototype, right? Didn't they make you as the genetic baseline for her and then clone your DNA? Come on, you know more than you're letting on, so just tell me!"

My heart races. I see madness in his eyes now; the same madness that always affects people who think about my sister. It's instinctive, I think – humans are so predisposed to fear death that we'll cling to the first mention of immortality.

I look Shane up and down, silently weighing him up.

"Shane, I don't have any power in the Project. Yeah, I live there, but that's just because I don't have anywhere else to go. Even if I took you to Lockless House, they wouldn't let you in. I don't have the authority to take you."

"Don't lie to me!" he yells. His voice bounces off the walls of the alley, and I freeze. This is a sudden departure from the affectionate man I've come to know. I jump away, my gaze flitting from him to the car. The keys are already inside, the engine still on to provide some light. All I need to do is outrun him.

It's not that I can't take him, if things turn violent. I can. But then I think about the shame on Rene's face if the media reports another 'attack', and opt to try diplomacy.

"I'm not lying to you."

"Yes, you are! I swear to god, this has been such a waste of time!"

I pause.

"What?"

"You think I didn't recognise you straight away? I was pretty sure I could get close to Alya if I used you. I've done everything you asked me to do. I pretended to be into you, sacrificed time I could have spent doing something worthwhile just to hang out with you. I gave you everything you wanted, and all I'm asking for in return is to meet her!"

Of course. Nobody ever wants me, do they? It's always about Alya. Shane moves closer, still ranting at the top of his lungs, and I notice that his hands have curled into fists.

"Listen," I tell him, "I'm nothing to the Project. If you'd asked me weeks ago, I'd have told you that. I'm not trying to deceive you."

"Stop lying!"

He roars the last word, sending a shiver of fear through me. Before he can bear down on me again, I duck under his outstretched arm and race towards the car.

"Oh no you don't!"

A hand grabs my shoulder, yanking me back. My sneakers slip on the wet tarmac and I tumble over, colliding hard with a trash can. Pain jolts up my spine.

"Ow!"

For a split second I see Shane standing over me, his eyes wild with rage, and then something strikes my face. The world turns white for a moment, and when it snaps back I'm slumped in the trash pile, my left eye throbbing.

"You should have just done what I told you, Reya!" Shane bellows. He spits as he speaks, and all the charm and charisma I've seen from him drains away. He's not the same smooth talker who convinced me to take a walk with him eight weeks ago. Now he's just a maniac like all the others, determined to do something, anything, to get close to Alya.

I bolt upright and he grabs at me, but this time I twist and drive my fist into his nose, which breaks with an audible crack. Blood spurts from his face and he falls back with an agonised cry. I take advantage of the opportunity and run, racing around the pickup and jumping into the driver's seat.

Something thuds at the back of the car – Shane, still chasing me. Crimson stains cover the front of his shirt, but he barely seems to notice. He smacks the car and screams something unintelligible.

The rear window shatters, and for a moment I hear nothing but Shane's barely-sane cries. I veer into the road and speed out into the city.

The moment I'm away from him, a terrible silence falls over me. Amare is quiet at night, so for a moment I'm left only with the sound of my own ragged breathing. I glance back at the shattered window and grimace. Sandra will be furious. It's not every day she lets me borrow her car.

I should have known this would happen. It always does. Any time I let someone get close, it ends the same way. Their interest turns out to have been false, and once I reveal that I can't help them get close to Alya or the Project, things turn nasty. I've lost count of how many false friends I've lost this way. Shane's the first to ever take it this far, though.

I tighten my grip on the wheel.

I pull up outside Lockless House and dump the pickup next to Rene's flashy red Porsche. I apply the handbrake, then delve into the passenger side footwell, plucking out a sizeable brick. So *that's* what Shane threw at the car. He really was trying to hurt me. I toss the brick aside as I step out, hoping nobody puts two and two together.

Lockless House is a vast white and silver building, shaped like a cube with a vast glass dome on top. It's protected by a large yard and chain-link fence lined with barbed wire. I step up to the security gate and scan my hand on a nearby panel. It emits a low beep, much to my relief. One of these days, I'll annoy Rene so much that he removes my security access altogether.

As the front door clicks open, I find myself wondering for the millionth time why we call it Lockless House. There's nowhere else in Amare with security this strict. Perhaps it's an intentional misnomer. Maybe it's meant to make the Project seem more accessible. Or maybe it was named long before the Project showed up.

The entrance hall is huge, leading off into eleven different, smaller laboratories. There's a glossy white floor to match the glossy white walls, and everything has been scrubbed to within an inch of its life. There's a strong scent of disinfectant in the air. I step inside and hear the door lock behind me. The heavy thud is another not-so-subtle reminder of how thoroughly entrapped I am in this place. I tug Sandra's keys from my pocket and step through the archway to my left.

This is the night lab, where the staff do shifts in the darkness. Soft purple lights fill the room, emitted from the underside of cabinets. In the middle of the room, tapping frantically at one of the small consoles, sits a plump, middle-aged woman with umber skin and a mass of dark curls that strain against her tight bun. She looks up as I enter, adjusting her white coat and pulling her thick-rimmed glasses from her head. She crams them onto her face and looks at me.

"You're back early."

I fire a weak smile her way and toss the keys to her.

"Yeah. I'm afraid the car took a bit of damage."

Her face falls.

"Are you kidding me with this, Reya? Again?"

"It's just the back window," I say, "should be a quick fix."

She looks me up and down and frowns. I look away, knowing how bad I must look. My hair is matted around my face and there's something revolting smeared across my jeans, no doubt from rolling around in a pile of trash. I take a deep breath. I stink, too. Sandra eyes me carefully.

"I thought you were going out to see a friend," she says quietly.

"I won't be seeing them again."

She stares at me for a long moment, then sighs and turns back to her computer. She pulls her glasses off and replaces them firmly on her head.

"For crying out loud. This is why Rene doesn't like you going out there. You need to stop antagonising people. Not everyone is out to get you."

I open my mouth to protest, but she pushes on.

"Every time you get into a scrap, the Project risks losing reputation and Sponsors. Lose too many investors, and we'll all be homeless. So you need to stop sneaking out, or learn a little diplomacy when dealing with the public."

Every part of me wants to shoot down her accusations, but I bite back on the words. It's not a good time to have this argument. She let me borrow her car. That's enough. It's not like I'll be needing it again, anyway.

I slink from the room, eager to get out of her sight. This isn't too bad as long as she doesn't tell Rene. As far as fulfilling his role as Project Head goes, he's exceptionally adept – but when it comes time to deal with me, not so much. I've found it's easier to avoid him entirely, if I can. Even the most basic conversations turn into arguments these days.

I head up the metal stairs to my room, which is situated next to Alya's. The Dome used to be one large room before Alya was made, and it was split down the middle. I slip inside, taking care to shut the door properly. There's no concept of privacy here; people barge into my room without a second thought. More than once I've considered slapping a chain lock on the door, but that's not a fight I'm willing to start.

My room is a perfect semi-circle, with the circular wall made of inches-thick glass. Our rooms are at the very top of the Dome, above the labs. From here, I have a brilliant sight of Amare sprawled out below us. For a moment, I'm pleased that the Project staff sleep on the floor below us. It provides a little distance from the labs, so my room is always pleasantly quiet.

Unfortunately, I can feel the presence in the room next to me. Alya should be sleeping now. They always make sure she gets her eight hours. Strange feelings well in my stomach, but I push them down.

I pull off my filthy clothing and stand in front of my cracked mirror, gingerly touching my face. There's nothing there yet, but I'm sure my eye will be bruised by morning.

I slump into bed. In the dim light of the city my room seems oddly desaturated, like I'm seeing in black and white. My gaze glides over the fluffy, decades-old rug in the middle of the room, and the pretty dresser I haven't sat at for years. It's the kind of room more suited to a teenage girl than a 24-year-old woman, but I spend as little time here as possible, so I don't particularly care.

I fall back onto the pillows and pull the sheets over my face. Most nights I'll sit up and look out over the city for a while, but I'm exhausted. What test are we doing tomorrow? Oxygen deprivation, I think. My *favourite*. Rene will probably yell at me if I'm tired for it. I push my face into the pillow, ignoring the way Shane's face flickers in my memory, and wait for sleep to come.

A sharp knock wakes me. I'm curled tightly into myself, the blankets still over my head, when I hear my bedroom door open. Light footsteps fill the room, quickly followed by an airy, sing-song voice.

"Good morning!"

Alya sounds happy today. This normally wouldn't be a problem but recently, whenever Alya is happy it turns out to mean something bad for me. She yanks my blanket away and I bolt upright, fixing her with a stern look.

I don't think anyone would doubt that we're related. She's only 17, but despite our age difference it's like looking into a mirror. We share the same pale skin and blue-black hair, though hers is shoulder-length and usually styled into delicate curls. I look her up and down. So much is the same – we're both on the slimmer side, though she lacks my muscle tone. Other than that, she's practically a carbon copy of me, even down to her stormy grey eyes.

Today, she wears a baggy jumper and denim shorts. Her hair is tied in two little bunches on her head, giving her the appearance of someone considerably younger. Makes sense. The Project often say we're both immature for our ages, given our sheltered upbringings.

Alya fixes me with a cheeky smile, and her face fills with colour. A healthy glow, Rene would call it.

"What the hell do you want?" I ask, suddenly aware that I'm barely clothed and still stink like a trash pile. She stares at me for a long moment, her expression odd, then shrugs.

"It's gone six. We should head down to the lab."

"You know, most teenagers sleep in."

"I'm always up with the sun," she beams.

I roll my eyes. Alya doesn't really need sleep, so it's unusual for her to stay in bed longer than the eight hours Rene mandates. I yawn. Unfortunately, not all of us are so lucky. I snatch my blanket back and pull it up to my chin. She frowns.

"Oh, come on. The sooner we do today's tests, the sooner we can have fun instead."

Fun. That's something else we differ on. While my idea of fun is driving through Amare or drinking with friends, she'd rather pay social visits to Project Sponsors. I've always hated watching her coo and giggle over everything she's told by the over-stuffed businessmen who come to visit.

"I need to shower first," I tell her.

"Fine. I'm going to go get breakfast, is that okay?"

"Do whatever you want."

"Alright."

She dances from the room and I watch after her. As always, I'm impressed and slightly peeved by her boundless energy. I returned to Lockless House at two in the morning, and I'm exhausted.

After my shower I step into my room, rubbing vigorously at my hair. It's long enough to hit my waist now, a look emphasised by how poker straight it is. That's never been a conscious decision on my part - more the inconvenience of getting it regularly cut.

I pluck last night's clothes from the floor and grimace. Shame. These were my favourite jeans. They're one of the few clothing items I have that aren't branded with the Project's name and logo. I tug on a pair of black leggings and reach for my trusty – if unattractive – Project-branded sweatshirt.

I rub at my sore eye and wince. Right. No wonder Alya stared at me like that. A glance in the mirror confirms it; the entire socket is the colour of red wine. There's no way they won't notice.

Sandra is right, as much as I hate to admit it. Every time I get into a fight, the Project takes the brunt of the consequences. The work done in Lockless House is already pretty controversial – not many groups can say they've made an immortal human – so people jump on any excuse to attack us. I may not be their precious 'Tomorrow Girl', but I look like her and I'm still an artificial human. In many people's books, that's more than enough reason to hate me.

I sigh. I don't want to leave my room, but there's no point keeping them waiting.

I step into the main lab to see today's test is already set up. Two large glass domes take pride of place over two metal tables, each one wrapped with tubes to suck out the air. It's a simple enough test, one they do every fortnight – place both of us under a dome, remove the air, and monitor our reactions. Alya, of course, flies through tests that would kill any normal person. To her, this is an enjoyable little game. She likes the way it makes her chest feel, tight and strange. Being the mortal baseline is considerably less fun. It's not too terrible until about sixty seconds in, when I reach my limit. They usually stop before I pass out, but it's all round a pretty horrible experience.

Alya's already here, perched on the table and surrounded by the others. At last count, there were about members of staff at Lockless House. The Project remained secret for a long time before Alya's reveal, and the pool of those they trust is still very small. Sandra is nearby, still tapping away at a computer. I can feel her eyes on my back, judging my every movement. She's the resident psychologist, tasked with keeping mine and Alya's mental health in check. I wonder how much she gleaned from last night's conversation.

I glance around the room. Everyone is here today. Even the Security head, Jonah, who watches more out of interest than anything. And Rene, who stands beside Alya, clutching a clipboard to his chest.

Rene is the kind of man who was clearly picked on as a kid. Still a little scrawny and specky despite his forty-something years, he's a rather unassuming figure, but there's something about him that intimidates me. Like a bullied kid who reached their limit, and is liable to punch someone in the face without warning. He sees me and pointedly looks away.

Nobody acknowledges me. I tell myself that's normal, that they're busy with their work and there's no need to address me. But after all this time, I know there's more to it than that. Nobody *wants* to acknowledge me.

I slump down on the table next to Alya and wait for the test to start.

The others have explained the tests to me before, but I only half understand it.

I'm a mortal, artificial human, and she was based off my genetic outline. The difference is, she's far from human.

What will kill me, she can shrug off. Aside from that, we're genetically identical. In other words, two sisters – one immortal, one not. Years ago, someone decided that testing our durability simultaneously was a good idea, and we've been doing that ever since.

Resentment builds in my chest, but I swallow it down. There's no point dwelling on what might have been, had they built us a little differently. This is my lot in life.

A tall, broad-set man with a stern face steps over to me. Neil's the Project's medical doctor, responsible – laughingly – for ensuring we don't die during tests. He sticks a series of tiny sensors on my arm, then nods.

"Ready."

Ready. That's all he says. Neil's a man of few words as it is, but I suddenly realise that I don't remember the last time he spoke to me. Nevertheless I obey, ducking beneath the glass dome and crossing my ankles. I may hate this test, but I'm used to it. By now the motion is almost automatic; shoulders back, chin up, deep breaths. In through the nose and out through the mouth.

What was my personal record, again? Ninety seconds, I think. That's without any air at all, until my vision starts to falter. Luckily they stop when they pick up on any major respiratory distress, so realistically, the worst I'll feel is slight discomfort.

I look over at the other table, where Alya is already perched. Unlike me, she seems thoroughly excited at the prospect of another test. I can't say I blame her. If I could survive literal suffocation, I'd be excited too.

The glass dome lowers around me, and I feel myself tense. I've done this dozens of times, so I'm not exactly scared. But I still feel that basic, instinctive fear at being trapped in a small space. I can hear speech outside the glass but the words are somewhat muffled, like I'm pressing a pillow to my ears.

"Are we jumping straight to full removal again?"

Rene lets out a small grunt.

"There's no point messing around. Begin at the count of fifteen, and pull out all the air."

I shift, suddenly aware of the countdown. I fire a glance across the lab. Alya mirrors my sitting position perfectly, her hands in her lap and her head up. She watches the lab with her usual form of intrigue. I resist the urge to roll my eyes. I used to be like that, too. Growing up around here inspires a certain type of curiosity, and though I seem to have grown out of it, I can still see it in her.

"Ten."

Rene glances at his watch, then signals to Alya. My back tenses.

"Five."

Damn. Why am I so on edge?

"Two."

I take the deepest breath I can.

"Beginning extraction."

My chest tightens and I lower my head, allowing my hair to form a dark barrier around my face. It hardly matters; nobody's looking at me. They're probably tracking my life signs on the screens, but that's about it.

After a while, the dizziness becomes overwhelming. I raise a hand – my signal that I'm ready to stop. It's several seconds before I realise that nobody noticed.

My vision briefly dips and I lean forward, pressing my hand against the glass.

Finally, they notice. As the dome is pulled over my head, the world comes clear again. I'm slumped on the table, cradling my head in my hands. I gasp, guzzling air as though it were water.

Neil tilts my head back, ready to carry out the normal post-test check, but his face falls. I realise with a start that he's noticed my bruised eye.

"Oh, this is..."

"How did you...?"

"It's fine," I tell him.

"It is not," a stern voice interjects. My heart sinks.

Neil fires me a warning look, then steps aside as Rene approaches. He doesn't need to warn me; I already know I'm in trouble. Any other day I might be tempted to storm out, but somehow I know I wouldn't get far before he blustered after me, red-faced and ready to explode. So as he steps up to the table, I do my best to look innocent. It doesn't work.

Rene nudges his glasses up his nose, looks me up and down, then pushes my hair from my face. He scowls at my eye.

"For christ's sake, what the hell did you do this time?"

"Nothing."

He runs a hand over his face.

"Don't screw with me. I know what you've been up to."

"What?"

He scowls.

"We had the police at our door again this morning. A young man reported that you attacked him. He has a broken nose and needed stitches. Is this true?"

I wave at the bruise.

"I think it's pretty obvious it wasn't a one-sided thing, Rene."

"What happened?" he asks coldly.

"I..."

I hesitate. I don't want to tell him the whole truth; how I trusted Shane, let him get too close for comfort, then broke his nose when things inevitably turned sour. I don't want to give Rene any more ammunition to use against me, or any further reasons to consider me wildly incompetent. So instead I shrug, still wary of the eyes watching our exchange.

"I got jumped."

His brow furrows.

"When?"

"Last night. I went out for a walk and I got attacked by some random thug."

He glares.

"You're supposed to be telling us when these attacks happen."

"What's the point?" I ask, "I handled it."

"Ah, yes. A black eye just screams 'handled it'."

"What do you want me to do, Rene?" I snap, "it's not like he can press charges against me, I'm not legally human. The guy wanted information about the Project and I refused to give it to him. What's the problem?"

Anger flashes in his eyes.

"The problem is that you didn't tell us. We could have carried out damage control – public apologies, offers of compensation. We could have curbed this before it really started. Now, he's free to go to the press and destroy this Project's reputation, thanks to you."

"Do you think that you could take my side just once?" I hiss, "believe it or not, I don't wander around picking fights."

"If it seems like the whole damn world is against you, maybe you're the problem."

"Well, I am so sorry..."

I bite my tongue, knowing I'm about to say something I'll regret.

Whenever I argue with Rene, I feel the urge to say something deeply personal. I want to throw his mistakes back in his face, rudely reminding him that the only thing wrong with me is the mistake the Project made before I was born.

But I can't do it, because Alya is sitting right there, listening to our heated exchange through the glass. Her head is tilted to one side, like a dog hearing a particularly strange sound. To her, the barely-concealed anger between us is something strange and almost alien. She could never understand. I bite hard on the inside of my cheek.

"Look, I get it," I say, "maybe I should have said something."

"Yes. You should have. You need to start taking your role around here more seriously. You're the world's first artificial human. People see you as a representative of Alya and the Project, so you need to set an example. Stop being so selfish."

A hundred different arguments fight their way up my throat, but I swallow them down. My anger is quickly replaced with sarcasm.

"You're the boss."

"Yes," he snaps back, "I am."

"If you say so. Now, if you don't mind, the test is over and I'm getting the hell out of here."

He fires me an unimpressed look, but reluctantly steps aside.

"Ice that eye while you're at it," he says curtly.

I just stride past him and out of the lab. As I walk, I feel the eyes of the lab staff watching me. I can only imagine what they're thinking as I pass. There goes Reya. The one who always makes things harder. The troublemaker. My chest tightens with rage.

Reya, the mistake.

Two

      I climb the stairs to the Dome, ignoring the ache still lingering in my chest.

      Just next to the Dome entrance is a set of metal steps. They lead out of the building, and to the top of the building's cube-like core. Here, the world opens up. The cold white corridors and glossy, sterile surfaces fall away to reveal a wide, if somewhat unloved, rooftop. The loose gravel is disrupted every so often by a batch of weeds. Particularly, dandelions. How they survive on the eighth floor, I'm not quite sure. But there's something nice about seeing them here, pushing through the mossy gravel.

      I slump onto the low wall around the rooftop and pull my legs up with me, allowing my feet to dangle off the edge of the building. Below me lies a sheer drop, easily enough to kill a man. Even Alya would take damage from this height. In all honesty, I should feel scared up here. But I don't.

      Because from here, I can see Amare spread out below me. It's far less intimidating in the daylight. The city has always been a little slow to adopt new technology, so it's an unusual sight. Instead of the glossy, metallic structures I've seen in photos of New York, or the solar panelled buildings of London, which light up at night with a ghostly glow, Amare is a little more grey. Or rather, a lot more grey. Our buildings are still made of concrete for the most part. Nearly every car on the road still has wheels, and the government have never installed a multi-level road system because of it. Jonah says it's like going back in time 250 years, compared to the rest of the world.

I take a breath, feeling fresh air fill my lungs. Sometimes, I wonder why the Project decided to make its home in Amare, instead of somewhere with a better grasp of technology. I'm sure lots of places would have been happy to have us. Anything to garner a little extra tourism.

Perhaps that's why. Amare is a working city; grey and dreary. Most people work in offices or at the solar farm, and few ever stop to consider their mortality. Here, the Project could work in relative peace, without an army of hysterical strangers at their door. Or at least, that was the theory. Turns out there are lunatics everywhere you go.

I shuffle closer to the edge and peer down. I lean a little more, until I feel the very slightest tip of my weight. Not enough to drive me off the ledge, but enough to send my heart racing and my breath to become ragged.

I shouldn't be doing this, but I can't help it. I feel more alive up here than I do in the building beneath me. I climb to my feet, still on the ledge, and reach both arms out as far as I can. A gentle breeze hits me, kicking up my now-dry hair and pulling it away from my face in strands. I inhale again. The air out here is always fresh, filled with a healthy dose of dirt; unlike the stench of bleach and chemicals that constantly fills Lockless House.

Before I know it I'm spinning on the spot, moving with little regard for the drop below. It's odd – every sane part of me screams that I shouldn't be up here, shouldn't be doing this – but I just can't help myself.

Being up here makes me feel alive. Like the dandelions poking through the gravel. Neither one of us is supposed to be here. Neither one of us is what people want us to be. But here we are, anyway. Unwanted and alive.

When the spinning stops I'm an inch from the edge, and it takes a moment to steady myself. When I do, I can hear my own breathing again – light, excited, ready for more. I touch one hand to my cheek. My skin is warm and flushed. My pulse is racing. This is it. This is how it feels to be alive. I cast an uncertain look across the city.

How could I have forgotten? It's been far too long since I've felt alive.

Something buzzes in my pocket. I tug out the device; a heavily-worn red phone with a number of deep scratches on its case. It's a spare of a spare, one that Jonah found for me after my first three were smashed during 'altercations'. I see the name on the screen and smile.

Nova. Just who I wanted to speak to. Her message is poorly spelled, betraying her genius, but the intention is clear. *Am I free tonight?*

I bite my lip. Rene would go spare if he thought I had plans to go out again – but then again, what Rene doesn't know won't hurt me. It's not like he's going to miss me, anyway.

I tap back my response. *I'm free if you are.*

She replies immediately, her message just as indiscernible as the last, but again I get the point. She wants to know how things went last night. My chest tightens. Right. Shane. I haven't given him much thought. He'd been a loose associate of Nova, someone she'd encountered a few times but had no real personal connection with. He had proven himself particularly helpful, she'd told me, in procuring some rarer materials for her inventions.

My fingers tighten around my phone. I don't feel like telling her everything. So I send back a simple missive. *It didn't work out.*

For several minutes, I receive no reply. Then, a sloppily written note – *at least your evenings are free again.* I chuckle at Nova's honesty. I suppose I have been neglecting her somewhat. Her latest project is nearing its first testing phase, and without me around to test it, she's probably losing patience. So I send a message telling her to meet me at the normal place tonight, then tuck the phone away.

I cast a cursory glance over the city. It's starting to rain, the kind of fine, misty downpour that doesn't really feel like much. But as I run a hand though my hair, I can already feel it growing damp. It won't be a fun walk into town.

Lockless House is eerily silent as I head downstairs. I pause at the door to the main lab, which is lit by a number of violet lights that are centred on Alya. She's perched on a stool in the middle of the room. Her jumper is gone, as are the shorts; she's now wearing her standard-issue examination clothes, a grey tank and cropped leggings.

One arm is stretched out in front of her, resting on a small table. In front of her, a robotic arm clutches a scalpel. The machine's other limbs hold blowtorches, needles, and rough rolls of sandpaper. Immediately, I recognise the test. Regenerative healing.

It's considered somewhat of a mainstay for Alya – the first thing people ask about. Can she really heal from anything?

I pause in the doorway, watching intently with a strange hunger in my stomach. She barely reacts when the scalpel touches her skin, slicing a half-inch into her forearm. I see crimson pool around the blade before streaming down her wrist. A clock starts on a nearby screen, and the scalpel pulls away.

In spite of myself, I start counting under my breath.

"One. Two. Three."

It's strange. I know exactly what'll happen once the clock reaches thirteen, but I'm still watching. The gnawing feeling in my stomach intensifies.

"Six. Seven. Eight."

Alya glances at her arm too. In the soft light, I see joy glistening in her eyes. She doesn't understand how incredible her body is. To her, this is normal. Expected.

"Eleven. Twelve."

My breath catches, and the world seems to shift. The cut is already starting to knit itself back together. The sight makes my skin tingle uncomfortably, but it's impossible to look away. It's similar to ordinary human healing, only accelerated - the pooling blood dries, hardens, cracks and falls away, revealing flawless skin beneath.

In an instant, there's no trace of the cut.

Rene steps closer, taking his hand in hers. His mouth moves, and somehow, I know exactly what he's saying. *You're amazing, Alya. Simply amazing.*

Amazing. He always tells her that. They all do. And why wouldn't they? It's true. Her face splits into a grin and Rene ruffles her hair, heaping even more praise on her. Pride comes off him in waves.

My fingers tighten on the doorframe.

I step into the street, zipping up my thick black hoodie. I've learned the hard way to hide any branded clothing if I go outside. It's far too recognisable. I fire a glance back at Lockless House, and the massive logo dominating the front of the building. A sideways '8' representing infinity, in a white circle. The word 'TOMORROW' is emblazoned below.

Sometimes, I forget that's our full name. We're not 'The Project' – that's just shorthand. To the rest of the world, we're The Tomorrow Project. It's a cheesy name for something so serious, but it seems to have stuck over the years.

The Project was founded decades ago. It's one of the largest independent projects ever established - three generations of geniuses working together for a single goal. And with the birth of Alya, their dreams have finally been realised.

Stepping out into the streets of Amare is always a strange experience. The real world is a far cry from the sterile labs I grew up in. We're based in a local industrial estate, so there are several white vans parked along the side of the road. Storage units fill the other side of the street, each secured by a half-dozen padlocks. Years ago, there were riots – people objecting to our existence – and since then, the unit owners aren't willing to take any chances.

I glance back at Lockless House. It seems out of place in a normal, dreary town, like it's been plucked from somewhere far more impressive and dropped here by mistake.

I tug my hood up as I walk. It's not that I'm scared of being recognised, but I can sense a bad mood brewing. If someone says the wrong thing to me, I'm liable to do something I'll regret.

Rene has never outright banned me from going into the city. I think he knows it's a fight he can't win. Nevertheless, he's open with his disapproval. He thinks I should be like the others, and spend all my time doting on my successor. I steadfastly refuse.

As I walk, I feel myself relax. My shoulders drop, all tension gone. I stuff my hands in my pockets, enjoying the sensation that comes with total anonymity.

Soon enough I see other people, and each one strikes me as completely, undeniably human. Some walk hand in hand with a friend or lover. Others carry bags of shopping. Still others walk alone, like me, their heads down low against the misty rain. And for the smallest of moments, trudging down the sidewalk, I almost feel like I could be one of them.

But then a bus passes me, and I feel everyone's eyes turn toward it; particularly, to the ad on the side. There, wearing a white and gold gown and smiling sweetly into the camera, is Alya. Of course. The Project has to get its funding somewhere – and in return, many corporations demand she support their brands. I quickly avert my eyes.

Nobody else looks away, though. All eyes linger on Alya's picture. The person nearest to me, a whiskered man in his fifties, bites his lip. There it is, again.

That insatiable hunger. The man glances my way and I hurry past, eager not to be recognised.

Once I reach the city centre, though, I pull the hood down. Here, in the crowds, I'm entirely anonymous. People hurry past, their mouths held in tight lines, hurrying to get wherever they're going. Nobody looks at me. Nobody looks at anything, except their own feet and their destination.

It's wonderful.

The screens overhead catch my eye. They flicker and flash, lighting up the drizzly day with a neon glow. They advertise a multitude of products; fancy perfumes, designer trainers, fizzy drinks. But most focus on the latest industry to make it big in Amare – computers. Computers that slot into your watch or glasses, or that float along behind you like metal puppies. Computers that track, and record, and communicate.

Historically, Amare hasn't been very technologically advanced. But things change, and though it's behind the times, it's slowly growing up. I catch myself glancing into the window of every shop I see, admiring the products. Realistically I don't need any of it, and I don't have any money so it's not like I could buy anything, but it's interesting to look.

I wonder what that would be like. To wake up and go to work, bring back your pay and choose how to spend it. To dish out a chunk on rent and bills and enjoy whatever remains. A hard slog followed by small blips of pleasure. That's how most people live. But it's always seemed so alien to me.

"Disaster!"

Someone shouts in the distance, and my heart sinks.

"A travesty has struck this city!"

I approach the source of the sound hesitantly. Sure enough, it's the same lunatic that's always hanging around these parts. A middle-aged man with an impressive beard stands on a wooden crate, ringing a bell. A crowd has gathered around him. I tell myself they don't all agree with him, that they're just there to taunt or humour the guy – but I barely believe it myself.

"Humans live, and they die!" he bellows, "that is how it should be. That is how nature intends it. We have no right to change that!"

A few cries of support rise up from the crowd, and I hastily tug my hood up.

"But some have tried!" he continues, "the so-called Tomorrow Project has taken it upon themselves to create an abomination – a creature that cannot die!"

His face is twisted with hatred, and there's vitriol packed into every word. He waves a meaty fist at the crowd.

"They have created a monstrosity – two, in fact. One, a plastic human, a copy of a person. A hollow shell, devoid of humanity and sense. But this Alya – this 'Tomorrow Girl' – is a mutant concoction of creatures, twisted into something monstrous! This unholy creation is little more than an empty chimera, feigning emotion to manipulate and toy with us!"

Another cry, this one louder and angrier. I tell myself that he's just one crazy guy, and that most people would see that. But then I see how quickly the crowd is growing, and it ignites my anger.

Even as I pull my hood down, I know it's a mistake. The man's gaze settles on me. His eyes widen.

"You!"

Eyes turn my way. I set my jaw.

I could argue with him. I could disprove all the bullshit he's spouting. I could tell him that every test has proven me to be entirely human. But he wouldn't listen. None of them would.

So instead I raise my middle finger high into the air, flipping off the entire crowd.

Rage erupts around me. The speaker hurls more abuse, screaming at the top of his lungs. I'm a monster, he insists. An unthinking, unfeeling shell with no emotion but hatred. I'm good for nothing – except viciously attacking the innocent citizens of Amare, like a feral dog.

I don't respond. Fury fills my chest, and I briefly imagine launching myself at him. I could probably get a few blows in before the crowd pulled me away. Maybe I could break his jaw. Perhaps having it wired shut would teach him a lesson.

Instead I turn and walk away, pushing the rage as far down as it will go.

There's a newspaper vendor nearby, brandishing the evening issue – but he pauses when he sees me, his hand curling around the paper to conceal the headline. Irritation flares in my gut and I snatch it from him, smoothing it out with one hand.

There, printed in black and white, is a photo of Shane. His injuries are admittedly horrific; his nose is bent to the side and there's an impressive split across his lip. Apparently, I punched him so hard that I bruised his entire face, right up to his eyes. I can't deny that it pleases me. It's not often that I get to see the results of my handiwork. But then my eyes drop to the headline.

'Plastic human assaults young passerby'.

I let out a growl. Is he really trying this? It's bad enough that he called the cops. Worse that he's resorted to calling me a 'Plastic Human' when he knows how much I hate that degrading nickname. But he actually went to the papers?! I toss the paper back at the vendor before taking off down the street.

Screw this. Screw him. Screw all the people who think a person must be a monster if they aren't exactly like them. I was made on a computer. That doesn't mean I am one.

And that's just me. What they say about Alya is worse. She's not just a 'Plastic Human'. She's an abomination, a disaster, a harbinger of doom. The Mortalists and religious zealots alike shout her down at every opportunity, and nothing the Project does ever helps.

The whole situation usually makes me mad, but I've never been consumed by hatred like this. When my fist connected with Shane's nose, I'd felt a distinct flicker of regret. I take no pleasure from hurting people, even those who deserve it – but now, seeing how he's twisted the truth, I'm nothing short of incensed.

I glance up. It's getting late. Stars peak through the clouds overhead. Any other time, I'd be calmed by the darkness. There'd be a wonderful rush of serenity and for a little while, I'd feel at peace.

Not tonight. I walk much faster than normal, swinging my arms with unnecessary force. The anger is still there, burning through me. A small part of me wishes I had smashed his nose even harder. Maybe then…

I pause under the soft glow of a streetlight.

Maybe… what?

There was nothing I could have done. I couldn't give him what he wanted. If I had, Rene would have lost his mind. No matter what I do or whose side I take, I always make the wrong choice.

My shoulders slump and suddenly, all the fight is gone from my body. I slide down the lamppost and sit on the pavement and pull my knees up to my chin.

What's wrong with me? I'm usually one to fight back. I take no nonsense. I shut down people's attempts to manipulate me. But when Shane had approached me, with his easy smile and contagious confidence, I'd allowed myself to be used.

Faintly, I hear footsteps. They're light and soft, like a ballerina walking on cotton, and I recognise them immediately. I fire an unimpressed look at the figure standing over me.

"It's not time to meet up yet," I say.

Nova beams.

"I know. I was coming back from the store when I spotted you."

She holds out a lithe hand and I take it, surprised by how easily she tugs me to my feet. To look at her, you wouldn't expect it; she's short and curvaceous, with deep, glowing skin and kinky black hair that shifts around her head like a halo. Tonight, she wears a tight-fitting top and long skirt.

She looks me up and down.

"You look terrible."

If it were anyone else saying that, I might be offended. But not Nova. Her honesty makes her one of my favourite people.

"You're one to talk," I retort, "a skirt in this weather – and are those sandals?"

She shrugs.

"My blood runs hot, but you already knew that much."

"Are you flirting with me, Miss Adebayo?"

She laughs and her hair bounces, as though to exaggerate her movement. The streetlight filters through it strangely, lighting up the tight curls and making her look goddamn ethereal. Her eyes narrow.

"So, why are you slumped on the floor two blocks away from my place?"

"No particular reason."

"You're a horrible liar. Is it something to do with the article in today's Amare Times?"

My heart sinks. My discomfort must show, because she snaps her fingers in my face and frowns.

"I knew it. That bastard upset you."

"That's not it," I insist, "look, don't worry about it…"

"Oh, hell no. I vouched for the guy, so I feel involved in this. Let's talk."

"Not here."

"Alright," she nods, "let's head back to the apartment. I need your help with something, anyway."

Nova's apartment has always been the source of envy, at least on my part. The décor is strictly white and black, tinged with red or orange as accents.

The floor is polished tile, the walls devoid of decoration aside from a single canvas on the far wall, which is expertly painted crimson. Her sofa is sleek and flawlessly white, and a massive television takes up most of the far wall.

I whistle as I enter.

"Shut it," she says, "nothing's changed since you last came over."

"I know. But it's just so *nice*. How loaded did you say your parents were again?"

She rolls her eyes.

"Not loaded enough to get me a place in a nicer area, unfortunately. Still, I make do. This isn't so bad."

"Not so bad?" I gasp, "this is a million times nicer than my room at Lockless House."

I glance at the floor and grimace. Several half-built computers litter the polished tiles, which are smeared with oil. Nova doesn't seem to notice, though. She just opens a cupboard and grabs two wine glasses.

"Are you drinking tonight?"

I consider this. Officially, I'm not allowed to drink, but that's another rule I ignore.

"Please."

She hands me a filled glass and I knock it back in one go, grimacing. I've never especially loved the taste of wine. I do, however, appreciate its numbing and memory wiping effects.

As I slam the glass down, Nova eyes me carefully.

"Okay, spill. You seem... bothered."

"You saw the article," I mutter, "I'm sure you know what's bothering me."

She strides to the sofa and pulls out a copy of the evening paper. She spreads it out on the coffee table and leans forward, glancing over the neatly-printed lies.

"A young Amare citizen states he was brutally attacked by Reya Mathis, the mortal base model for Alya Mathis, otherwise known as 'The Tomorrow Girl'. Both women are artificially created individuals with no genetic links to existing humans, and as such are not recognised as human by the state. This report is the latest in a long line of accusations against their creator, The Tomorrow Project..."

"This is painful," I interject, "just tell me what Shane said."

"Oh, right. Hmm... the young man tells a chilling tale of meeting the woman in an alleyway. When questioned about the Tomorrow Project and its intentions, the Plastic Human proceeded to attack him with a length of pipe."

I gape.

"Pipe?! I didn't use a pipe!"

"He reports attempting to calm the woman," she continues, "however the attack continued, resulting in a broken nose and multiple facial wounds. At this point Miss Mathis fled, seemingly to avoid the consequences of her latest vicious attack on an innocent citizen."

I slump down next to her.

"I can't believe this. It didn't happen like that at all."

"I figured not. You might be tough, but you wouldn't beat a guy with a pipe."

She tosses the paper aside and leans back, planting both feet on the coffee table.

"I wanted your thoughts on the platform's progress," she says, "but I think we need to clear this up first. What really happened?"

She watches me with expectant eyes, and eventually I sigh.

"Turns out he only wanted to meet Alya. I said no and things got violent."

She gapes.

"He attacked you?"

"Well, first he started yelling so I tried to get away, and then he attacked me."

"Is that why you've got a black eye?"

"Shocker, I know."

"No pipe, then?"

"For the last time, no. I had to hit him pretty hard to get off me, and he still chased after the car and shattered the window."

She runs a slim hand though her hair.

"Wow, Reya. I'm sorry. I vouched for the guy. He always seemed okay to me."

"Not your fault. Alya always makes people crazy."

"What's the Project going to do about it?"

I laugh – and immediately realise that was the wrong choice. Nova's face is creased with concern, and she leans over, squeezing my knee gently.

"What's so funny?"

"You know the Project," I shrug, "Rene assumed it was my fault. They're probably going to pay him off."

Her mouth falls open.

"Wait, you came home with a black eye and they blamed you?"

I peel her hand off my knee, suddenly uneasy. Nova's a good friend – sometimes too good. She doesn't understand how things work at Lockless House, or why I'm willing to put up with things she wouldn't be. So instead I shrug, waving one hand dismissively.

"It's fine."

"No, it's not," she sighs, "did you tell them what really happened?"

"More or less. I didn't go into detail, but…"

Nova leans back, pouting.

"Same old story with them, huh. I don't like the way they treat you."

"It's not one-sided," I admit, "my temper gets the best of me more often than I'd like. I really don't help myself."

She crosses her arms, shaking her head so hard that her hair bounces.

"You shouldn't go back."

"Nova, come on. We've been through this. I can't just leave."

"Why not? You could come and live with me. I'd get so much more work done if I had my assistant here 24/7."

"There's a hundred reasons why I can't," I laugh, "but I appreciate the offer. Really."

I lean forward, eager to change the subject.

"So. You've done something else on the platform?"

"Ah, Yes! Follow me. I wanted to wait until the crew was all together to show you, but since you're here, you can give me your thoughts."

She prances across the room with all her regular grace, and I watch with amusement. When I was small, Rene demanded I take ballet lessons, hoping it would grant me a similar natural elegance. It didn't. I plod after her on flat feet, stuffing my hands into my pockets.

Nova leads me into her workshop. It's a far cry from the rest of her stylish apartment. The walls are lined with metal panels and there are rubber grips underfoot to keep us from slipping on the oil on the floor. A clunky metal table takes pride of place in the middle of the room, surrounded by more half-built engines and humming computers. On the table is a large metallic frame, several feet wide. One of its four sides is missing. The opposite edge is lined with clamps, which hold it firmly at the table's edge. It's similar to when I last saw it, only considerably slimmer and more compact.

"Wow," I say, "you've made so much progress since last time."

"Of course, I'm a fast worker. If you hadn't spent so much time wrapped up in Shane's arms, you'd have been able to watch it come together."

I resist the urge to laugh, instead gliding my fingertips over the cold metal of the frame. Nova is a freaking genius. She could have had her pick of careers and been pretty successful, but she stuck to her inventions instead, even recruiting me and the others to help build, transport, and test her creations.

"It looks practically done," I say. She shrugs.

"Not quite. I still have quite a bit of work to do cosmetically, plus the additional strengthening we talked about last time. Right now, the two exterior limbs are a little fragile. But in essence, yes, I think it works."

"Show me," I plead. She grins, an excited twinkle in her eye. It's not often she gets to demonstrate her creations to a willing audience. She secures the clamps and plugs the device into the wall, then leads a second plug over to a small generator and plugs that in, too. She must see me watching, because her face flushes.

"I, uh, still haven't fixed the energy usage problem. It's a work in progress, alright?"

She taps at her computer and the frame begins to hum. I lean close and watch as small tendrils of air blow from little holes lining the inside of the frame. It's pushing the air out fast enough that I can see the lines crossing and knitting with the air coming from the other direction. In a few short minutes the centre of the frame looks like a tapestry, a thousand tiny worms of air twisting together to form a translucent, almost clothlike surface.

Nova catches my eye and winks.

"Watch this."

She rips a page from a nearby notebook and screws it up, then tosses it onto the frame. I expect it to fall through, or perhaps to get kicked around by the airflow – but it doesn't. Instead the paper just sits there, floating idly. I duck my head below the frame and gasp.

"Wow! It's actually working!"

She fires a satisfied grin my way.

"Yep. I can keep something afloat for about ten minutes with this setup."

"This is awesome," I grin, "imagine it, Nova! Invisible walkways between buildings. Air roads that don't need us to give up petrol cars. You could flip this thing into a wall and create a clear barrier for security – hell, Jonah would use that at Lockless House! It's a game changer."

"Not yet. Like I said, it needs to be reinforced, and it still uses too much power. Also, it only works with the paper because I turned on a pre-set."

"Pre-set?"

"Basically, if I tell it the estimate size and density of what it's holding, it works. But if I put something it doesn't expect on there…"

She yanks her keys from her pocket and places them next to the paper, where they drop clean through and hit the floor with a clang. She frowns.

"It can't handle anything new or unfamiliar. Stuff just falls through. That means it won't work in any practical sense as it is now."

I lean against the wall and cross my arms.

"Okay, I'm with you so far. How can I help?"

"Well, I've got a theory. I'm writing a programme that can scan for density automatically, and adjust its settings to hold whatever I put on it. I've even tested it once or twice, and the results are promising. But I'm not sure how that's going to work when I fasten this thing to the side of a building. Accounting for air pressure, wind, humidity…"

"You don't know if it'll work?"

"No. But it's too big to move on my own, so I was wondering…"

"Sure," I shrug, "I'll help move it."

"Thank you. That's not all, though. I plan to try it out on the auto-scan setting. Toss a few things out there and see how it holds up. Besides, if it can handle inanimate objects, then maybe it can handle a full-grown woman."

She looks at me again, a mischievous look playing in her eyes. I sigh.

"Are you asking me to stand on this thing while it's hanging off a building?"

"Well, I mean, you don't have to…"

"Sounds fun, I'm in."

"Are you sure? It's pretty dangerous."

"I regularly do far more stupid things for far less valid reasons."

Her face lights up and she crosses the room, resting a hand on my shoulder.

"I knew I could count on you. Any excuse for a rush, huh?"

I shrug. She's not wrong.

"What about Charlie and Spencer?" I ask.

"I was going to ask them to help, too. Or Spencer, at least. You two are the muscle."

"Hey now. Charlie is good at... making tea. And providing emotional support."

She chuckles.

"Wouldn't think they were related to look at them, huh? Much less twins."

I return her easy smile, then glance at the window. It's completely dark now. I've been out too long. It's not like I have a curfew, but Rene usually flips if I'm out too late. At least they won't come looking for me; they never do, even though they could track my cell phone. Normally I just slink back to my room and wake an hour or so later, ready to accept whatever punishment awaits me.

Nova follows my gaze and frowns.

"It's getting late, huh? Do you want to stay the night?"

I shake my head.

"Yes, but I'd better not. I've already annoyed the Project enough today."

I step towards the door, and she throws out an arm to stop me.

"What's wrong?" I ask.

"Nothing. Just... be careful out there, alright? You haven't heard what some people are saying about the Project. I know it's your sister they want, not you, but you look pretty similar and I doubt they care who they hurt. So keep your wits about you, okay?"

I draw my face into what I hope is a confident smile.

"I can handle myself, Nova."

"I know you can. But the crazies are starting to get organised, you know. Crazy on its own isn't really a threat – but when crazy meets intelligent, that's when things turn bad."

"Are you talking about the Mortalists, or you?" I taunt.

"I'm serious! Look, I'll text you where to meet next time. Until then, do *try* and stay out of trouble."

"No promises," I grin, ruffling her hair as I head out.

Three

It's nearly four in the morning when I step into Lockless House. For a long moment I stand in the hallway, unsure where to go. Logic tells me I should go to bed. But then my stomach lets out an anguished growl and I head for the kitchen.

The kitchen is one of the few welcoming, home-like areas of Lockless House, though I suppose that's appropriate considering how many people live here. I pull open the nearest cupboard, half-hoping to find a bottle of wine hidden behind the tupperware. No such luck. Alcohol is banned on Project premises.

Tonight, I'm in luck. Someone's made a few batches of food and frozen them. I dig around in the freezer and pull out a small tub of something that looks vaguely soup-like. Once it's heated, I pour the soup into a large mug and clutch it with both hands, marvelling at the warmth against my icy fingers.

When I enter the night lab, it's aglow as always. But tonight, it's not Sandra working the late shift. Instead it's Jonah, a broad-set, weathered-looking man with a shock of slicked back hair that's retained its brilliant darkness despite his age. He stares at the large screen at the head of the room, which displays Lockless House's security systems. He looks up when he hears me, and for the briefest of moments, I think I'm in trouble. I would be, if it were anyone else.

But then he just waves, and I allow myself to relax.

"Hey, Jonah."

"Evening," he rumbles, "where have you been?"

I shrug.

"I went out for a walk."

"For the whole day?"

"It was a really long walk."

"Of course. And I'm sure it had nothing to do with the article in tonight's paper."

My chest tightens, but I brush the feeling aside and sink onto one of the benches that line the night lab. In the dim light, I can see dozens of photographs stapled neatly to the wall. They fill it entirely, each a perfect glossy square. I stare at each one.

This is from some kind of event; Alya wears a periwinkle ballgown, flanked by Rene and Neil in suits. Here's one from one of her early birthdays, balloons, streamers and all. Another photo shows everyone in the Project standing in front of Lockless House.

I stare at the photo and find myself. I stand at the edge of the crowd, arms crossed. Oddly, there's no sunny smile on my face. Instead I stare off into the distance, watching the horizon with a quiet, longing look. My chest tightens.

Behind me, Jonah stands. He runs a hand over his tired face and steps closer. He perches awkwardly beside me, eyes gliding across my red hands.

"Cold out tonight?"

"I guess so."

He looks away, and I feel his discomfort rising. Jonah's a good one – he'll tell me things I probably shouldn't know, and talk to me a little more frankly than the others would. After all these years, he knows why I'm here.

"What did you want to talk about?" he asks softly.

"Maybe I just wanted to sit quietly for a while."

"After today, I know there's something you need to talk through. It doesn't help to keep it bottled up."

"You're not my psychologist, Jonah."

"You're right, that's Sandra's department. But as Head of Security, I have a responsibility to keep everyone safe. If you're not thinking straight, you're more likely to get in trouble and someone will wind up hurt. I can't have that. Now, tell me what's bothering you so we can write it off."

I turn back to the wall of photographs and grimace. There's no point trying to wriggle out of this. Not when Jonah's made up his mind. If I try to resist, he'll just drag it out of me.

"I was in town today. There was a guy screaming about the Project."

"Oh?"

"He was saying some... really awful things."

"That's not a new development, Reya."

"No, but I've never seen such a big crowd supporting it before."

He gives a small, knowing nod.

"Yes. I've heard that the Mortalists are building their numbers lately. So this man's words, they bother you?"

"No," I snap, "The Project hasn't done anything wrong. They're all crazy."

"Then why are you worried?"

"Because they're probably going to try something."

He shakes his head.

"If you're worried about them trying to hurt you..."

"I can handle myself just fine," I say defensively, "but what about the rest of you? Alya's so sheltered. She doesn't have a clue what people are saying about her."

"Lockless House is the safest place in Amare. I set up the security myself. We have over a dozen Saferooms, each with a fully-stocked arsenal. Handprint recognition just to gain access to the building. 20 safehouses in the event that Lockless House becomes unsafe. Every Project staff member is trained in basic self-defence and has a licence to conceal carry if needed. Nothing can happen within these walls."

"It's just..."

I trail off, but he gives an encouraging nod.

"I've been thinking," I mutter.

"About what?"

"Well," I bite my lip, "do you think things would be different, if it were just me? If I were her."

His lips suddenly tighten.

"Reya. We don't talk about that. You know Alya has no idea..."

"Please, Jonah. You're the only one around here who even acknowledges what was supposed to be. Everyone else likes to pretend it didn't happen, but it did. I remember, even if everyone else has forgotten."

I gaze at the photos, my heart aching.

"It was supposed to be me."

It feels good to say it. 24 years ago, when I was born, Rene's father lifted me up to the lab's fluorescent lights and swore that I would live forever. I was supposed to be incredible. Able to survive anything. I was the culmination of decades of research. I was meant to be Reya Mathis, the first and only immortal human.

"Everyone told me I was The Tomorrow Girl," I breathe, "you all raised me to think I was."

Jonah doesn't respond. He's too busy avoiding my eyes.

"I still don't know what went wrong," I say, "I was supposed to grow into my abilities, right? I was meant to start healing and stop needing sleep and food. That's how it should have gone. But it just... didn't happen."

I look down at my hands, which still clutch the mug of soup. This is all wrong. Being cold or hungry or tired shouldn't affect me the way it does. But here I am, 100% human.

"It was a coding error," Jonah finally says, "in the programming of the computer that pieced together your DNA. We had no clue that it would remove the traits we'd built into your genetics."

Coding error. That's always the reason. A simple mistake, a zero in the place of a one – and yet, as a result, I'm not the Tomorrow Girl.

My heart hurts at the thought. For the first seven years of my life I was told that I would live forever and had no reason to fear death, only to find out that I was wrong, broken somehow, and would never be what they wanted. Then they made Alya by cloning my DNA and fixing the mistake in her code, and she turned out perfect.

"Hey, now," Jonah says softly, "don't pout like that. You're still involved, aren't you?"

"Yeah. As the body double for the real Tomorrow Girl. Bit of step down, don't you think?"

"It's the best we could do. You still have identical genetics, so your presence is helpful for our research."

"Yeah, right. All I do is cause trouble."

"True, but you usually have good intentions. I'm willing to bet that young man from the paper deserved everything he got?"

I let out a small chuckle.

"That and more."

"Did you use the boxing techniques I taught you?" he asks hopefully.

"Sorry," I shrug, "I wasn't that graceful about it. But that's not the point. If there weren't two of us – if I'd turned out right – do you think any of this would be happening now?"

He frowns.

"I think they'd hate us just as much whether it was you or not."

I heave a sigh.

"You don't have to lie to me, Jonah. Things are messed up, and I just make it worse."

I lean against the wall of photos, allowing my body to melt into the bench. I'm tired. Tired of all the crap going on in the city, and all the crap in Lockless House.

Jonah's still talking, but his words sound distant. My eyes have slipped shut, too, seemingly of their own accord. A dim voice tells me I shouldn't sleep in the lab, but I can't help it. I'm exhausted, and the soft glow of the lights is so comforting.

I try to pull myself back into the moment, to continue talking to Jonah about what could have been, but I don't have any fight left in me. Thoughts of seeing forever are frightening and intense; the thought of not seeing forever is even more so. I'd rather not think about it right now. Not when my eyes feel so heavy, and my body is so relaxed.

I hear a dull thud as the mug slips from my hand, and then nothing.

I'm woken by Alya barging into my room again. For a moment I consider throwing my pillow at her, then think better of it and settle for firing a scowl from under the covers.

Wait. How did I end up in bed? I'm still wearing last night's clothes, too. I don't have time to ponder this latest mystery, though, before Alya starts talking.

"Reya, come on. Hurry up!"

"Tell me," I grumble, "is there going to be a single morning when you don't let yourself into my room?"

"You don't mind."

"I really, really do. Unlike you, I need sleep."

Her eyes glitter.

"You wouldn't need so much sleep if you didn't stay out all night."

I kick off the blankets and stand. Her gaze drops to my shoes and her eyebrows raise, but I ignore it.

"What do you want?" I say coldly.

"Rene asked me to wake you up."

I promptly sit back down.

"I'll be down later. I'd rather put off the inevitable screaming for a little while."

"He said it's important. He told me not to leave until you agreed to come downstairs."

I consider refusing again, but there's no point. She always gets her way.

"Fine."

I plod down the stairs after Alya. She'd stood and watched as I dressed. When I'd huffed at her and reached for my jeans, she pushed a wadded-up blouse and skirt into my hands and told me to tie my hair back. I feel a little foolish to be honest, but I learned long ago to just do what Alya asks rather than try to fight a losing battle.

Rene stands in the main lab, waiting for us. He wears a pressed white shirt with a blue tie pulled as high as it will go, and glossy black dress shoes. As we near, he fixes me with a cold look.

"Are you ready?"

"Yes," says Alya, glancing at me with expectant eyes.

"Rene," I say, "what's going on?"

"One of our main Sponsors is arriving soon for a monthly update on the Project's progress, and how we can both benefit from our relationship in future."

"Wow, that's fantastic," I joke, "have fun with that."

"Not so fast."

He fiddles with the cuff of his shirt before addressing me.

"After everything you've done lately, I'm not letting you out of my sight. You're sitting in on the meeting."

My heart sinks. I can't stand these kind of events – there's something about the smug faces of the rich and famous that makes me feel especially punchy.

"Please tell me you're kidding. You can't possibly want me there."

"What I want doesn't matter. This way, Jonah and I can keep a close eye on you."

"You have got to be kidding me," I complain. He just fixes me with a cold look. Beside me, Alya beams. I glance at her. She's wearing a white dress with bell sleeves, and sandals braided up to her knee. Her messy hair has been pulled back into a number of thin tendrils that knot together behind her head, the remaining length tumbling loosely over her shoulders. In short, she looks mildly ethereal.

The sponsors arrive soon after, dressed in suits more expensive than anything I own. As they enter the main lab their eyes snap toward Alya, and I see the same glimmer of insanity that I saw in Shane's furious eyes. It's always the same.

For many of them, this is their first time seeing her in the flesh. One or two pull out their phones, eager to tell everyone that they saw the Tomorrow Girl. Others recoil as we near, afraid to get too close. One or two even scowl, shaking their heads like they're about to launch into a rant about 'everything wrong with the world'. Alya doesn't seem to notice, and Rene and Jonah don't react either – but I make a point to glare until they avert their eyes.

Once again, I find myself wondering. If I had turned out right, how would I have handled this? The Project hides anything from Alya that might frighten her; but they can't hide anything from me. Would I have confronted them? Would I have taken the high road and stalked past them, nose in the air? Maybe I'd have still felt this defensiveness flare in my stomach, the animalistic instinct to snarl at the slightest threat.

Finally, we're greeted by a pudgy man in a three-piece suit. He's got the same grizzled look one can only get from working long hours for too many years. He waves as he spots us and Rene hurries over, extending a hand in greeting.

"Mr Clarington. Good to see you again."

Rene's voice sounds strange, suddenly; clipped and professional. It's a far cry from how he speaks to me. The man shakes his hand jovially.

"Always such a joy to visit your facility. And hello to you, too, Miss Mathis."

He turns his gaze to Alya, and I stiffen. There's a look in his eyes that I've seen far too often; a sort of intrigued, excited glimmer as he looks her up and down. His round cheeks fill with colour and he bites his lip before planting a slightly-too-long kiss on her cheek. It's all I can do not to retch.

It's always been like this. Nobody knows how to react to her. Whereas people are either indifferent or hateful towards me, she's different. Alya is a freak of nature and a goddamned sweetheart – so inevitably, people want to fuck her or kill her. Looks like Clarington is the former.

Finally, Clarington looks at me, and his expression falters.

"Ah. This is the base model, correct?"

"Reya," Rene says simply. He fires me a warning look over Clarington's shoulder. Rebellion stirs in my chest, but I bite back on it.

"Hi," I say.

He watches me for a long moment, taking in the traits that Alya and I share; the black hair, pale skin, light eyes. But then his gaze drops to my chest, and I cross my arms. He stiffens.

"This is our first meeting, if I recall correctly."

Rene replies, still pointedly avoiding my gaze.

"Reya is often very busy with tests, so she doesn't normally attend Sponsor meetings."

I nod politely, but Clarington's face doesn't change. He still watches me with a strange curiosity, like he's confused by my presence. I guess that makes two of us.

Rene clears his throat.

"Shall we?"

"Yes."

The older man blusters past me and the others fall into line behind him, delving into the lab and through to the back office. Clarington has called Alya to his right-hand side, and they're chatting as we walk. I can't quite make out his words, but she's smiling, so it seems innocent enough. What seems less innocent is his oversized hand, which lingers on her lower back. She doesn't seem bothered by it, but she likely doesn't understand why it's so damn creepy. I look at Rene, trying to catch his eye, but he's still ignoring me. So I stare at Jonah instead.

"What's wrong?" he asks, falling back a half step to hear me better.

"This guy," I mutter, "who is he, exactly?"

He frowns.

"Mr Clarington owns one of the largest research facilities in the country. He also happens to be one of our most generous financial Sponsors. I thought you knew that."

"I don't like him."

"Of course you don't," he sighs, "and why is that?"

I glance at his hand again. Why does it keeping getting lower?!

"Just keep an eye on him, alright?"

Jonah rolls his eyes.

"Don't. Just don't. If you antagonise our biggest sponsor..."

He trails off mid-sentence, his eyes settling on the man's hand. He's just seen it, too. I expect him to comment, or perhaps to rip Alya from Clarington's grip, but to my surprise, he doesn't. He just lifts his gaze and keeps walking.

By the time we arrive in the meeting room, I'm seething. They're clearly aware of who this guy is. Why aren't they saying anything?

As everyone sits down, Clarington clears his throat.

"Alya, over here, please."

He drops down onto the nearest leather seat and pats the one next to him. She obeys immediately, thanking him – and again, I feel my anger building. I catch her eye, but she doesn't react. She just sits with her head down, her hands folded neatly in her lap.

She's uncomfortable. Anyone could see that. Why isn't Rene stepping in?

"So," Clarington beams, "I'd love to hear an update on the Project's progress."

"Of course. So far, Alya has met or exceeded our expectations for every experiment. Wound healing remains at thirteen seconds. She continues to have little to no need for sleep or nourishment. So far she's managed 62 full days without sleep, and there's everything to suggest that she can go longer."

Clarington looks at her with renewed interest.

"That is impressive. And you say her body remains fully functional?"

"Entirely. It really is remarkable."

"I agree. But how does this compare to the base model's limitations?"

And with that he looks straight at me, fixing me in his gaze. I stare back for several seconds before he winks. Yuck. I slump in my chair, thinking how I'd rather be on the rooftop right now. Or hanging out with Nova. Or shooting myself in the foot.

"The base model is as human as you can get," Rene says, "requiring your standard eight hours of sleep and 1600 calories a day. We designed this model to be your typical human, to serve as a good comparison to Alya."

"As human as you can get?" Clarington muses, "fully.. anatomically correct, yes?"

Rene nods.

"Yes. As I was saying..."

"Has the base model reached sexual maturity? I understand young Alya isn't quite there yet."

"Um... yes, I believe so. As you know, Alya's body should stop aging as soon as she reaches full maturity, at around 25 or so. She should remain around Reya's age in appearance."

"Marvellous. Capable of doing everything the average human is?"

"Of course. Reya was designed to be entirely average, so..."

Lies. They slip from his mouth so easily. He tells Mr Clarington how I was made to be basic, to be normal – but nothing could be further from the truth. I remind myself that the world doesn't know what I was meant to be. They think that my creation was the first step in hers. The thought is almost as agonising as Clarington's attempts to gauge how fuckable I am.

Then, they move on to discussing Alya's education. I'm constantly floored by how much they're teaching her – she studies literature, does complex mathematics, and knows science I could never hope to understand. And that's just the core of it. Ballet, singing, musical instruments; a dozen different talents they hope to imbue her with.

On some level, I understand. Times move on, and sooner or later the world might need her. She'll be expected to use her wisdom, grace and talent to keep a little peace in the world. It makes sense for her to be knowledgeable.

But then Clarington eyes me up again, waggling his brows, and things click into place. He'd like nothing more than to fuck Alya, but she's just 17. I, on the other hand...

"Mr Clarington," I say curtly, "I have a question."

The room falls silent. From the corner of my vision, I see Rene's face contort with fury. Jonah's words echo in my head. We need this guy. Don't antagonise him.

But then Clarington's face breaks into a smile.

"You go right ahead, sweetheart."

"If you don't mind me asking, why do you support the Project?"

Rene shuffles uncomfortably.

"Reya, that's rude."

"Not at all," Clarington scoffs, "this is our first meeting, after all. I'm happy to answer any questions this young lady might have."

His gaze dips briefly, and I set my jaw.

"I was just wondering," I say, "because I'm struggling to see how this partnership benefits you. What does your research company specialise in?"

"We run group studies on nutrition, mostly."

"The data collected from the Tomorrow Project relates to genetic engineering, mainly – nothing that would benefit your company. So I'm loath to believe that you're in this for the research aspect."

He doesn't respond. Nobody does. The tension is building, and something tells me that I should stop talking. Drop it. Leave it here. But then I catch Alya's eye, and she seems as sick of this as I am. I push on.

"But then again, you're a research company. Not the type of business that would advertise on billboards. So I don't think you would benefit from having Alya as a spokesperson, either. And considering that you're one of the largest contributors to the Project, I simply can't understand how you benefit from this arrangement."

I meet his eyes coldly, allowing me mouth to twist into a sneer.

"Or," I say slowly, "is there some personal reason you feel so invested?"

Rene curses under his breath. I know he's going to scold me for this later, but frankly I don't care. Someone needs to call him out.

"I understand your curiosity," Clarington says, "I do have a deep personal interest in the Project and the amazing things it does. I want to put a lot of trust in Alya."

I snarl.

"I'm sure that's not the only thing you want to put...."

"Reya!"

Rene slams both hands on the table, his face twisted with anger. The room falls silent in an instant. He fixes me with a furious look.

"You are out of line."

"Nonsense," Clarington says, "she's just curious about our arrangement, that's all. I'm sure it's entirely innocent. Isn't it, sweetheart?"

"Don't call me sweetheart," I spit. The room falls silent.

I open my mouth to comment further – but Rene interjects.

"I am so sorry for her behaviour," he says, "Reya doesn't often get the opportunity to leave the lab so I'm afraid she's inexperienced with people. She lacks a filter."

More lies. I spend less time at Lockless House than he does.

"That's quite alright," says Clarington, "let's continue, shall we? No need to get side-tracked by a petty argument."

Rene sinks into his chair, his eyes fixed on mine.

"Let's."

The conversation starts again, and this time I don't bother interjecting. I sit with my arms crossed, watching with a bored expression. I only pull myself from my stupor to look at Alya. As our eyes meet, she fires a grateful look my way.

In spite of myself, I smile.

Rene charges into the main lab, cursing at the top of his lungs, drawing everyone's attention. Jonah and Alya follow him, both walking with their heads down. I lift my chin high and stride in after them, ready for the inevitable scolding.

"I have never been so humiliated!" Rene snaps, "how dare you speak to one of our Sponsors like that?!"

My skin crawls, and I realise that everyone in the lab is watching.

"What on earth were you thinking?" Rene demands. I set my jaw.

"A better question would be, what are you thinking? The guy's a creep, and you know it."

His face promptly reddens.

"That's our biggest Sponsor! How dare you..."

"I know I may seem wonderfully innocent," I joke, "but I'm not actually a moron. I understood exactly what he was asking about me and Alya. I can handle myself, but she's a kid. Don't you think it's your responsibility to defend her from that?"

"You don't understand anything about this Project or our responsibilities! It's you, Reya. You just start fights wherever you go. What is *wrong* with you?"

I glance at Alya, who watches with wide eyes. He follows my gaze.

"Alya, go to your room."

"But..."

"Please."

She bites her lip. It's clear she'd rather stick around and see how this plays out, but she won't oppose Rene. I suppose 17 years of seeing us at each others' throats has taught her better than that. So she nods, shoots a concerned glance my way, and darts from the room.

Rene turns his attention back to me. The light glints off his glasses, momentarily hiding his eyes.

"Reya. Do you understand the importance of what we're doing here?"

"Of course I do."

"Then do you understand that we need money? Lockless House is one of the largest labs in the country, full of incredibly expensive equipment. It costs a small fortune to keep this place running. We rely on support from people like Mr

Clarington to survive. Without them, the Project could be forced to shut down. Do you want to live on the streets? Because I don't."

"So that's it, then?" I growl, "get the money, and damn the consequences? Isn't it better to have less funding if it means we're actually standing for something?"

"It doesn't work that way! We need that funding to provide Safehouses, equipment and security. Everything falls apart without that."

Suddenly, my face burns.

"Come on, Rene. You can't pretend you didn't notice what he was doing. Why didn't you speak up? Maybe not in my defence, but in hers?"

"I'm not going to antagonise our Sponsors."

Rage consumes me for a moment and I realise that I'm slipping. Any second now, I'll say something I'll regret later.

"She's clueless!" I bark, "you have to teach her to protect herself, or you need to protect her! What happens when the Mortalists come after her?"

"That won't happen!"

"They're getting organised, Rene. That's what everyone keeps saying. If you can't keep her safe from some creep with wandering hands, what makes you think you can keep her safe from those maniacs? She needs to know how to handle herself!"

Anger flashes in his eyes and he steps closer, mouth contorting with rage. Now *this* is the Rene I know. The one with barely-concealed hatred in his eyes.

"Handle herself?" he scoffs, "like you? You want her to vanish every night and come home injured and angry, with another police report logged about her violent behaviour?"

"It's better than being a victim!"

He turns his back.

"I'm done with you. Just get out of my sight. I have a lot of work to do to repair the damage you've done."

"Sure, that seems fair. Alya and me, we're just a means to an end, right?"

"Don't pretend you understand this, because you don't."

"Of course not. Who cares how we feel, right? It's not like we're human."

"I didn't say that."

"You didn't need to," I snap.

His eyes widen, and he opens his mouth to speak – but I'm done. My anger suddenly ebbs. I gaze into Rene's disappointed eyes, and feel the first stab of shame.

I step into the gym, pulling my hair behind my head.

Aside from the roof, the gym is my favourite part of Lockless House. It's nothing spectacular; just a small-ish room lined with mirrors on one side and windows on the other. Even the word 'gym' isn't entirely accurate. The only equipment is a treadmill, stepping machine, a few weight racks, and a small, cordoned-off area we use as a makeshift boxing ring.

As I load up some weights, I catch sight of myself in the mirrored wall. It feels somewhat vain to admire the definition in my arms, but I'm quietly pleased by the sight. I'll never be able to build large amounts of muscle – it's just not in my genes – but I've done well, considering.

"Trying to beat your personal best?"

I pause, glancing up as Jonah sidles into the room.

Unlike me, Jonah has plenty of muscle. It's only when he wears shorts and a tank that I really see it; what looks like a broad-built, somewhat chubby figure when clothed is actually a wall of muscle built over a couple of decades. My eyes trace the tattoos on his arms, lingering for a moment on his bicep, where mine and Alya's names are written in script, then come to rest on his face.

"I thought you guys had another meeting," I remark. He shrugs.

"Rene wanted to talk about damage control, and how to assuage Clarington's frustrations following your... outburst. I'm not really needed for that, so I figured I'd come find you."

I sit up, my shoulders slumping.

"How'd you know I was here?"

"You're a lot like me, Reya. Sometimes the best way to get rid of frustration is to tire yourself out."

"Well, you've got that right."

He eyes the weights behind me.

"How much are you lifting?" he asks. I eye him curiously, my lip curling.

"Depends. How much do you weigh?"

I half-expect him to change the subject, but instead he chuckles.

"Try 250lb. Let's see how you do with that."

"Alright, challenge accepted," I smirk, "load me up, let's see if I can bench press you."

He strides over, loading up the weights, and shoots me a curious look.
"After this, how about a bit of training? You still need practice."
I sigh.
"I'm *bad* at boxing, Jonah."
"You're not a natural, sure. That doesn't mean you can't get better."
"Rene would be furious if he thought you were teaching me how to fight," I sigh.
"I'm not teaching you how to fight. Boxing happens to be excellent cardio, that's all."

He fires me an amused glance.
"If you happen to transfer those skills into self-defence, well, that's on you."

I laugh and lay back. Jonah hovers overhead, one arm outstretched.
"You don't need to spot me," I tell him, "I can do this."

He doesn't respond; just widens his smile and motions for me to continue.

Two weeks slip by quickly. Each morning I reach for my phone, hoping to see a message from Nova. We usually see each other more frequently, and though I know I can visit anytime, I don't like to interrupt her work. Once or twice I exchange messages with Spencer or Charlie, but it doesn't compare to seeing them in the flesh.

It takes a week before Rene can stand to be in the same room as me. After about ten days, he can even look me in the eye during tests. The tests themselves are repetitive and dull – the same dozen experiments repeated weekly, always with the same result. On some level, I understand why they're doing it. They need to make sure that Alya's reactions remain consistent.

Once, I asked Neil to explain the science to me. I vaguely understood the part about 3D printing human DNA and growing it in an artificial womb – but then it got a little intense, and I quickly gave up. Nowadays, I leave the science to them.

The media continues to talk about my 'vicious attack' on Shane. It's clear he's trying to cash in on it. In interviews, he's even demanded to meet Alya as some sort of peace offering. The Project hasn't agreed to this. In fact, nobody has been in touch with him.

On a particularly quiet morning, I approach the large TV in the kitchen and flick it on. The Project insists that Alya can only watch educational documentaries, so it's rare that I get to watch something interesting. A newscaster tidies a stack of paper and peers over the rim of her wire-framed glasses.

"The so-called Mortalist movement seems to be gaining traction lately," she says curtly, "the movement runs on its core beliefs relating to what constitutes humanity, and what variations, if any, should be permitted to exist."

I lean forward, curious. It's not like I don't know what Mortalists think of us, but it's interesting to see how they present to the public. She clears her throat.

"The main subject of discussion is Miss Alya Mathis, an artificial human expected to have a near-infinite lifespan. Miss Mathis also possesses increased regenerative ability, as well as an unnatural resistance to hazards that would kill most humans. This includes poison, suffocation, starvation, and even nuclear radiation."

The newscaster does a quick double-take at the news prompter, briefly stunned, then regains her composure.

"The Mortalist movement believes that Miss Mathis, along with her genetic base model, should not be permitted to remain in society. Some go even further, and request the extermination of both individuals and the bio-geneticists that created them as part of the Tomorrow Project."

The screen briefly flicks to a recording of last year's protest. Several hundred people stand outside Lockless House, brandishing banners and signs. I try not to read the text, but my eyes are drawn to the logo on every banner. The same infinity symbol used by the Project, only with a small blade held against it. Ending eternity.

"What are you watching?"

Sandra drops down beside me and for a moment, I think she might scold me for putting the news on – but instead she pushes a cup of something warm into my hand.

"What's this?" I ask.

"Coffee. You drink it black, right?"

Suspicion fills my chest and I open my mouth to question her – but then the scent of the coffee fills my head, and I decide against it.

"Thanks."

For a moment we sit in uncomfortable silence, eyes fixed on the TV. The newscaster speaks over the clips, talking about the latest petition handed to the city council to evict the Project. It failed, of course – but that certainly won't stop them.

"It's really heating up out there, isn't it?" Sandra says suddenly. Her voice is soft, like she's half-hoping I didn't hear. I nod.

"Yeah."

"Are you scared?"

She looks over at me, her expression unreadable, and I realise that I'm being evaluated. Sandra is responsible for tracking mine and Alya's mental states, and picking up on psychological issues before they develop. She gave up trying to drag me into therapy sessions years ago, but she still does this sometimes – frames an evaluation as casual conversation.

"No," I tell her, "I can handle myself."

"You seem pretty confident."

"I've run into enough lunatics to know how to deal with them."

"You mean like that man in the paper?"

"Yeah. I know his story sounds bad, but he really didn't leave me any choice."

"So that type of thing, it happens a lot?"

I shrug.

"Often enough."

"Are you going to keep going out?"

"Sandra, why are you evaluating me?"

She pauses, biting her lip.

"Rene was worried about you."

"I find that hard to believe."

"The Mortalists are becoming dangerous. We need to make sure that we all know how to deal with any future confrontations. You can't imagine how bad we would feel if something happened because we didn't rein in your worst instincts."

I laugh.

"That's awfully flattering. I'm not a total psychopath, you know."

"I know. But I fear that there are some among the Mortalists who toe that line themselves. You see, we've been getting threats."

"That's nothing new."

"But the content has started to change. They're becoming more violent. I think they're intentionally trying to get a rise out of us."

"What are they saying?"

She shudders.

"Let's just say that there have been some especially graphic threats made against Alya."

"Graphic?"

"Please don't make me go into detail. Let's just say that they're especially revolting threats, considering that she's a minor."

I crinkle my nose.

"Has anyone warned her?"

"No. No good would come from that. She'd just be frightened, and that's the last thing what we want."

I feel a flicker of irritation, but fight the urge to disagree. Repeating myself isn't going to change anything.

"Why are you telling me this?" I ask. She chews her lip for a moment, then leans closer and presses something into my hand. I glance down, gliding my fingers over the smooth black plastic of a small device.

"A taser? Where did you get this?"

"From the defence arsenal. I want you to keep it on you at all times."

"Why? These things need a licence, and I don't have a clue how to use it safely."

"Listen to me."

She fixes me with a stern look.

"Reya, I know you have a tendency to get mixed up in things," she says warningly, "and I'm not giving you this so you can get into fights. But the Mortalists are likely to make a move. They might come after you. Or, they might come after Alya."

I stare at her, and she pushes on.

"We intend to protect her. We really do. But you've encountered these people before and you know how to deal with them. So if something happens, and you're around – I want you to take charge. I want you to grab Alya, run, and keep her safe."

"But Jonah's security protocol..."

"Jonah is an excellent Head of Security, but even he can overlook things. There's a possibility that the Mortalists will break through his defences. If that happens, we'll need a final line of defence. I'm trusting you to protect her."

Confusion fills me. Rene doesn't trust me with a butter knife. He doubts that I'm capable of defending myself, much less Alya. But Sandra doesn't seem to be lying. Her expression certainly seems earnest. So I slip the taser obediently into my pocket.

"Alright. I understand."

"Good. Don't let anyone else know you have it. Especially Rene."

I smirk.

"Don't worry. What Rene doesn't know won't hurt me."

Her lips tighten, but she doesn't say anything. She just reaches over, switches the TV to a documentary about penguins, and heads back into the lab.

Four

    I knock on Nova's door with a smile. It's been far too long since I've seen my friends, and I'm starting to go a little stir crazy without someone to speak to. There's a small commotion on the other side before she opens up, grinning.
    "You made it."
    "Of course."
    I look her up and down, then giggle. She's wearing a heavy grey boiler suit that's thoroughly stained with oil along with, chunky gloves and a pair of goggles perched on her head. She glares.
    "What's so funny?"
    "Nothing. Now can I come in, or am I spending the night on your doorstep?"
    She rolls her eyes, but steps aside. Her apartment is in chaos – the air platform is in the living room now, perched haphazardly on her delicate coffee table.
    The door opens behind me, and two familiar figures step into the room.

Charlie and Spencer are twins, though you'd never think it. They share the same dark skin and eyes, but that's where the comparison ends. Spencer's a regular at the gym, and it shows; he's a relatively hulking figure with a shaved head and a hefty chunk missing from one of his pierced eyebrows. He scoops me into a strangling embrace.

"Long time no see, Plastic."

"Hey," I choke, "can I breathe, please?"

He drops me, then messes up my hair before addressing Nova.

"Alright. I've cleared some room in the van, so we should be able to put it right in."

"Thanks," Nova smiles.

A hand finds my arm and I turn, flashing a bright smile at Charlie. He's half the size of Spencer and somewhat lanky, with a certain awkwardness about him that makes him seem much younger than he really is. His hair falls in tight coils around his eyes, shielding them from view. I flip back one of his locks and smirk.

"You need a haircut bad, Charlie."

"I-I know," he stammers, "it's on my to do list."

"How's it going?" I ask him, looping an arm through his. Normally, I'd pull away from anyone who tried to touch me too casually. I even hate it when the Project staff touch me during tests. But with these guys, contact is okay. It feels natural.

"We've been really busy with work," he says.

"Aren't you guys tempted to go into drone delivery?" I ask, "I'm sure most major cities abandoned vehicle delivery services years ago."

"People appreciate the old-fashioned touch. You'd know that if you took up our offer of a job."

"Believe me, I'd love to. But the Project would have my head if they found out. Besides, haven't you been watching the news? I'm a 'violent thug' these days. Not the best look for your business."

"I heard all about that. His name was Shane, wasn't it?"

If it were anyone else, I'd change the subject. But I trust these guys.

"Yeah, he turned out to be a creep."

"Did you really break his nose?"

"Would you be mad if I did?"

He simply laughs. Charlie's not normally one to endorse violent behaviour, but he's never preachy about it. If he were, I doubt we'd be such good friends.

Spencer crouches beside the platform and locks something around it.

"That should do it. I've affixed some handles so it's easier to get it downstairs."

"Downstairs?" I ask, "I thought we were fixing it to the roof."

Nova shakes her head.

"Nope. That was the original plan, but apparently my landlord has an issue with me doing experiments on the roof. Something about not wanting the place to be considered a suicide hotspot if someone falls through and dies."

"So that's a no go," I say, "but having a fully kitted out lab in your second bedroom is fine?"

"My parents pay a hefty surcharge so that he doesn't mention the lab. Technically, this whole set up is very, very illegal."

She pokes out her tongue.

"So don't tell anyone, alright?"

I nod, though there's really no need. If I told anyone about her inventions, then I'd have to reveal where I've been going at night. Rene knows that I sneak out, but if he ever found out what I do with the guys, he'd lose it.

"So where are we going, then?" I ask.

"To the inner city. There's an area by the old bus station that will work. We can fasten it over the top of an apartment block and angle it so the platform hangs over an alley. That way we won't interfere with traffic, and if we set it far back then nobody will start freaking out if they see someone about to step off a three-storey building."

"Hold up," Spencer interjects, "when you said Reya was your guinea pig, I thought you meant she was testing it on the floor, not when it's actually on a building."

"Nope."

He stares wildly at me.

"Are you crazy?"

"Depends who you ask," I retort.

"You do realise that Nova made this?" he says, "and historically, well... Nova's inventions..."

She fires him a stern look.

"Be very careful how you finish that sentence, Spencer."

He opens his mouth, then closes it and looks pointedly away.

He's not wrong. I remember the various bumps and bruises sustained during previous tests; from auto-mapping shoes that plan your route and force you to walk it, to an electric baton designed for athletes and gymnasts, which had a nasty side effect of shocking the user. I've lost count of how many times Charlie's had to administer first aid after an invention gone wrong. Nowadays, I fully expect to take a beating during the first test or three.

"There'll be a cushion or something, right?" I ask, "Not that a three-storey fall onto solid concrete doesn't sound like fun."

She waves dismissively.

"Calm down, will you? The garbage hasn't been collected, so in the worst-case scenario, you fall into a pile of rotting food."

"And the good news just keeps on coming."

Between the four of us, we manage to carry the platform down the stairs of the apartment building. Along with the attached handles, Spencer's covered the thing in a tarp. He insists it's for protection, but we all know it's to disguise it. From this, Nova's neighbours would think we were moving a table or something equally innocuous.

It's not that inventors are frowned upon in Amare. With the recent boost in tech, some of Nova's inventions would be considered wildly useful. The platform in particular excites me – if she perfected it, we could create multi-level roads without having to switch to hovercars. Not to mention isolated walkways between city blocks, or private access points to make the whole city safer. Her invention could change everything.

"Will this thing fit in the van?" I ask Spencer as we heave the platform through the front door.

"It should. I might sit in the back and hold it upright, though. It's not worth my life if I turn too fast while driving and it falls over."

"If you're doing that, can I drive?"

He rolls his eyes and lets out a barking laugh.

"Any chance to get behind the wheel, huh? Fine. Take the keys."

He presses them into my hand and I take them gleefully. Nova chuckles.

"You really love driving, don't you?"

I simply beam at her. As we clamber into the van, Charlie slips into the seat next to me.

"I meant to ask," he says quietly, "who taught you to drive? I thought you couldn't get a licence."

"Jonah taught me when I was a kid. He figured that if Lockless House ever got attacked, I might need to pile people into a car and escape. As for the licence, only humans need them."

He visibly pales, so I laugh it off.

"Don't worry, Charlie. You're in no more danger with me behind the wheel than with your drama queen brother back there."

"Hey!" Spencer barks, "focus on the road, not on my personal life."

"How *is* your personal life?" Nova asks him.

"Actually, pretty good. Me and Sean have booked a vacation."

"Sean? Wait, who's Sean?"

"Spencer's latest fling," Charlie chuckles. Nova gasps.

"You broke it off with the last guy, then. What was his name, again...?"

"Geoff?"

"Yeah, Geoff. He was an asshole."

I burst into laughter, and the others quickly follow. I adore Nova's brutal honesty. If I tried to be half as blunt I'd send the Project into a fit.

We arrive at the apartment block and somehow carry the device up the fire escape. I'm briefly tempted to ask Nova if we have permission to be here, then stop myself. If we had permission, we almost certainly wouldn't be going up the fire escape.

Once we reach the top, I relax. The chaos of the city falls away here, and there's a pleasant quietness. I take a deep breath, marvelling at the fresh air that fills my lungs. There's one major benefit to living in Amare, rather than a larger city. Sometimes, the air still tastes clean.

I approach the edge of the building and peer down. There's nothing barring me from the sheer drop below, no railing to prevent a sudden fall. My legs quiver.

It's higher than I thought. Normally, heights feel good – exhilarating, even. But for some reason, I don't like this. I won't just be standing at this edge. I'll be stepping off it.

"Getting nervous?" Nova says tauntingly. I fire a stubborn look her way.

"Please."

"Well, get used to the view. This'll take a while to set up."

I sit on the edge of the building, letting my legs dangle towards the street. Occasionally, I glance at Nova. She's hard at work getting the generator and computer set up. We've already heaved the platform onto the edge of the building and clamped it down. Now, there's nothing to do but wait until it's ready.

"Aren't you cold?"

Spencer slumps down next to me, mirroring my pose – but then he glances over the edge and pulls back, unnerved by the drop.

"Is it cold?" I ask. I'm wearing my favourite black hoodie tonight. I learned years ago that head-to-toe black is a great way to avoid notice, and the hood helps hide my face. The other upside is that it's thick, so on nights like this I can hardly feel the cold. Spencer pulls his own jacket a little tighter around himself.

"It's bloody freezing. Do you have super-human heating, or something?"

"I'm an artificial human, Spencer. Not an alien."

"Hey, I'm not a scientist," he shrugs, "you could be anything and I wouldn't know."

I roll my eyes. When Alya and I were first unveiled, there were similar rumours; that I might have inhuman abilities due to my DNA being printed by a computer. Unfortunately, if I have any fantastic abilities, I've never uncovered them. Unless you count a heightened capacity for pain, of course, but I suspect that's from experience rather than genetics.

"How's it going at the Project?" he asks.

"Same old. Rene's pissed at me."

"What did you do this time?"

I let out a long breath, watching it cloud in front of me.

"A Sponsor paid a visit to Lockless House, and he was being super creepy. So I may have said something inappropriate."

"You, saying something inappropriate? Shocker."

I playfully slap his hand and he pulls back.

"So, what did you say that was so bad?"

"It's not what I said so much, it's more what I implied..."

"Which was?"

I flush madly.

"I... may have insinuated that our biggest sponsor was a pervert."

His laughter rings across the street – and in spite of myself, I join in. I love Spencer's laugh. It's the kind of big, booming laugh that just brightens my mood. He wipes a tear from his eye.

"Priceless."

"It's not funny," I insist, trying hopelessly to stifle my laughter.

"You're something else, you know that?"

"There were better ways to handle it."

"Have you told Rene that?" he asks.

I fall silent. Rene and I have a precarious dynamic as it is, and admitting my mistakes would only hand Rene more power. If I confess that I fucked up this time, he'll have even more ammo the next time something happens.

"No," I say slowly, "and I'm not going to."

"Why not?"

"It's not worth it. I shouldn't have antagonised the guy, but there was a point that needed to be made. I'll undermine that if I apologise now."

Spencer opens his mouth to respond, only to be interrupted by Nova. She stands, cupping both hands around her mouth as she yells over the wind.

"I think I've got it!"

As we approach, I take in the new setup. The new generator's half the size of the one she was using before, and there are about two dozen wires running between it, the device and the laptop she's set up in the gravel. She taps at the keys, murmuring.

"I'll just put the auto-scan on..." she mutters, "and then we'll test it out."

A particularly strong wind blows through, and I bite my lip.

"Have you accounted for the weather?"

"It's auto-scan, remember? In theory, it should automatically adjust for the wind."

She hands me a piece of paper.

"Same test as before, please."

I do as I'm told, crumpling the paper into a ball and tossing it onto the platform. I expect the wind to carry it away, but to my surprise it doesn't. The paper just sits there, floating three storeys above the ground, lightly bobbing as though affected by a light breeze.

Nova lets out a satisfied grunt.

"Alright. Are you able to get it back?"

Charlie reaches out for it, but I touch his arm.

"I've got it."

As he shifts away, I take the chance to eye up the alleyway below us. Nova's right; there's been no collection today. A number of large metallic bins lie below us, each overflowing with glossy black garbage bags. I can smell them from here. *Fantastic.*

"Next."

We spend another ten minutes tossing random items onto the platform to see how it responds. Each time, to my surprise, it handles the item perfectly. It holds a brick, a pen, even a mobile phone. Finally, Nova turns to me.

"I think there's only one test left."

"Are you sure about this?"

"Yes," she says, "it's worked for everything else, right? Besides, it's programmed to be able to hold the weight of a small car, so it should have no problem with you. Barring some catastrophic failure, that is."

"You do realise that 'catastrophic failure' is my middle name, right?"

"I thought your middle name was Gabriella."

"You know what I mean."

She rolls her eyes.

"Are we doing this or not?"

I take a hesitant step towards the edge. The wind picks up a little, kicking up my hair and blowing it in front of my face. I shove it aside and stare at the platform. It looks fairly solid; a tapestry of fine flutes of air, bound together as though neatly stitched. I take a deep breath and cast a glance over the city.

It's peaceful tonight. It's not raining, at least, and for Amare, that's often as good as it gets. I fight to clear my mind. I trust Nova. Just in case, though, I close my eyes tight.

My first step is light. I point my toe, searching desperately for a semi-solid surface – and find one. The air platform feels almost like a thick rug. I can feel something akin to fibres under my foot, not quite solid, but substantial enough. Gently, I place a little weight onto the foot.

It holds. Behind me, Nova begins typing furiously. The others stand in utter silence, as though they're afraid a single noise might cause it to fail.

"Alright," I say, more to myself than them. Slowly, I place all my body weight on the foot, then bring the other to rest beside it.

When I open my eyes, my heart pounds like a jackhammer in my chest. There's nothing at all beneath me – the tendrils of air seem to flatten out a little, leaving the space under my feet oddly clear. I remind myself that it did that with the paper, too, and lift my head.

The city is still peaceful. I've not broken the calm by screaming bloody murder, at least. A strong wind kicks over the roof and I lock my knees to keep from being blown away.

"You can move around a little," Nova says. Her voice is somewhat hushed, like she's waiting for something to go wrong.

I shuffle slightly. Nothing changes. Slowly, I turn to face them. They're watching with nervous expressions, their faces pale. Nova fires me a sick expression and lowers the laptop.

"Well?"

"I'm not dead, am I? I guess that's a good sign."

I glance down.

"This is kind of awesome, Nova."

"How does it feel?" Charlie whispers. I flash a grin his way.

"It's like... standing on a really, really fluffy rug. Like liquid static. Does that make sense?"

He pauses.

"Not really, no."

I turn away as the wind picks up again, and this time I open my arms wide. Now that the initial fear has subsided, this feels incredible. I step forward, nearing the edge of the platform.

"Hey, be careful!" Charlie whines.

"Oh wow," I say, "guys, you have *got* to try this."

Another gust of wind. I throw my arms out again, marvelling at the feeling. It's like I could float away any second, swept up into the sky. I stare into the darkness, half-wishing it would actually carry me off.

After the test we sit on roof, chatting. Spencer reaches into his rucksack and fills a few tumblers, pressing one into my hand.

"Can't go without a drink, huh?" I tease, then take a sip. Vodka.

"Drinking is the best coping mechanism I've ever found," he tells me, "after sex, of course. But I feel that might be inappropriate in this situation."

"I'm sure that between the four of us we have a lot going on, but what in particular is the coping mechanism for?"

He leans back, grinning.

"Your legs were shaking when you got off the platform."

"That's a natural reaction," Nova interjects, "and she did a good job."

"Not as good as you," I say, "it's amazing that you can keep coming up with these ideas, Nova. The platform could change everything."

She promptly reddens, turning her gaze back to her drink.

"Do you think so? Really?"

"Uh, yeah? Some cities have already migrated to hovercars and multi-level roads, but that's not affordable for most people. With something like this, Amare could have multi-level roads without forcing people to re-mortgage their homes to buy a new car. It'd be awesome."

The guys nod their assent, and Nova smiles sheepishly.

"I'm really happy you said that, because... I *may* have been approached by a Sponsor."

I give her a round of applause and Charlie leans forward, grinning from ear to ear.

"That's amazing," he says, "congratulations, Nova."

"Seriously," Spencer booms, "that's incredible."

"Now, don't get ahead of yourselves," she warns us, "they haven't made an offer yet, and I haven't even met the guy. But he found my site and decided I was worth investigating. Apparently, he wants to meet before the Show, and if he likes what he sees he'll fund everything I need to display the platform properly."

The others seem excited by the thought, but my heart sinks.

The Amare Creation Show is an annual science conference that happens on the other side of town. Young geniuses share new discoveries there, and inventors display their creations. It's not a small event, given the city's recent efforts to modernise. Nova's managed to rent a table this year, which is a huge opportunity for her. Even so, my chest feels suddenly heavy.

"I was wondering," Nova says, "I know that I dragged you guys into helping me out of friendship, but things are starting to happen fast and frankly, I'm getting cold feet. Maybe instead of it being just me, it can be all of us. We can come up with a group name, or something. We should all go and meet the Sponsor together, and we should all attend the show."

Charlie tilts his head.

"But that isn't fair, Nova. You do all the work, you should get the credit."

"I couldn't have come this far without you guys. You two have been great at helping me find parts and doing research. Not to mention Reya..."

She smiles at me, and my chest feels warm.

"How many times have you risked your neck testing one of my more dangerous creations? You deserve some of the credit, too."

I ignore the heat building in my face.

"Look, that sounds like fun. I definitely think you guys should go to the Show and blow everyone out of the water. But I can't join you."

Her face falls.

"Wait, what? Why not? We could have you test the platform in front of the entire show, it'd be fantastic. Everyone would love it."

"The Project wouldn't," I say sullenly, "they always attend the Creation Show. If they spotted me there with you guys, they'd figure out what I've been doing every night when I leave home."

"What do they think you're doing?"

"Getting wasted and having punch-ups, I guess."

"This is better though, right?" she smiles wryly, "you've been working on an important project with friends. Maybe they'd be impressed."

The laugh slips out before I can stop it.

"Hey!" she snaps.

"Sorry," I say, "but it doesn't work like that. If they knew I'd been working on something – anything – outside the Project, they'd lose their minds and probably stop me from seeing you. I can just imagine Rene now. 'You're not fully dedicated to the Project if you're busy playing with your delinquent friends'."

"Hey, we're not delinquents," Charlie complains, "well, except Spencer."

His brother fires him a stern look and he laughs. Nova frowns.

"They need to give you a little breathing space. Not everything can be about the Project."

"I wish it were that easy."

"I don't get it," Spencer says, "they don't need you anyway, right? They have your sister."

His words sting and he must realise it, because he fires me an apologetic look.

"What I mean is, she's the main focus of their work. So why can't you live a little?"

I stare into the tumbler, resisting the urge to scowl at my own reflection. Not the Tomorrow Girl, bound to inspire the world. Not a human, free to choose my own way.

"Because I'm not human," I say icily. Nova touches my shoulder, but says nothing. She knows all too well how much I hate saying that. Charlie leans forward.

"I never really understood why it's so awkward with you and the Project. You've told me before, but it just… doesn't make sense to me."

"Charlie…" Nova warns. I shake my head.

"It's alright. In short, they hate me because I turned out wrong."

He tilts his head and I push on.

"Basically, the Project decided to make the Tomorrow Girl. It was meant to be a one and done kind of situation – it had to be perfect first time. After all, they're the third generation working toward this goal. My face, my name, everything was planned out years before I even existed. I was the culmination of decades of work."

My chest throbs. How many times have I told them this story? They're the few people outside the Project who I trust with the truth. Nobody else knows; not even Alya. I push on, certain they'll understand. They always do.

"When I was born, they figured I'd grow into my extra abilities. They told me I'd probably live forever."

"Probably?"

"The Tomorrow Girl has infinitely-regenerating cells. That's what speeds up healing and provides resistance to disease. Alya's expected to live for at least 10,000 years. Potentially much longer."

He nods, and I push on.

"Anyway, my abilities never appeared. Once they realised they'd failed and I was just human, they made Alya, and she came out perfect. They couldn't hide me, though, so they pretended it was intentional. They weren't just trying to make the Tomorrow Girl; they were also trying to make a fully artificial human, and they succeeded on both counts."

"So they moved the goalposts."

I nod.

"Pretty much. They use me as a comparison to Alya, since we're genetically identical. They can pretend it was planned all they like, but the fact is they screwed up when they made me. I'm pretty sure that's why they hate me so much."

An uncomfortable silence settles over us, and Nova tightens her grip on my shoulder. I know what she's thinking. She wants to ask again, to beg me to move in with her. The guys have offered me a job more times than I can count, promising I could live like a human. I have to admit, the idea is tempting.

But like it or not, the Project made me. I belong to them.

So instead I knock back the rest of the vodka and slap Nova on the back.

"There'll be time for moping later. Congrats again, Miss Adebayo! If you want company at this meeting, just let me know. Even if I can't be at the show in person, I'll happily play the part of bodyguard to make sure this Sponsor doesn't get too handsy!"

Spencer laughs.

"Haven't had your fill of fighting pervs, Reya?"

"Never," I grin. Nova smiles.

"Actually, I'd really appreciate you guys coming with me. The Sponsor wants to meet next Saturday at some seedy bar downtown. I wouldn't feel safe going alone."

"Not to worry, we'll be your entourage," I say. She laughs, and suddenly the heaviness in my chest is gone.

I wish I could stay here forever. Right here, with my friends, drinking on a rooftop.

My room fills with steam as I fling open the bathroom door and step out, nude aside from the towel wrapped around my head. Dimly, I remember that half my room is made of glass, and I should probably be worried about being seen naked, but dismiss the thought. Few buildings are as tall as Lockless House, and if anyone has a camera with fantastic zoom, they'll be too busy snapping pictures of Alya to care about me.

I toss on a t-shirt, drag a brush through my hair, and reach for the cell phone on my bedside table – then stop.

I could have sworn I put it there. That's where I always put it; tucked between the lamp that barely works and an ancient bottle of painkillers from that time I broke my leg. Briefly, I worry. Should Rene, Sandra or Neil find it, I'm in trouble.

So I pull on some leggings and head into the hallway, my hair still dripping down my back.

Alya steps out of her room. As always her steps are slow and measured, graceful as all hell, and a total opposite to my heavy clumping. She walks with her hands together, just like she was trained to. She lifts her head.

"Hey," I say, "have you seen my cell phone?"

She averts her eyes, gives a tiny nod, and unfolds her hands. There, sitting neatly in her cupped palms, is my phone. I stride over and snatch it up.

"Thanks," I say bluntly, turning away. I get about three steps before she clears her throat.

63

"Reya."

"What?"

"Who's Nova Adebayo?"

I spin on the spot, heart hammering.

"You looked at my phone?"

Her expression changes, and I recognise it with a start. Guilt.

"Hold on," I snap, "did you take this from my room?"

"You were in the shower," she tells me, "I planned to put it back before you got out."

"Why would you take my phone?"

My chest tightens.

"Did Rene tell you to spy on me? Because I swear to god..."

"No," she insists, "he didn't. I was just curious."

She steps forward, bouncing lightly on her heels. The dreamy, far-off look in her eyes suddenly gives way to something much more mischievous. She fixes me with a smug look.

"You're going to meet your friends at a bar tonight, right?"

I don't answer; just glare. Alya's never approached me like this before. I'm used to her being a barely-there presence or a helpless soul in need of constant protection. But this? I'm not sure what to make of it. She smirks.

"Can I come?"

"Not a chance," I say coldly. Sneaking Alya out of Lockless House sounds like a pain in itself, but accompanying her to a bar? Never mind that she's only 17; I wouldn't inflict her saccharine personality on my friends in the first place.

But then she rolls her eyes – another uncharacteristic act.

"Alternatively, I could... tell Rene about your work on Nova's inventions."

My heart pounds.

"You wouldn't."

"Are you sure?"

Our eyes meet, and I feel my hackles raise.

"I don't care what Rene thinks."

"But if he knew about your friends," she muses, "he'd probably stop you seeing them. Right?"

Heat fills my face, and I'm suddenly grateful that only the two of us live in the Dome. It means nobody's listening.

"This is bull," I spit. She cocks her head.

"It's a simple choice. Take me into the city with you, or I'll tell Rene everything."

"You're seriously blackmailing me? I thought you were supposed to be sweet and innocent."

Her smirk intensifies.

"There's a time and a place for sweetness. But I want this."

"Why?"

"I have my reasons," she says. I rub my head frantically.

Damnit, she's got me. If I have to entertain her for a while, I'm sure I can manage. But I won't allow her to interfere with Nova's chance at getting this sponsorship. The last thing Nova needs is the Tomorrow Girl stealing all the attention.

"F.... fine," I say, "I'll take you into the city."

"To the bar?"

"Not a chance."

"But!"

"It's a bar. Nobody's going to believe you're old enough to drink. I'll take you out next time instead."

Disappointment fills her face but she recovers quickly, replacing the unimpressed scowl with a wide smile.

"Thanks, Reya!"

I blink at her, confused by the sudden shift. She doesn't seem to notice my discomfort though, instead heading back to her room. I stare after her.

"Hey. Are you going to tell me why you're doing this?"

She stares back with deceptively-cute eyes.

"Perhaps I just want to spend time with my big sister."

"Sure," I say, "and I'm going to a bar for the atmosphere, not the one-dollar beers."

If she finds that funny, she doesn't show it. Instead she just keeps walking, hands folded just like they were before. For a brief moment I watch her, and wonder for the millionth time if we'd have turned out similar, had things gone differently.

The bar Nova mentioned is surprisingly packed. It's somewhat old-fashioned; there's a wooden bar lined with red stools, with dim yellow bulbs lighting up the bottles of liquor behind it. I step inside and take a deep breath. It smells like worn leather and cigarette smoke.

"Hey! Over here!"

Nova. She waves madly from the bar, where she, Spencer and Charlie are already waiting. I approach and she throws a strong arm over my shoulder, then pushes a glass of liquor into my hand.

"Took you long enough, Reya! Where have you been?"

"Sorry. The Project's been on high alert lately, so they work a bit later – it's harder to sneak out without being spotted."

"High alert?" she asks, finally releasing me, "what for?"

I open my mouth to reply, then shake my head.

"You know what, it doesn't matter. We didn't come here to listen to me bitch about the Project. We came for you. So, where's this mysterious Sponsor?"

She flushes.

"He's not coming for an hour or so. I just wanted a drink first to calm my nerves."

"There's nothing to be nervous about," I tell her, "he's going to love you."

"Reya's right," Charlie adds, "anyone would be proud to sponsor you, Nova."

Spencer finishes his drink, slams down the glass and sighs.

"Besides, you've already got one foot in the door. This is your first meeting, and you're accompanied by the world's first ever artificial human! That's got to give you a bit of scientific street cred."

I press a finger to my lips and he fires me a sheepish look. It's not that I'm scared to be recognised – it happens often enough – but the last thing I want is to derail their meeting by talking about the Project. The lower profile I can keep, the better.

I glance at Nova. She's somewhat paler than normal, toying anxiously with a loose strand of hair. It's strange to see her so nervous. I fire her a warm smile.

"Don't you dare start getting anxious on us, Nova. Remember, you're the brains of the operation."

"Oh!" she says, "I forgot to tell you. The 'operation' has a name."

The guys lean in, curious, and she blushes again.

"I was thinking something like Quad Creations, since there's four of us. Or maybe not. Maybe it sucks. I can't tell anymore."

"It's great," Spencer grins. She frowns.

"Are you just saying that to be nice?"

I laugh.

"Have you ever known Spencer say something just to be nice?"

He lets out an offended tut and pushes another drink towards me.

"Shut up and drink."

After half an hour, I feel the slight fuzziness that accompanies one drink too many. I'm not drunk, per se – still aware of what I'm doing and where I am. But I find myself repeating jokes two or three times, unable to remember whether I've already told them or if the others laughed. Luckily, they're all considerably more drunk than I am. They barely even notice.

"So, guess who got blackmailed tonight?" I say, staring at the bottom of my glass.

"Aww," Nova frowns, "and I thought I was the only one with blackmail material on you. What did they use?"

"You."

"Huh?"

"It's Alya," I sigh, "she stole my phone, read about you guys, and threatened to tell Rene everything and have me put under house arrest if I didn't play along with her ridiculous request."

Spencer hoots with laughter, but Nova cocks her head.

"She always seems so sweet on TV. Who knew she had a manipulative streak?"

"If you were told you're amazing ten times a day, you'd be good at manipulation, too."

"So, what did she want?"

"To come out with me, into the city. She seems curious about what it's like. I suppose I can see why - the Project doesn't let her out without an entourage – but it's not like I can show her much at night. Rene always says I should be a role model for her, but what am I supposed to teach her?"

My head hits the table with a dull thunk.

"The last thing she should learn is how to be like me," I say bitterly.

To my surprise, Nova laughs.

"Just bring her out with us, then, stupid!"

"Huh?"

"We have fun. Inventing, games. Fireworks again, soon. Bet that would satisfy her – plus we'd all be there to make sure nothing goes wrong."

I stare. I hadn't even thought of that. For years I've battled to keep my friends and the Project separate; but intentionally combining them would solve my problems, at least in theory.

"You guys wouldn't mind?"

Spencer shakes his head.

"Hey, we already have the Plastic Human. Let's complete the collection."

I smile and raise a hand to request more drinks, but someone steps up behind Nova and I pause.

The man is perhaps a little older than Rene, with sherry-flushed skin, heavy brows and a square chin lined with stubble. His face is wrinkled, though not necessarily in an ugly way – he has several fine lines around his eyes and mouth, and three strong creases across his forehead. He strikes me as familiar, but I can't place him.

"Miss Adebayo?"

That voice, too. Deep and gravelly. Almost sickeningly familiar, like a whisper heard in a dream. Nova turns.

"Ah! Are you Mr Gregory?"

"Call me Marcus," he says, smiling. She nods fervently, then glances at the nearby stack of empty glasses.

"Oh! I'm so sorry, we were just..."

"Not to worry," he says, "I actually arrived a little early with the same goal. More drinks, please!"

He waves down the barman and points to each of us in turn. When his gaze settles on me, he fixes me with a curious look.

"Well? What's your poison?"

I shake my head. I'm the perfect degree of drunk right now; tipsy, but not so wasted that Rene will figure out come morning.

"I'm done with the booze for tonight," I tell him, "but I'll have a soda, if you're offering."

"Heh. The last time I saw you, you were too young to drink. It feels strange."

I frown.

"Last time? Sorry, but I don't know you."

"Well, I wouldn't expect you to remember me. It's been a long time since I was part of the Tomorrow Project."

I stare at him for a moment, searching my memory for his face, his voice, his name. Vaguely, images of the local library appear. Someone used to take me there, when I was still very young. They'd sit me on the colourful plastic chairs and read story books with me. They'd put on silly voices for each character and make me giggle maniacally.

The name rushes back.

"Marc?"

His face splits into a smile.

"So you do remember me."

"Of course I do."

He steps closer, and I instinctively move into his outstretched arms. I'm not sure why – hugging a stranger isn't something I'd normally do – but to my surprise, it feels good. Marc pulls me close and in spite of myself, my chest swells with happiness.

"It's wonderful to see you again," he says, "I'm surprised you recognise me."

"Me, too. I was, what, six when you left?"

His expression falters momentarily, but he quickly replaces his smile.

"Well, I recognised you instantly – though you've grown up since we last spoke."

He looks me up and down.

"You're a grown woman now, aren't you? My, that makes me feel old."

"Don't be silly," I laugh, "you don't look any different from how I remember you."

"Oh, I'm very different."

He releases me. I stuff my hands into my pockets and grin at him.

"So. You're Nova's mysterious Sponsor?"

"I realise how this looks," he chuckles, "but I assure you I had no clue you were involved with Miss Adebayo. I found her site detailing her plans, and wanted to meet with her to see if she was interested in being funded."

I glance at Nova, who watches our exchange with wide eyes.

"Reya, you know Mr Gregory?"

"He used to work for the Project, years ago. You were in the genetic editing team, right? You helped make me."

He nods fervently.

"Yes, but nowadays I pick up young geniuses and give them a head-start. Somewhat like a parent company, only it's just me. Oh! Mind my manners."

He takes Nova's hand, shakes it, and grins.

"Well, my mind is made up. If you're good enough to be friends with Reya Mathis, then you've obviously got your head on straight as far as I'm concerned."

"Reya's part of Quad Creations," she says sheepishly, "it's all four of us."

"Wow, impressive! Four young adults in the middle of Amare, creating miracles. I'm sure I can market the hell out of that – though you are the leader of this little enterprise, I assume?"

She nods and lets out a nervous squeak, but he doesn't seem to notice.

"Well, your creations have ignited my curiosity, alright. How about this? Before we go signing any contracts, we run a trial. I understand you're hoping to attend the Amare Creation Show this year?"

"Yes," she says, "but there are some kinks I need to work out…"

"How much?"

"Pardon?"

"How much funding would you need to get a finished prototype for the show?"

"About… $20,000, if you wanted to be absolutely certain. With that, I could provide an extra strengthening layer and fix the fuel consumption issue…"

"It's a deal," he smirks, "I'll be in touch to transfer the money within the next few days. No obligation on your end. I do hope you'll keep me abreast of your progress in the meantime."

"O-of course."

Spencer lets out a booming, half-drunk laugh.

"See, Nova? It was that easy! More drinks!"

The guys strike up their own conversation; Nova stares blankly into the distance, like she can't quite believe what just happened. Marc turns my way.

"So, you're part of Quad Creations."

"Not in any meaningful way," I shrug, "I'm the team guinea pig, that's all."

"Well it's certainly fitting, considering your background. Seems like you've been up to a lot since I left the Project."

I shuffle uncomfortably. In truth, I have nothing exciting to tell him. He left before Alya was made, before everything fell apart back home.

Perhaps I could tell him about everything he's missed. About how I was replaced, how I fight with Rene every day, how my friends are a secret because I can't trust the Project. Maybe he wouldn't judge me for it.

But then I recall Shane's face, twisted with rage as I desperately tried to calm him. Telling the truth didn't work last time. I don't know who Marc is anymore.

"Unfortunately not," I smile.

"No? Shame. I always expected you to make something of yourself."

Irritation flares in my gut, but he just laughs.

"It's a joke. I'm sure you'll change the world yet."

He knocks back the rest of his drink.

"I should head out. Don't want to run into trouble out there. I've been hearing some disturbing stories about terrorists on the streets of this city."

He eyes me carefully.

"Listen, Reya. I don't know if you're interested or not, but I'm going to be in town for a couple of months. If you're not up to anything, I'd love to catch up with you."

Immediately, I balk.

"I have no power in the Project," I say, my voice hard, "I can't help you come back."

He blinks.

"I don't want to come back. Frankly, the Project and I didn't part on the best of terms. I have no plans to work with them again, nor do I want any information about them."

"Then why..."

"Because I helped make you," he says, "and helped raise you too, for a little while at least. You can't raise a child without developing some attachment. I want to get to know you again. See what I've missed."

For a moment, I'm speechless. I'd expected excuses – insistence that he only wants to speak to the others, or that he just wants a photo op or two – but not this. The thought of anyone wanting to get to know me is unnerving. Experience tells me that it never works out.

So I step away, shaking my head hard.

"Thanks, but... no. I don't think so."

To my surprise, he shrugs.

"Can't say I didn't try, right? It's a shame, but you're a grown woman and I respect your decision. I'll be in touch with Miss Adebayo, either way, so if you should ever need me..."

"I won't."

He gives a short nod and heads for the door, but not before firing me another small smile. I watch him as he leaves, ignoring the strange hunger that's just started burning in my gut.

Five

Three days later, the plan is in place.

The others agree to let Alya come along, just for one night. Nothing too weird, they promise me.

It wasn't too long ago that they were helping ease me into life on the outside. While there were times when I felt like I'd been tossed into the deep end, they never let me down. They won't let her down, either.

Before we go, I warn Alya about staying quiet on the streets. I wrap my largest sweater around her and thread a scarf under her hair, making her swear to lay low. She rolls her eyes, but ultimately agrees.

We wait until midnight before sneaking out. With the Project on high alert, they're staying up later, if only to scour the news for possible problems. I can feel their concern every time they look at Alya; the worry that something might happen, and they could be unable to protect her.

As I scan my hand to open the door, guilt fills my stomach. I shouldn't be doing this. She's not just an ordinary girl. Even if she does learn how to protect herself, it isn't going to change anything. I could teach her how to win a one-on-

one fight, but that won't help much if the Mortalists get organised and form a small, ignorant army.

I pause with one hand on the door and open my mouth to tell her that. She can't go outside because it's dangerous. It's not worth the punishment Rene would dish out if anything happened to her. She's too precious to them, too important. If she got so much as a scratch, the Project would have a collective aneurysm. But then she fires me a hopeful look, and I imagine how pleased Rene would be if I sided with him.

"Come on," I say, "let's go."

We reach Nova's block quickly, and luckily don't encounter anyone in the darkness. Alya seems to have taken that as reassurance; she strides ahead, gazing around like she's never seen the city before. Which, I suppose, she hasn't. Not like this, anyway.

"Have you never visited downtown before?" I ask her.

"No. I haven't even visited Main Street. Only a couple of boutique shops, photo studios, and office buildings for some of our Sponsors."

"Have you ever asked to go anywhere else?"

She falls silent at that, blinking as though she'd never considered asking before.

"Never mind," I say quickly, "let's head up."

She gazes up at the block of flats, her lips tight.

"So this is your friend's house? It's huge."

"No, no. This block has about forty flats in it. Four on each floor. And I'm sorry to say it, but Nova said to meet her on the roof."

She heaves an unhappy sigh, but follows. The front door to the block is always open, allowing access to the stairwell and hallways. How they don't suffer more crimes, I'll never know – but we're able to head up to the roof.

As we walk, I become more aware of Alya's presence. I hadn't realised it before, but we've never really been alone together, not really. Sure, she lets herself into my room with an impressively cavalier attitude, and there are some lab tests that require some small amount of interaction, but we've never done anything like this. Suddenly, I'm not sure how to act around her.

"Listen," I mutter as we reach the door to the roof, "you understand that this has to be kept secret from the Project, right?"

"I know, already. I'm not going to tell them we sneaked out..."

"I don't care about that. Look, Rene knows I go out at night, but he has no idea where I am or who I'm with. He doesn't know about my friends and if he did, he might try to stop me seeing them. I can't have that. I'd lose my mind without them."

Her face creases.

"You really like these people, don't you? Why is that?"

"You'll find out soon enough."

We emerge onto the rooftop as a biting wind rushes through. Alya shudders and nestles into her jacket, but I don't care. My attention is elsewhere.

The others are waiting for us. They sit on overturned crates around an old plastic table, chatting idly. The table itself is covered in red solo cups and half-empty bottles of beer. Beyond them, closer to the edge of the rooftop, sits a hefty box of fireworks.

I stride over to the table and slam my hands down, firing them my most sarcastic smile.

"Got the party started without me, huh? I see how it is."

Nova simply chuckles, and I realise what she's been drinking. Wine sends her into a daze, but beer has barely any effect on her. She looks totally sober.

"Sorry," Spencer says, "we figured you wouldn't be drinking tonight, since you're babysitting."

"It's not babysitting," I snap, waving for Alya to come closer. To my surprise, she stands in the doorway with her hands together and a nervous look on her face. She glances at me and bites her lip. The normally smiling, social Tomorrow Girl has fallen away to reveal an awkward, self-conscious teenager. I fire her a reassuring look.

"Come on, I promise they won't bite."

"Much," Nova adds, winking.

Alya steps closer, and the others lean forward. I just know they're comparing our faces, our builds, or way of standing. Drawing unwanted comparisons. I ignore them, motioning for Alya to sit down and pushing a drink her way.

"What have I missed?" I ask, dropping down on a spare crate. Nova's smile widens.

"Not much. We were talking about my next great invention."

"Wait, your next one? Don't you have to finish the platform first?"

"Of course, but it's always good to have an idea in the planning stages while you finalise your current project. I think I'll make something to assist with the guys' delivery service. Something to give them the edge, you know?"

"Like what? The guys are oddly determined not to use drones, and I'm not sure what else would work."

She pauses, chewing on her lip.

"I... don't know yet. Give it time. I'll figure something out. Can I rely on you to help?"

"Of course," I say, "it's not like I have anything better to do with my time."

We share a laugh, and I feel Alya's gaze on me. Perhaps I'm acting differently; it wouldn't surprise me. Now I'm with my friends, my shoulders drop. I can breathe easier. That awful, constant weight in my chest vanishes.

"How's business going?" I ask the guys. Spencer shrugs.

"Same old. We've been thinking about closing up for a few days and taking a trip to the beach. Are you in?"

For a moment, my heart soars; I've always wanted to visit the ocean. Nova showed me some photos of the last time she went. Golden beaches, crystal water... it sounds wonderful. A far cry from grey, drizzly Amare.

But then I glance at Alya, and doubt creeps in. Rene would never allow me to leave the city, even for a day or two. I suppose I could go anyway, but he'd be beside himself when I came back. It's not worth it. So instead, I heave a sigh.

"Sounds wonderful, but I don't think I can swing it. Too busy with the Project."

"Right, testing."

His lips curl.

"We know how much you *love* testing."

Alya remains silent, but I feel her shuffle beside me. Is she surprised? I don't make a secret of it.

"Ooh," Spencer says, "Nova, have you heard from your Sponsor?"

She nods.

"Yep! True to form, he sent full payment over about an hour after we met him. Now I can really get to work. It's odd, though. Most sponsors won't fork over that kind of cash without a robust contract in place first."

"Maybe it's because he knows Reya?"

I shrug.

"Marc used to work for the Project, but that doesn't mean we're close."

"Marc?" Alya interjects, "I don't recognise that name."

"You wouldn't. He left before you were made and when I was just a kid, so I don't remember him especially well. Besides, you know what Rene's like – if someone ever left of their own accord, he'd make damn sure they remained forgotten."

She must hear the bitterness in my voice, but to my surprise, she doesn't point it out. Instead she toys with a lock of hair, twirling it idly around one finger.

"Why did he leave?" she asks.

"I don't know. He was just gone one day. Jonah told me he had decided to pursue a different career. It's a shame, because I always liked him."

"He seemed nice enough at the bar," Nova says, "is he back in town to stay?"

"I think so, but I told him I won't see him again."

"Why not?"

I peer down at my hands, which are clasped together against the cold.

"Call me paranoid, but after what happened with Shane I don't feel like trusting another stranger any time soon."

Nova claps me on the back.

"Not everyone is going to be like Shane. You met us, right? And we're awesome, if I do say so."

"You are one of a kind, Nova."

Charlie stands suddenly, fixing me with an excited look.

"Reya. Let's set up the fireworks now. Please!"

I glance at Alya, worried to leave her alone – but the others just smile reassuringly at me. They'll take care of her.

"Sure thing," I say, standing, "Alya, you're going to love this."

Once we've set the fireworks up, we call the others over. I glance at our setup and grin. After driving, this is my second favourite hobby. There's something brilliant about watching them explode. Something satisfying.

As the others wander over, I'm pleased to see Nova's arm around Alya. The embrace isn't protective or even supportive – it's the same way she touches me, casually, easily, like the contact means less than nothing. Alya flushes red, but she doesn't seem altogether displeased.

I glance at the sky. It's a pitch black, clear night, the perfect backdrop for our display. Charlie stands beside me, a satisfied smile playing on his lips. He's the one who taught me how to set up displays – a hobby of his that he's happily shared with me. I've always felt it clashed with the rest of his personality, but he seems to enjoy it, so I've never questioned it.

"All done?" asks Spencer. Charlie nods.

"Yes. Though maybe next time, we should go for the bigger pack..."

"Hold up. We're not made of money."

"But..."

"It's fine," I interrupt, "this'll be great."

Alya fixes me with wide eyes.

"Fireworks? What are we celebrating?"

"Nothing."

"Then why...?"

"Why else?" I chuckle, "it's fun."

We perch on the edge of the building, and Charlie lights the fuses. The smell of burning fills the air, and Alya shifts beside me. She glances at the others sitting on the edge, booze in hand, and frowns.

"Is that safe?"

"Is that relevant?" I tease.

The first firework catches and soars into the air, leaving a stream of silver glitter behind it. It reaches its limit and bursts, crackling into a hundred tiny white sparks. Alya tenses beside me, and I realise that she's never seen fireworks up close before.

She knows what they are, of course. Some corporate Sponsors invite her along to displays. But those are different; professional events that impose a distance between the explosions and the viewers. But this time, there's nothing to protect her.

I half expect her to be afraid, but when I look over, she's smiling. Her mouth is open, her cheeks flushed, and her eyes are so wide that when the next firework explodes, I can see the sparks reflected in them. I look up, watching the colours dance above us. I take a deep breath, inhaling the scent of ash and smoke.

We sit there for a long time, watching the fireworks. I pull my legs up to my chest, wishing I could experience the same light feeling as Alya.

But instead, I'm thinking.

I yawn loudly, much to Rene's dismay.

We stand in the sports hall at Lockless House, ready for the morning's tests. We finally got home at four in the morning, and while Alya had the sense to wash her clothes and bathe, I completely forgot. As a result, I stepped into the room only to have everyone instantly notice the stench of smoke lingering on my skin.

Rene glowers at me, then waves the stopwatch.

"Unfortunately, we still have to test, regardless of your... extracurricular activities."

"It'll be fine," I mutter sleepily, "I've still got it."

He frowns. He hasn't asked where I was last night, but I can feel his irritation growing. In his mind, I'm not taking this seriously. And, well, I guess I'm not. Frankly, I'm still a little giddy from last night.

Alya stands by, also in her gym clothes, watching me from the corner of her eye. She fights to keep her expression neutral, but it's clear she's struggling. Rene's face twitches.

"Let's just get this over with."

We both straddle our cycles and slide into position. I don't hate this test quite so much as the others. Racing around on bikes until one of us tires is supposedly a good way of comparing Alya's endurance to an ordinary human. I glance over and giggle. We both know I'm going to lose, and I'm tired anyway so their data won't be accurate. But I'll do it, regardless.

As soon as Rene flags us to go, we're off. I pedal softly at first, like they taught me to. Ease your way into it before going full bore. Alya pulls away easily, even at her slowest pace.

The Project has always been very clear about this. I'm not here to compete. I'm here to serve as a comparison, and every successful test should result in my loss. If I were ever to beat her, it'd be a dark day for the Project.

But then my gaze settles on her back, and in spite of myself, I pedal faster.

She looks up as I whizz by, her eyes wide. I cackle.

"C'mon, Tomorrow Girl. Catch up!"

To my surprise, she laughs.

"I'm coming for you, Reya!"

In an instant she's beside me, pedalling almost casually. She fires a smug look my way, igniting a competitive fire in my chest. We reach the first corner of the course and I veer forward, cutting in front of her and taking the inside lane.

"H-hey!" she barks, "that's against the rules!"

"Wait, there are rules?" I call, zooming down the length of the room. She lets out a sound that's somewhere between a growl and a giggle, and I soon hear the sound of frantic pedalling as she fights to catch up.

Despite my exhaustion, this is fun. There's a faint sensation of static in my legs, a pleasant electricity caused by movement. It crackles through my body, urging me on. I can still hear her, faintly at first, but quickly nearing.

"Come on," I taunt, "you're supposed to be better than me, remember?"

She doesn't reply; just lets out a whooping laugh. She sidles up next to me. We both pedal flat out, shooting sidelong glances at one another. She looks how I feel – bemused and entertained, aware that we're breaking the rules. Oddly, she seems to enjoy it.

We reach the next corner and turn – but the wheel on her cycle skids and catches mine. We're flung into a heap on the floor, a tangle of limbs and bike parts.

I sit up, checking myself over. No injuries. As Alya climbs to her knees beside me, she seems unhurt, too. I open my mouth to ask if she's okay; but laughter comes out instead. She quickly joins in, and I'm surprised to find that I enjoy the sound. It's unlike her normal polite, withdrawn chuckle. This is a true laugh, punctuated by the occasional cute hiccup. I wipe a tear from my eye and clamber to my feet and offer her a hand.

"Alright, already," I wheeze, "you win."

She grasps my hand and stands, still laughing.

"What *was* that, Reya? Honestly."

"If we have to do tests, they'd better be fun, huh?"

The door to the gym slams open, and my heart sinks. I forgot about Rene.

"What the hell do you call that?!"

He rounds on me, anger flashing in his eyes.

"These tests are serious, you know. Actual, scientific research. This is not a game!"

"Your results were already skewed," I point out, "I got an hour of sleep last night."

"So because you've already messed it up, it's okay to go overboard?"

I open my mouth to fire something witty back, but no retort comes. He's right. I don't take this as seriously as I should. Part of me feels guilty about that, but it's drowned out by another, louder part. Why should I take it seriously? I never asked for this.

Rene looks at Alya.

"Alya, go back to the main lab," he barks.

When she doesn't react, he hesitates.

"Please," he adds, firing her an apologetic look. Of course he won't scold her for this. It's all on me.

She does as she's told, but not before shooting me a fearful look. As the door closes behind her, Rene growls.

"Must you always do this? Throw off the research we've spent decades working on?"

"I wasn't trying to do that."

"Well, you did. And you do it constantly. This research is unimaginably important. Not just to us, or to Alya, but the whole world. Creating an immortal human is something that's never been done before, and thanks to you, the data will never be complete."

"What's that supposed to mean?" I ask, suddenly defensive.

"Every time you sneak out and come home tired, or drunk, or injured, it affects our studies."

"You can study Alya without me."

"But not as effectively. Without a basic human to serve as a comparison, her abilities seem far less extraordinary."

Something about that rankles; I feel my hackles raise.

"I don't know what else you want from me, Rene. Would you rather I sit upstairs in my room, like a good little girl? Never go out, never speak to anyone? Would you rather I exist purely for the sake of being a comparison? Because that's no life worth living."

He stares at me for a long moment, grinding his jaw, then sighs.

"Just get out of my sight."

"I want an answer."

"Well, you're not getting one. Just go."

He strides past me, muttering under his breath.

"Honestly, Reya? I've given up on you."

The door closes behind him and I stand alone, the echoes of laughter still filling the air.

I walk the streets in a rage, anger snaking through me. I've been wandering for hours now, and the sky has turned dark overhead, but I don't care.

Soon my cell will start ringing, and Sandra, Neil or Jonah will demand to know where I am. I don't know if I'll answer that call.

Rene and I have been arguing for years, and every time, one of us says something awful. When I say something regretful, I try to forget it. It's easier than admitting my mistake. When Rene says something hurtful, I shrug it off.

This time, I can't.

Something about what he said today has struck a nerve. The indignation I felt back in the gym has faded, replaced by hopelessness and anger. Rene's one of the few people who can take what I dish out – and there's something disheartening about knowing that he's lost patience.

I can't say I'm surprised. I've always been waiting for them to get sick of me. Waiting for the day when they'll say they've had enough and turf me out onto the street, finally ridding themselves of my wretched presence. Maybe if I'm not around anymore, they can forget about their first, failed attempt at a miracle.

For what feels like the millionth time, I consider leaving. It wouldn't be hard. I could get Spencer and Charlie to drive me out of the city, then hitchhike. If I made it far enough, the Project would never be able to find me. A good disguise is all it would take.

But I can't. Even if I didn't feel some kind of obligation toward Alya, it would be too hard to live away from Amare. I'm not legally human, so I can't get a job. Can't rent an apartment. I suppose I could get a fake ID, but I wouldn't know where to start with getting one.

My frustration builds and I turn into a side road. Here, there's nobody to witness my tantrum. I let out a furious growl and lash out, kicking over the nearest trash can and sending it rolling into the middle of the street.

Damn it, Rene. Give up on me? Fine! I don't need you, anyway.

Suddenly, footsteps. They're heavy and fast, like someone's scurrying behind me. I whip around. Nobody.

I pick up the trash can and put it back in place, then keep walking.

There it is again. The sound of someone behind me. This time, I keep walking and glance back – just in time to spot a figure darting into the shadows. *Brilliant.*

This is the worst time to encounter some anti-Project goon. I'm still angry as hell, and I'll gladly take up any offer to take that out on someone.

"Look," I call into the shadows, "whatever you want, try again tomorrow. I'm not in the mood, and I don't want to hurt anyone. So just fuck off, okay?"

I walk a little further, but the footsteps grow louder. I don't look back again, instead just listening. Fine. They want a fight? I'll give them a fight.

But then the footsteps echo, and I realise that there's not just one set. As I walk, the sound seems to multiply, until there could be ten or twelve people behind me.

Can I take that many? Even well-rested and calm, I don't think I could. I check my pockets, praying I brought the taser Sandra gave me. No luck. I bite my lip. Do I run? Should I race to the end of the street and see if I can make it to a busy place, or somewhere better lit? I briefly consider pulling out my phone and ringing the Project, just so they know where to find me after the inevitable beating.

I can't do it. Calling for help would be like admitting to Rene that he's right – that I'm just a screw up who can't take care of myself. The thought reignites my fury.

I quicken my pace, eager to make it back to the main road. The sounds behind me grow faster, too. I look up, planning my escape; but there are figures in front of me. They stand at the alleyway's exit, arms folded, blocking my escape.

I start running, hoping I can barge through and make it out unscathed – but a hand grabs my shoulder.

"-Hey!"

Hands find me from all directions, countless people converging on me. They lock my arms behind my back, force me to the floor, grind my face into the gravel. I fight them with all my strength, but it does nothing. I'm outnumbered, pinned by the weight of several shadowed strangers.

"Get the hell off me!" I bark, but a hand locks itself over my mouth, silencing me. I bite hard into their flesh, grimacing at the taste of oil and dirt, but they don't release me.

It's strange. I've been mobbed by strangers before. Had them screaming in my face, shouting that I'm a crime against nature. It's rare that I feel afraid. But there's something about these people – their total silence, the efficiency with which they pin me down – that sets my heart racing.

Mortalists. They have to be.

One arm is pulled out from behind me and pinned to the floor, a bulky knee forcing my hand down. I strain against their grip, but they hold fast.

Someone covers my eyes, and a pair of hands squeeze the sides of my head. For a long time, I see and hear nothing. All I can feel is something cold being dragged across the skin of my inner wrist.

And then they're gone, racing into the shadows without so much as a backwards glance. For a moment I stay curled on the floor, frightened they might come back. I stare at the ground, listening to the sound of my own ragged breathing.

Once I'm sure there's nobody watching, waiting for me to move so they can continue their attack, I sit up. A quick glance down the alleyway assures me that they're gone.

I pat myself down in the darkness. No injuries. Not even a graze. My phone is still in my pocket, too. What did they do to me? Right, my arm.

There's a ray of pale streetlight nearby, so I lean into it and turn my arm over. I'm expecting a cut. I wouldn't put it past them to slash my wrist and hope I bleed out. But as I squint through the darkness, I don't see blood. The lines on my arm are thick and black.

As my eyes adjust to the dim light, I make out the word they've drawn on me in marker.

PLASTIC.

My first reaction is laughter. How ridiculous. They obviously put time and effort into tracking me down and catching me somewhere isolated – why waste that effort on something stupid like this?

I snort and toss my head back, laughing into the cold night air. Idiots. They're all idiots!

It's only when something hot drips from my chin that I realise I'm crying.

I rub madly at my face. What's happening? Why am I upset?

In the Project, it's common knowledge that people hate us. I've grown used to it, and I figured nothing they could do would affect me. I can walk down the street without fear of the Mortalists who scream on every street corner. I can argue with them, defend my humanity without an iota of concern for what they think.

But as my throat grows tight and my face becomes hotter, I have to admit it. This hurts.

Growing up, I was constantly warned that people would do this. That humans would act as gatekeepers, trying to bar me from humanity if I didn't fit their mould. The Project had assured me that I was human, in every practical and measurable sense of the word, and I believed them.

I glance down at the letters and let out a strangled sob. Suddenly, it's all too much. I remember the abuse screamed from street corners, the hatred twisting on Shane's face. Rene's voice when he said he'd given up on me.

I bury my face in my hands. Why do I do this to myself? Why am I never good enough? I couldn't be the Tomorrow Girl. I can't be human, either. I can't stay, or go. All I can do is drift amidst it all, praying that the next confrontation won't be the one that finally ends me.

"Reya?"

My head snaps up, instinct taking over; but before I can jump to my feet, I recognise the voice - and the figure standing across the alley.

Marc stands in a brown trench coat and matching hat. He holds a red umbrella over his head. I hadn't even noticed it was raining.

Instinctively I look away, hoping he hasn't seen my tears. But I know he has.

"What are you doing here?" I ask.

"I was just out for a walk. But I heard someone crying and thought I'd check things out. I had no idea it would be you."

His face creases with unspoken sympathy. I ignore it.

"Well, I'm sorry to disturb your evening."

Despite my best efforts, it's clear I've been crying. My voice is thick, and I can tell that my face is puffy and red. Marc looks me up and down then steps forward, holding the umbrella forward. As the rain streams down his face, I frown.

"It's okay. I don't need your help."

"I know you don't," he says softly, "but maybe a warm drink and a change of clothes?"

I bite my lip. I can't exactly go back to Lockless House like this. It's obvious that something has happened – I peer down at the word scrawled on my arm. I wonder if it's permanent marker. Certainly something that the Project will notice, if I don't scrub it off first.

So when Marc offers me his hand, I take it gratefully.

The marker won't come off.

I sit in Marc's living room, scrubbing madly at the stain. I wear a t-shirt that's several sizes too large, but it's served its purpose while my soaked, dirty clothes are cleaned.

The apartment Marc lives in is as luxurious as Nova's – though I suppose it would be, considering how rich he is. The rooms are lined with wooden panels and furnished with red, leather sofas. There's a roaring fire in the corner, which helps get rid of the chill in my bones.

Marc rests a warm drink on the table beside me, then glances at my arm. Until now he's been careful not to mention it, instead busying himself with hosting, but now there's nothing else to talk about. He didn't even comment when I dug into his kitchen, helping myself to a bowl of water and a scrubbing brush.

He crosses the room, warming his hands near the flames. Some part of me says that I should thank him for his hospitality, or offer to help clean up the mess I made dripping water across his floorboards, but I don't care right now.

The tears have gone, but the anger remains. My skin protests and I let out a frustrated growl.

"You'll hurt yourself if you keep that up."

Marc's voice is low, barely more than a whisper. I shrug, but don't reply. I just keep scrubbing. After several minutes of silence, he speaks again.

"They're wrong, you know."

I pause.

"What?"

"Whoever did that to you. They're wrong."

I let out a snort.

"I know."

"I'm sure you do. But that doesn't mean you never doubt it."

He leans forward, resting his elbows on the table between us.

"The day you were born, Rene Mathis Senior lifted you up to the lights of the lab and declared that you would be something amazing. I guess that can give you high hopes, huh? You start to think that life is going to be some kind of dream, and then something like this pulls you back to Earth with a bump."

Right. He knew me back then. Back when I thought I would be like Alya.

"I wouldn't worry about that," I mutter, "I was brought back to Earth years ago."

"So I heard. I've seen some concerning things in the local paper."

Any other time, I might insist that the articles are lies, or describe exactly what happened during each alleged attack. But after today, I don't have the energy. So I shrug again and carry on scrubbing.

Marc sighs.

"That isn't going to work, you know. You're just going to rub your skin raw, and then you'll be in pain on top of everything else."

He reaches out with a gentle hand, taking my arm and running his thumb over the ink. I shudder at his touch; at how it feels both nostalgic and new. He frowns.

"Looks like permanent marker. That won't come out with hot water, but I think I have something that might do the job."

He wanders off for a moment, then places a bottle of rubbing alcohol in front of me. I dab some on and slowly, the ink starts to come away. Relief floods my chest.

Once it's off, I stare at my arm. Now, it's like it was never there. Like I imagined it. But I know I didn't, because that uneasy feeling in my stomach is still very much there.

"So," Marc says, leaning back, "your clothes are nearly dry. Do you want me to drive you home?"

"I thought that you and the Project left on bad terms."

"Oh, we did. But I can drop you off a street or two away, if you'd like."

I heave a sigh. I've already been out too long. Despite my conflict with Rene, I never actually intended to abandon the Project. I tug my phone from my pocket, expecting to see several missed calls from the others.

Nothing yet.

"I'm in no rush to go back," I hear myself say. He nods.

"Then would you like to catch up a little? I know you refused my offer back at the bar, but given the circumstances..."

I consider this. While it's true that I refused to speak with him again, it wasn't out of hatred. I'd been concerned that he might dig for secrets. I glance around his apartment. If things turn nasty here, I'm trapped.

"I won't talk about the Project."

"Ground rules, huh?" he chuckles, "seems fair to me. What else would you like to talk about?"

"Why did you leave Amare?"

He pauses.

"I thought you didn't want to talk about the Project."

"So you left because of the Project."

He gives a dismissive wave.

"No, no. I left because I had personality clashes with good old Rene Junior. I quickly figured out that we had very different ideas of how to run things, as well as how we wanted to approach raising you. It soon became clear that we couldn't sort out our differences, so I made the decision to leave before things turned ugly."

"You clashed with Rene?"

"Oh, all the time," he chuckles, "he was always a bit prickly for my taste. Frankly, most of our 'discussions' ended with me politely suggesting that he remove the stick from his..."

He trails off suddenly, then looks at me as though he's expecting a scolding. I just laugh.

"Believe me, Marc. I get it."

"Actually, would you mind calling me Marcus?"

"Yeah?"

"You're the only one who's ever called me Marc," he says, "and that was when you were a little kid. You had trouble with the 'us' sound, so I never had a problem with it, but I do go by Marcus amongst my social circles."

"Sure thing."

His smile broadens.

"So, tell me. What has my wonderful girl done with the past 18 years, aside from growing up?"

"Nothing," I admit, "I just help out with the tests as Alya's human counterpart."

His mouth twitches.

"Ah, yes. The Tomorrow Girl. I was so sorry to hear about that."

"What do you mean?"

"After all our hard work to give you the life we had promised, it didn't work out. I can only imagine how much you must resent her."

I open my mouth to deny it, but the words die in my throat. Do I resent her? Does it hurt a little to see her paraded around, held as the pinnacle of perfection, a pinnacle that I could never hope to reach?

I push the uncomfortable thought aside and fix him with a stern look.

"So, why did you really come back?"

"What do you mean?"

"You don't honestly expect me to believe that you came across Nova's inventions by chance."

He rubs his chin for a moment, then laughs.

"You're as sharp as ever, aren't you? Even as a kid, you wouldn't be fooled. Fair enough, I'll admit it. I honestly did come across Miss Adebayo's work by chance, but at first I was only mildly interested. Then, I spotted a photo of you in the background on her blog – and that may have stirred my interest in her work."

The hair at the back of my neck prickles. Great. Another trap. I look at the door, planning my escape – but he just leans forward, pushing a drink towards me.

"Now, now. Don't look so panicked. I'm not going to hurt you."

I pick the mug up hesitantly. The warmth is pleasant against my fingers, but I don't dare drink what's inside. Not until I'm sure.

"So you wanted to see me again. Why?" I ask, dreading the answer.

"It's a long story."

"I have time."

He watches me for a long moment, then stands and wanders over to a nearby bookcase. There, he flicks through several books before pulling out an album, which he drops on the coffee table.

"After I left the Project, I was a little lost," he explains, "my father had worked alongside Rene Senior when the Project was founded, so much like the others, I was raised amongst them. Stepping into the world without that support system was unnerving, to say the least."

He flips open the album and starts fingering through the pages. All the photos are of him; some of him looking scrawny and underfed, others seeming powerful in a three-piece suit. He ages as the photos progress, changing from the man I once knew to the one I see before me. His brow furrows.

"I travelled the entire world searching for something worth my time. I made many friends and saw some incredible places. Eventually, I settled into investing in small inventors. My career quickly became my main use of time and for the past twenty years, I was more than satisfied with that."

His hand pauses on the album suddenly, falling limp against the pages.

"Until about six months ago, when I went to visit an old friend. I hadn't seen him in well over fifteen years, so when we met again, I was surprised to see how his life had changed. When I'd known him, he spent every moment at work while his wife stayed home to raise the kids. I'd really respected that, at the time. But when I went back for a visit, everything was different. He spent more time at home. He had grandkids. He'd play with them, he'd take them places. And even from that brief encounter, I could tell that they simply adored him."

I fight to remain motionless as he pushes on.

"That day, I realised I didn't have anyone like that. Nobody who would spend time with me, or enjoy my company, or miss me when I'm gone. And I started to wonder what I'd spent my life doing. I didn't have a partner or kids. I was set to die without ever leaving a legacy."

He raises his eyes to meet mine, and his expression changes. It's the slightest, most imperceptible change, but suddenly he seems much older.

"Then, a few months ago, I had a thought. There was someone, once, who I cared for greatly. A little girl I once thought of as a daughter."

He flips to the next page, and this time I lean in. The next few photos aren't of Marcus. They're of me.

Me as a kid, cross-legged in the library, smiling toothily at the camera. Me blowing the candles out on a birthday cake. My chest aches.

I turn the page. These photos are different. They're paper clippings, articles about the Project. I spot the words 'Plastic Human' and look away.

"I don't understand," I whisper. He smiles weakly.

"I left the Project because I felt unwelcome," he says, "and I don't regret doing that for my own happiness. But the more I thought about it, the more I came to regret leaving you behind. With all that pressure heaped on you and no outlet. So I looked you up."

My chest tightens.

"You found out..."

"That you're not the Tomorrow Girl? Yes, though I'd known about it when I lived at Lockless House. At that point, it was just becoming a discussion amongst the Project. A simple web search told me that you had been relegated to someone else's genetic base, and they had been pronounced the Tomorrow Girl. But that's not what interested me the most."

"It isn't?"

"No," he says, his eyes glimmering, "I was interested in the trouble you keep getting into. I was able to find over thirty articles about different fights you'd had. Several people have started petitions demanding your arrest."

My heart sinks and I lower my head, waiting for the inevitable scolding. But to my surprise, Marcus leans forward. He rests his chin on his hands and watches me with intrigue.

"It seems that I'm not the only one who's a little lost."

I stand up and take several steps back.

"This is getting a little weird."

He sighs.

"I know how this must look. It's strange that I've come out of the woodwork like this after 18 years. Believe me, I understand. But when I saw that you were struggling, I knew that I needed to see you again. I thought maybe we could help each other."

"So that's why you came back to Amare?"

He nods.

"I truly am keen to support Miss Adebayo's inventions. Following our correspondence, I've grown to rather like her. And I trust your judgment. If you like her, then she's probably a stand-up worker."

"She is. Nova's incredible."

"Seeing you again is just an added benefit. I've really missed you, Reya."

He scoops my hands into his and smiles – but I feel my hackles raise.

"This isn't some new idea, Marcus. You wouldn't be the first person to try and manipulate me to get to Alya. It's never worked before and it won't work now."

Shane's face flashes in my head.

"I'm not falling for this again," I growl.

For a long moment, we stare at one another. Then, his face creases.

"You poor thing. What happened to you?"

I don't reply – I'm too distracted by the sympathy in his eyes.

"You were always so spirited," he continues, "and remarkably optimistic. What changed?"

"I grew up."

"There's more to it than that. It's like you've totally given up."

I shake my head.

"I haven't…"

"It's okay."

He fixes me with a small smile.

"You don't have to tell me anything. I won't force the issue. Look, I've discussed it with Miss Adebayo and agreed that you can visit anytime and provide me with an update on her work. I'd like as many updates as possible. Photos, too, if you can swing it."

"And that's all?" I ask, "you don't want anything else from me?"

"I want to get to know you again," he says warmly, "but I understand if that's off the table. Either way, I hope you'll stay in touch. Who knows? I may be able to find some extra funds for your friend's projects."

I step out onto the street with conflict burning in my chest. Despite refusing Marcus' offer of a drive home, I hadn't been able to outright refuse his request for contact.

Dimly, I tell myself that it's stupid to see him again. That it's been 18 years and in that time, he may have done anything, become anyone. I have no real reason to trust him again after all this time. But I silence the voice. There had been a strange sadness in his eyes when he looked at me. Perhaps he really missed me.

I look up. Night is nearly over; there's a strange shade of periwinkle blue on the horizon, slowly rising to meet the indigo above it. Soon, it'll be time to enter the main lab for today's tests. By the time I get home, the others will be awake. Who's on the night shift? Will they have woken Rene yet, and told him that I haven't returned?

I tug out my phone, expecting a dozen missed calls from the night shift. I always end up with irate messages if I'm not back by five in the morning. But as I flip open my phone and stare at the screen, my heart sinks.

Nothing.

I've been gone all damn night, and there's not even a single phone call.

I stuff the device back into my pocket. There's no way they didn't notice I'm gone. No chance they thought everything was okay. There's never been a time when I'm not back before morning.

For some reason, it irritates me. Don't they know I just defended them? Just stood up to someone and told them, unequivocally, that I wouldn't go against the Project no matter what? Granted, he didn't ask me to, but the point stands.

For the briefest of moments, I consider walking off in the opposite direction. I wonder how far I could walk before they realised I was gone. Whether I could make it out of state before they thought to look for me. But I don't dare. There's always the possibility that they wouldn't bother.

I ignore the heaviness in my chest and head for home.

Six

    I step through the door to Lockless House. Though the sun is out and birds are chirping, I can't help but feel a sense of forboding. Like there's a bomb buried somewhere nearby, and if I make the slightest move in the wrong direction, it'll go off.
    As the door locks behind me, someone marches from the main lab. Rene sees me and stops, adjusting the lapel of his lab coat. Our eyes meet, and his gaze turns stony.
    "Are you gracing us with your presence today?" he asks coldly.
    I open my mouth to fire back at him, but words fail me. I recall the concern in Marcus' eyes as he asked what had changed me, and suddenly my chest is filled with hatred.
    In a single movement I've passed Rene by. I drift up the stairs, my gaze fixed on the floor.
    "We have tests to do," he reminds me. He's right. I have responsibilities, whether I want them or not. And there's no getting out of this; if I told them I

didn't want to take part, it wouldn't change anything. I should lower my head in submission and go into the lab.

But as I reach the top of the stairs and slam my bedroom door behind me, I find I don't care.

I'm woken several hours later by thunder.

I sit up groggily and push the hair from my face, staring out at the city. It's even darker now. Another rumble licks through the building, making the floor shake a little.

My stomach lets out an audible growl and I stand, ignoring the wave of lightheadedness that washes over me. Now I think about it, I've not eaten much lately. It seems like that would be hard to forget about; but after fasting so much for tests, I've grown used to ignoring normal hunger pains.

I glance at the clock. Three in the afternoon. Tests should have stopped by now, right? Maybe I can sneak into the kitchen and grab a snack. I never learned how to cook, and as a result I don't remember the last time I ate a proper meal. Even so, there should be something in the kitchen I can eat.

My resolve falters halfway down the stairs. If I run into Rene, we're bound to argue. After what Marcus said, I don't know if I'll be able to resist throwing his words at Rene. I swallow hard before stepping into the lab.

Silence. The room is empty and oddly peaceful.

"They've gone to a Sponsors meeting."

Jonah. He sits in the corner of the room, clutching a steaming mug of coffee. He eyes me with a curious look.

"You decided to come down, then. What happened?"

"I got hungry."

He chuckles.

"Want me to throw something together?"

"I can manage."

"Nonsense," he says, "I haven't eaten yet either, so it makes sense to cook for both of us. Come on, you can help me."

He heads into the kitchen and I trail after, uncertain but driven forward by the thought of real food.

"Aren't you going to yell at me?" I ask him.

"Why would I do that?"

"Didn't anyone tell you?" I say, "I stormed out yesterday morning and didn't come back until today. Rene was furious."

Jonah pulls a ceramic pan from the cupboard, then fires me a bemused look.

"Honestly, I think he was just relieved to see you safe."

"Sure, that sounds about right. We all know that Rene is the pinnacle of concern for others."

Normally, even Jonah would narrow his eyes at that level of sarcasm. But to my surprise, he ignores it.

"Grab some bowls, will you?"

I do as I'm told, as surprised by my own sudden obedience as I am by his attitude. I tell myself that this is Jonah; one of the few people I can talk to openly. I open my mouth, then close it. I don't know what to say. Luckily, he beats me to it.

"I heard what you did yesterday. During the test."

"You did?"

"Yes. Turning it into a race, huh? I must say, you surprise me all the time."

"It was just a bit of fun. Alya enjoyed it, too."

"I know she did. Why do you think I'm not mad?"

I stare, but his smile simply widens.

"That girl doesn't get a great deal of fun these days," he explains, "too much pressure, too much responsibility. Alya's going to have a rude awakening one day, when we're all gone and she's left to fend for herself. Maybe it's good to let her have a little fun before that."

And with that he turns away, flicking on the tap and lifting the pan. I think of a million responses, but bite back on them. Instead, I think of all the times Jonah's told me the hard truths. Like why I didn't come out right. Or what happened to Rene's father. I bite my lip. Surely he'd tell me this, too.

"Jonah. Can I ask you a question?"

"Shoot."

"Why did Marcus leave the Project?"

He pauses, placing the pan down and turning to face me. He grabs a dishcloth and runs it anxiously through his fingers, but he's trying a little too hard to seem casual.

"Marcus? He left when you were just a kid. I didn't think you remembered him."

"Well, I do. So why'd he leave?"

Jonah watches me uncertainly, like he's not sure how much to divulge.

"Why are you asking this, Reya?"

"I..."

I hesitate.

"I heard someone say the name earlier and suddenly remembered him, that's all."

"I see. Well, the short version is that he left because his aims didn't match the Project's."

"What's the long version?"

He tosses the dishcloth aside, suddenly stern. His jovial attitude dissipates as he looks me up and down, like he's searching for some tell-tale sign that I'm lying. And it's true – if he digs too deeply, I'm bound to slip up. So when he picks up the pot again and demands I tell him why I'm asking, I know better than to lie.

"The truth is," I mutter, "I may have... bumped into him in the city."

In an instant, the kitchen is filled with the sound of shattering ceramic and colourful swearing. Jonah leaps away from the remains of the pot, and I jump out of my seat.

"Jonah, are you okay?"

"What did he do?!"

Jonah doesn't even glance at the broken shards. Instead he rounds the table, locking his hands on my shoulders. When I lift my gaze to meet his, I'm stunned to see a host of new emotions in his eyes. Anger. Confusion. Even a hint of fear.

He grips my arms tightly.

"Reya, tell me. What did that psychopath do to you?"

"Huh? What..."

He slaps one hand against his forehead, then drags it over his face.

"I should have known he'd come back. We've been complacent. No wonder you were gone all night! Are you hurt? Should I get Neil to come home?"

He lifts my chin, stares into my eyes, pushes back my hair.

"Jonah, I'm fine!" I laugh. He doesn't laugh back.

"You need to tell me what happened. Every last detail, do you understand me?"

"It's nothing," I say, pushing him away, "I just ran into him and we said hello."

He steps back, still breathless.

"He didn't try anything?"

"No. Why?"

Finally, he seems to relax. He sinks into the nearest chair, clutching his chest. I step closer.

"Jonah. What's with that reaction?"

"Are you sure you're okay?" he asks. I nod, and he lets out a long sigh. He cups his head in his hands and sinks forward onto the table.

"I'm sorry, Reya. I didn't mean to frighten you. But that man... I don't trust him one bit."

"Why not?"

I feel my resolve harden.

"Why did he leave? Is that why you're scared? What did he do?"

Jonah shakes his head, then reaches out and grasps my hand. I ignore the discomfort in my chest and allow him to pull me closer. As he meets my gaze, I'm confused by what I see. I've never seen Jonah like this before.

"Listen to me," he says firmly, "that man might seem friendly enough, but he does not have your best interests at heart. Or anyone's, for that matter. Marcus will tell you anything if he thinks it'll get you on his side, even if he has less than honourable goals."

I remember how gentle his touch was, how supportive his smile was, and sigh.

"I don't know what to tell you, Jonah. He seemed totally sincere to me."

"And? What did he ask for? There has to be something."

"Nothing."

I chew my lip.

"Well, not nothing. He asked if I'd speak to him again. But that's fine, right? He might be bigger than me, but I'm pretty sure I could fight him off if anything took a turn."

"No."

Jonah fixes me with a hard look.

"This isn't a case of trying it out, and seeing if he's changed. He's dangerous and you'd be stupid to see him again. I need you to promise me, Reya. Promise you will not speak to him again."

"But..."

"Please!"

His voice cracks and just like that, I take him seriously.

"A-alright. I get it."

"Just trust me, okay? This is for your own sake."

He heads back to the kitchen, his attention now turned to the broken ceramics on the floor. He grabs the dustpan, but I can see his fingers shaking.

"Are you going to tell me why he's so dangerous?" I ask.

"I can't. Not right now."

He leans down to start sweeping, disappearing from my view.

I guess I shouldn't be surprised that Marcus is a psycho. I've encountered enough of them over the years to have been suspicious anyway. But I can't deny that flicker of sorrow in my chest at having lost yet another potential friend.

Jonah stands up, eyeing me carefully.

"I know this doesn't make much sense right now," he says softly, "but it'll come clear soon. I need to speak to the others, and gather some information. Then, I'll tell you what you need to know. Until then, don't tell anyone else that you've met him. We don't want to cause a panic."

"I understand."

"Good. Your strength has always been reading people, and playing off them. You're clever like that. I need you to utilise that skill now. Protect yourself. Trust nobody."

"Not even you?" I joke. His mouth twitches.

"Maybe not."

Alya and I sneak out again that night. Though I'm still a little nervous following Jonah's outburst, I hadn't been able to refuse when she'd knocked on my door, pleading with me to take her somewhere interesting. Apparently, meetings with Sponsors no longer thrill her the way they used to.

I text the others on our way out, asking if anyone's free. Luckily, they are. Nova tells us to meet her and the guys outside her place for a drive through the city.

As we walk the shadowed streets, Alya fires me an excited look.

"What's got you so worked up?" I ask. For once, I wish she'd be a little calmer. Jonah's warning earlier has me on edge, and I need the silence. I walk a half-step slower than her, glancing nervously around. Each distant footstep or car horn sends uncomfortable shudders through me.

That group yesterday was so quiet. I hadn't realised they were there until it was too late. I glance at Alya. She darts ahead, marching happily, her dark hair swishing as she walks.

"Hey."

She finally pauses, glancing back at me with a confused look.

"What? We're nearly there."

I stare at her for a moment; at the jet black hair, the pale face. Her icy grey eyes, her slim body hidden by a loaned, oversized sweater. Even in the dim streetlight, it's clear she's not a randomer. There's something inhuman about her.

I swallow hard. Consciously, I know what's best. I should tell her what happened to me last night. All of it – from the attack and the scrawled words on my arm, right down to encountering Marcus. I owe her that much. But for some reason, Rene's face flashes in my head. That warning look he always gives me. I shouldn't say too much.

So instead I walk past her, reaching out to ruffle her hair.

"We had better hurry. It's not safe out here."

"What are you talking about?" she laughs, smoothing out her locks, "I thought you knew these streets."

"Maybe not as well as I thought."

She steps up beside me, face filled with curiosity. I bite my lip.

"Look, last night..."

"Right. You went somewhere, right? You were out really late."

"...the point is, last night something happened."

Her brows furrow.

"Huh?"

I roll the words around in my head for a moment, trying to find the right combination. Something that will get my point across without sending her into a panic. Finally, I settle for the basics.

"I got jumped again last night," I explain, "I got away, but this time it was... different. There were more of them, and they were organised. Like they'd been following me."

Her face drops and she steps closer, hooking an arm through mine.

"You were attacked again? Are you okay?"

"I'm fine. But it was eerie. I didn't hear them coming, and suddenly there were a lot of them. We need to be careful."

"Should we go home?" she asks, looking around nervously. I shake my head.

"No. If we go home, they win. At least for tonight. Is that what you want?"

"No."

I fire what I hope is a confident look her way.

"I didn't mean to make you worry. Just keep your wits about you."

"I don't know how to fight, Reya."

"You won't have to. That's why I'm here."

She seems somewhat comforted by that, to my surprise, and falls into line beside me. I find that my own breathing has calmed a little too, every step a little easier in her presence. Knowing that she's listening out for danger, too.

"Hey," she says suddenly, "what's the big deal with driving Nova's car, anyway? You seemed so excited about it earlier. I didn't even know you could drive."

"Of course I can drive. I learned how a long time ago, in case of an emergency."

"And you enjoy it?"

I shrug.

"It's fun, I suppose. Especially at night. The roads are clear and you can really pick up some speed around the edge of the city. As for Nova's car, well..."

We step onto the car park of Nova's building. She's waiting nearby, leaning heavily on a particularly glossy convertible – the latest birthday gift from her parents. It's not quite the same level as Rene's flashy supercar, but it's a far cry from Sandra's beaten-up truck or the twins' white van.

As we near, someone waves from the back seat. Charlie and Spencer lounge in the back of the car, their arms dangling over the edge like they're celebrities being chauffeured. Nova rolls her eyes theatrically as we near.

"God, *finally*. I wondered when you two were going to show up."

Alya mumbles an apology, but I just chuckle.

"Sorry about that, Nova. See, some of us have responsibilities."

She cackles at the joke, then waves at the driver's seat.

"Your throne, madam. I figured you'd want to do the driving tonight."

My fingers itch with the desire to leap in and start up the engine; but then my gaze is drawn to Alya. She watches politely, eyes wide as she admires the sleek vehicle.

I was taught to drive in case something happened, and I needed to make a quick getaway. It makes sense for her to learn, too.

"Actually," I smile, "how about we let Alya drive tonight?"

The others fire stunned looks my way.

"Hold up," Spencer gasps, "Reya doesn't want to drive?!"

Nova leans forward, pressing a hand to my head.

"Are you sick?" she teases. I push her away.

"Alright, alright. I get it."

"Why do you want me to drive?" Alya squeaks, "I don't know how."

"Now's a damn good time to learn," I tell her, "the roads are quiet this time of night, and it's not like you need a licence. So long as Nova's happy with it, that is."

She glances at Alya and smirks.

"I hope to god you're a better driver than Reya. She's smashed up my car so many times I've lost count."

I settle into the passenger seat, Nova perched awkwardly on my lap. Any other time, I might insist she sit in the back – but Spencer's huge form is easily taking up two seats, forcing Charlie against the door. This is probably safer.

Alya sits stiffly in the driver's seat, looking like she'd rather be anywhere else. Nova talks her through the first steps, but her panic doesn't fade.

I get it. When I was a kid – when I was the Tomorrow Girl – the emphasis was always on knowledge. You didn't have to be able to do something, just as long as you understood *how* to do it. At the time it had seemed so simple; it's only after meeting Nova and the others that I learned my lesson. Alya's never been taught to do something for herself before, and it shows in the terror behind her eyes.

"You've got this," I tell her. She glances from me to the steering wheel, then nods. The first time she nudges the pedal, the car roars but doesn't move. Spencer leans forward.

"You might want to take the handbrake off."

"Oh! Right."

A click. Another nudge of the pedal.

The car jolts forward, and Charlie's head promptly hits the back of my chair.

"Hey, are you okay?"

He pulls back, rubbing his temple.

"Yeah. Sorry. I wasn't belted in."

No wonder. He can't even reach the belt.

Alya fires me a pleading look.

"I-I don't think this is safe."

"Don't worry," I coo, "the first couple of tries are always terrible. Take it from me."

Nova shuffles on my lap, looping one arm around me.

"Can't be any worse than Reya was!"

"Thanks for the input, Nova."

She grins, then gives Alya an encouraging nod.

"Try it again. Softer, this time."

Alya chews her lip for a moment, then fixes her eyes on the road ahead. I can tell she's trying to psyche herself up, building her confidence for one major push. She glances my way and I smile.

The next time she tries, the car takes off at a steady, if slightly slow, pace. Spencer cheers while Nova politely claps.

"You've got it! Keep going!"

Alya's eyes widen and her mouth falls open in shock.

"Oh, god. Reya, it's moving. What do I do?"

"Relax," I tell her, "you're doing great."

Spencer slaps the back of my chair.

"Let's get some speed going, shall we?"

She glances at me, eyes wide. I just laugh.

"It's alright. Signal left here. I'll guide you to the freeway."

"But..."

"You're the Tomorrow Girl, right? You've got this."

She still seems terrified, but seems to steel herself. Perhaps it's the pressure of living up to the title. She veers onto the main road, suddenly confident. The others voice their approval, but I watch her for a moment.

The fear in her eyes has vanished. Instead she fixes her gaze on the road, checking the mirrors like a seasoned pro. I open my mouth to tell her that she's picked it up better than I did, then catch myself.

Why is she *trying* so hard?

We pull onto the freeway and her expression briefly falters - but with a few encouraging words, she floors it. My neck jolts as we shoot forward, her instincts unused to the pedals. She fires an apologetic look at the rest of us.

"This is harder than it looks."

"Are you joking?" Spencer booms, "you're a total natural! Are you sure you haven't already had lessons?"

"No. I've never even sat in the front seat before."

Surprisingly, there's a hint of bitterness in her voice. Something aches in my chest. Understanding, perhaps. I fix a smile on my face.

"You're amazing, Alya."

The words are gross – a sickly sweet combo I'd never normally use. But for once, I mean it.

Colour fills her cheeks, and she looks pointedly at the road.

"T-thanks."

Nova leans closer, whispering into my ear.

"That made her really happy, huh? Why don't you say stuff like that more often?"

I don't reply; I'm too busy asking myself the same question.

We pull up outside a fast food joint and sit by the car, sipping on some sugary, brightly-coloured ice drink. Though I'd normally prefer to go to a bar, there's something nice about this. Just the five of us, propped against Nova's flashy car. Gentle laughter fills the air.

"I still can't believe it," Spencer says, "Alya, you're a goddamn superstar."

Her chest is puffed with pride, her face still flushed. Idly, I wonder why. All she ever hears from the Project is how incredible she is. Why would it please her so much to hear it from us?

"I wonder what else you're a natural at," Nova wonders aloud. Alya shrugs.

"I don't know. The Project teaches mainly academic subjects, but a lot of them don't have much real-world application. Like Latin."

"Latin?! For real?"

She nods, and Nova looks at me.

"Do you speak Latin too? Is that the kind of stuff they teach you at Lockless House?"

I let out a cold laugh.

"Please. The Project gave up teaching me anything years ago."

"I always wondered about that," Alya says, "why you were never in classes with me."

"That's because I'm unteachable. Or at least, that's what Rene says. I never showed up to lessons anyway, since I was having way more fun with these guys. Of course, he always figured I was out getting into fistfights."

"To be fair, a lot of the time you were getting into fistfights."

"Well sure, technically. But it's not like I look for trouble. Trouble just finds me."

"How did you learn to fight?" she asks, her eyes glittering. I shrug.

"Sink or swim, I suppose. Jonah tried to teach me boxing a few times, but I never really clicked with it. Spencer taught me a thing or two about self-defence, too."

He winks.

"Always go for the crotch. Guaranteed win."

"Any options that are less... gross?" she squeaks. He fixes her with a curious look.

"Do you want to learn? I can teach you."

"Come on, Spencer," I interject, "leave her be. She's just a kid."

"I thought you were teaching her how to survive out here."

"Not by sterilising people!"

Alya rounds on me suddenly, her pale eyes flashing with indignance.

"You warned me about the Mortalists! What if they try something?"

"You'll be okay. Rene and the others would rather die than let anyone lay a hand on you."

Her eyes fill with tears.

"That's what I'm worried about."

"Huh?"

"The rest of you aren't built like me," she says shakily, "humans are all so... fragile. One gunshot, one stabbing, and... look, I know Jonah used to be a boxer, but even he isn't superhuman. If I can defend myself, then nobody has to die trying to protect me."

She whips round to face me, fury in her eyes.

"Teach me how to fight."

"But Alya..."

"I'm asking you to help me. I know you can fight. You'd have been hurt a lot worse by now if you couldn't."

"I haven't fought anyone properly in years," I tell her, "just drunken yobs. I joined a street fighting tournament a few years ago and did pretty well with it, but I had to stop."

"Why?"

"Someone complained about me not being human. Evidently, it's considered an 'unfair advantage', whatever that means."

"So you do know how to fight. Show me."

I take a moment to study her expression. It's somehow familiar, like a look I've seen a million times before. Her brows are furrowed and her lower lip juts out. There's a peculiar emotion burning behind her eyes.

Suddenly, I recognise that face. It's the same face I pull when I'm arguing with Rene.

I reach out and pat her arm. I can't believe I'm about to do this.

"Alya. Punch me."

Her face drops.

"What?"

"Punch me. Right here, as hard as you can."

I point at my cheek and she backs away.

"What the hell are you..."

"I'm trying to teach you, idiot. It's easy enough to learn the basics. How to use someone's weight against them, how to break free. Spencer could teach you that in a day. I'm no good with the technical side. But what I can teach you is how it feels."

I open my arms wide, egging her on.

"Spar with me."

"Right here? In the car park?"

"Don't worry," I laugh, "just throw a couple of punches and we'll see what happens."

She hesitates, then curls her hand into a fist. For a moment she stares down at it, like she's never made the motion before. Then she looks up at me, her lips tightening into a thin line.

"I'll dodge it," I reassure her, "promise."

I expect her to refuse, but she doesn't. To my surprise she pulls back, aims squarely at my jaw, and throws her weight forward.

Damn. She's faster than I thought.

I twist aside, narrowly avoiding the blow. There's not much strength behind it and her technique is god-awful, but I still feel the air shift as I move away.

"Not bad," I chuckle, "try again."

She does as she's told, but this time I'm ready. I catch her fist in my hand, easily taking all the force from it. She gasps.

"How did you do that?!"

"Look how fast you are!" I grin, "light on your feet, too."

She pulls back and glances down at her feet. Then, after a moment, she starts to bounce on her heels, jumping slightly from side to side. I can almost see the wheels turning in her head. She's trying to figure out how to utilise her natural grace.

"Once more," I instruct. She nods, pulls back, then dodges to the side. It takes a moment for me to realise what she's done – and by the time I do, she's already on me. Her fist collides with the side of my face, and I freeze.

That didn't hurt in the slightest. Her hands are too soft, her will too weak.

But she did it.

She pulls back, panic in her eyes.

"I'm so sorry! Are you okay?"

I rub at my face, surprised by how light the blow was.

"Are you kidding me? I barely felt it. I thought a butterfly had landed on my cheek."

Her face fills with colour, but I grab her shoulder.

"You're fast, though. Clever, too – you really got me with that feint."

"I wasn't sure if it would work."

I glance at Spencer.

"Well? What's your verdict?"

The others have been standing by silently, but now they finally react. Nova's eyes fill with amusement, but she covers her mouth with both hands to keep from laughing. Charlie sits on the kerb, still clutching his drink, looking for all the world like he doesn't belong. Spencer, on the other hand, leans in. His face is flushed with excitement.

"You're right!" he booms, "she's fast as hell. We can definitely teach you a thing or two."

At that, Alya brightens.

"Really?"

I fire a pointed smirk at Spencer and he frowns.

"Oh, hell. You want to show her the throw, don't you?"

"It's saved my ass a few times," I shrug, "plus it's useful when someone sneaks up on you."

"Does it have to be me?" he whines.

"You're the biggest one here, so you're less likely to get hurt."

Spencer sighs and steps up behind me, shifting into position. One hand wraps around my shoulder, the other near my face as though he were an assailant trying to gag me from behind. I glance at Alya and nod.

"This is a useful one. If anyone tries coming up behind you, just do this. Watch."

In an instant I've grabbed Spencer's arm, wrapped my other hand around his neck, and shifted my weight forward. For a split second, he's airborne – and then he hits the ground hard, flung forward over my head.

He lets out a pained whine, then starts giggling.

"Oh jesus, that hurts," he laughs, "you couldn't have gone easy on me, Reya?"

"Sorry," I mutter. I glance at Alya, who watches me with a stunned expression.

"Did you see how I did that?"

"But he's so much bigger than you," she gasps, "how did you toss him like that?"

"It's hard to explain. I guess you just use momentum?"

"How did you learn to do that?"

I shrug, cheeks burning, and fire her a sheepish look.

"By the way, do me a favour and never tell Jonah I can do that. He's not a fan of any combat that doesn't have rules and he'd lecture me for hours about structure and the importance of discipline."

"I'll keep it secret if you show me how you did it," she says, "but I don't think I can throw Spencer."

I wind up my shoulder and flash a grin her way.

"Alright then. We're about the same weight, right? Let's see how you do with me."

We slip into Nova's apartment in the early hours, still giggling. Alya grasps my arm. Her face is red, partly from laughing and partly from the speed she was driving at a few moments ago. Her dark hair is tousled, briefly destroying her ethereal appearance. For a brief moment, she looks like any normal teenager.

Nova yawns and Spencer elbows her.

"Hey, what're you doing? You promised us an update on the platform."

"Fine, fine," she says sleepily, "please, follow me into my workshop."

"Workshop?" Alya asks, tilting her head. I grin at her.

"Nova's working on something incredible."

We pile into her spare room, and Alya eyes up the platform. Her mouth falls open as she surveys the new, sleek coverings, the reinforced underside, and the smaller-than-ever generator.

"What does this do?" she gasps. Nova smirks.

"It's an air platform. It jettisons thin tendrils of air out and weaves them together, and can be used as an invisible floating floor or wall. My main plan is to use it for a multi-level road surface."

"Wow! I bet the Project would use something like this!"

"I told you," I tell Nova, "anyway, this looks great. You've made so much progress!"

"The grant from Marcus has been really helpful. It's almost ready for showing."

"You'll make one hell of an impression at the Creation Show," I tell her, "and then you'll be drowning in Sponsorships."

Spencer hooks an arm around me.

"Have you figured out a way to attend, yet?"

I glance at Alya. I'm willing to share plenty of my secrets with her, now – my friends, my hobbies, even Nova's inventions – so I suppose I can trust her to know about the show, too.

"I haven't got a solution yet," I admit, "but I'll keep trying."

Alya doesn't speak, but I feel her gaze settle on me. Charlie frowns.

"You have to find a way, Reya. It won't be the same without you."

"Sure, it will. I'm not a supplier or the brains of the operation, after all. I'm just the guinea pig."

"Don't sell yourself short," he says, "every successful venture needs a good guinea pig."

I laugh, and he promptly reddens.

"Th-that's not what I meant!"

"Too late, Charlie-boy! You already said it."

He buries his face in his hands, and Spencer claps his brother on the back.

"Alright, come on. If you're done calling our friends rodents, we should head home. We've got a couple of early deliveries tomorrow, and I'm definitely a little over the limit."

Nova turns towards me.

"Do you and Alya want to spend the night?"

I sigh.

"I'd love to, but we can't risk it. Alya can't be gone all night, or Rene will have my head."

"Then sleep a couple of hours, set an alarm for about 4am, and head home before the Project wakes up."

"I don't wake up to alarms," I say, "I just sleep through."

"Then I'll stay up," Alya interjects, "you know I don't need sleep. I can just stay awake until 4 and then wake you. That way, we can leave without disturbing Nova."

"Don't be silly, you can't go without sleep."

She fixes me with a defiant look.

107

"What's the use of having these abilities if I can't use them? I can go a month without food, but the Project still makes sure I eat three square meals a day. It's ridiculous."

"Consider yourself lucky. They don't give a crap what I do and nobody ever taught me how to cook, so I barely eat enough to survive."

It's meant as a joke, but the room falls silent. Nova shifts uncomfortably.

"I'm heading to bed. You guys can have the sofa. You're free to stay all night but if you go, make sure you lock the door on the way out. I don't want to be burgled if I can help it."

With that she heads from the room. Alya clutches my sleeve.

"Can we stay just a little while? Please."

I stare into her wide, grey eyes, and something stirs in me.

"Fine."

She grins and heads for the living room. I watch her, confused by my own reaction. Damnit. When did I start liking the little weirdo?

"Here you go."

I press the cup of cocoa into Alya's hands. She takes it with a grin.

"You even put whipped cream and sprinkles on it."

"Yep. I may not have a clue how to cook, but I'm somewhat of an expert in beverages. Though most of my expertise is limited to the alcoholic kind..."

I sink down next to her, my back against the wall. Really, we should be on the sofa – but for some reason we're perched on the deep sill of Nova's window. The rest of the apartment is bathed in darkness, silent aside for Nova's snuffly breathing in the other room.

I lean forward. From here, there's a glorious view of the city. Buildings crowd the lower half of my vision, blending into a mass of black and blue shadow. Overhead, thin grey clouds roll over a starry sky.

"Pretty, huh?" I chuckle, "can't get views like this during the day."

Alya tilts her head at me.

"Reya? Why can't you cook?"

"What kind of a question is that? I can't cook because I never learned."

"Why not? Rene started teaching me when I was just a kid."

"Rene can cook?" I ask, incredulous. She nods.

"He's really good at it! He makes dinner for everyone all the time."

"He does?"

"Yeah. You'd know that if you ate dinner with the rest of us."

"I thought everyone ate at different times."

She frowns.

"Most days, sure. That makes sense when people work in shifts. But Rene cooks a big batch of food once or twice a week and we all have dinner as a family."

My heart sinks.

"Oh. I didn't know about that."

"Really? I just figured you didn't want to join us."

"Well," I say, "it's news to me, but I guess it's fine. If he wanted me there, he'd have asked. The last thing I'd want is to intrude on family time."

I fight to keep my voice light, but in truth, the news hurts. I've known for a while that the Project excludes me from certain things, but this seems especially cold. It would be nice to be asked, even if it was only out of obligation.

Suddenly, I remember being a kid. We'd cover the kitchen counters in finger foods, like a small buffet, and sit cross-legged on the floor of the lab to eat. Back then, nothing made me happier than being with everyone for a 'lab picnic'. The Project knew this, and I could tell they did it more often because it made me happy. Then again, that was back when they thought I was something special.

I look over at Alya, who once again looks celestial in the moonlight.

Of course they do it for her. She's their whole world. Alya never gets into fights or brings shame to the Project. She's pretty and polite and perfect. What's more, she turned out exactly how she was supposed to. I can't blame them for loving her more than they ever loved me.

"Reya?"

She leans in suddenly, her face creased with concern.

"Are you crying?"

I blink, surprised to find she's right. Droplets have formed in the corners of my eyes – not enough to spill down my cheeks, but certainly enough to make my eyes glisten. I wipe my face and laugh.

"Nah, of course not. You know I don't cry."

"Everyone cries," she shrugs, "I cry all the time."

"What do you have to cry about? Your life is pretty perfect from where I'm sitting."

She snorts.

"Perfect? Please. I'm 17 and I have no friends. Until recently, I'd never been out of Lockless House after dark. Even in the day, I can't go anywhere without an entourage. I've literally never been entirely alone, not in my whole life!"

She lets out a low, frustrated growl.

"Every second of my life is recorded, tracked and logged. I can't sneeze without a report being written on the subject. Hell, I'm not even allowed to talk to the Sponsors!"

"You're not? But they always talk about how much they love you."

"Yeah well, why wouldn't they love me?" she sighs, "I hardly ever say a word to them, not even when they're doing something wrong. Like Mr Clarington."

She lifts her head.

"That's why I made you bring me out here. I never meant to threaten you with blackmail, honest, and I wouldn't have actually told Rene anything. I just wanted a taste of how most normal 17 year olds get to live."

I sigh.

"I guess I can understand that. The Project can be a little overbearing."

"Not with you, though. They let you do whatever you like."

I take a sip of cocoa.

"It's not as fun as it sounds, trust me."

"I know you hate the Project, Reya. It's okay. I get it."

I pause.

"You think I hate the Project?"

"It's pretty obvious."

"I don't hate it," I snap, "the Project made me, remember? I literally owe them my life."

"Is that why you stick around, because you owe them? The way I see it, you have some pretty great friends out here. If you have all this, why do you bother coming back to Lockless House when you just argue with Rene?"

Her words hurt, but I shake them off. In truth, I've asked myself this countless times.

"Look, Rene and I haven't always been at each other's throats. We used to be really close."

She leans forward at that.

"Are you for real?"

"It's true! When I was a kid, the Project was run by his dad, Rene Senior, and Rene was one of the Project's youngest members. He'd always take time out to hang with me, even though I was a little brat. We were so close the others used to tease him and say I was like his daughter."

"So what changed?"

My stomach churns. What changed? He realised that I was a failure and moved on.

"Reya?"

I blink hard. The tears are fighting me again.

Why am I sad? I've known for years that Rene doesn't like me. I've made too many mistakes. Things will never be like they were before.

"I... guess he had more important things to focus on," I choke.

She watches silently for a moment, then clears her throat.

"Reya, do you hate me?"

"What?"

"It sounds like things were happier for you before I was born. Like I ruined it. You know I'd never want to do that, right?"

My chest hurts. I've lost track of how many times I've blamed her; cursed her out in my head, dreamed of telling her every secret about her birth and the Project's intentions, watching betrayal fill her eyes as she realises that not only was she the backup, but that in merely existing, she'd effectively ruined my life.

Then, I reconsider. It's not her fault. Neither of us asked to be born into this mess. No matter how much my throat aches with envy, or how often I watch them love her more than they used to love me, I can't blame her.

"No," I say softly, "I don't hate you."

"I wouldn't blame you if you did. You can hate me as much as you hate Rene."

At that, I balk.

"I don't hate Rene," I tell her, the softness vanishing from my voice. She stares.

"Yes, you do."

"I don't hate anyone, especially Rene," I repeat, "the only thing I hate is constantly letting him down. I've never been good enough for him."

When I glance over again, she's smiling.

"What's so funny?"

"Not funny, exactly. It's just sweet that you care so much about what he thinks. But you're the only one who thinks that you're not good enough."

I snort and she sighs.

"Honestly. Why do you think that?"

I don't respond; just pull my knees up to my chin. We're getting too close to the bone. I can't imagine Rene's reaction if I told her the big secret, even if she does deserve to know. The churning in my stomach grows stronger.

"Reya?"

She leans in.

"I mean it. I really want to know. Why do you think you're not good enough?"

"You don't want to hear this story."

I keep my face buried, half-hoping she didn't hear me – but of course, she did.

"Yes, I do."

"Rene will kill me if I tell you."

"Great," she huffs, "another Project secret I'm not allowed to know. They always do this. They treat me like a toddler who can't understand anything beyond bells and whistles. It's not like I'm the sole purpose for the Project's existence, or anything."

At that, I lift my head. A glance tells me that she's just as sick of it all as I am, albeit for a very different reason. For the first time, I put myself in her shoes. She exists to test, every breath monitored and logged. When not testing, they educate her at a rate of knots, filling her head with useless trivia, or sell her image to companies for a quick buck. There's no doubt in my mind that they adore her, but their love can be just as strangling as their disapproval.

Suddenly, I want to tell her everything.

"You weren't."

"I wasn't what?"

"The purpose of the Project," I say, "it wasn't meant to be you."

She tilts her head.

"What are you talking about?"

"Look," I sigh, "this isn't just a Project secret. This is *the* Project secret. Telling you could get me sent away forever, do you understand? They can never know I told you."

She nods, so I push on.

"The truth is, years before you were born, the Project tried to make their precious Tomorrow Girl. They planned everything meticulously, and spent years preparing for it. They planned her name, her face, her voice. Everything. And they made a little girl, who seemed to be everything they wanted. At first."

Alya stares, wide-eyed, but allows me to continue.

"The girl was supposed to change as she grew up. Her abilities were supposed to develop with her body, and be traceable by the time she was a few years old. You know the traits. Healing, resistance, survival. But they never appeared. The girl was a perfectly average human, and as she grew up she remained just that. A normal human. Artificial, sure, but nothing special."

"Reya."

"So they tried again. Second time round, it worked. Alya Mathis became the Tomorrow Girl, and she was absolutely perfect."

I pause, but don't raise my head to look at her. I can't stand to see it; the look of dawning realisation and disappointment. I push on but my voice cracks, betraying me.

"The other girl – the first, failed attempt – wasn't legally human, so they couldn't send her away. Instead, they pretended that she was always meant to be like that. So they claimed that she was a genetic base instead, made to serve as a comparison for the Tomorrow Girl. The shadow of the real miracle."

Something hot streams down my cheek, but I ignore it.

"That girl... had to deal with always being second best. A failed attempt. She had to resign herself to being a footnote in someone else's story – and a depressing footnote, at that."

I bite my lip, and in an instant Alya is on me. She leans in so close that our noses nearly touch. To my surprise, her eyes are wet with tears.

"Reya... I'm so sorry."

She loops her arms around me, pulling me close, and I don't fight her.

"Why didn't you tell me sooner?" she whimpers, "I had no idea."

"The Project don't want you to know. They figure it would upset you."

Her embrace tightens.

"Is it a little disappointing to find out that I wasn't the first? Sure. But I can move past it. But what happened to you..."

"I'm fine," I lie. Suddenly I want nothing more than to change the subject – to get rid of the ache in my chest and the heartbroken expression on Alya's face. I draw my face into a smile, but my lip wobbles, betraying me further.

"That's why you're so angry all the time," Alya mutters. I give a weak chuckle.

"Hey, I'm not angry all the time. Just *most* of the time."

"I don't blame you. Did they tell you everything when you were a kid?"

"Yeah," I shrug, "until I was six, they told me I was going to be like you. Guess it was kind of a shock when it turned out to be a lie."

Alya sits beside me, clutching my hand tightly.

"For what it's worth, if I could make you just like me, I would."

"It's alright," I tell her, "as it turns out, you're actually a great Tomorrow Girl. I think I was the wrong fit for the role. I couldn't do it - all the smiles and diplomacy. I'd probably have destroyed the Project's reputation single-handedly. Most likely by punching the Sponsors in their smug faces."

She giggles, but her hand tightens around mine. My chest feels warm for a moment, and the heaviness vanishes.

"Besides, if I'd been the Tomorrow Girl, they'd never have made you, would they?"

She smiles.

"It doesn't make you sad at all, that you're not like me?"

"Course it does. If I could push a button and be everything the Project wanted, I'd do it in a heartbeat. But I'm not cut out for it."

"Nobody is," she admits, "they expect so much from me. Sometimes I wish I had turned out more like you."

Shock washes over me.

"You want to be like me? Are you absolutely insane? Do you have any idea how much the Project adores you? People are constantly amazed by you. You never have to be scared of anything. I'd kill for even half of that!"

"You have friends, and hobbies, and confidence," she breathes, "I'd kill for that. Hell, even just the friends."

I scoff.

"You need to start paying attention. Nova and the guys obviously like you, and I wouldn't be spilling my gross feelings to you if I hated you. What makes you think we're not your friends?"

Her head snaps up.

"Really?"

"Uh, yeah? Now stop being sad, alright? You're okay. I'm okay. We'll survive whatever the Project throws at us and whatever the rest of the world wants to put us through."

I flash her another smile, but this time it's far more genuine.

"We've got this."

Seven

When we slip into Lockless House, I motion for Alya to head upstairs first. She hesitates but obeys, taking the softest steps possible to prevent the steps creaking. I poke my head into the main lab.

"Evening."

Jonah looks up and frowns.

"You went out again."

"You know me," I shrug, "can't sit still for two minutes."

"Aha. And is this a habit you're looking to teach your sister?"

I pause, then decide to hedge my bets.

"It's fine, Jonah. What she doesn't know…"

"I know Alya can be a little naïve," he says firmly, "but she's not stupid. Considering that she accompanied you on your last few trips – and yes, I have CCTV footage to prove it - I'd say she's well aware of what you're up to."

I swallow hard. Jonah stands, rubbing a hand over his face.

"What have the two of you been doing?"

"Nothing dodgy, if that's what you're asking," I snap, suddenly defensive. He sighs.

"You'll have to tell me, Reya. Otherwise I'll have to inform the others, and you know that Rene won't take kindly to your actions."

I lean against the wall. If it were anyone else, I might try and lie my way out of this. Sandra or Neil are usually easily distracted. Even Rene could be angered to the point of forgetting why he was mad in the first place. But Jonah knows all my tricks, and he won't be fooled.

"Look, it's fine," I tell him, "she just asked me to show her a few things. Life skills, you know."

He raises one eyebrow.

"Life skills?"

"Yes. Like tonight, we went out driving."

"You let Alya drive?"

"Why not? She's good. A damn natural."

He purses his lips, then steps around the table. His expression is almost unreadable and in spite of myself, I shrink back. But then he folds his arms, looking me up and down.

"Anything else?"

"I introduced her to some of my friends."

"Friends?"

"No," I interject, "not thugs or criminals. Just normal people."

He considers this for a moment.

"Are you being safe? Are you staying with your friends? Public places? Staying aware?"

I nod.

"Yes. I know the Mortalists are getting organised, so I'm being careful. It's a short walk to my friends' place. They know how to handle themselves, too."

"And if something had happened?"

"How many times have I had to fight off some asshole who wants me dead?" I shrug, "I can look after both of us. Besides, all the usual tricks are in force. Speed dial on my phone, complete with tracker. If anything happened, you'd be the first to know."

His lips part, and I expect him to start yelling – but instead he digs into his pocket and strides past me. I hear the jingle of keys as he drops them onto the table.

"What are those for?" I ask, dreading the answer. Luckily, he smiles.

"You. Well, you and Alya."

"I don't understand."

"I learned a great many years ago that I can't keep you from doing things," he admits, "you're like a tornado. You cause chaos and speed away without consequence. So as much as your actions concern me, I'm not going to try to stop you. Instead, I'm going to make sure you're both safe."

He points at the keys.

"Those are the spare keys to my Jeep. I know it's not exactly stylish, but it's the official security vehicle so it's safe as all hell. There's a tracker built in, along with emergency contact with Lockless House at the push of a button. If you're going into the city with Alya, then I want you to take it."

I stare.

"You want me to take your car?"

"I expect it back in one piece," he warns me, "any damage will get you in trouble. And if I find that you've been doing anything dangerous – anything at all – I'll withdraw the offer and tell Rene exactly what I've found out. Do you understand?"

I pick up the keys and turn them over in my hand.

"No. Not even a little bit. Why are you just letting me do this?"

"Because, as much as I hate to admit it, you're right. About one thing, at least. Alya does need to learn about real life. I've tried convincing Rene of that but so far, no luck. Now, let me be clear. You learned how to handle yourself by starting as many fights as you finished. That's not okay. Alya is not to learn in that manner. But I also think that you're her best bet at developing those skills."

My chest tightens.

"So, you think she's going to have to fight soon, too."

"Perhaps. Perhaps not. Maybe she won't have to fight for years. But it'll come around eventually and when it does, I don't want the thought of fighting to paralyse her. It shouldn't feel natural, of course – but it shouldn't be totally alien, either."

"Rene would be furious if he knew you thought that."

Jonah winks.

"Well then, I suppose that neither one of us should relay the contents of this chat, should we? Now put those keys away before I change my mind. And keep them hidden when you're not using them. If the others assume they're stolen, I won't be jumping to defend you."

I slip them into my pocket and grin.

"Hey, now. I know everyone thinks I'm crazy, but theft? That's a stretch."

"Crazy?" he asks, bemused, "is that what you think?"

"Well, yeah. Don't get me wrong. I don't blame you, but you guys are definitely scared of me."

He chuckles.

"Of course. 24 year old women are simply terrifying. For now, though, go to bed. You're bound to be tired for tomorrow's tests and I doubt Rene will be as forgiving as I am."

I turn towards the door, then hesitate, remembering our last conversation. The panic in Jonah's voice as he'd demanded to know about Marcus. I glance back at him.

"Jonah? A quick question."

"Fire away."

"The last time we spoke, you said you'd tell me something important. About Marcus."

His expression falters.

"I hoped you'd forget about that."

"I didn't."

"No. No, of course you didn't. As you know, I needed to get the approval of the others to tell you what happened with Marcus 18 years ago."

"And?"

His face fills with some unknown emotion, and when he speaks, his voice is oddly sad.

"The executive decision has been made. I'm not allowed to tell you. All I'm allowed to say is that he's dangerous, and isn't someone you should trust."

Irritation flares in my chest.

"I don't get it," I complain, "if you guys had a disagreement then I can see why you don't like him, but why all the secrecy? You understand that just makes me more eager to find out the truth, right?"

"Yes. I tried to explain that, but..."

He chews his lip.

"Look, our decision is final. I won't tell you, and neither will anyone else."

"But!"

"I know it's hard to understand," he says firmly, "but I need you to trust us on this. We know what's best."

With that he turns away, sinking back into his chair and continuing with his work. It's clear the conversation is over so I slink away, ignoring the burning determination in my chest.

I knock the door to Marcus' apartment and draw myself up to full height. Jonah would lose his mind if he knew I came here, let alone without warning. I take stock of everything I brought with me – my phone, prepped to call for help at the push of a button; my taser, ready to go; and finally Jonah's spare keys, which I hold between my fingers, ready to use them as a weapon if needed.

I definitely shouldn't be here. This is undeniably stupid, yet I can't help myself. If Jonah won't tell me the truth, I'll have to hear it from Marcus himself.

I tense as the door opens. Marcus yawns and rubs a bleary eye.

"Reya. Good evening."

"Is this a bad time?" I ask, still on edge. He yawns again.

"No, no. It's just been a long day. Come on in."

He steps aside and I enter, glancing around nervously. His apartment is much the same as it was during my last visit. Nothing to raise my suspicions. Marcus strides into the kitchen, where he pours out a cup of coffee and takes a hefty glug. He waves it at me.

"Coffee?"

I hesitate.

"Sure?"

He chuckles.

"Always a suspicious one, aren't you? Look, I'm drinking it. If it were poisoned, you'd know. Now, how do you like it?"

"Strong and black."

He pours it out and slides the cup over to me.

"I see you're a woman after my own heart."

The clock in Marcus' living room is almost deafening.

We sit across from one another, politely sipping our coffee. He watches me carefully, like he has a lot to say but he's waiting for me to speak first. My chest tightens.

This is harder than I thought. It's just a question, right? I open my mouth, but nothing comes out. Marcus' lip curls.

"Go ahead. Whatever you need to say, you can say it. I won't judge."

"I... I wanted to ask..."

I hesitate.

"Why did you really leave the Project?"

"I'd have thought the Project would have told you that already."

"They did," I lie, "but I want to hear your side."

He leans forward, smiling over his coffee.

"Well, now I'm intrigued. I'd love to hear what they told you. How they framed it."

I fall silent and he laughs.

"I thought so. You're not a very good liar, are you?"

"Fine. They didn't tell me. I asked, but it's all hush hush."

"So you thought you'd get it out of me?" he asks, "that's fine. If you really want to know, I can tell you."

"I know that whatever you tell me will be biased," I say firmly. He nods.

"Well, of course it will be. We all think we're the good guys, Reya. We all tell stories framing ourselves as the heroes and those who oppose us as villains. In truth, it's never that black and white. What happened 18 years ago certainly wasn't."

He leans back, swilling his cup gently.

"By the time you were five years old, we had started carrying out tests. Small things, like seeing if you could keep up with us when running. Monitoring scraped knees and the like. It wasn't anything like the kind of tests you're doing now – it was simpler than that. But it was already becoming clear that things weren't right."

My stomach squirms. I remember those days vividly. Minor tests disguised as playtime, followed by stints of awkward silence as they tried to figure out what was wrong with me. I hadn't realised what was happening at the time, but now it seems obvious.

"You weren't healing quickly enough," he says, "and you seemed to tire just as quickly as any kid your age. Initially, we had a few theories on why that might be – delayed reactions, perhaps, or something you needed to grow into – but as time went by, we were forced to acknowledge our mistakes. For whatever reason, you weren't the Tomorrow Girl. You were a 100% ordinary, healthy human child."

He looks me up and down, a strange expression crossing his face.

"And that was the start of the problem. The Project quickly split into two camps; those who wanted to set you aside and try again, and those who – like me

– wanted to see if we could 'mend' our mistakes. You can imagine what side Rene was on."

"Yeah. I can."

"Well, that just added extra strain onto our less-than-stellar relationship. Things became hostile. Personally, I think that Rene was struggling more than most. He had just lost his father, you see, and the leadership of the Project was at stake. It became more and more likely that Rene was going to take up the mantle and I knew that if he did, he would be able to override me and proceed with the creation of a 'new' Tomorrow Girl. I'' admit, I became a little panicked by the whole situation. I became determined to become the Project Head instead, to try and control things."

"Why were you panicked?" I ask. He shakes his head sadly.

"We had brought you into the world and raised you with promises of an eternal life and a shining future. I loved you like a daughter, and the thought of snatching that away without even trying was just... unacceptable to me. Besides, I was worried for you. If the Project made someone else, they wouldn't need you anymore. There were even talks of adopting you out."

My heart sinks.

"They wanted to get rid of me?"

"Some did. Rene was the main supporter of that idea. I was against it. You don't create a child, then skip out on them when they don't meet your expectations. I worked to find a way to fix whatever had gone wrong, instead. I thought if I could bring out your latent abilities, the others would stop this nonsense about sending you away."

I roll my eyes.

"Am I really supposed to believe that? Everyone else was saying these awful things and you alone were fighting for me? I wasn't born yesterday."

"No," he chuckles, "I guess you weren't. At first, the sides were fairly even. Jonah sided with me the most; you know he's always had a soft spot for you. Sandra joined us – at least, some of the time. The others dithered a little more, but it certainly wasn't just me. And I can't say that my intentions were entirely noble. I also didn't want to admit defeat. I had put an immense amount of effort into your creation, and pride was definitely a factor. I maintain that my actions were primarily for your sake, though, even if my own ego did get a little too involved at times."

I pause, stunned by his candour. He pushes on.

"Then, I told them about my theory. That your abilities lay dormant for some reason, and that we just needed to crack open your DNA and fix whatever wasn't working. That was, of course, a rather serious thing to suggest given your age, but I presented it nonetheless. People were enraged, of course. Things heated up, arguments started, regretful things were said. That day, the others refused to side with me any longer. Rene was selected to lead the Project and he declared that the following day, they would start work on a new Tomorrow Girl. One who would be better."

His expression darkens suddenly, and his hands clench around his cup. My stomach tightens.

"What did you do?" I whisper, already scared to hear the answer.

"First, let me tell you. I'm not proud of what I did that night. I was furious and desperate, and I couldn't see any other way out of the situation. I saw everything slipping through my fingers and I only had a few short hours to change things. So, while you slept, I put you in my car."

I lower the cup to the floor, fixing him with a steady gaze.

"You kidnapped me."

"I wouldn't call it that. I was still part of the Project, after all. And it's not like I went against your will. When you woke up and asked where we were, I just said we would be home soon. I took you to one of the Safehouses – this old, decrepit-looking warehouse on the edge of town..."

"Safehouse 17."

"You know it?"

"Not exactly," I mutter, "I know we have Safehouses, but I've never had to go to one. Especially not 17. That one's been out of action for as long as I can remember. That's because of you, I assume?"

He nods.

"You're probably right. I took you there because it had a fully-stocked lab, so I could carry out my work in total privacy. In my head, it was so simple. I'd do some tests, get you fixed up, and then take you home before the others even stirred. They'd never have to find out what happened – they would just think you came of age and your abilities had finally manifested. I'd spent the past few weeks developing a serum that could be used to 'unlock' your DNA and reform it slightly, just like how we adjusted your DNA back when you were still developing. I strapped you down, then used long syringes to inject the serum into your spine..."

I stand suddenly, my heart pounding. My gaze flits to the door.

"You... you ran experiments on me?!"

"No! No. I ensured you were fully drugged before doing anything. I wanted to make sure you wouldn't remember a thing come morning."

"Like that makes it better?"

"You didn't feel anything."

"I was a kid!" I shout, "you don't run experiments like that on children!"

I head for the door and yank it open, terror building in my stomach.

"Jonah was right to warn me about you. You *are* a psychopath."

"Reya, please. Just wait."

A hand hits the doorframe and I freeze. Marcus looms over me, the difference in our sizes painfully apparent; but there's no anger in his eyes. Instead, they glisten with unshed tears.

"You're right to be angry. Just like the others were. They caught me, you know, before I could finish my work. I've never seen Rene so furious. Jonah almost put me in the hospital, and I was lucky he didn't beat me to death right then and there."

"You deserved it," I spit. He nods.

"I know I did. That and more. They took you back and kicked me out of the Project. They forbade me from contacting you or anyone else at Lockless House. They said my life wouldn't be worth living if I ever decided to come back to Amare."

"So why did you come back?" I growl. He sighs.

"Because I saw an opportunity to help you."

"Yeah. Sounds like you really helped me last time."

"What happened before was awful. I've never stopped regretting it. I wasn't thinking straight. I acted out of fear and desperation. I thought that's something you could understand."

"No," I snarl, "I might do stupid things, but what you did was cruel."

I whip around and walk back inside, making a beeline for the window. I'm not sure what floor we're on, but there's bound to be a fire escape somewhere. He charges after me, still shouting.

"Listen, I don't know what convinced the Project to keep you. After what I did, I expected them to send you away, like they said they would. But instead they kept you around, and it's pretty clear that hasn't worked out."

"That's none of your business!" I bark, prising open the door to the balcony. It opens a half inch then sticks, and I pull harder. Great. There's no easy way out. My thoughts linger on the taser in my pocket. I shouldn't use it. Rene would kill me if he knew I was here, much less that I'd attacked someone after his latest warnings. But if he gives me no choice...

"You're clearly unhappy."

Marcus stands in the middle of the room, both arms held open like he's inviting me into an embrace. I scowl.

"I shouldn't have come here. I don't know why I even bothered. People always do this. You pretend to care about me, and then it turns out you're just out to screw me over. What the hell am I supposed to do with that?"

I'm snarling now, anger forcing tears from my eyes. He recoils.

"I don't know what you expect from me," I shout, "the Project already wishes I didn't exist. You can keep me here if you want. You can torture me and demand a ransom if you want to, but it won't work. They won't care."

I wipe my eyes furiously and lean against the window, fighting to calm myself.

"Look, I get it. For whatever reason, you hate the Project. Plenty of people do, and it sounds like you have more reason than most. But if you think I'm going to be a bargaining tool, you're a moron. There's only one person they care about, and that's Alya. If you're not the Tomorrow Girl, you don't matter to the Project. So whatever you're planning, just give up. I'm not playing these games."

He stares at me for a long moment, then nods.

"Alright. Look, I don't have any impure intentions with you, but I can see you're not going to trust me."

He steps aside, waving at the door.

"You can go. I won't approach you again. I'll keep my contact with Miss Adebayo to a minimum and I won't ask her about you. Don't worry, this won't affect her funding."

"That easy, huh?"

"It's not easy," he sighs, "I really wanted to be part of your life again, but I won't force my way in. What I did to you 18 years ago was clearly unforgivable. I understand."

I swallow hard, then start walking. As I pass him, though, heading for the door, he sighs.

"It's a shame, though. I truly thought I could fix you this time."

I stop in the doorway, head spinning.

"What did you say?"

"It doesn't matter. You should go."

I fix him with a stern look.

"Don't screw with me. You just said you could fix me. What does that mean?"

He sinks onto the sofa and picks up his coffee, taking a small sip.

"That was supposed to be a conversation for another time. Once we'd built some trust. But that clearly isn't going to happen."

I stare at the doorway for a moment, my stomach swirling. This is a trap, right? It's a trap so obvious that I feel stupid for even considering walking into it. But 'fix' can only mean one thing.

I slink to the other sofa and sit down, fighting to still my racing heart.

"You have sixty seconds," I say, my voice hard, "tell me everything. Including what your end goal is. No games. Just tell me what you want."

He takes a slow breath, then lets it out even slower.

"Reya. Do you know why the Project was founded?"

"I asked for an explanation, not questions."

"Humour me."

"Fine. Why?"

"Legacy," he says simply, "the notion that something will live beyond us, will carry our memory and voice into the future, even when nobody else remembers us. It's a very human obsession, and one that kickstarted the Tomorrow Project. Creating our own legacy has always been at the heart of our work."

"So you want to live forever."

"Not at all. Just to be remembered fondly."

I suck on my teeth, allowing him to continue.

"You once meant the world to me," he says, "and I think it could be that way again. I want to prove I can do this, and I want to see you smile again, and I want to see you finally become accepted in the Project after all these years. But mostly, I want my legacy. Like I was promised, when I joined the Project decades ago."

"You're chasing the wrong person, then. It's Alya you want."

"No. It's you. Listen to me, Reya. Years ago, when I was running those tests, I believed that your body would adapt. And mere seconds before the others arrived to stop me, I started to see... results."

I sit up a little straighter, finally meeting his gaze.

"Results."

"Yes. The more I pushed your body, the more it fought back. It was like your DNA was changing."

He leans closer, a serene smile playing on his lips.

"I believe that if I had continued, even for a few minutes, you would have become the Tomorrow Girl. I was stopped, of course – and rightfully so – but I still believe that to be true."

My hands tighten into fists.

"What are you saying?"

"You're a grown adult. You can consent to tests now. What the Project says doesn't matter – you're your own person. I want to run those tests again. This time, with your permission and input. No sneaking around. No lies. Just you and me, working together to fix something that should never have been broken in the first place."

His smile broadens.

"I want to make you immortal, Reya. Like you were always meant to be."

I curl up under the covers, thoughts swarming like a hive of angry bees. Marcus had let me walk away after his proposition, promising not to approach me again. He'd reminded me, softly, that I knew where to find him should I change my mind.

I raise both hands and lightly thump the sides of my skull. Immortal. I've imagined it a thousand times – waking up with all the advanced abilities I was supposed to be born with. I've fantasized about wowing the Project with them, about Alya's delight at no longer being the only one. I've even dreamt of flashing those abilities in Rene's face, asking him who's worthless now. But those thoughts have always just been that – thoughts. Idle fantasies that have no place in reality.

Until now.

I can understand why Jonah didn't want to tell me the truth. Kidnap and forced experimentation aren't exactly normal misdemeanours; and if he sided with Marcus at the time, he might feel ashamed now. I would hardly blame him.

Still. The temptation is immense, especially given the Project's current situation. Wouldn't it be better for everyone if I were just like her? Fights would be easier. Protecting Alya would be a breeze.

Maybe, if I were immortal, Rene wouldn't be so keen to dismiss me. Perhaps I'd finally earn his respect – and maybe a little affection. At the very least, I wouldn't be a source of embarrassment anymore. I'd be an important part of the Project.

And it's not like Alya would complain. Knowing her, she'd be pleased. It'd be nice for her to not feel so much pressure.

I bury my face in the pillow. This all seems perfect; too perfect. It's bound to be a trap.

Even so. I want to try.

I slump around Lockless House the next morning, watching the others perform their usual routines. As usual, nobody tries to speak to me. That used to make me feel uncomfortable, even unwelcome; but it's been so long that I barely register it. I've grown used to feeling like I barely exist.

Then they pack up, donning suits and ties. I wander over to Alya, who sits politely while Sandra pulls her hair behind her head.

"Tests over already?" I ask. Alya nods.

"We're going to visit Clarington this afternoon."

"All of you?"

"Most of us. I think it's just you and Jonah who are staying behind."

I balk at that. Rene has never trusted me to stay home alone. I'm not entirely sure what he thinks I'll do – throw a party and trash the place, maybe? But he always leaves someone here with me. Watching me.

At least it's Jonah.

"So what's with the big visit?" I ask.

"Some kind of conference. I don't know much about it."

Of course she doesn't. I doubt Alya ever knows what the discussions are about. She's likely there to smile and look pretty. Luckily, that's something she does well.

She watches me for a moment, and her expression changes. Perhaps she can tell that I'm deep in thought, still lost in memories of Marcus' promises.

"Do you want to come with us?" she asks, "I can ask Rene."

"No," I answer, almost instinctively. I used to watch in envy as they left, wishing I could somehow be involved, but nowadays I know better. Being dragged to events is akin to punishment. Even so, I try to laugh it off.

"I get the feeling Clarington and I aren't going to be best buddies."

Sandra lowers the brush to the table, fixing me with a warning look.

"You almost lost us one of our biggest Sponsors, Reya. You should be more careful."

"He was being a creep."

Sandra bites her lip, then looks away. I know she agrees with me. I've seen the way randomers treat her. They take one look at her pretty face and look her up and down, like they're eyeing up a particularly juicy piece of meat. It's the same expression creeps have when they look at Alya.

I may not be conventionally attractive, but at least I don't have to deal with that. Nobody in their right mind would consider me centre fodder. Good thing, too. I'm not as well-composed as Sandra or Alya. If someone tried to touch me up, I'd probably break their hand.

The others leave for the conference, and I stand bored in the lab.

What now? With Jonah around I can't exactly slip out; no doubt Rene told him to watch me like a hawk. I suppose I could take the opportunity to watch TV while Alya's gone. The Project limits what she's allowed to see, even banning the news unless she's gone.

But then Jonah strides into the room with a stack of boxes in his arms, and I step forward to help.

"Thanks," he grunts as I take the top two.

"What are these?" I ask, bouncing the boxes in my arms.

"This week's mail. Rene told me to make myself useful and gave me two options. I could either sanitise the equipment or sort the mail. You know how I hate the smell of that cleaning fluid."

"Good choice."

We tip the boxes out onto a nearby table, and I gape at the sheer number of envelopes.

"That's a lot of mail."

"This isn't too bad, compared to normal. At least I don't have to answer it all. Just sort it into stacks."

I hesitate.

"Want some help?"

"I'd love it, but don't worry. This is boring administrative work."

I pluck an envelope off the table, flipping it over in my hand.

"It'll take less time if we do it together."

At that, he nods.

"Fine. If we do it quickly, we can watch something on TV later. Sound good?"

I smile.

"Alright. Where do you want things?"

We work for a solid hour, sorting only a small pile of post. Jonah instructs me to work on the more official-looking envelopes first, stacking them according to sender and department. Any other time I might be curious about the letters' contents, but today my eyes slide right over them.

But then I spot an envelope with my name on it, and my curiosity builds.

I pick it up. My name is hastily scribbled on the front of the envelope in thick, black marker. The handwriting looks somewhat familiar, but I can't quite place it.

I slip my hand under the flap and something slices my palm.

"Fuck!"

I fling the envelope aside and clutch my bleeding hand. The cut is deep, running from my thumb to my pinkie. Blood fills my palm. Jonah rushes over.

"What happened?"

"I think there was something in there," I say, wincing. He glances over at the now-bloody envelope and frowns.

"For crying out loud, why did you open it?"

I fix him with a fiery look – or as fiery as I can make it, through the pain.

"It has my name on it."

"Plenty of post has your name on it, but that's the stuff we don't open."

I must seem confused, because he just sighs.

"Let me look at that."

I sink onto a lab chair and Jonah kneels beside me, pulling out a medical kit and dabbing away the worst of the blood. He peers down at the injury and grimaces.

"Looks pretty deep. That razor got you good."

"Razor?"

"It's an old trick. Not a very good one, at that."

"Great," I say, rolling my eyes, "the one envelope I happened to pick up and some lunatic sent me a blade."

He doesn't say anything, but his brow furrows.

"What's that look for?" I ask.

"There's a reason I told you to get the formal-looking post, Reya. All the handwritten stuff is addressed to you or Alya, and it almost always contains something like this."

For some reason, this surprises me.

"Wait, are you saying that people regularly send me razor blades in the post?"

"And death threats, cryptic messages, you know the type."

He indicates a pile behind him. He's stacked them on a separate table, far away from the rest of the letters. My heart sinks.

"That's all hate mail?"

"Mostly. We do receive the odd piece of post for Alya with less-than-appropriate propositioning, and I suppose that's slightly less harmful than a death threat, but no less unpleasant."

He sprays my hand with antiseptic and I yelp.

"Sorry," he mutters, "can't let it get infected. Who knows what the crazies are putting on the blades."

As he bandages my hand, I stare at the envelope I'd opened, my gaze fixed on the writing. My chest hurts when I recognise it.

The same handwriting. The same thick, black marker.

That's the same person who wrote 'PLASTIC' on my arm.

"Bastards," I growl. Jonah nods in agreement.

"We've always had people disagree with us, but lately their actions have taken a dangerous turn. We decided about a year ago to stop opening post addressed to either of you – but especially you."

"Let me guess. My charming personality has failed to win over the public?"

He shoots me a disapproving look, but there's no real weight behind it.

"You seem to make enemies easier than most, I'll give you that. It's still no excuse."

He steps back, kit in hand.

"How does that feel? I'm no doctor, but I've done my best."

I look down. My hand is heavily bandaged – probably a little too heavily – but the pain has eased. I flex my fingers, and they move fine.

"It'll do."

"Good. I'll have Neil check you out properly when he's back. Let me go restock the medical kit while I remember."

He steps from the room, and I do the mental maths. He has to go to the storeroom on the second floor to get more supplies. I have a solid ten minutes.

I eye up the stack of handwritten mail.

Eight

By the time I've opened every letter, my hands are littered with cuts.

My hate mail is stacked in piles on the table, separated by type. One pile of razor blades, one of dog shit. Another two or three containing small explosives. But all those seem like small fry compared to the largest of the piles – the death threats.

Initially, I find them funny. I imagine the kind of person who would take time out of their lives to write this stuff. They can't have much going on if another person existing is enough to stir this much anger.

Then, I hesitate. Some letters are written so poorly they resemble children's handwriting. Some letters don't threaten me so much as they implore me to top myself. One envelope is empty, save for a length of rope tied into a noose.

Finally, I pull out a pretty piece of cloth. Someone has lovingly cross-stitched the words 'Die bitch' across it, complete with tiny pink flowers and green leaves.

As if on cue, Jonah returns. I hear his footsteps slow to a stop behind me.

"Oh, Reya. You opened it all."

He steps closer, resting a hand on my shoulder.

"What on Earth were you thinking?"

"Hey, Jonah. Look at this."

I wave the cloth at him, laughing.

"Someone took the time to cross-stitch a death threat and mail it to me. I mean, who cares this much? I'm almost flattered."

"Reya…"

"You know, I always imagine Mortalists as bald, angry drunks. That's the type I meet in the city, anyway. But no, some little old lady spent hours painstakingly crafting this thing, just to tell me to fuck off."

His hand tightens on my shoulder.

"This is why we didn't tell you about it."

"I'm not Alya," I breathe, "I don't need you to protect me."

My voice cracks, and I'm not sure why. It's not like I care what strangers think. Rene's always said that's my problem – that I just don't care enough. Why would I care now?

Frustration overwhelms me and I fling the cloth aside, making sure it lands in the dog shit. I stalk from the room with my head buzzing. Jonah follows.

I burst into the kitchen and head for the cupboards, pulling each one open. There's a strange quivering in my stomach that's not entirely unfamiliar, and I know of only one way to silence it.

"Do we have vodka anywhere?" I ask Jonah. It's not like me to be quite so outright with my rule-breaking, but I don't care right now. His face creases with sympathy.

"They're idiots, Reya. The whole lot of them. They don't deserve your time."

"I'm not retaliating," I snap, "be happy that I'm taking this out on my liver rather than their faces."

"People hate what they can't understand, that's all."

I slam my hand on the counter and he jumps back.

"Look, Jonah. I'm sorry, alright? But I just…"

"You'll be okay," he tells me softly.

"I know."

"If they try anything, we'll protect you."

"I don't know if you can," I sigh.

"Just… don't be scared. It'll be alright."

I turn to face him, fighting the heat in my face.

"I'm just... so sick of being angry. Why does it never let up? I know they'll never accept me, but why won't they just give me space to breathe?!"

I let out a rattling sigh.

"I just need a break."

After several seconds, he nods.

"How does bourbon sound?"

I slump on the floor, my back pressed against the sofa, a glass of booze in my hand.

"This is good stuff, Jonah. You've been holding out on me."

He pours his own glass, drops down on the sofa and switches on the news.

"Alcohol is banned on Project premises, remember? It'll be confiscated if Rene finds out."

"I won't breathe a word," I tell him. Gratitude fills my chest as I take another sip. Nobody else would have done this for me. I wouldn't have even believed Jonah would, if I hadn't just seen it for myself.

"The mail still needs sorting," I pipe up. He nods.

"It can wait a few minutes."

"I'll help you clear it up."

"Later."

We sit in silence, and I'm surprised that he's not pushing me to talk.

I close my eyes. Being hated is such a normal part of life that most of the time, it really doesn't bother me. A week ago, I could have read every letter and felt entirely at ease. I wouldn't feel sick to my stomach or angry as all hell. I certainly wouldn't feel tears prick the back of my eyes.

But then I remember what Marcus said in his apartment, and my stomach twists.

I don't care if people in the city hate me. I don't care if they send me death threats and razor blades, or if they pummel me in an alleyway, or if they go to the papers with false stories. I've survived that so far, and I can keep surviving it.

Can the others?

If I ruin the Project's reputation enough, will we lose Sponsors and have to shut down? What happens to us then? What happens to Alya?

And even if we don't shut down, what if the attacks spread? The others can't fight like I can. It's only a matter of time before someone gets hurt.

Briefly, I consider telling Jonah about the attack in the alley. How I'd been pinned in total silence, held down by a dozen strange figures and released with an insult scrawled on my skin. No doubt it would disturb him. That attack was nothing like the others.

"Have you always had to deal with the anger?" I ask. He grunts.

"People got angry from the first day we revealed Alya. It sits ill with some people, you know. They're worried they'll be replaced as the apex species. But the rage didn't get really bad until a few years ago."

"About the time I started going out alone."

"I suppose so."

"That explains it."

He sips his drink, then frowns.

"You know I have to tell Rene that you read all that mail, right? I'll also have to tell him about your hand."

"Ugh. Seriously?"

"He needs to know what's going on."

"Rene doesn't need any more reasons to think I'm a screw up."

"You're not a screw up. You're just aimless and desperate to find a goal."

"Thanks for the psych evaluation, Jonah. I thought you were Head of Security, not a psychologist."

He smirks.

"No, that's Sandra's job. Though she often tells me I overstep my boundaries with her work."

"Oh?"

He pauses, like he's considering whether he should tell me, then nods.

"If you were to access my private console right now, you'd find plans for a whole new security system. Not just for Lockless House, either, but a city-wide security system that could be used to protect everyone, rather than just us."

"Why do we need to protect other people?" I ask, "in case you haven't noticed, other people suck."

"I suppose some do. But others are just ordinary folk trying to get on with their lives. I have a theory that the Mortalists base their anger on what they don't understand. They see the Project sealed away in here, working away at something top secret. They see Alya as this silent, beautiful, inhuman kind of girl. It's all too close-knit, too suspicious. That's why the public latches onto negative stories, and prefers to paint you as a violent thug rather than a troubled victim of circumstance."

"I'm not a victim," I insist, but he ignores me.

"I believe that opening ourselves up to the world would be a good idea. Transparency, you know. Public presence. Openly accessible data. Maybe, if we allowed people to meet you and Alya, they wouldn't be so afraid. Maybe they could see past 'not human' as a definition and respect you as people."

He sighs.

"It's a pipe dream, of course. I've brought it up to the others more times than I can remember, but they never support it. Rene says it's idealistic, and Sandra often tells me to stick to security rather than trying to psychoanalyse the public. Apparently, one shouldn't be learning how to think like their enemies unless one is actively seeking to destroy them."

"Huh," I grunt, "I wouldn't be against destroying the Mortalists."

"You don't mean that."

"Wouldn't life be easier without them?"

"Well, sure. But if we got rid of someone any time they caused a hassle, we'd be pretty terrible people, huh?"

I let out a low, throaty laugh.

"I guess. If you took that approach, I'm sure you'd have sent me away years ago for causing trouble. Not that I wouldn't deserve it."

Jonah doesn't reply, but I can feel his gaze settle on the back of my head. I look away, turning my attention to the TV.

They're airing live coverage of the conference. Rich folk in designer suits step out of cars worth more than most people's houses, walking up to a large, glass-fronted building. Security rope lines the path to the doors. There are dozens of people standing around the entrance, but they don't look like they belong. They hold signs and banners, and for a second I think they're positive.

Then, I spot a logo on a banner. The Project's 'infinity' symbol with a small blade held against it. I recognise it instantly.. Jonah follows my gaze.

"Mortalists."

"Yeah," I breathe, "are the others already inside?"

A second later, the Project's cars slide into view. The crowd shifts.

"Surely they're not stupid enough to step into that," I say. The car doors open.

"But I've been wrong before."

The camera view changes, switching to street level. Someone's head blocks half the screen, but I see clearly as Alya and the others step out. The crowd erupts. They roar over one another, blocking out each other's words, but their intentions are clear. Insults. Threats. Hatred.

For a brief second, the camera zooms in on Alya's face. Her eyes are wide as Rene leads her towards the doors. They walk as slowly as they can, fixing their gaze ahead. Rene's lips move, and somehow I know he's warning Alya not to react. React, and it'll only get worse.

I spot the gun before Jonah does.

"Top left," I spit, "someone's got a gun."

His gaze flits to the corner of the screen – to the figure wearing a balaclava and clutching a pistol – and he fumbles with his phone.

"I'll try to warn them."

I rise to my feet, staring at the screen, my heart pounding in my ears. Please don't do it.

The figure raises the gun, aiming it squarely at Alya's back – and squeezes the trigger.

"No!"

Jonah and I scream in unison. I lunge at the screen, terror ripping through my chest.

The crowd scatters. People run away in a blind panic, screaming. An alarm blares. In the chaos, the camera is knocked from its stand, falling sideways onto the pavement. I spot the others.

Rene's arms are locked protectively around Alya. A streak of crimson marks her back; blood streaks down her shirt. Her head is low, one hand on her shoulder. She's crying.

In an instant, I'm incensed.

Rene scoops Alya into his arms, yelling something at the others. They turn toward the building and run at a dead sprint. It's only when the door swings shut behind them that the TV falls silent.

Rage snakes through me. I'm mad. Madder than I've ever been during a bar fight or an argument with Rene. The feeling is both terrifying and exhilarating. I ball my hands into fists, imagining how good it'd feel to pummel the guy who hurt my little sister.

I barely hear it when Jonah lowers the phone and steps closer.

"They're okay," he huffs, "it was a short call, but Neil says they're fine. Alya's already healing. She won't even have a scar."

"That's not the point."

He doesn't reply. My anger intensifies.

It's one thing to come after me. I can handle myself. It's one thing to go after the Project staff. They're trained for this kind of thing. But Alya...

For a moment, I imagine how scared she must be. I fight the urge to punch a wall.

"Where's the conference centre?" I ask Jonah. He frowns.

"If you're thinking of going..."

"Damn right, I'm going! He won't get far before I track him down."

"They'll be fine! They'll lay low until it's safe and then they'll come straight home."

"That's not the point!" I yell, "that asshole deserves..."

I trail off, unsure how to end my sentence. I can see Jonah's expression changing. He can sense my anger, and it scares him. I take several deep breaths and step away.

"I'm borrowing your car, okay?"

"No chance. I'm not letting you run off after some gun-toting maniac. You'll be killed."

"So we just let him get away?"

"He endangered human lives. The police will track him down."

Human lives. Just the humans matter. I clench my jaw.

"Jonah, please. Let me help her."

His face settles into a stony expression.

"You can help her by staying here. Give her one less thing to worry about."

I step back again, trying to push the anger down, but my hackles raise. She's scared. She's hurt. Rene might be holding her right now, whispering empty promises into her ear, assuring her that he'll always be around to save her. Even though he – and the Project as a whole – just failed to do so.

The others will never understand how it feels to be hunted. It's not the same as being hated for your beliefs or actions. The feeling of being despised for what you are, of knowing that people don't even consider you a person, is something they can never comprehend.

Just like that, the anger turns inwards.

I should have been with her.

It's another five hours before they come home.

I'm waiting on the bottom step when they enter the lobby. They look exhausted. Alya walks in under the protection of both Rene and Neil. They march at her sides like prison guards, stiff and silent. Her head is lowered, her hair falling forward to hide her eyes. Her shirt is stained with blood.

Rene reaches out for her, but she shakes him off.

"Right," he croaks, "you should go and clean up. Take a shower and put on a clean shirt."

She passes silently, then looks up to meet my eyes. Her face is carefully blank, like she's holding in a million emotions, and it's a feeling I know all too well. In the Project, we're supposed to be better than anger and sadness. She's spent years watching me rage, and she's learned how it ends. Even so, I can see it in her eyes. Staying silent is killing her.

So I pull my lips into a half-smile.

"Hey, fuck all of those people."

Rene gives me a death-glare, but Alya seems relieved. If she can't bring herself to be mad, then I'll do it. I'll rage for both of us.

"Don't worry, karma's gonna get that asshole," I tell her, "hopefully before his own stupidity. Surprised he knew which way to aim the gun."

In spite of herself, she smiles. Rene growls.

"Reya."

"Nice job protecting her, Rene. Stepping out into that crowd, are you serious? A kid could have told you that was a dumb move."

He deflates at that. I feel Alya relax. These things need to be said, but she can't say them. She takes my hand and squeezes it.

"You should have heard the awful things they were saying," she says softly.

"We need to talk about this," Rene states. He steps forward, touching her arm – and she pushes him away with as much force as she can muster. He staggers back, his face a picture of shock.

"Alya... I'm just trying to help. I understand that you..."

"No!" she spits, "you don't."

With that she races past me, tearing up the stairs. I hear the door to her room slam shut.

Rene rounds on me.

"That poor girl has just been through hell and back, Reya! How dare you speak to her like that?!"

"You don't get it, do you?"

His expression falters. Perhaps he can sense my own anger.

"You don't know what it's like for your humanity to be a TV debate. For people to discuss whether you have feelings. Whether you bleed. You haven't got a clue how it feels to be her," I snarl.

"And you do?"

He steps back, eyes wide. Stunned by my fury.

"I was her," I spit. He falls silent.

"I'm going to talk to her," I tell him, "and you need to give her some time to come to terms with this on her own. Use that time to come up with a new way to keep her safe, alright?"

With that I turn tail and head upstairs, determined to be there for my sister.

Alya's on the roof. She sits in the gravel with her knees pulled up to her chin. She hasn't bothered to change her shirt. When I approach, she looks away.

"I'm sorry I raised my voice. Is Rene angry?"

I shrug.

"Probably, but I think that's more at me. He could never be angry with you."

"I shouldn't have been rude to him."

"Don't worry. He's a big boy. He can handle it."

I drop down beside her, but don't try to touch her. I remember how I feel after every attack; skittish and tender, like every touch could burn me. She sighs.

"I think something's wrong with me, Reya."

"Well, you were raised by a bunch of weirdo scientists and you're related to me," I smirk, "I'd be shocked if there wasn't something wrong with you."

"I mean it. When they shot me, it barely hurt. But I burst into tears anyway."

"It's okay, you were just scared."

"No."

She wipes her eyes with the back of her hand, sniffing deeply.

"I was angry."

She fixes me with a worried look.

"I wanted to scream at the man who shot me. I wanted to chase him down. I wanted to tell him that he doesn't know anything about me, and ask him why he thought it was okay to hurt me like that."

I lean closer, watching as she flexes her fingers in front of her face. Worry rolls off her in waves, and I get the impression she doesn't want to tell me any of this. But she needs to get it off her chest, so I'm not going to interrupt.

"Why do they think I'm not human?" she says, her voice cracking, "is my existence really such an insult to them?"

I stare at the sky.

"Humans think they can decide what defines humanity. Truth is, they don't know a damn thing. Their idea of humanity is twisted."

"But you're human."

"Not to them."

Alya buries her face in her knees.

"What's the point? They're never going to leave us alone."

She lets out a low sob.

"I wish I didn't have this stupid body. I'm the wrong person for it."

"That's not true."

"It is. The Tomorrow Girl should be someone stronger. She should be willing to fight when she needs to. Someone who deserves immortality wouldn't have cowered when that man shot her. She'd have marched over to him and broke his jaw."

She lifts her head. Snot drips down her chin.

"Rene always says that someday, I'll have to take charge and help people. But I don't want to. I'm not a leader. I'm not wise and I'm not strong. And whenever that day comes, everyone I love will probably be gone. I'll have to do it all alone."

"You won't. There'll always be someone."

"But not the Project. Not you."

Her gaze slides over to me, and her face creases.

"We're mixed up, Reya. I've always thought it."

"I'm sure you're right, but how?"

"You should have been the Tomorrow Girl. You're perfect for it. I think everything would be much easier if it were you instead of me."

I reach out, and when she accepts my touch, I wrap an arm around her.

"Listen to me," I tell her, "you are the best person for this job, and do you know why?"

"Why?"

"Because you care. You care so much that when someone tries to kill you, your first reaction is to cry because they don't like you. That's amazing."

"It's pathetic."

"It's incredible. Do you know how many humans could do that? Listen, Alya. There'll be fights in the future, and plenty of them. Someone like me, sure, I'd be leading the charge every time. But anger isn't what gets us through tough times. It's people like you who do that."

She buries her head against my shoulder and I nestle closer.

"About today," I whisper, "I'm sorry I wasn't there."

I tighten my grip on her. If I had been there, I'd have noticed the gun in time to warn them. I'd have had chance to position myself between Alya and the gunman. Then she'd be safe, but I'd be...

Marcus' face flashes behind my eyes.

He could fix me. Make me an immortal shield.

I stare down at Alya's tear-stained face, and my resolve hardens.

"I won't let this happen again," I tell her firmly, "I promise."

Marcus hasn't looked away from me since we started driving. I stare straight ahead, ignoring him. His car is a stick shift, and it's taking all my focus.

"I'm surprised you called me, Reya."

His voice is soft.

"Nova gave me your contact details," I retort.

"Excellent. Her work is coming along brilliantly. I half-expected her to cut contact with me after our last conversation, but her updates are just as regular as ever. You must have decided not to tell her about our history."

"If you're only funding Nova to get to me, then she doesn't need to know that. Just keep supporting her and I'll keep dealing with you. Got it?"

"Got it. Though I must admit, I didn't expect you to insist on driving."

I shift into a higher gear, face carefully neutral.

"I need to memorise the route, just in case I have to find my way back alone."

"I'm not going to hurt you," he starts, then hesitates. I chuckle.

"That's exactly what you're going to do."

He tears his gaze away.

"Turn right here."

I do as I'm told. We're near the city limits, veering through an industrial estate. Large, abandoned factories line the roads. I map things out in my head, and it suddenly seems familiar. This whole area is owned by the Project, kept clear in case of an emergency.

"We're headed towards Safehouse 17," I state.

His brows raise.

"Well noticed. Yes, we are."

"You know we're trying to keep this secret, right? Using a Project Safehouse doesn't seem like a good idea."

"I know. I've been looking for somewhere to carry out our tests, and this place came to mind. It seems the Project has disconnected all the passageways to and from the Safehouse. They also left it fully stocked. Nothing has changed since the last time we were there."

My hands tighten on the steering wheel. The last time we were there.

"I imagine they wanted to get the hell out of there, after what you did to me."

He frowns.

"That makes sense. Too many bad memories. Still, it benefits us now. They've left thousands worth of equipment in there, including everything we need."

"How long will it take to get this done?" I ask as we pull up outside another non-descript factory. Its only defining feature is a '17' of flaking paint on one wall. I hop out of the car, my stomach swirling. Should I be feeling something? I was kidnapped and brought here. I almost died here.

Now I'm back, eighteen years later, and my kidnapper stands beside me, ready to do it all over again.

Marcus doesn't seem to notice my discomfort.

"It'll take a few weeks. I have a plan in mind, but we need to perfect some details. Shall we talk inside?"

"Yeah. How do we get in?"

He waves at a nearby panel – a black, glossy, thing set into the wall – and I step closer. This is the same kind of access panel we use at Lockless House. I fire a confused look at Marcus.

"Will either of us have permission to use this?"

"You should. As long as the security system has been updated regularly, that is. Knowing Jonah, I doubt he'd let it slip. I'm sure he's maintained some minimal degree of communication between here and Lockless House. He wouldn't allow hoodlums to break in and start using the place for their own nefarious purposes."

I hesitate, then press my hand against the panel. It lets out a tired groan, then a low beep, and the door swings open. I stare at the dusty handprint for a moment before Marcus touches my arm, leading me inside.

The first several rooms are full of pallets and old crates. A front, I suppose, in case someone ever tried to break in. I frown.

"How did you know this place is fully stocked, if you don't have access?"

He doesn't respond; just fires me a warm smile and waves for me to open the next door.

The lab is a near-duplicate of the main lab at Lockless House. The equipment is smaller and coated thinly in dust, but I recognise most of it.

We have dozens of Safehouses. A little overkill, perhaps, but Rene always said they were necessary. Right along with the Saferooms in Lockless House. If something major happened – a fire, a bombing, a violent attack – we need to be able to go somewhere safe, and keep working from there. Luckily, we've never had to use them.

No thanks to me, I suppose.

"So," I mutter, "what's this brilliant plan of yours?"

He eyes me carefully.

"I need to strap you into a chair and administer the serum. I've got a batch here – luckily, it wasn't too hard to remember the components – so it's just a case of injecting the serum into your spine."

"Why my spine?"

"It needs to hit bone marrow as well as blood vessels, so that's the best place. I'll hit multiple places down the spine at varying depths. I think six needles should do it."

"Sounds like it'll hurt."

He nods.

"The needles are several inches long and quite thick. Yes, it's going to hurt."

I must seem uncomfortable, because his expression changes.

"It's not too late to back out, if you're scared."

"No," I snap, "I have to do this."

"What changed your mind?"

I look away. He nods.

"The attack on your sister, right? I saw it on the news."

"I should have been there. I could've helped."

"You don't trust the Project to keep her safe."

It's a statement, not a question. I let my hands curl into fists.

"No."

"So you're doing this for her."

"Not exactly. I'm doing it for me, too."

He waves at a nearby piece of equipment. A white, plastic chair sits in the middle of the device. Restraints hang off the arms, ready to be fastened around someone's wrists. I recognise it instantly; we have a similar one back at Lockless House. It's used to deliver short, harmless shocks. We mostly use it to compare recovery times and reactions to pain.

"You're using that?"

"Don't worry, I'll disconnect the shock pads. They won't do us any favours. But the setup is practically perfect, even with the holes at the back of the chair. I plan to set up an automated system to insert the needles, but that will probably take a couple of days. Tonight, I'll inject you manually, just to ease you into it. That way we can go slowly."

"How do I know you won't strap me down and kill me?" I ask. Marcus turns away.

"You don't, I guess. You'll just have to trust me."

The thought terrifies me, but I force myself to sit. As he tightens the straps around my wrists, I notice he's avoiding my gaze. The thought strikes me that there's still time to run. I can rip free and escape, steal his car, and head home. I can spill everything to Rene. I'm sure he'd try to keep me safe, even if was only out of obligation.

Then I remember the look of shame in his eyes.

I can't let him down anymore.

"Do it," I instruct Marcus. He steps back, fiddling with a long, thick syringe.

"I'll take it as slowly as I can, alright? To get you used to the pain."

"Why do I need to get used to it?"

"Unfortunately, this isn't a one and done situation. Your DNA was first adjusted while you were still developing, so we had a full nine months to make changes. You're less fragile now than you were as a foetus, so it shouldn't take that long, but it'll still be a couple of months until the final test."

The term 'final test' is a little unnerving, but I don't call him out.

He steps up behind me, then hesitates.

"Reya. Are you absolutely sure about this?"

I grit my teeth. No. I don't want to do this. But it's the only way to make the Project happy. To keep Alya safe. To have a purpose. To make Rene proud of me for once in my goddamned life.

"Just do it."

Nine

    The pain is paralysing. Incredibly, I can feel it; each needle popping through the skin, forcing its way through flesh and deep into my spine. The flood of iciness as he pushes the plunger – followed by a surge of heat as the serum seeps into my bones, scorching everything along its path.

    Air leaves my lungs and I strain for more, unable to stop the reflex. My body stiffens, and I try to curse him out. I'm certain the words are coming out, but I don't hear them.

    The next needle breaks the skin, and this time I'm cognizant enough to cry out.

    "It's okay," he tells me, "not much longer. Try not to move."

    After what feels like the longest 30 seconds of my life, the pain stops. I slump in the chair, gulping down air like I haven't breathed in days. The pain vanished as quickly as it had started, but my energy is drained. The moment I have control over my mouth I'm swearing, shouting at Marcus, calling him every name under the sun.

    He watches coolly, arms folded. When I finally tire, he nods.

"That was good. Well done."

"That was horrible!"

"I warned you that it would hurt."

He reaches behind me and dabs at my back with a cloth. It comes away crimson.

"Doing that every night will kill me," I croak. He chuckles.

"No, it won't. It'll hurt and you'll be very tired, but you won't die."

He fires a sly look my way.

"Unless you think you can't cope?"

Rebellion flares in my chest.

"I grew up with tests. This is nothing."

He seems pleased with that as he reaches for the straps on my wrists.

I slump into bed at 3am, aching all over. Marcus drove me home as soon as I was able to stand, but my legs still shake violently. I don't bother changing my clothes – just kick off my shoes and bury my face in the pillow.

Just as sleep threatens to take me, someone knocks my door.

"Yeah?"

Alya pokes her head around the door, watching me with wide, reproachful eyes.

"I've been waiting for you to get back."

"What are you still doing up?" I ask, forcing myself to my elbows. She shifts uncomfortably, and even in the dim light, I can see the streaks on her face. She's been crying.

"Have you slept?"

"Yes," she whispers, "but…"

My gaze drops to her shaking hands.

"Bad dreams?"

"N-no, I can't have bad dreams. Rene says they're a sign of an unhealthy mind."

"Rene wouldn't know healthy if it punched him between the eyes. Come here."

I toss my blanket back as she nears, patting the mattress beside me.

"You can sleep here tonight, if you think it'll help."

She seems confused, and I realise that this is new to her.

As a kid, I'd have nightmares constantly, and the only solution was slipping into bed with Rene. He never refused me – just rolled over and allowed me to clamber in beside him.

Alya crawls in beside me, nestling herself in the crook of my elbow. I lean back on the pillows, my body still throbbing. If she notices my heavy breathing, she doesn't say anything.

I force myself to stay awake for a while, waiting for her to either start talking or crying, but nothing happens. When I glance over, she's not moving. In the dim light, she looks almost peaceful. In spite of myself I roll closer, wrapping a protective arm around her.

My baby sister nestles into my arms and I let the silence carry me off.

I wake to the sound of a click, followed by giggling.

Opening a bleary eye, I see three shadows standing over the bed. One of them clutches a camera.

As my vision comes clear, I recognise Sandra, Jonah and Rene. Sandra's the one clutching the camera. She looks down at the photo she just took, a broad smile on her face. Jonah stands beside her, clearly bemused. Even Rene seems to smile – or at least, as close to a smile as I've seen from him.

I open my mouth to ask what's so funny, but something shifts beside me. Alya is still wrapped in my arms, her head buried against my shoulder. She sleeps soundly, a half-smile on her lips. My face burns.

Sandra chuckles.

"Oh no, we woke you up!"

"What are you doing?" I whisper. Jonah grins.

"We couldn't find Alya this morning, and panicked."

"So you broke into my room?"

"Sorry. But this is pretty cute."

Alya shuffles against me, letting out a low sigh. Damnit, he's not wrong.

"What time is it?" I ask. Rene replies.

"Long past time we were doing tests. It's throwing off our data."

I reach up, toying with a strand of Alya's hair.

"I think you need to give her a day off, Rene."

"We can't just..."

"She had a nightmare last night," I tell him, "what happened yesterday really scared her. Just... give her some time, alright?"

His lips tighten, and for a moment I think he's going to argue with me, but he just nods.

"Alright. W can skip the tests, just for today. I suppose we need that time to come up with a new defence plan, anyway."

"Good idea," I whisper, opting not to point out that he's following my suggestion. There's a worm of guilt in my stomach, reminding me how I spoke to him yesterday.

"Is everything okay?" I ask him.

"The media is blowing up, of course, but the police are hot on the tail of the gunman. For now, we're not doing any public appearances."

"That's sensible."

The others file from the room, but Rene hesitates. He shoots a concerned look at Alya.

"Don't worry, Rene," I coo, "she'll be alright. I've got her."

He doesn't look especially comforted by that but he nods nonetheless, following the others out.

I slip out of bed and leave Alya dozing. By the time I get downstairs, the others are already gathered around a table in the main lab. They've pulled out the blueprints for Lockless House and are poring over them, searching for weaknesses in our security. They look up when I enter.

"Is Alya still asleep?" Sandra asks me.

"Yeah. I couldn't bring myself to wake her up."

Her face creases with unspoken sympathy. I step closer, eyes flitting to the large red blocks on the blueprints. Saferooms.

"Are you guys beefing up security?"

"Yeah," says Jonah, glugging on a coffee. The smell makes my stomach rumble but I ignore it, turning back to the paper.

At this point, the plans for Lockless House are ingrained in the memories of everyone here. We know every escape route, every fire extinguisher, every button for the silent alarm. Jonah insists on annual reviews. All staff are trained in basic defence as well as handling firearms – which is good, because there are a dozen or more sealed away, just in case.

"The security here is intense," I grumble, "it's the security outside that's the problem."

To my surprise, they nod.

"How do we keep her safe outside?" Rene says, more to himself than anyone else.

I drop my gaze to the table. This doesn't concern me. I'm not as smart as them, nor do I have any real status here. But for some reason, I feel eyes settling on me. They don't have a single reason to listen to me, but they seem willing to hear me out. I chew my lip.

"Everyone should carry some kind of protection. A taser, a handgun. Something."

I look up at Rene.

"All Project staff have a licence to conceal carry, right?"

He nods.

"Then everyone should start carrying when you go outside," I mutter, "We should also refresh everyone's self-defence skills with some training. And that includes Alya."

His brow furrows.

"If there's going to be a fight, then I don't want Alya anywhere near it."

"What if they manage to get close to her? It doesn't hurt to refresh her training."

"She's never had any training."

"I've taught her the basics."

His jaw clenches at that – but I shrug it off. He doesn't need to know that I've taken her into the city, or that I've sparred with her on a car park. If I leave it at that, he'll think I just gave her some pointers. Nobody could fault me for that.

"We also need a way of communicating from a distance," I push on, "Jonah and I spotted the gunman before you did, thanks to the camera angle, but we had no way of warning you. Perhaps some kind of alarm?"

Jonah replies this time.

"There are remote alarms available. We could set them up on a private network and give everyone a device. One click, anywhere, and it would alert everyone else who held one. It could be used as a warning or a call for help."

Rene nods, seemingly keener on this idea when it's coming from Jonah.

"Look into it. Anything else?"

An awkward silence falls over us, and I feel eyes on me again. They're expecting me to say it. I make eye contact with Sandra, and she gives a small, encouraging nod.

"I think... I think that Alya and I need to know how to use a gun."

"I just told you, no," he replies, "she's not fighting, and neither are you."

"We may not have a choice."

He promptly turns red – a sure sign he's about to explode.

"You speak so casually about fighting off assassins, Reya. But this isn't the same as your drunken bar brawls. And Alya isn't like you."

"Everyone else can defend themselves, why not her?"

"You call what you do 'defending yourself?" he snaps, "I call it pointless, vacuous violence. You go around this city breaking noses and crashing cars and drawing more hatred to the Project. If not for your selfish actions, we wouldn't even be in this mess."

I feel my hackles raise.

"Hey! What happened yesterday wasn't my fault."

"Perhaps not directly, but you encourage it. With the trouble you cause, more people than ever hate and distrust us. That's what drives them to try and hurt her."

"The only person to blame for the gunman's actions is him."

Even as I say it, guilt twists like a knife in my gut. He's not wrong. Every time I confront someone – fairly or unfairly, in self-defence or not – the Project's reputation worsens. We lose another Sponsor. Another handful of people take up the Mortalist label.

The realisation hits like a truck. Was the attack my fault?

Rene's lip draws back in a sneer.

"Your behaviour is the root cause for all of this. People will always disagree with us, but they'd have gotten over it eventually. It's thanks to you that this kind of thing keeps happening."

I step back, wounded by his words. He's not wrong; but it still hurts to hear it.

"You know I would never want this."

"Intention doesn't make a damn bit of difference. If you want to help, you need to do more than just talk. You need to stay out of trouble."

He fixes me with those cold, intelligent eyes, and my anger crumbles into shame.

"Rene, come on. You know I'd do anything to stop this."

The others shuffle uncomfortably, stepping back as though afraid we're going to start screaming. Rene fires me a filthy look.

"I don't know if you can stop it. It's out of your control now."

My chest tightens.

"I'll fix this, one way or another."

His eyes remain cold as I turn away, marching from the room with my spine straight and my chin held as high as I dare hold it.

I'm dressed to meet Nova and the others when Alya knocks on my bedroom door. She looks me up and down, frowning. It's clear I'm going out. I'm not wearing any Project-branded clothes. I've thrown on a pair of too-tight jeans – the only ones I own since Shane destroyed my other pair – and my trusty black hoodie over the top. I've tugged my hair back into a ponytail. I don't particularly like tying my hair back, but it's harder to grab this way. It's sad that I even have to consider that.

"Where are you going?" she asks.

"Nova and the guys want to meet me. We're checking out the next prototype and testing it."

"Can I come?"

My breath catches.

"You'd best not."

"Why?"

I fiddle with a loose strand of hair, carefully avoiding her eyes.

"I don't think it's safe for you."

"What? But that's why we're doing this. I need to learn..."

"Spencer and I already gave you the lowdown on self-defence. You've got the basics down pat. There's not much else to teach you."

She stares, but I can see pride in her eyes. She's a fast learner. Much faster than I was. Within an hour of practising she was able to successfully pin Charlie – and while he's the easiest target out of all of us, it's a vast step up from the butterfly punch she delivered on her first attempt.

"Rene got to you, didn't he?"

Her voice gives me pause. She's watching me with an uncharacteristically stern look.

"What do you mean?" I ask.

"Rene doesn't want me to go outside until things calm down. I tried telling him that it's a bad idea, that hiding is what they want, but he wouldn't listen."

"He's just trying to protect you," I tell her, confused. Suddenly, I seem to be defending Rene. That's never happened before. She clicks her tongue.

"I'm not going to hide in Lockless house, feeling awful and alone, while the world keeps turning. It's not fair."

I want to put my foot down and tell her that life's not fair. That staying safe and alive is more important than being happy. But on her face, I see a strange, somehow familiar look of defiance. Then it hits me. She's using my own rebellious glare against me.

"Don't pull that face," I sigh, "it's eerie, coming from you."

"You never do as you're told."

"Yeah, and look where that's got me."

"Not the point. Do you regret it?"

I consider this. No. As much as I hate to think I've brought this on the Project, I don't regret going out. If I hadn't, then I'd still be here, all alone. If I hadn't met Nova, Spencer and Charlie, I'd have lost all hope years ago.

Alya steps closer, and in her face I see everything I used to be. Desperate and alone, clinging to any vestige of the outside world. Anything to retain her sanity in a place where everything is so sterile, and reality only comes in deafening, painful bursts.

I sigh.

"I don't know if I can protect you if they try something."

"You've always kept me safe before."

"This is different. They're organised. They already hurt you once."

"Please, Reya."

My hands clench at my side.

"If you come with me, then we have to set some ground rules."

She nods.

"Whatever you say."

"We're taking Jonah's car. I'm driving. You'll keep the windows up so nobody recognises you while we're travelling."

"Alright."

"When we get to Nova's, you'll stay by my side. I don't want you out of my sight. Got it?"

"Sure," she shrugs, rolling her eyes. I step closer.

"And if I tell you to run, you'll do it. Doesn't matter what else is going on. If I throw you the car keys and tell you to drive home, you won't argue. You won't question me. You won't stick around to help anyone. You'll just do it."

I don't like giving her orders. It doesn't feel natural for either of us. Her mouth falls open and I expect her to argue with me, but then she pulls it shut and nods.

"Alright. Agreed."

We pull up outside Nova's apartment and I sigh. Being out here after everything that happened has me on edge. I glance over at Alya, but she seems at ease. She reclines in the passenger seat, watching the road with a casual demeanour.

"Ok, we're about to go in," I tell her.

"Alright."

"Remember the rules?"

She winks at me.

"Yes, I do. Honestly, Reya. You're almost as much of a basketcase as Rene."

"Where did all this sarcasm come from?" I tease. She chuckles.

"Oh, that? I got it from my big sister."

Nova throws open her apartment door and flings her arms around me. She squeezes my cheeks and laughs.

"Look at you! I'd almost forgotten what you looked like."

"It hasn't been that long," I say. She just laughs.

"You brought Alya, too? Wow, it's a full house! Come on in, guys."

We step inside and I do my usual bit of whistling and asking how rich she is. Nova just rolls her eyes, slapping me gently on the back of the head as she passes. Charlie and Spencer are already sprawled on the sofa, sipping some kind of sweet-smelling liquor.

Nova heads to the kitchen.

"Want a drink?"

I open my mouth to accept, then reconsider.

"No, thanks. I'm driving."

"Really? Whose car did you steal?"

"I didn't steal it," I insist, "one of the Project staff let me borrow it."

"Wow. How charitable of them."

"Well, after everything that's happened, it's safer than walking."

Her face falls, and she stares at Alya.

"Oh, my god. I can't believe I didn't ask about that!"

"It's alright," Alya shrugs.

"No, it's not. Are you okay? I mean... did you...?"

Nova trails off suddenly, unsure how to continue. Alya just tugs her shirt off her shoulder, revealing flawless porcelain skin. I glance over, realising that our bodies are identical, right down to the freckles on our collarbones.

"It healed up in a few seconds. Look, no scar!" Alya says. Her face smiles, but her eyes don't. I know she's recalling our conversation on the roof.

"That's amazing," Nova tells her, "you really are something else, huh?"

"Thanks," she replies hollowly. I opt to change the subject, steering her into the living room.

"Hey, guys. Look who I brought with me!"

Spencer grins his enormous, toothy grin. Charlie gives a small wave.

"I feel like it's been forever since we've seen each other," I say. Spencer nods.

"I think we've all been kind of busy. Weird how life does that, huh?"

"Tell me about it."

I sink to the floor and lean against Charlie's legs. He doesn't seem to mind.

"How goes business?" I ask.

"That's boring," Spencer says, "I'd rather talk about the shooting."

Alya tenses. Nobody else notices.

"Let's skip it," I mutter, "it's not important right now."

"Okay, but the gunman..."

"Still on the run. The cops will track him down."

"I'm surprised you haven't found him yourself," says Nova, joining us, "when I saw it on the news, I half expected to see Reya burst out of the car and chase the guy down herself."

"Trust me, I wanted to. Jonah wouldn't tell me where they were, or I'd have gone after him."

That anger is back now, snaking through my veins, unpleasantly hot. My pulse thumps in my ears.

Alya lifts her head, watching me closely. Perhaps she can sense my anger, too. I hope she can't tell that the rage is laced with anticipation. A few more weeks, I tell myself. A few more weeks and I'll be able to fix everything.

Nova leads us into her workshop, where the platform is set up on the edge of the table. Its design is sleeker than ever, and she fires a prideful look our way as she plugs the cord directly into the wall. I whistle.

"No generator!"

"Nope," she grins, "the extra funding has been unbelievably useful. I was able to get hold of some high-cost alloys to strengthen the frame and thin it out, and it uses hardly any power compared to before! Besides, look at this."

She types something into her laptop, and the tendrils of air begin to spread. Only this time, they spread much farther than the edge of the frame. I touch Alya's hand, tugging her aside as the air extends right up to the workshop door. Her eyes go wide.

When I look back at Nova, she's smiling wider than I've ever seen. Excitement pours from her.

"What do you think?" she asks, her voice thick with anticipation.

Before I know it, I'm clambering onto the table.

"It looks good," I tease, "but let's see if it works, shall we?"

Alya fires a worried look my way, but Nova laughs.

"I was hoping you'd say that."

I stare down, the fear from last time gone entirely. This time I take a small jump onto the platform, which feels as firm as concrete beneath my feet. I spin on the spot.

"Well?" Nova demands. I spin faster.

"It feels… different. Firmer."

"After you mentioned this could be used for roads, I thought I'd add a road-like surface. Does it work?"

"Fantastically," I grin, before stepping further down the platform. She tenses.

"Don't go too far from the centre of the frame. I haven't found a way to keep the surface tension consistent over 10 metres."

I nod and walk slowly, both arms spread out for balance. It's hardly necessary – my shoes grip the surface as easily as if I were walking on concrete. I walk until it wavers underfoot, then take another step.

My feet pass through the platform and I hit the floor, both knees pulled up. I straighten my back and turn to face Nova, who now stands on the opposite side of the room.

"Nova, this is incredible!"

Relief floods her features.

"You think so?"

Charlie nods frantically and Spencer steps closer, admiring the new, lighter frame.

"You're really going to make it big with this one, Nova."

She flushes madly.

"Really?"

"Uh, yeah," I remark, "we've been telling you that for years."

"I never really believed it before, but... with this extra funding, I've been able to do so much more. Maybe we really will do well."

"You'll be a millionaire," Alya tells her. Nova nods.

"We'll all be millionaires. I can't take all the credit when I have a team behind me!"

"You do most of the work," Spencer reminds her, "we just source things and help move stuff."

"You're my suppliers and lab assistants," she replies. I laugh, and she glares at me.

"And you're my guinea pig, Reya. One mustn't forget to credit the test subject."

I stride over, looping an arm through hers.

"It hardly counts. I don't do much compared to you guys."

"You're still getting your share if this all works out. Enough for a small flat and a car, maybe."

She knots her fingers with mine and squeezes.

"Maybe it'll be enough to get you out of there."

I fall silent, ignoring the pang of longing in my chest. I can hardly talk about this in front of Alya; especially as I don't quite know what to say.

Do I want to leave Lockless House?

Absolutely, and absolutely not. I barely understand it myself.

Nova tilts her head, curious, and I cover my worry with a smile.

"You'll be awesome at the show."

"Are you coming?"

"At this rate, we'll be lucky if anyone from the Project attends," I admit, "it's a pretty public event. They probably wouldn't let me go, even if I wasn't taking part."

Alys steps closer, plucking at my sleeve.

"The Creation Show?" she asks. Nova nods.

"That's where this is being unveiled, if everything goes according to plan."

She smiles.

"You should have approached the Project, Nova! They run an annual fund for young inventors. They'd have probably sponsored you."

I stare.

"Wait, the Project does that? Since when?"

"The last few years. You really need to start paying attention."

I scratch my head, unsure how that would work – after all, the Project itself is almost entirely Sponsor-funded – but before I can think too deeply about it, Nova replies.

"Actually, my Sponsor has been brilliant through all this. He's even contributed some ideas on how to improve the frame, and he's more than willing to send funds my way whenever I need them. Half the time he doesn't even ask what it's for, he just trusts that I'm not out for the money."

She fires a warm look at me.

"I guess I have you to thank for that, huh?"

"What do you mean?"

"Marcus told me why he really approached me. He wasn't planning on sponsoring me until he saw that you were involved. That gave him the final push. I know you didn't really do much, but thanks anyway!"

I smile, but my stomach twists. He's made no secret of the fact that he wants to get close to me, even going so far as to tell Nova. And of course Nova's okay with it. She doesn't know our history. In her eyes, we're both getting exactly what we want.

Thoughts of Marcus fill my head – his kind words, his promises – and I search the room for a clock.

I'll need to leave early if I want to get to Safehouse 17 in time. I guess sleep will have to fall by the wayside tonight. I'll drop Alya off early and head back out on foot. Since I can never drive after a round of serum injections, I can hardly take the car.

"So," I say, eager to change the subject, "have you tried this baby outdoors?"

"Not yet," Nova says, "I haven't had the manpower, or my guinea pig."

I fire a sly look her way, and she waggles her brows.

"...Really? You want to test it now?"

"Why not? We could snap it onto your balcony, so the drop's only two storeys. It would be, um, beneficial to your research."

Nova snorts.

"Yeah, right. And it's got nothing to do with you wanting to mess around on it, right?"

I reach over, loosening a clamp on the platform, and Nova's smile widens.

"Well, if you're that eager, it'd be selfish of me to decline. Fine. Guys? Can you help us move this?"

Nova switches on the platform, and I watch as the tendrils extend out into the cold night air. I'm standing on the railing of her balcony, clutching Charlie's shoulder for support as the platform boots up. Although we're only two storeys up, it's enough to make my heart race; more than once I tilt towards the edge, lifting one foot, shifting my weight just enough to generate a surge of adrenaline. If the others notice how much fun I'm having, they don't point it out. Spencer steps out with mugs of something sweet-smelling – one of his fruit teas, perhaps – but I wave him away.

"Are you sure?" he asks softly, "it's cold out tonight."

"Maybe when we're done," I smirk. He lowers the tray, firing a sweet smile at me.

"Alright," Nova says, "we're ready."

I leap onto the platform, landing heavily on the tendrils of air. They hold just as firm as before, as hard and smooth as concrete. I spin a few times, firing Nova a thumbs up. Beside her, Alya watches nervously. Her gaze flits from Nova's laptop to me, then to the ground.

"Hey," I say, "don't look so worried. It's fine."

"Just be careful."

I roll my eyes and reach down, hoisting her up beside me. She yelps and drops to her knees – but after several seconds, she realises she hasn't fallen. Lowering her hands, she reaches out, touching the platform gingerly. Awe fills her features.

"It can hold two people," I tell Nova. She stares at me, slightly flustered.

"I really wish you'd warned me before you did that."

"Sorry."

"It's okay. Just... don't push it too far."

I nod and motion for Alya to stay where she is, then start stepping backwards, away from the frame.

"How far did you say, again?" I call to Nova. She bites her lip.

"10 metres, but it could be less outdoors. Wind could weaken the outer section, so don't..."

I don't hear the last part of her sentence. I'm too distracted by the sudden shuddering underfoot. I spin around, panicked. The platform wavers and flickers, suddenly feeling less like concrete and more like jelly.

"Nova, what the..."

"Get back, quickly!"

"Wait, I..."

"Reya!"

I whip around, catching sight of Nova's frightened face – and my feet pass through the platform.

Something locks around me, and I fall.

Ten

"Reya! Alya!"

I bolt upright, gasping hard. Cold. Shit, I'm so cold. I look down. My clothes are drenched from landing hard in a puddle, but otherwise, I'm miraculously unharmed. I look up.

The platform has malfunctioned. From the ground, I can no longer see it shimmering. I try to see if anyone's standing on the balcony, but see nothing. Perhaps they're on their way down.

"Ouch..."

I look down and my face burns.

I'm sitting on top of Alya, who's sprawled on the tarmac. She seems to have taken the brunt of the fall; her face is bruised, her lip bloody. One arm is twisted in the wrong direction.

"Oh, crap."

I leap aside and she sits up, rubbing her head. I expect her to see her arm and panic, but she fires it an unamused look before turning back to me, concern in her pretty eyes.

"Are you okay?"

"Me?" I gasp, "your arm is..."

"It's fine, it's already healing."

She points at the extremity, and she's right. We watch in silence as the bone straightens itself, locking back into position. Within seconds, every bruise is gone from her face. She's pristine again, albeit soaked through, and still watching me with a worried look.

"Are you hurt?" she asks. I stare.

"I... I don't know what just happened."

"Something went wrong and you fell," she tells me, "so I fell with you and cushioned your fall."

"Cushioned my...?"

"Stop freaking out and just tell me you're not hurt," she snaps. I nod, rubbing my arms and face.

"No pain. I think I'm okay."

"Good. Nova would panic if something happened to you."

"Thanks for the save," I say, standing. When I extend my hand she takes it, grinning.

"I know how helpless you are," she teases. I roll my eyes.

"It was just a two storey drop, you know. The worst I'd have gotten was a broken leg."

"Yeah, well. This way, nobody gets hurt. Well, not permanently, at least."

The door to the apartment block flies open. I hear footsteps in nearby puddles and Nova heaves herself at me, grabbing my face with both hands.

"Are you okay?" she yelps, "do you have a concussion? Any broken bones?"

Charlie and Spencer follow after her, their brows furrowed with concern.

"Do either of you need an ambulance?" Charlie squeaks, waving his cell phone in one hand.

"We're both fine," I say, "but I'm not sure what happened back there."

"Just a glitch with the platform," Nova says, "the edge of the surface seems much more susceptible to wind resistance and air pressure. I have a lot more work to do before it can be used outside."

She fires me a worried look.

"Are you seriously not hurt?"

"I had a fantastic cushion," I joke, hooking an arm around Alya. She blushes madly.

Charlie looks us up and down, frowning.

"You're both soaked through. Come inside and dry off."

"Yeah, that could make Rene suspicious," I agree. Spencer nods at Nova.

"I'll help you move the platform back inside while these guys get dry."

"Alright."

The rest of the evening passes uneventfully. Nova sets up a heater in her living room and places me and Alya in front of it. Charlie pushes the fruit tea on us a little more forcefully than before, and we sit and chat while the two of us slowly dry off.

When the others take a break, heading into the kitchen to refill their glasses, I pull out my phone. Marcus has sent me a time and place to meet. I reply with a simple agreement.

I give it another hour before standing. We're sitting in the living room, laughing at Spencer's slightly-drunk impression of some local celebrity I've never met. I glance at the clock, then reach for my hoodie.

"We'd better head out. C'mon, Alya."

Her face falls.

"What? But I was having fun!"

"Sorry. But we need to get you back before anyone notices."

"The lab won't open for another three hours. What's the rush?"

The others watch me carefully, too, and I wonder if my discomfort is that obvious.

"I... look, I need to go somewhere else tonight."

"Where? I'll come too."

"No!" I snap. For some reason, I feel that mixing Alya and Marcus would end in disaster. Her face falls.

"What's with that reaction? Are you doing something you shouldn't be?"

"No."

"You're lying."

"I'm not."

"So why can't you tell me where you're going?"

The others watch in silence, clearly unsure what to say. I scratch my head.

"Look, I... it's just private, alright?"

Nova frowns.

"Is everything okay? Maybe we can help."

"Don't take it personally," I say, "I just really, really don't want to discuss it."

She rolls her eyes.

"Well, I'm not going to push you if it's so private. If you have to go, then go. I was going to ask you to stay the night, but clearly you've got more important things to be doing."

Irritation fills her face and I reach out, squeezing her hand. She softens a little.

"I haven't seen you in weeks, Reya. Do you have to go so early?"

"Sorry. This is important."

"Something for the Project? For Alya?"

"For me."

She blinks.

"A secret project, huh?"

I fire her a tight smile.

"I'm really sorry."

"I get it. I mean, I don't, because you're so secretive about it, but I get it." She smiles.

"Go on. We'll catch up another time."

Alya hops into the passenger seat and buckles up. As I jump in beside her, I feel her eyes on me.

"Quit staring at me," I mutter.

"What's the big secret?"

"If I told you, it wouldn't be a secret, would it?"

I reverse out of the car park, heading for the freeway. It's the longest way home, but also the safest.

As we drive, she keeps asking. Her questions slowly become more pointed.

"Are you trying to track down the gunman?"

"Is it more experiments, like the ones you do for Nova?"

"A secret boyfriend?"

I ignore all her guesses aside from the last one, which warrants a derisive snort.

"What?" she says, "why is that so funny?"

"My last boyfriend gave me a black eye and ran to the papers," I say bitterly, "I'm not going to make that mistake again any time soon."

"Surely you haven't given up on finding 'the one'?"

"I'm 24. Most people my age haven't found 'the one' yet," I laugh, "besides, why do you care about my love life? Can you even imagine Rene's reaction if I brought someone home and introduced him as my boyfriend? I can almost hear them loading the guns."

She just giggles and turns toward the window. I can almost feel her smiling as we pull onto the freeway and get up to speed.

For a moment, a peaceful silence falls over the car.

"Reya. I know it's private. I don't want to force you to talk about something you'd rather keep to yourself. But, you'd tell me if you were doing something dangerous, right?"

I glance over. Alya's staring at me with wide, pleading eyes, her head tilted to one side. I open my mouth to tell her that no, of course it's nothing dangerous, but the words die in my throat. Instead, I hesitate.

"Reya?"

"Look, it's just..."

The back window explodes.

"Shit!" I cry, grabbing the wheel and veering back toward the road. In my shock, I'd crossed lanes. Someone honks angrily behind me.

"W-what just happened?!" Alya gasps. I glance in the rear-view mirror. Nothing remains of the back window, save for a handful of glass shards still stuck in the frame. I squint and spot a dark car moving behind us. It drives dangerously close. It has windows tinted to near-total blackness. Most importantly – that damn symbol is painted on its bonnet.

Something glimmers near its side mirror. The barrel of a gun poking out. My heart pounds.

"Get down."

"What?"

I grab her head and push it down, forcing her to the floor of the car.

"Keep your head down!"

Another shot. This one blows through the headrest, where the base of her skull just sat. The pounding fills my head. Can she survive a headshot?

"Damnit," I growl, "don't you dare sit back up."

I floor Jonah's car, veering in and out of the moving traffic. Something flashes overhead and I'm sure I just broke at least a dozen traffic laws, but I don't care. Not when the black car shifts behind us, matching our speed.

Mortalists.

"How did they find us?" Alya yelps. I don't reply; just slam my hand on the control panel. This is the security vehicle. It's tracked, and there's an oversized red button on the dash for calling the Project. I hesitate only a moment before pushing it.

I can't protect her in this situation. We need help.

The line crackles open, and Rene's bleary, tired voice fills the car.

"Jonah, what's going on? Why aren't you at Lockless House?"

"It's Reya!"

"Reya... you took Jonah's car?"

"Not important! We're on the freeway."

"We?"

I grit my teeth. God, I'll regret this later.

"Alya's with me."

He curses at the top of his lungs, all exhaustion gone in an instant.

"What is *wrong* with you?!" he screeches, likely waking up everyone at Lockless House, "how dare you take Alya, steal a car... this is the last straw, Reya!"

His rage is palpable, and even a little frightening. Alya lets out a whimper from the footwell.

"Rene, just listen..." I start.

"I can't believe you would do this!"

"We..."

Another shot hits the car, this time smashing the windscreen. Glass shatters in my face, littering my skin with cuts. I must cry out, because Rene's tone changes.

"What happened? Reya!"

My vision blurs but I shake my head, forcing myself to focus.

"We're under attack," I tell him, straining to sound calm, "Mortalists are on us. They're shooting the car."

"Is Alya okay?"

I glance at her. She's curled up in the footwell, both hands twisted in her hair, her eyes shut tight.

"Yeah. She's out of line of the shots."

"Are you injured?"

I ignore the blistering pain in my face.

"I... I don't think so."

"Keep her safe," he instructs, "we'll track the car and meet you at the end of the Freeway. We'll bring guns."

Alya sits up, suddenly lucid. She glances out of the window.

"Th-they're still coming."

"Get the hell down!" I screech. She folds in an instant. Apparently, my fear is contagious.

How far away is the end of the Freeway? Why can't I remember? I swerve between cars at top speed, scraping several and denting a few others. Some small part of me screams that this is dangerous, that I'm just as likely to hurt someone this way than if we just confronted them, but I don't dare stop.

Who knows how many people are in that car. Who knows how many have guns.

Suddenly, I'm ashamed of my earlier cockiness. Who was I to think I could keep us safe?

Maybe if I were like her. Then we could pull over and face them. I could take a dozen bullets without issue and we could walk away unscathed. But right now? When I'm one well-aimed gunshot away from dying behind the wheel? I'm worse than useless.

A shot whizzes past, grazing my arm. The pain is minimal, but bloodstains blossom across my sleeve. Alya squeaks.

"Reya, you're hurt."

Rene starts yelling again, and this time his voice is different, like they're already in his car.

"We're on our way. What's going on?"

"You're bleeding," Alya whimpers. Rene starts with the questions and I turn my attention back to the road. Ahead of us is a bulky red low loader, the type of wide load that takes up both lanes with little room to spare. My stomach tightens. If we can squeeze through and get ahead, then maybe we can lose our pursuers.

I position the car, and Alya's eyes widen.

"Woah, woah, what are you going to do?!"

I floor it. We shoot down the outside lane, zipping past the low loader's motorcycle escorts. They honk loudly, and I resist the urge to flip them off as we pass. I don't have time for this.

"Reya!" Alya cries, "it's too tight, we can't..."

I force Jonah's jeep through the gap between the concrete barrier and the lorry. It's not really wide enough and in the first few seconds we lose the wing mirrors. Sparks fly as the doors scrape concrete. I tense, praying the sparks don't make it into the car. Alya screams.

And then we're free, zooming ahead of the lorry with ease.

"We did it," I gasp, "Rene, I think we lost them."

I glance at the spot where the wing mirror used to be.

"Tell Jonah I'm sorry about his car. I don't think a fresh coat of paint will do the job."

He laughs, but I suspect it's more from relief than anything. Alya lifts her head hesitantly, letting out a heavy sigh.

"Are we okay?"

"Yeah," I say, reaching out for her, "we're..."

Pain splits my body and my vision turns red.

Eleven

Screaming.

I recognise Alya's voice, but I can't make out her words. Her tone is frantic, desperate, terrified. The car lurches and I double over, clutching my burning shoulder. Something hot streams down my front, saturating my clothes. Someone else starts yelling. Rene?

I reach out to grab the wheel but my arm falls limply to the side, sending a shockwave of pain through me. The car veers off course and honking fills my ears before pale hands grasp the steering wheel, correcting our course. Alya stares at the road for a moment, then turns to face me.

"Reya?!" she cries, "Are you okay? Jesus, there's so much blood..."
"Girls," Rene's voice echoes, "just stop the car. We're close, we can..."
"They shot Reya!"
"It's alright, I promise. Just listen to me."

Rene's voice shakes madly. Her fear is contagious, and it's affecting him.

I look up from my bloodied shoulder, fixing my eyes on the road. I feel like I've been hit with a goddamn shovel. My vision blurs, then clears. I shake my head to clear it and instantly regret the choice.

"Oh god, oh god, what do I do...?"

Alya's voice breaks through the agonising thump in my ears. I grab the steering wheel with my one good hand, fighting to hold the car steady.

"Alya. Can you see if they're still chasing us?"

She glances back.

"I... I can't tell."

Rene's voice burns through the car.

"Reya, are you still with us?"

"I damn well hope so," I tell him, "because if this is heaven, I am sorely disappointed."

I let out a bitter laugh, but the pain intensifies. I weave between cars clumsily, terrified.

"Rene, please tell me you're close."

"We're within sight. Start moving across. You can pull over soon."

I fight to focus on the road, ignoring the thump in my broken shoulder. My hand wobbles and the car swerves again – but then Alya's beside me, grabbing the wheel with one hand, stabilising us.

I look over to thank her, then pause. Her face is paler than I've ever seen it. Her dark hair is messy and knotted, wrapped around her face and stuck to her lips. She watches me with wide, reproachful eyes.

I snap back to reality.

"Shit!" I cry, swerving to avoid another motorcyclist. The road suddenly clears ahead, and the rear-view mirror flashes blue. My head is filled with the sound of sirens.

"What's happening?" Rene barks.

"We're fine," I lie. My hands tighten on the steering wheel. I can see my knuckles turning white.

"Pull over," instructs Rene, "we're close enough now."

"What if they're still following us?" I mutter. Alya's eyes widen.

"Rene, what do we do?!"

"Just pull over. We've got a plan to surround the car and we're all armed. Nobody will try anything."

Sound fills my ears, and I realise I'm gasping for air. My hands shake.

"I thought I could keep us safe, Rene, but I can't. I can't do this."

My voice comes out barely above a whisper, but he hears it. When he responds, his voice is firm.

"You don't need to. We're here."

I grit my teeth and veer across the lanes. Pressing the brake feels like a betrayal; like I'm willingly driving into danger. But I know I can't win this one. My body is racked with pain, my skull pounding like someone's drilling it with a jackhammer.

We slow to a stop and I slump against the wheel, cradling my bloody shoulder. I hear the familiar roar of Rene's convertible as it pulls up alongside us. Familiar voices fill my ears and my shoulders drop. They're here. We're safe.

"Are you okay?"

I open a bleary eye. Alya sits beside me, one hand on my knee. Her face is a picture of concern. It takes all the effort I have to smile.

"Yeah. Are you?"

She shudders.

"I'm scared, Reya."

I cast a cursory look over the dash. It's littered with broken glass and small metal shards – probably from the cars we collided with. The driver's seat is drenched with blood. Red handprints clutch the steering wheel.

"Yeah," I say glumly, "me too."

Someone shouts orders outside the car, and I hear guns being drawn. The passenger door bursts open and Rene clambers inside, scooping Alya into his arms. She clings to him, burying her face in his shoulder and promptly bursting into tears. On my other side, Neil pulls open the door. His eyes glide across the bloody dash.

"It's alright," Rene coos to Alya, "we're here. They can't hurt you."

And then his eyes snap toward me.

"I can't believe you," he says icily, "how could you be so reckless, so *stupid*..."

"Not the time," Neil interjects. Rene falls silent, but I can still feel him watching me.

Neil tilts my head back, peeling me off the steering wheel as gently as he can. I inhale sharply as he tugs back my hoodie, examining the wound in my shoulder. My breathing is heavy, my nose still filled with the stench of blood, and I wonder if I look half as bad as I feel.

He exchanges a look with Rene, who speaks softly.

"How is she?"

"Don't pretend to care," I slur.

Neil fires me a stern look and I stop talking. He presses a hand to my cheek and frowns.

"Bones and muscle look okay. Not too much blood loss. But there's definitely signs of shock."

Shock. That makes sense. It would explain why I'm suddenly so cold even though I'm drenched in sweat, and why I can't seem to level my breathing.

Rene lets out a small grunt.

"What do we do?"

"Get her warm and dry. Patch up the wound. Some rest wouldn't go amiss, either. We need to take her home."

"I don't think that's going to happen. The cops have formed a blockade while they figure out what's happening."

"She'll need treatment sooner rather than later."

Rene heaves a sigh.

"Put her in my car and do what you can with the mobile medkit. We'll try and calm things down here and maybe we can clear a route to take the girls home."

Neil steps back and I turn, trying to step out of the car – but his hands find me, pulling me against his chest and lifting me with ease. My face burns and I'm tempted to tell him to put me down, but my legs are quaking so badly that I'm quietly grateful I don't have to walk.

I'm carried across the highway, which is now filled with honking, frantic traffic. I think about all the damage I caused, the chaos that's just taken place down the length of the Freeway. I think about Jonah's trashed car – something he either hasn't noticed yet or is carefully trying to not think about, judging by the efficiency with which he instructs the others. Something soars overhead, filling my head with a deafening thump, and I realise it's a news helicopter.

The whole city is watching the aftermath. My heart pounds faster, terrified by the thought. Neil must sense this because he crouches low, covering my face from the view of the cameras.

Neil places me on the backseat of Rene's car, pulling a blanket from under one of the seats and wrapping it tightly around me. He grabs a small medkit and tapes a wad of gauze to my shoulder before instructing me to put pressure on it. And then he's gone, slipping into the front seat to turn the blower up to full.

I should probably thank him. For coming to save us, for helping me even though I messed up. But instead, I'm bowled over by exhaustion. It washes over me like a tsunami, and suddenly it's almost impossible to keep my head above water.

He touches my arm gently.

"Don't fall asleep."

I don't respond, and he shakes me harder.

"I mean it, Reya."

My eyes flicker open. I'm so tired that my vision has started to blur, reducing everything to vague, fuzzy shapes. Neil watches me from the front seat, his brows furrowed in concern. Another door opens and dimly, I hear Rene's voice. He and Neil exchange muffled words, and then someone slides into the seat next to me. They pull me into their arms, laying my head on their chest.

"Shh, it's alright. You can relax now."

I do as I'm told, my fuzzy vision making it impossible to recognise them. All I know is that their arms feel secure and somewhat nostalgic, and they don't seem to mind when I curl into them, desperate for their body warmth. The distinct scent of coffee and disinfectant fills my head, relaxing me further. I haven't a clue who's holding me, and for the moment, I don't care. This is a safe place.

"How many fingers?"

Rene holds his hand in front of my face.

"Four. Two. Five. One. Three."

I recite the numbers dully, more out of habit than anything. After all these years, I know that Rene always uses the same pattern. He gives a low grunt and pulls back, typing something into a nearby console.

I'm sitting on a metal table in the main lab, my arm wrapped in a sling to support my busted shoulder. The others bustle around us, taking calls, saving data. Damage control, I assume.

"I told you a million times Rene, I didn't hit my head."

"We can't be too careful. Given the circumstances, it's fortunate that you got off with such a clean wound. The bullet went right through you. No shrapnel. No muscle damage. Very lucky."

"Right," I grunt, though I've never felt less lucky in my life.

"Don't underestimate how dangerous that situation was. If they'd shot a little closer to your centre, or if they'd severed an artery, things could have ended very differently."

"Yeah."

He watches me for several seconds, a million emotions on his face. Anger, concern. Maybe a little bit of relief, too.

"How's the pain?"

"Bad," I mutter. Neil gave me something for it earlier, but it's starting to wear off. I can feel a steady throb down one side of my body, plus an agonising stiffness in my spine. Rene grabs a towel and dabs at my head, wiping away the dried sweat.

"I've never been angrier in my whole life, Reya. I can't believe you would put Alya and yourself at risk like that."

"You don't seem particularly angry," I remark.

He hesitates.

"Well, you did get shot. I'd say that's more than enough punishment."

"Bit extreme for just sneaking out, if you ask me."

He fires me a cold look and I recoil.

"Right. Sorry."

"You should be. This never should have happened. You stole Jonah's car, you went into the city without telling anyone. You took Alya with you, for some nonsensical reason. I don't know why you thought that would be okay. After everything that's happened…"

He rounds on me, anger flickering into life.

"You know, the Core Project constantly defend you. Any time I'm mad at you, they scold me. They tell me I'm being unfair. That you're not perfect, but you're loyal and smart. Do your actions last night sound like the choices a smart, loyal person would make?"

Shame fills my chest and his face crumples.

"Alya insists that she shares the blame for what happened tonight. Apparently, you tried to leave without her and she begged until you caved. Not that it's an excuse, mind you. Even if she hadn't gone with you, those… people would have still tracked you down."

He pauses, suddenly contemplative.

"If Alya hadn't been with you, the car would have hit the barrier when you got shot. You'd probably be dead."

"Remind me to thank her when I see her," I say. Oddly, nobody has said much to me since we got back. Initially I thought they were angry, but their worried glances say otherwise. I think Rene's easing me into conversation, searching for any change in behaviour from my injury. He clicks his tongue.

"While you're at it, apologise to Jonah for his car. It's absolutely wrecked."

I know. I remember the mirrors tearing off, sparks flying off it. The windows were all shattered, and I can't imagine how many bullets hit the exterior. There'll be no salvaging it. In retrospect, taking the security vehicle was probably what saved us. The reinforced exterior made all the difference.

Rene glances at me.

"Look, I have to go. We have a lot of work to do to fix this."

"Fix it?"

"This isn't like the assassination attempt at the conference. We all know what really happened tonight, but the media is already trying to spin it and throw blame. I feel confident we can clear any accusations against you, but it'll take work. Your driving caused a lot of property damage and injured a couple of people. In the meantime, you're off tests until I say otherwise. And I have to warn you, Reya. This is your last chance. One more outburst. One more fight. One more time when you endanger someone else…"

His expression hardens suddenly, twisting into something unpleasant.

"I'll be forced to do something you'll hate."

"What does that mean?" I ask, dreading the answer.

"You currently have the privilege of being part of the Core Project. Along with me, Alya, Sandra, Neil and Jonah, you have full access to all our security systems. So far, Jonah has refused to let me take away your security access in case of an emergency, and I haven't pulled rank on him because he seemed confident that you would be sensible about it."

"But…"

"But," he says warningly, "if you cross the line again, I'll remove you from the Core Project. You won't be able to access weapons and alarms, or unlock any doors. You will not have access to a phone, or the web, or any means of accessing the outside world."

"So, house arrest."

"I don't want to do it. But if that's what I have to do to keep everyone safe, then I will."

I look at him for a long moment, then nod.

"I see."

"This is your last chance, Reya. You're only getting this because Alya vouched for you. Don't make me regret it."

With that he strides over to a nearby chair, where my blood-stained hoodie hangs. He delves into the pocket and my stomach flips.

"W-what are you doing?"

"Taking your phone," he says, nonchalantly pulling it out.

"What? Why?"

"Don't panic. Jonah's trying to figure out how they found you tonight. They must have tracked some kind of signal. Could be the car, could be your phone. Either way, we're going to check this over and make sure it's untraceable except by us."

He flips it open, blinking at the screen.

"My, that's a lot of missed calls."

I try to snatch the phone with my good hand, but he steps out of my reach.

"45 missed calls from Nova," he mutters, "whoever that is."

"That's none of your business!"

His lips tighten.

"I'll text them and tell them you're still alive, shall I? The news reports did leave your condition somewhat unclear."

I open my mouth to object, but I'm momentarily distracted.

Sandra leads Alya into the room, and it's obvious they just finished a particularly hard-hitting therapy session. Alya's eyes are puffy, her face flushed, and she seems to hesitate when she sees me.

I pull my face into the broadest smile I can manage.

"There you are! I was starting to think you'd forgotten about me."

I mean it as a joke, but she doesn't laugh. Instead she stops a few feet away, her hands folded neatly together. Her lip wobbles.

"How do you feel?" she asks, her voice still weepy.

I shrug.

"Hurts like hell, if I'm honest. But I can cross 'late night car chase' off my bucket list, so I suppose that counts for something."

Her lips twitch, and for a moment I think she's going to smile – but then she steps closer, collecting my free hand in hers.

"You're going to be okay, right?"

"Why are you asking dumb questions?" I laugh, ruffling her hair, "I'm tougher than that! Neil said I'll be back to normal in a few weeks. And besides..."

"Reya."

I pause. Alya's hands are shaking.

"Hey," I say, "don't be upset. I know it was scary, but you're safe now. They can't get you."

"I'm so angry."

Her fingers tighten.

"It's just like last time. I saw the blood, and I saw you were in pain, and I was just... so angry. I thought about the person who hurt you and I... I wanted to hurt them back."

"That's normal," I say, "you're not insane. Just human."

With that she looks up, and behind the fear I see a glimpse of my sister. I keep pushing.

"You're awesome, did you know that?" I tell her, "I couldn't lift my arm and you managed to steer the car back onto the road."

"We were going to die if I didn't," she says, her lip curling. I smile wider.

"You're such a badass. Casually saving lives and you don't even take advantage of it. You can make me do anything you want now that you've saved me. Come on, what do you want me to do? Anything you like."

I expect her to make a nice, easy request, or perhaps demand something sarcastically outrageous. Instead, she fires me a pretty smile and squeezes my hand.

"Anything?"

"Anything."

She looks around the lab, as though to check that nobody's listening, then meets my eyes.

"Don't die," she pleads. I squeeze her hand back, my chest suddenly aflame.

"Alya, I don't..."

"Promise me. Promise you'll stay with me."

I hesitate, then nod.

"I promise."

Twelve

My phone is returned to me the next day. I search the messages frantically, worried they've found out about Marcus, but there's no sign they have. Luckily, I'd had the sense to save his number under 'M', and none of our texts are especially incriminating. Just dates and times. Suspicious, but nothing damning.

Rene frowns at me.

"Your friends have been texting you constantly."

I don't react. I'm sitting upright in bed today, feeling a hundred times better. I reply to Nova and the others, giving them a quick update, and letting them know I won't be going out for a while.

"So," Rene mutters, "these friends of yours."

I drop my phone and stare at him. No. Please, no. For years I've kept them secret out of fear that Rene might forbid me from seeing them. I must seem horrified, because he steps back.

"Calm down. I'm just asking who they are."

My shoulders hunch. I'm hardly in a position to refuse him.

"Nova's an inventor from the inner city," I tell him, "she's incredible, Rene. You'd be amazed if you met her. I've never met anyone so intelligent outside of the Project."

He raises an eyebrow, but says nothing.

"Spencer and Charlie are brothers. They run a delivery firm in town, and they help Nova with her inventions."

"How do you know them?"

"I help with the inventions, too. I'm the test subject."

His eyes widen.

"Test subject?"

"It's fine, Rene. It's not like here. I'm not doing anything dangerous. In fact, most of the time we're just drinking or playing cards, or watching fireworks."

"Fireworks?"

"Charlie taught me a bit about pyrotechnics."

"Doesn't sound especially safe."

"They're not bad people, Rene. They aren't criminals, or drug lords, or thugs."

"I didn't say they were."

Irritation flares in my chest.

"We both know what you think I'm up to whenever I leave Lockless House."

An awkward silence falls over us. Eventually, he sighs.

"Well, tell your friends goodbye. You won't be seeing them anytime soon."

"I know. I can't really go anywhere with a busted shoulder."

"That's not the only reason. I don't want you going out until things have calmed down."

"Come on Rene, that's not fair. They're my friends. If I wait for all this to blow over, it could take years."

"Yes, it could. But surely you understand the weight of the situation now. This has gone far past harassment and stories in the paper. Lives are at risk."

"I can be more careful."

"No. They've targeted Alya and they've targeted you. How long before they try and kill someone else? Alya can't cope with much more. She was so scared when they attacked her. And you heard her screaming when you got hurt."

Yeah, I remember. My stomach twists painfully.

I don't want her to be scared like that again.

"You're losing colour," he says suddenly, "have you taken your painkillers?"

"Yeah."

"What about lunch? When did you last eat?"

"Um..."

"That's all the answer I need," he sighs, "I'll throw something together. Fair warning, I'm not exactly on the ball lately. Too much to worry about. But with any luck you'll avoid serious food poisoning."

I give a weak laugh and he heads from the room, leaving me alone with my thoughts.

Three weeks later, I call Marcus. I don't have to wear a sling anymore, which is a relief, but the stack of pill bottles on my bedside table remind me that I'm still far from healed. I've grown used to the steady, unpleasant thrum of my own pulse in my shoulder.

He picks up instantly.

"Reya. How are you?"

"Sore," I admit, "I'm still loaded up on painkillers."

"Try to be patient. From what you've told me, that was a nasty injury."

I bite my lip. I've told Marcus every detail of the attack, even more than I've told Nova and the guys. I'm not quite sure why, but when I first rang him I just blurted it all out. Perhaps it's because I know it won't get back to the Project. I can say anything to Marcus.

"When can we carry on with our tests?" I ask.

"We should wait until you're fully healed. And that's if we continue at all. Perhaps it's not the best idea right now, considering everything that's happened."

My pulse quickens.

"No! No, we need to keep going. Please."

"I'm surprised you're so keen to leave Lockless House," he says, "aren't you scared you'll be targeted again?"

"That doesn't matter."

"Of course it does."

I bite my lip. Am I scared of being attacked? Sure. I hate to admit it, but Rene's right. My experience is limited to street fighting and snapping the arms of handsy drunks in bars. When it comes to organised crime, that's a whole other ballpark. I don't know how to use a gun. I've never had a single real self-defence class. I'm not scared of fighting hand to hand – but I don't know how to fight someone who's armed.

Damn right, I'm scared.

"I have to do this," I sigh, "I have to fix myself."

"What's the hurry?"

"If I wasn't mortal, I could have avoided the car chase. I could've just pulled over and beat them up. They could have shot me and it wouldn't matter. Alya would have been safe. I wouldn't have put strangers' lives at risk trying to escape. If I were just how I was meant to be..."

"Won't the others be angry if you sneak out again?"

Yes. Rene gave me a final warning. One more slip-up, one more reckless decision...

"They don't have to know," I tell Marcus. He sighs.

"Either way, this could throw off our tests. You should heal fully, first."

"Every day I waste waiting for these stitches to dissolve is another day when they could attack," I snap, "I'm wasting time! Who will they target next time? Sandra? Jonah?"

"Logically, the next target would be Rene," he replies curtly.

My breath catches. Rene?

It would make sense. He's the Project Head, after all. Of course he'll be third priority to anyone wanting to harm the Project. Against my will, images fill my head. Sirens. Paramedics. The long, drawn-out beep of a heart monitor. Alya slumped on the floor, her body wracked with sobs. In an instant, it's hard to breathe.

"Just fix me, already!" I shout down the phone, "please. I can't stand this."

I can't lose Rene. I can't lose any of them.

After several seconds, Marcus agrees.

"Fine. We'll get back to it tonight."

"Have you set up the automatic injection system?"

"Yes, but it's a massive step up. Maybe we should hold off..."

"No. Let's use it tonight."

"Reya," he tells me, "it'll hurt a lot more if we switch straight over. Besides, we were looking to increase the dosage and we can't do both. I don't know if your DNA will hold its structure well enough."

"If you gave me the choice, I'd do it all tonight. One massive dose would do the job."

"If I gave you that much serum, you'd die."

"Then increase the dosage and use the new system," I growl. He sighs.

"Alright, you're the boss. I'll see you soon."

He hangs up and I stare at the phone for a moment, terror rising. I don't want to increase the dosage. The experiments are agony. I don't want to do this.

But then I remember Alya's eyes filling with tears, and fling my phone across the room.

I don't have a choice.

A week passes, and we fall into an uneasy routine.

Our tests become more intense, just as we agreed. As the gunshot wound heals there's less pain, but it's quickly replaced by a constant ache in my bones. I sleep long and hard during the day, desperate to regain some small amount of energy. Nobody in the Project points it out. Perhaps they think I'm still recovering from my injury. Maybe they're just happy I'm not awake enough to start trouble.

Marcus' tests are increasingly unpleasant. I've grown used to the sensation of needles in my spine, of the waves of cold and subsequent burning that accompany each dose. Marcus has rigged up a machine to track my movements and inject me, which is supposedly much more accurate than his bare hands. The downside of this is that they're faster now and shoot much harder into the skin, resulting in sharper pain.

One night, after a particularly hefty dose of serum, I fall asleep.

When I come round, I'm propped up in Marcus' car. I bolt upright.

"Woah," he says from the driver's seat, "take it easy."

"What happened?"

"You fell asleep. Figured I could drive you most of the way home without disturbing you."

I grit my teeth. Any other time, I'd be mad. I'd remind him that I don't need his sympathy, that I'm perfectly capable of finding my own way home. But a yawn forces its way out, and I'm suddenly grateful I don't have to walk.

"How are the tests going?" I ask.

"Good. I'm starting to see changes on a cellular level. At this rate, I expect we'll be finishing up in about a week."

Finishing up. The 'final test'. A massive, singular dose that might finalise these changes – or potentially kill me. My entire being balks at the idea, but I swallow it down.

Marcus must sense my discomfort, because he fires me a small smile.

"Hey, now. Don't look so worried. You know I'll be there the whole time."
"That's comforting," I joke.
"I'll do my best," he retorts.
I turn my attention to the road, still yawning.
"Hey. Can I ask you a question?"
"Shoot."
"Why me?"
"Huh?"
I lean back, stretching both arms over my head.
"If you just wanted a legacy, you could get it. You could worm your way into Alya's life somehow. You could create a new Tomorrow Girl. A Tomorrow Boy, maybe. They could keep each other company in the long, cold forever."
He chuckles at my joke, but doesn't reply.
"Well?" I urge, "why is it so important that I'm the one? You know more about me than most. I'm a disaster of a person. What makes me so special?"
"I've told you everything already," he says simply, "it's up to you how you apply that knowledge."
We slow to a stop at our usual corner, and I stare at the pavement. Two blocks to Lockless House. I'll have to be more careful than ever, now.
My stomach swirls. Rene made it clear that my next screw-up would be my last.
"What's wrong?"
Marcus watches me with curious, intelligent eyes. I shrug.
"I guess I just don't want to go home."
"You don't have to, if you don't want to."
I look at him, and his smile widens.
"I was trying to think of a way to bring it up. We have a week until the final test. 7 days. Instead of going back to Lockless House and having the added stress of trying to keep our work a secret, why not stay with me?"
"In Safehouse 17?"
"No," he laughs, "at my apartment. I have a couple of spare rooms, so you could take your pick. I'd cook for you every day. I've never been especially good at domestic life, but I do try."
His gaze drops to my body.
"I notice you've been wearing the same outfit all week, too."
"This? Yeah, my other ones got all bloody..."

"Then let's go shopping. I earn more than enough to buy you a new wardrobe. You could have your pick of the rack."

I let out a laugh.

"Oh, right. Sure. I'll move right in with you, and let you feed and clothe me. What next? Do you want me to start calling you Dad?"

I expect him to join in my laughter, but instead he sobers up. I gape.

"What, really? I'm a grown woman, Marcus."

"I know. I missed your entire childhood, didn't I?"

He lowers his hands to his lap. His face is suddenly filled with some strange, otherworldly emotion; something I barely recognise.

"I'm so sorry."

My skin prickles.

"What are you talking about?"

"I'm sorry that you had to grow up without me around. I'm sorry you feel like you're a failure. I'm sorry you were always so lonely."

Heat fills my face and I look away.

"Thanks, but I'm alright. I can look after myself."

"You can now, sure. But there was a time you couldn't."

He leans closer suddenly, sending shivers up my spine.

"Did the Project treat you well, Reya? They never hurt you, right? They never made you feel bad?"

I open my mouth to tell him that no, of course they didn't. That if anything, I hurt them. But suddenly my eyes fill with tears, and I don't know why.

"Reya?"

"I'm fine."

I rub my face, confused.

"You're upset," he says, his face crumpling with sympathy. I shake my head.

"No. Really. I'm fine."

He watches me for a long moment, then reaches out. One hand finds my cheek, tilting my head up. A rough thumb brushes my tears away.

"Why do I get the feeling that you always say that?" he breathes, "why does it seem like you'd always say you were fine, even if you were moments from falling apart?"

My instinct is to pull away. My entire body aches to leap from the car and run home. Anything to escape the sympathetic look in his eyes. But his hand is warm against my cold skin. His steady breathing counteracts my own heavy, post-test panting.

The tears come faster.

"L-leave me alone."

He chuckles again, but pulls back.

"You're not what I would call emotionally intelligent, Reya."

I wipe my eyes madly.

"What, now you're calling me stupid?"

"Everyone's clever in their own way. Some people are intellectual. Some have street smarts. Others have skill at understanding feelings and what to do with them. All I'm saying is that when it comes to emotions, you don't really get it."

I pout and look away. He just smiles.

"You don't even understand how you feel right now, do you?"

"I'm feeling kinda hungry, if that's what you mean."

He doesn't laugh at my joke – just lets out a low cluck.

"Deflecting with humour. Classic. You used to be much more in tune with people."

"I was?"

"Absolutely. As a kid, you had this wonderful ability to charm everyone. It was nothing short of amazing. I'm sad to see that the Project stopped encouraging that."

"It's not their fault," I tell him, "I did nothing but cause trouble, so it's no wonder they didn't want to keep teaching me. Besides, that would mean talking to me."

His brow furrows.

"What do you mean?"

I chew my lip. Memories are already flooding back; memories I've tried to ignore for years. I consider waving him away, telling him I don't want to discuss it. But then he leans closer, his eyes pleading. I swallow hard.

"After... after you left, everyone went back to work. I didn't realise it at the time but looking back, they must have been making Alya. I didn't mind that they were suddenly busy, or that they stopped tucking me in at night. They stopped talking to me so much. It was fine. I figured I was just growing up."

I hesitate, but he gives an encouraging nod, urging me on.

"Then, one day, I came downstairs and went into the main lab. Nobody had come to wake me, so I'd got up on my own. I walked into the lab and everything was dark. They were using that old machine in the corner – the one you used to make me – and it was making weird sounds. I stayed in the doorway because I didn't understand what was happening."

My chest tightens at the memory.

"Then, Rene leaned over the equipment and opened that big, parachute-like part..."

"The artificial womb," Marcus interjects. I nod.

"Yeah. He reached inside, and pulled out this tiny baby."

"Alya."

I close my eyes for a moment, remembering it. How Rene's face had lit up in amazement. Alya was born smiling, something they talk about to this day. The few times they talked about my birth, they always say that I was born shrieking.

"Of course. They clipped the cord and it healed in an instant. Everyone was overjoyed. Rene held Alya up to the lights and made this big speech..."

"Declaring that this infant would see forever, and would serve as a grand symbol for the future."

I fire him a curious look.

"How did you know that?"

"That's the same speech Rene Snr made when you were born. So, what happened next?" he asks, apparently eager to hear the whole story.

"Well, nobody ever explained to me what had happened. I was left to figure it out for myself. That I had turned out wrong and they'd replaced me. It was years before I was able to get Jonah to discuss it with me. But the day Alya came along, everyone just... stopped. Nobody talked to me. Nobody looked me in the eye. And whenever they did, whenever they paid me the slightest bit of attention..."

The tears are back with a vengeance.

"They just seemed so ashamed of me."

Marcus' eyes soften.

"Oh, Reya..."

"I started sneaking out because I thought I'd go mad otherwise. But that just made them angrier. Rene thinks I'm just an irresponsible mess who puts everyone in danger, and the more he believes it the truer it becomes."

"That's why you're so lonely."

"I'm not lonely. I have Nova and the guys."

Not that I'll be able to see them much from now on.

"And Alya," I add, "the more time we spend together, the more I realise we're much more alike than I thought. I know I've never had a family, but it's what I'd imagine that feels like."

I lower my hands to my lap, breathing deeply. Marcus watches me silently. Those quick, intelligent eyes have softened into something rather different.

"I have you."

My words are quiet, and for a moment I hope he didn't hear. But he does. His face breaks into a smile.

"Yes, you do."

I wipe at my runny nose.

"You really want to help me?"

His smile widens.

"I just want to see the little girl I love smile again."

Love. Somehow, the word aches. It fills me like water, warming the tips of my fingers and sending a pleasant shudder down my spine. My head drops to my chest.

"Are you alright?"

I open my mouth to tell him that I'm fine, then realise how that'll sound. I consider cracking a joke, but no doubt that's deflection. I stare up at Marcus, remembering the few years before Alya came along. The years I was happy. My throat tightens.

"No," I breathe, "no, I'm not."

He opens his arms and I fall against his chest, allowing myself to cry for the first time in years. I mean, I've cried before – out of anger, out of sadness. But not like this. He holds me against his shoulder as I bawl, the frustration of the past 17 years bursting from my throat. The feeling is agony. Every part of me pleads to get up and move away, to apologise, to pretend it never happened. But I need this.

The memories flash in my head. Days in the library, nights spent crawling into others' beds, lessons on subjects I could never understand. The sight of Rene holding Alya up to the fluorescent lights, awe consuming his features. Alya herself, gleaming and beautiful, charming everyone without even trying. How it feels to stand behind her. How cold it is in her shadow.

His hand finds my head and I cry harder. I'm so sick of this. I don't want to be alone anymore. I don't want to be unhappy anymore.

Marcus lets out a low hush.

"Shh, shh. It'll all be okay. One more week."

His voice comforts me somewhat, and I'm able to finally pull away.

"I need to fix this, Marcus. I need to be what they want me to be."

He watches me with soft eyes, then nods.

"We'll make sure of it. I promise."

I sit up in the middle of the night. Alya shifts beside me. She's taken to crawling into my bed regularly since that first night, often waiting until I return in the early hours. So far, she hasn't asked where I've been going, but I'm sure she will soon.

The Dome is dark, and entirely silent aside from the sound of our breathing. I strain my ears, listening for sounds from downstairs. Nothing. Even the night lab is utterly silent.

I sigh. This is the first time in weeks that I've felt somewhat relaxed. I'm not sure why. All my problems are still there, just as desperate as ever. My mortality, our safety, the external threats. But suddenly, I feel calm.

Perhaps it's because I'm thinking about Rene.

Not grumpy, argumentative Rene. His father. Rene Senior.

While Rene Jnr has the look about him of a bullied nerd who never quite filled out, his father was the kind of man who looked like he had always been tiny, bespectacled and ancient. He had the same dark eyes as his son once, apparently, but they'd paled as he aged, fading to a grey that almost matched my own. When I pointed that out, he'd been quietly pleased.

I cast an eye across the room. So much has changed since then. The far corner was once filled with cushions and beanbag chairs. It was the same spot we would sit in while they read books to me. Everyone had their own preference; I still remember Sandra singing and Marcus' serious dedication to every part. Rene Senior read poetry.

To this day, I don't understand poetry. The way the words lilt and sing has always seemed strange to me, not unpleasant so much as alien. Sure, it's beautiful, but I've never been able to find a deeper meaning in it.

Even so, I loved it when he'd read to me. He'd let me nestle in the crook of his elbow while he read, and encouraged me to read along with him. Oddly, the most memorable part was his enunciation. I've never met anyone who spoke so clearly, every word crisp and delightful, like he was pouring his entire being into the simple act of speaking. Even when I didn't understand a single word, I'd cuddle against him and listen to his voice.

What I'd give to hear his voice now.

I stand, pacing the room uneasily. Why am I thinking about this?

Perhaps it's Marcus' fault. He mentioned the speech Rene Senior made when I was born. I close my eyes, imagining Alya's birth – but replace the man holding the infant up. I imagine the sparkle he must have had in his eyes at that moment, the smile that filled his features as he made me a million wonderful, impossible promises.

What would he think of me now?

He died before they figured out what was wrong with me.

Suddenly my feet move, seemingly of their own accord. I leave the Dome and clamber up to the roof, where the icy night air bites at me. I didn't think to don more clothing before venturing outside, so I wear just a tank top and a pair of too-short sweats. The gravel is rough under my bare feet, but I hardly notice.

Amare is dark. I'm reminded for the millionth time that this isn't some bustling metropolis like New York or London. This city doesn't live 24-7. It sleeps long and heavy, awakening under a thick cover of fog each day.

I sit on the wall and more memories surface, distracting me from the cold.

Rene Senior used to bring me up here. In his mind, I think he wanted to give some epic speech – a kind of 'look down at the world you get to shape' deal. In reality, he just founded my love of heights and quiet places.

A particular memory strikes me as important, and I dive into it.

In an instant I sit beside him, our legs hanging off the edge of the building. If he's afraid to be so high up, he doesn't show it. Amare is lit by soft, early morning sun. Nobody else is awake yet – that's when we liked to come up here.

He talks to me in a low, gentle voice.

"You really are fearless, aren't you Reya?"

I giggle in response and his smile widens.

"Good. You'll have to be fearless. Tough times are ahead for all of us. Not everyone will understand what we're trying to do here."

My adult mind races with questions I wish I'd asked. What are we trying to do? What was the goal? Money, fame, a legacy? He smiles so widely that his eyes crinkle.

"Humans are strange creatures. We don't always understand what's best for us, and we're liable to lash out at things that we can't comprehend. Hatred, rage, violence. All manner of terrible things caused by the simple trait of being human."

Young Reya doesn't have a clue what those words mean, but I feel her sober immediately. I never knew what he was talking about when this subject came up, but his tone had been clear as day.

"Your job isn't to save the world or anything like that," he says, "that would be too much to ask of anyone. I have a simple job for you. The only thing you ever need to do."

He reaches out, toying with a strand of my hair.

"Be good to people, Reya. Try and make them happy. If you can do that, you'll make me proud."

Then the memory is gone, leaving me with an ache in my chest and a familiar heat behind my eyes. I want to cry; but for once, they're tears of joy.

I remember him. I'm not sure why it's been so long since I thought about him. I don't know why I stopped.

I remember a lot about my childhood. The lessons, the training, the tests. I'd tackled everything with a certain rigour, determined to be whatever they needed. How had I forgotten my favourite parts? We had been so happy back then.

I look out over the city, aware that Rene Senior has vanished from beside me. I'm alone, again. Like always. My gaze sinks to my hands. I miss him. I miss them all; even the ones I see every day. They feel like perfect strangers now.

Something stirs in my chest, and my resolve hardens. I'll make them all happy again. I'll be what they always wanted me to be.

There used to be so much love in my life. Out of everything I'll get back once these tests are over, I think that's what I'm looking forward to most.

Thirteen

Three days later, my phone buzzes. I glance at the caller ID before picking up.

"Hey, Nova."

"Hey. How's the injury?"

I reach up, touching my shoulder gently. The pain is almost entirely gone now, and I've had a full range of movement for a while.

"Almost back to normal," I tell her, "but something tells me the Project isn't going to let me drive anymore."

"Nor should they! I saw the footage on the news. You hit so many cars."

"I feel a bit bad about that."

"It's nothing compared to what you've done to my car in the past," she says, and I can hear her grinning.

"You let me drive," I shrug, "what's up, anyway?"

"I wanted to ask if you're allowed out yet."

I bite my lip.

"Probably not. Why?"

"Well, do you remember when you and Alya had to leave in a hurry?"

"Oh, that. Listen, I'm sorry..."

"Ah, never mind. The reason I was so upset is because we had a surprise for you, and you left in such a hurry that we didn't get chance to give it to you."

I sit up straighter, pressing the phone to my ear.

"A surprise?"

"Yeah. It's your birthday tomorrow, right?"

"It is?"

She heaves a sigh.

"Honestly. I can see you forgetting someone else's birthday, but your own?"

"I don't do birthdays," I remind her. Not since I was a kid, anyway. Once Alya came along, they stopped feeling so important.

She huffs.

"Well, me and the guys wanted to do a big show of telling you about your present, but since we can't see you face to face, I guess this will have to do. You know how we'll need to stay overnight at the Creation Show, since we can't set things up on the day?"

"Yeah, I was going to meet you there if I managed to get away."

"Well, we pooled our money. We booked an extra hotel room, including all meals, so you can stay with us for the night!"

My chest aches.

"W-wow, Nova..."

"That's not all! We came to an agreement. The first round of profits from the platform is going directly to you, to fund an apartment and a car. You can finally start your own life. Marcus donated a ton of extra cash, too, once I explained the situation."

The thought is incredible. I imagine living in my own place, working a job like any other normal person. Four months ago, I'd have never dared to dream about such a life.

"Nova, that's amazing. I really appreciate the thought."

"But?"

"But, things are crazy right now. I can't attend the show and I certainly can't move out."

"You're an adult. You can do whatever you like."

"Now's not a good time. I'm sorry."

"But we booked it just for you."

"Sorry," I tell her, my heart aching, "I love it, really, but I can't."

"You need to do something to make yourself happy, once in a while."

"It's just, after what happened on the freeway…"

She lets out a long sigh, and I know I'm starting to talk her round. I don't want to. We've been talking about the show for months, and I always hoped that somehow, I'd find a way to be there. I imagine Rene's reaction if I asked permission to go.

"Look," she says, "maybe I can talk to Rene for you."

"As it is, you wouldn't get within 50 yards of Lockless House."

"Then just come to my place. Come live with me."

I bite my lip so hard it hurts. This is a conversation we've had a thousand times. Nova moved out as a teenager and she's always been self-sufficient, aside from in a monetary sense. It baffles her that I would willingly stay somewhere I didn't like. But then, that's Nova – she just gets up and walks when she's not happy. Maybe that's why she's never miserable.

"You know I can't do that."

"You absolutely can. I know, I know. You're not legally 'human'. Whatever. The guys will give you a job delivering parcels and you can stay with me as long as you want. Indefinitely, maybe. I don't care. We can get a bigger place and throw parties every night. It'd be great."

My hand tightens on the phone.

"I'm being hunted, or have you forgotten that?"

"We can protect you."

"I wouldn't want to put you guys in danger."

"You're not a superhero, Reya. Nobody's going to kidnap your girlfriend and force you to expose your secret identity."

"As funny as that is," I say, "these people are crazy. They shot me, Nova. What part of that tells you they're sane, normal people who can be reasoned with?"

"I guess so."

A long pause.

"So you're not coming with us?" she sighs. My chest aches.

"No. I wish I could. I really wish I could."

"I suppose I can understand. And I guess you need to stick with Alya, right?"

"That too. You know what she's like. Can't do a damn thing for herself."

We share a laugh, even though we both know Alya's more capable than both of us combined. Nova sighs.

"That means we're going to miss your birthday."

"I don't mind. But I want you guys to keep us updated about the show, alright? I mean photos, videos, phone calls. Everything. I'll even text you the number for Alya's phone, so send them to her too, okay?"

"She has a cell phone?"

"Strictly in case of emergencies. I'd say that this constitutes as one, wouldn't you?"

She laughs, and I feel myself join in. It feels good to laugh. Like I haven't in a long time.

"How long before you can come over?" she asks, still chuckling. I frown.

"Whenever things are safe, I guess."

"When will that be?"

My gaze is drawn back to the city, and I think about the people gathering there. Planning the next attack. Who will they target next? Who will they try to kill?

I stand, feeling my hackles raise. They're not going to get a chance.

"With any luck," I tell Nova through gritted teeth, "it'll all be over soon."

I draw back my fist, driving it at Jonah's face.

He dodges me easily, knocking my hand aside and laughing.

"You're slow, today."

"Give me a break," I puff, "I'm still working with a busted shoulder."

He rolls his eyes. Jonah knows as well as I do that my shoulder's practically back to normal. He's been encouraging me to keep training while waiting for the go-ahead from Neil to start testing again. It's helped, somewhat; the pain is minimal, my range of movement entirely back to normal.

Jonah circles me, raising his gloved hands. In a sense, it feels good to be back in the gym. Even though my body is tired, and every session wipes me out for days, the normality is reassuring.

He steps closer and I jump back, blocking my face with my arms. He grins.

"You're out of practice, Reya."

"I'm doing my best," I tell him. Just to emphasise my point I bounce harder on my heels, feeling my ponytail flick behind me. It's tougher than expected to keep up the energetic façade, but I'm trying.

Briefly, I wonder how much better it'll feel when this is over. When my body is back to full force, when I no longer have to worry about exhaustion or injury. Despite plenty of practice, I've never been able to best Jonah in a fight. That might change after I'm fixed.

For a moment, my mind goes blank – and when I snap back to reality, Jonah's fist is flying towards my face. I brace for impact, but nothing comes.

When I open my eyes, I see Jonah's fist hovering an inch from my face. He sighs and pulls back, fixing me with an uneasy look.

"Alright," he says, "what's going on?"

"Nothing."

"That was an easy dodge, Reya. Well within your capabilities. You weren't focussing."

"Guess I'm having an off day," I say, suddenly defensive. He frowns.

"You're distracted."

"No, I'm not."

He watches me for a long moment, then steps back.

"There's no point training today if you're not paying attention."

"I can keep going."

"No. Take five."

I roll my eyes and turn away.

"Forget it. I'm going to wash up."

"Hey."

He grabs my wrist, holding me still.

"Look, Reya. I know things are tough right now. You're worried. We all are. And it's obvious you've got some things you're working through."

He's got that look on his face again. The look he gives me during every heart-to-heart. He's silently asking me to sit down and talk to him about my gross feelings. I shrug, fixing a half-smile on my face.

"I don't feel like talking misery tonight. How about we get back to training?"

"Training's no good if you're distracted. Something's clearly going on. Have you spoken to Sandra?"

"No," I reply tersely.

"Alright. That's fair."

He reaches out, resting a hand on my shoulder.

"Reya, I've always done my best to keep your secrets and help you out where I can."

"I know."

He squeezes my shoulder.

"You know you can talk to me about anything."

I look up, meeting his eyes. I hadn't expected this to be so hard, but he's right. Jonah has always been the least judgemental person in the Project. He's always tried to help, even if he doesn't truly understand. If there's anyone I could trust with the truth...

Then I remember the panic in his eyes when I mentioned Marcus. He damn near lost his mind at the sound of his name. If he knew what we were doing – if he had any idea what I've been up to – he'd stop me. Jonah, who always understands, wouldn't understand this.

"I know."

I reach up, gently peeling his hand from my shoulder. Hurt crosses his face but he shifts back, giving me space. I sigh.

"It's not that I don't trust you," I tell him, "but some things, I need to figure out for myself."

His expression falters, but only for a moment before he smiles again.

"Alright. I get it. But I'm here if you need me, alright?"

"Sure. I'm gonna go wash up."

"Nope. Come here."

He walks over to the gym bench, sinks onto it, and taps the spot beside him. I frown.

"I just said I don't want to talk about it."

"And I said I understand. But you still need training."

"Really? Come on, Jonah, I'm exhausted. I was doing a crap job today, anyway."

His eyes glimmer.

"Exactly. You're overthinking, that's why you can't focus. So we're going to distract your mind, instead."

"Huh?"

He simply pats the spot again, his smile widening. I hesitate, then drop down beside him. He reaches up, mopping the sweat from his face.

"I need you to memorise some codes."

"Codes?"

"Security codes," he tells me, "everything in Lockless House works using hand prints, but that's not always the most effective method. If there were ever an attack, you might be tied up or trapped somewhere, unable to reach a panel. In that case, you'll need to use a verbal access code."

"Nobody's going to bust into Lockless House, Jonah. Even if they did, you'd be here. I doubt anyone would get past you."

"I am excellent, I'll give you that, but even I'm not infallible. I can't protect everyone all the time. But that car chase proved one thing – in a crisis, you focus on protecting your sister."

I don't respond, but my cheeks burn. Jonah had greeted me enthusiastically after the incident, and though I'd expected rage following the destruction of his car, I instead received praise for my quick thinking. Apparently, forcing Alya to the floor was the right choice – even if it had felt cruel at the time.

"Different codes will grant different levels of security access," he tells me, "and I want you to memorise them all. Just in case."

"You're literally prepping me for an attack."

"I can't control what you do outside these walls, Reya. But what I can do is make sure that when you're in Lockless House, you're as safe as possible. And as well-prepared as possible to help protect others."

"Protecting everyone is your job," I joke. He stares me down, suddenly serious.

"We're all responsible for protecting each other. That's the promise we all made when we joined."

"You did?"

He ruffles my hair, apparently opting to ignore my question.

"Alright. Codes. Let's get them memorised, and then I can give you a low-down on the alarm systems, basic armoury contents and security protocol."

I open my mouth to tease him, to ask why he's suddenly so paranoid – then stop. There's an uncharacteristic seriousness in his eyes, like he's trying a little too hard to appear nonchalant. Whatever's going on, he's more worried about it than he's letting on. The urge to taunt him vanishes.

If teaching me protocol will give him some sense of control, I'll learn it. So I draw my face into what I hope is a casual smile, and encourage him to continue.

We're starting tests again today. I try not to yawn as Neil leans over me, carrying out the usual pre-test checks. I've been banned from the main lab during tests while I was recovering, so it feels strange to be back.

He pulls back, lowers the light he was just shining in my eyes, and nods.

"You're good."

"Ever the conversationalist, Neil," I grin. He doesn't reply, just moves away. I can't say I'm surprised.

The others pull out the equipment for today's test, and my stomach churns. It's the same equipment we've been using during my tests with Marcus – only without his modifications. This is the original setup; a wooden chair with small nodules on the arms to deliver shocks through the wrist. I glower at it.

"Electrocution? Are you serious?"

"It's a mild one to ease you back into it," Rene says, somehow hearing me across the lab, "just a couple of short shocks to check your refractory period. Nothing that will put strain on your shoulder."

"My, the consideration!" I gasp. He rolls his eyes. Rene has never appreciated my humour.

"Just sit down."

I sink into the chair beside Alya, who sits with her arms already against the metal nodules. She watches me with a cheery smile.

"Why are you so happy?" I ask.

"I missed you during tests. It feels good to have one thing go back to normal."

Rene stands in front of us, talking more to Alya than to me. He wears his normal lab coat – a small detail that somewhat pleases me. It's better than all those suits he's been wearing lately.

"Okay," he says matter-of-factly, "we'll be doing a couple of short bursts, just to test your reactions and recovery from a brief flash of pain. Alright?"

Alya nods. Rene watches me, waiting for me to nod too before he turns away.

I relax in the chair. This is the same machine I've been strapped into a dozen times before, only without Marcus' modifications. No device at my back, ready to inject me with gallons of mysterious, DNA-altering serum. Just two tiny pieces of metal at my wrists, prepped to deliver low-level electric shocks. Comparatively, this seems rather tame.

They count down to the first shock and when it starts, I barely feel it. I think about the agony I've experienced lately - not just from Marcus' tests, but from the gunshot, too – and suddenly the shock is little more than a mild tickle.

Rene watches me with curious eyes. Perhaps he's noticed my lack of reaction.

"Let's take it up a little."

The second burst forces Alya to gasp. I feel a tingle in my wrists.

"Again."

She lets out a low whine beside me. I stare down at my arms, wondering what's wrong. It doesn't hurt. Not even a little. Rene's eyes narrow, but he doesn't say anything.

I glance at the monitors tracking our vitals. Alya's heartrate has increased slightly – her standard reaction to minor pain. Mine is as steady as ever. For the first time ever, I've outlasted her.

The room falls silent, and I realise they're all watching the monitors. This has never happened before. I stare at the back of Rene's head. This is unusual, but a relatively minor blip. They'll probably explain it away, perhaps referring to recent stressful situations as an reason for my lack of response.

Neil nears, unhooking my wrist and turning it over. My breath catches as his fingertips graze the skin, tracing the veins in my arm. Rene steps closer, too, watching Neil with curious eyes.

"Well?"

"There's nothing wrong."

"The machine is working just fine, though. Is she positioned properly?"

"Yes."

"Then, scar tissue. Something has to be blocking the current."

"Nothing."

It takes everything I have to remain silent as they exchange confused looks.

What I'd give to tell them that I'm growing stronger every day. That my recovery period is already practically zero. The thought ignites something deep inside me. God, I wish I could tell them everything.

I'm changing. I can feel it.

Finally, Rene steps back. His expression is unreadable as his gaze flits from Neil to Alya and back to me. He glances at the console.

"We're going to step it up again," he says slowly, "is that okay?"

This time, he doesn't wait for my answer. I watch as he crosses the room in silence, taps in a few numbers, and activates the machine. As it starts up, I realise they've unhooked Alya. Neil tugs her away from the testing area. Every pair of eyes has settled on me.

My chest swells with excitement. I long for the pain the shock will bring. I'm desperate to show them that I can take it. That I can do anything they want me to.

When the shock arrives my spine straightens instinctively, but the pain is barely worse than a muscle cramp. I breathe through it, like how Marcus taught me. My pulse remains remarkably steady.

And then it's over, and the room is silent. I feel countless eyes on me. When I lift my head Rene stands in front of me, confusion swimming in his gaze.

I give him a small smile.

"Did I do it right?"

"Did you really say that?"

Marcus leans back in his chair, chuckling. He brought along a bottle of fine scotch tonight, claiming it's the perfect precursor to a little testing. Once I explained that it'd take more than a bottle to get me drunk, he'd admitted it was more for his own sake.

I knock back the remainder of my own glass and place it on the counter, the sound echoing through Safehouse 17.

"I didn't know what else to say!" I tell him, "they were all just staring at me!"

"Well, I can understand that. You've measured up against average humans your whole life, right? It's impressive that you can handle that much pain without much reaction."

"I've always been good with pain," I retort, "they just never noticed before."

"And our tests have nothing to do with it?"

"I do feel different."

His eyebrows raise.

"Different?"

"I can't really explain it. Things just feel... new."

He pours me another glass and I clutch it with both hands, smiling.

"Something's definitely changing. I can sense it."

His lip curls.

"You seem happy tonight, Reya."

"I guess I am. It was amazing, Marcus. They were blown away. Is that what things will be like when I'm fixed? Will everyone react like that?"

His smile grows bigger.

"Well, how do they react to Alya?"

"Everyone who meets her is blown away. Even the people who claim to hate her want to be near her. It's like she's intoxicating."

He gives a knowing nod.

"That's perfectly natural. Humans have an innate fear of death. The thought of escaping that – of anyone escaping that – is certainly the type of thing that could drive one to obsession."

"Just imagine it, Marcus. In a few days' time, once we've fixed me, we can go back to Lockless House. We'll explain what we've done, how we did it, how amazing everything is now. They'll be so happy. For the first time ever, they might even be proud."

His expression falters briefly, but he quickly replaces his smile.

"Well, even if they aren't, I'm proud of you, Reya."

"You are?"

"How many people would go through literal torture to accomplish a destiny they were handed by strangers? I'm amazed by your dedication. And listen..."

He leans closer, peering at me with those dark, intelligent eyes.

"...After all this, you can still come and live with me."

"As your daughter, right?" I joke.

"Yes," he says softly. I frown.

"Hey, we've been through this already. I'm 24."

"25, actually."

He leans back, chuckling.

"Happy birthday."

"You remembered my birthday?" I ask, genuinely stunned. He chuckles.

"What kind of person would I be if I forgot your birthday?"

"What do you mean? Everyone at the Project forgets it."

His face pinches.

"Really? Every year?"

"I guess so," I shrug, "nobody's mentioned it for years, so I assume they all forgot."

Either that, or they don't care. But I don't need to voice that concern. He knows exactly what I'm thinking. An uncomfortable silence falls over us, and I don't bother breaking it. Eventually, he clears his throat.

"Well, then. Does that mean you don't want your present?"

"Present?"

He stands, yanking open a nearby cupboard and pulling out a thin, plastic packet.

"You know, most people get presents on their birthdays. Or didn't they teach you that, either?"

"I know that much," I say, flushing red, "Nova paid for me to attend the Creation Show with Quad Creations. Man, was she disappointed when I said no."

"You're not going?"

"This is more important."

He strides over, pushing the packet into my hands.

"Now, I know it's not gift-wrapped, and I'm sorry. I've never been very good at things like that, and I admit I figured you wouldn't care."

"You figured correct."

I take the parcel hesitantly, somewhat nervous. Even with Nova and the guys, 'gifts' are special nights out. Most years we go to karaoke or that one fancy nightclub on the edge of town, or we save up for weeks and buy an enormous box of fireworks. We've never done physical presents before.

I've seen classic birthdays, of course. I'm sure I had them when I was very young, though I don't really remember. Project staff get a card signed by everyone else on their birthdays, and they'll bring in a pack of donuts or order a pizza. Alya gets proper birthdays, of course; they decorate the lab with streamers and banners, sing 'happy birthday', and make everyone wear silly hats while she blows out candles on a multi-coloured cake.

I stare down at the plastic-wrapped gift, then around at the cold, empty lab. Somehow, this doesn't have the same kind of excitement to it. Still, it's a first.

Fourteen

I pull open the packet and tug out a mustard-yellow hoodie. Marcus smiles.

"I noticed you haven't been wearing your black one lately."

"Yeah," I croak, "it got stained with blood during the crash."

"I hope I got the right size. I've never bought women's clothes before."

I stand up and pull the hoodie on. The sleeves are a little long and the colour is somewhat vile, but it's warm and fleecy. I zip it up and snuggle into it, pulling the hood up over my hair. Warmth travels down to my fingertips, making everything tingle. My lip curls.

"This is brilliant."

"Are you sure?" he asks, "I can return it for something else, if you like. I wasn't sure about the colour. You normally wear Project gear or all black."

I walk over to a nearby cupboard, which has a glossy steel door. My reflection is blurred, but I can see myself clearly enough. Perhaps it's the distortion but for a moment, I see someone else.

I see a woman in her mid-twenties, pale with dark hair, light eyes, and a permanent line between her brows from scowling, with an uncharacteristic smile on her face. I lean closer, wondering why my eyes are glossy. This shouldn't make me want to cry.

"You look nice," Marcus offers. He's almost as awkward as I am, perched uncomfortably on the edge of his seat.

"Thanks," I say, and I'm surprised to find I mean it.

I make my way back over to the chair and sink into it, lowering the hood. Marcus raises his glass.

"Oh god," I interject, "please don't do a toast."

"Not a fan?"

"Rene used to use the rooftop at Lockless House to practice speeches for events. I can't tell you how many times I had to find somewhere to hide and listen to him recite the same words ad nauseum."

"Well, if you're sure. I was just going to wish luck on our latest endeavour."

I glance at the setup in the corner, and my stomach spins. This is what I want. This is what's best for everyone, even if they don't know it yet. But that doesn't mean I'm not terrified.

"You won't let me die, will you?" I ask him, "like, for real die?"

"We both know there are no such things as guarantees in this line of work. But I promise I will not let anything happen to you, not as long as I have the power to stop it."

Something in me balks at his answer, but I silence it. I've heard the Project say this a million times. 'To the best of our knowledge'. 'As far as evidence shows'. What sounds like excuses and disclaimers in plain English are actually just science talk. Since nothing is ever certain beyond a shadow of a doubt, they can't state it outright. As far as Marcus can, he's just promised me I won't die in three days.

"We should get to work soon," he says.

"Why so eager?" I ask.

"My goal is to take you home as early as I can. With the local lunatics on the lookout for you, it's not safe to keep you here any longer than absolutely necessary."

"I can handle myself," I retort, wondering how many times I've said this in the past few months.

"I'm sure you can. But nobody is supposed to be leaving Lockless House, correct? If you return with so much as a black eye, Rene will know you've been going out. He won't take kindly to that."

He's not wrong. I glance at the setup again.

"This is going to hurt."

"Most likely, yes."

"You're being really sympathetic right now, did you know that?"

He winks.

"I know you rather well by now, Reya. You'll spend several minutes telling me how you don't want to do this, and then I'll tell you that you don't have to, and you'll leap into the seat without further prompting, begging me to continue the tests."

I promptly deflate.

"Am I that predictable?"

"Every single time," he smirks, "so why don't we just skip the hesitation and jump in feet first?"

"Damn. When did you get so good at reading me?"

"Consider it a skill."

My legs wobble violently as I enter Lockless House. Tonight's tests were particularly brutal.

On an emotional level, I don't care. This is all necessary. But my body is running on fumes. I'm tired, hungry, thirsty, and ready to rip someone's head off if they look at me sideways.

I sneak past the night lab and upstairs, clutching the railing to keep myself upright. To an onlooker, I must appear drunk. This would hardly be the first time I've tried to navigate these steps while intoxicated.

I step into the dome, yawning.

"There you are."

Alya reaches over and switches on the lamp, which sends a flicker of pain through my head. She sits cross-legged on my bed, a look of conflict on her face.

"Have you been waiting for me?" I ask, "more nightmares?"

"No," she snaps, then hesitates, "well, yes. But that's not why I waited up."

Her gaze drops to my feet, lingers on my wobbling legs, and finally settles on my torso.

"Where did you get that jacket?"

"Oh, this?" I chuckle, "it's a gift from my sugar daddy."
She promptly pales. I laugh.
"Calm down, I'm kidding. It's from a friend. A birthday present."
Her eyes widen.
"It's your birthday?"
"Apparently."
"I thought you hated your birthday."
"Who told you that?" I ask, then roll my eyes. Of course the Project would tell her I hated my birthday, rather than explain the truth. I stifle another yawn and her stares deepen.
"Where have you been?"
"Why do you care?" I retort, a little more harshly than I intend to. She doesn't back down.
"You've been going out every night. I know it's not with Nova and the boys; she's been texting me non-stop ever since you gave her my number. You're not bruised or anything, so I don't think you're out getting into fights. But you don't smell like alcohol, either. So what gives?"
"Does it matter? You've never cared where I go before."
"It's not safe anymore. And even if it was, you're exhausted. You sleep all day and you still look like you could collapse any moment. I'm not the only one who's noticed. The whole Project's been talking about it. Everyone's worried about you."
I roll my eyes again, this time making sure she sees. She pushes on.
"You and I are supposed to trust each other. Why won't you tell me what's going on?"
At that, I balk. She's got me. I sigh.
"Do you remember the night of the car chase, when we had to leave Nova's early?"
"Yeah. You were acting weird all night. You said you had to do something private."
"Exactly. Well, I'm trying to fix something important and I enlisted an old friend to help me. I go out at night to work on it and it's tiring. That's all."
"Well, what's broken?"
Me, I think, but I daren't tell her that. So instead, I shake my head and walk towards the bathroom.
"Are you trying to fix yourself?" she asks.
I freeze, one hand on the door handle.

"W-what are you talking about?" I whisper, praying I misheard her. She twists to face me, re-crossing her legs and fixing me with a calm look.

"Are you trying to become immortal like me?"

I whip round to face her, heart gunning. She gives a triumphant grin.

"I knew it. I'd thought it was a long shot. But if it wasn't risky, you'd tell me what was going on. And if it were anything else, you wouldn't be prioritising it like this. I'm right, aren't I?"

I hesitate.

"Yeah."

"Who's helping you?"

"Do you remember we talked about Marc Gregory? Nova's new sponsor."

"Right," she nods, "he used to be Project staff. That makes sense. Why are you doing it?"

"Why else? If I can fix myself, not only will the Project be happier, but I'll be *better*. During the car chase, I was useless because I'm mortal. If not for that, I'd have been able to protect you better. This is just... the logical solution to all our problems."

"How are you doing it?"

"I don't really understand it myself. All I really know is that I'm exhausted. But I'm nearly done."

Her eyes are round now, glittering in the half-darkness.

"Really?"

"Yep. A couple of days and it'll all be over."

I don't fight the grin that works its way across my face.

"A couple of days and I'll finally be able to protect you. You won't have to face forever alone, either. I'll be there right alongside you for as long as you need me. Everything will finally be how it was meant to be."

Alya watches me thoughtfully, like she doesn't quite understand what I'm saying.

"Just trust me," I say, stepping into the bathroom.

The fluorescent light is blinding, and in an instant my head spins. I teeter towards the sink, trip over the bathmat I never bother to lay properly, and collide painfully with the side of the tub.

"Ow..."

I push myself to my knees, fighting off the worst of the fatigue. Marcus warned me this might happen – moments of dizziness, sensitivity to light – but I need to handle it better.

The bathroom door opens behind me.

"I heard a crash," Alya says, "are you okay?"

I give myself a once over, and my gaze settles on my arm. There's an impressive scrape running down to my wrist, shallow but seeping blood. I touch it and wince.

"Oh, that's just marvellous."

Alya drops to her knees beside me, brows furrowed.

"What happened? Did you pass out?"

"No," I snap, "I just got a little disoriented."

She watches me closely, pursing her lips, and I wonder if she's about to call me out. Luckily she seems to think better of it, instead turning her attention to the scrape.

"That looks sore. Should I call for Neil?"

"Don't be daft, he's asleep. I know how to treat..."

My breath catches. The subtle sting of the graze is growing into a strange, burning sensation. Like someone's holding a lit cigarette to my skin. The feeling intensifies until my whole arm is aflame.

"Reya?"

Sweat streams from my head and I double over, a cry escaping my lips. I tell myself it's just a graze. But suddenly, I feel terrible. The pain is all-consuming, making it almost impossible to draw breath.

I expect Alya to panic, but when I look up, she's frozen. She holds my arm in both hands, eyes wide.

"What the..."

I drop my gaze to the scrape and my stomach knots.

I'm healing.

The change is slow, the skin regrowing at a snail's pace, but it's happening.

Suddenly, the pain makes sense. I feel waves of agony as the skin stitches itself back together, as the blood pools, hardens and cracks, and the scar fades. Accelerated healing; just like her.

The moment it's over I slump against the tub, gasping for air. Alya pulls away, visibly shaking. I touch the now-healed skin. It's red, irritated, and somewhat thinner than it was before – but it's healed.

Triumph fills my chest. It's working. It's actually working!

"Are you okay?"'

She leans in and I beam at her.

"Did you see that?"

"Yes. I did."

"It works," I gasp, "he's actually fixing me. God, there was a part of me that thought he was full of it. I can't believe it's working."

Her expression wavers.

"That looked like it hurt."

"It was absolute agony. But look! It worked."

"But Reya..." she breathes, "it's not supposed to hurt. You shouldn't feel anything during healing."

"We're not done yet," I remind her, "we haven't done the final push. This is just... the development stage, I suppose. It'll be better soon. Faster, less painful. Then..."

She steps back suddenly, shaking her head.

"Listen to me, Reya. This isn't normal."

"I was meant to be immortal."

"But you're *not*," she snaps, "this isn't normal for you. I thought you were about to have a fit or something."

Her eyes flash.

"We need to tell the Project. I'm sure they can reverse this."

She turns to leave and I find the energy to stand, grabbing her by the wrist.

"No. No, you can't tell them."

"I'm scared for you," she confesses, "you're not being logical. There's no way this isn't damaging your body. If we don't do something soon..."

"Look."

I hold out the healed arm, shaking it at her.

"Do you see this? This is the single most amazing thing that's ever happened to me. I never thought I could be this happy. My wildest dreams are finally coming true, Alya. I can finally be the person I was always supposed to be."

My chest aches.

"This is the only thing I've ever wanted. Please, please, don't ruin this for me. It's the only dream I've ever had and it's finally real."

My little sister stares tearfully at me for several seconds. Her lip wobbles slightly, and then she nods.

"Okay."

I release her wrist, grinning.

"Thank you."

She fires me a sideways glance.

"Reya, forgive my bluntness but... you look horrible."

"Yeah, yeah. I know. I'll sleep it off."

I make my way to the bed, where I collapse fully clothed onto the mattress. When I don't move to grab the blanket I feel Alya do it, tucking me in like a small child. Some dim part of my brain suggests I should thank her, but exhaustion washes over me and I allow my eyes to slip shut.

As my senses die down, I'm left with the sound of breathing. My own, calm and steady, and Alya's – which is decidedly less so.

Fifteen

I wake alone. Light streams through the Dome, falling across my face. I'm still sprawled on the bed, exactly where I fell last night. For several seconds, it's peaceful.

Then I remember what happened last night and bolt upright, grabbing my arm. I examine the skin carefully. It's still a little tender, but otherwise perfect.

It really happened. I'm changing.

I need to tell Marcus.

I delve into the pocket of my hoodie, searching for my phone. Nothing. Did I leave it at Safehouse 17? No, I checked before I left. Perhaps I left it in Marcus' car? I don't think so. I bite my lip.

I hope I didn't drop it somewhere in Lockless House. Rene's already made it clear that my messages are his business – and he's unlikely to turn down an opportunity to snoop. I wrack my brain, trying to remember if I sent Marcus any especially incriminating messages lately. But on that front, at least, we're safe. We've both been careful to only text in code. Rene won't be able to figure out that I'm meeting 'M' at '17'.

I drag a brush through my hair and head downstairs, pleased that my aches have eased. I'm still not especially energised, but I feel okay. And okay is about as good as I've felt in months.

Lockless House is oddly silent. Normally at this time, the place would be bustling. I step into the side labs, poking my head in. Nobody.

I walk into the main lab, scratching my head.

"Hey, guys? Has anyone seen my..."

I freeze.

The entire Project is gathered around a large screen in the centre of the room. Data flies by on it; showing locations and times, displaying various messages. But I don't care about the screen. What worries me is what I hear.

Marcus' voice, clear and unmistakable. My own, snapping back at him. He tries to reason with me, encouraging me to rest after my injury. I insist we continue testing.

This is our conversation from the roof. The call I made on my Project Cell. Which records every call.

My heart thumps like someone's taken a jackhammer to my torso.

Everyone's facing away from me, but they know I'm here. I can see Rene's shoulders clenching, his agitation building with every second of the conversation. Beside him, Alya fires a guilty look at my cell, which is plugged into the console. My head spins.

She sold me out.

The conversation ends with a click, and a horrible silence falls over the room. I steal a glance at the front door, wondering if I should just book it. Run away. Head out and never come back – not that Rene will ever let me back after this, anyway.

Slowly, I feel eyes shift toward me. They fix me with looks of shock, disgust, anger. I shrink back when I see Neil's face – contorted with the kind of rage I always thought he was incapable of. Then Rene turns around.

I've seen Rene angry plenty of times. I've heard hurtful words leave his lips. I've seen frustration build behind his otherwise meek features, threatening to erupt. But I've never seen this before.

He looks at me with pure, venomous hatred. My heart sinks.

This isn't how this was supposed to go.

"Reya."

His voice is remarkably calm, despite the vitriol burning behind his eyes. I gulp.

"Don't freak out. I can explain everything."

"How..."

He trails off and shakes his head, apparently so blinded by rage that he can't formulate a sentence. Luckily, Alya interrupts. She steps forward, her face a picture of panic.

"What have you been doing?!" she cries.

"Woah," I say, "it's alright. Listen, everything is..."

Jonah shouts next, his voice booming across the room and making me flinch.

"You promised, Reya! You promised you'd stay away from him!"

Rene rounds on him in a flash.

"You knew about this?!"

"I..."

"Of course you did!" Rene snarls, "you just couldn't resist keeping in touch with your old buddy, could you? What part did you play in all this?"

"He didn't," I interject, "Jonah didn't know anything."

Jonah shakes his head.

"Look, I knew he was in town, that's all. We discussed it and I told her to keep away from him."

"And you didn't think to tell me about this?"

"I thought I'd handled it."

Rene rolls his eyes.

"All these years and we still can't trust you."

He swoops away with an air of disgust, and I see Jonah's face crumple. The last thing he'd ever want is to disappoint the Project. I open my mouth to apologise, but fall silent when I realise how many people are still glaring at me.

"So," says Rene coolly, "what did Marcus promise you?"

"Huh?"

"I know that manipulative bastard better than most, and I know that even you aren't stupid enough to do this willingly. There's no way you'd agree unless he promised you something. I want to know what it is."

"He..."

I pause, humiliation filling me. What am I meant to say? He said he loved me, and I folded? He promised he could make you love me? I can't say that.

"Listen, Rene, if we can just talk this over..."

He slams a hand on the table and everyone jumps. Even Sandra backs away, frightened by his anger.

"What has he been doing to you?"

He steps closer, and my frustration grows.

"I get that you're angry, but you don't have any right to stop me doing this. I'm a fully grown adult and if I want to consent to things I couldn't before, then that's my business."

"Reya," Alya interjects, "just tell us what you've been doing."

Oddly, Alya's voice calms Rene. He glances at her, takes several deep breaths, and steps back. My skin crawls; I can still feel his anger.

Somehow, the request doesn't seem too unreasonable coming from Alya.

"He's created a serum that can disassemble my DNA and put it back together a little differently. It's supposed to fix whatever went wrong with me before I was born."

Rene's rage returns in an instant.

"Are you really that stupid?!"

"I'm not being forced, if that's what you're mad about. This is a choice I've made."

His eyes narrow.

"Marcus doesn't care what you choose."

His anger ebbs for a moment.

"That man doesn't care what you want," he tells me, "he's cruel, and manipulative, and he doesn't give a crap about anyone but himself. I'm willing to bet that everything he told you was an utter lie. A way to manipulate you into thinking he was trustworthy."

"He didn't lie to me."

"You wouldn't know it if he did!"

I let out a low growl.

"If you must know, Marcus is the only person I can trust! He told me everything that you never did. He told me how the Project was split when I was a kid. About his theories."

I stare him down, anger scorching my tongue.

"He told me how you planned to send me away, once you realised I was a mistake."

Rene's anger fizzles out.

"Woah, hold on..."

"Are you going to deny it? Because Marcus told me more than that. He told me about the kidnapping, the tests, everything. All the horrible secrets you never told me."

I step forward, power filling my chest. Rene and I have argued a thousand times, maybe more – but never have I felt in control like this. I always slip up and say something hurtful, but not this time. This time, I have the truth on my side. Rene stares.

"Marcus told us about his theory years ago," he says, "there's no science to back it up. It won't work. He's relying on the fact that you don't understand the science, and using that to manipulate you."

"He's not lying, Rene. It's working."

"He's tricking you. There is no way it's working."

"Happy to put that to the test?"

Before he can respond I pull open the nearest drawer, searching for something sharp. Even as I pull the scissors out and prise them open, my heart is thumping. I don't want to do this. But I learned a long time ago that I'm not capable of convincing Rene of anything. My best bet is cold, hard proof. Once he sees this – once he sees how far I've gone – everything will be okay. The world will fall back into place. Even if it's not perfect, this will be enough. It has to be.

Rene's eyes widen when I put the blade to my arm.

"Wait, what are you...?"

"Just watch."

I drag the blade down the inside of my arm, slicing deep into the flesh – and in an instant he grabs my hand, forcing the scissors away. His other hand grips my arm above the wound, tightening enough to hurt. The scissors clatter to the floor.

"What the hell are you doing?" he shrieks. His anger is palpable; my skin crawls.

"Rene, listen."

"Someone pass me some gauze. We need to stop the bleeding."

"Rene!" I snap. He stares at me and I lean closer.

"Please, just watch."

An unsettling silence falls across the lab as Rene's eyes drop to the cut on my arm.

The burning has set in again, only hotter this time. Much, much hotter. Within seconds I feel sweat streaming down my face. I throw out my free arm and lean on a nearby table, desperate to stay standing while the wound heals. My breathing falters, then levels, then falters again. I ignore the dark spots in the corners of my vision.

This is crazy. I know that. But if this is what it takes for him to understand, then I'll do it. He'll see how hard I'm trying. Surely, then, he'll finally be happy.

Rene's eyes widen as the wound begins to knit itself together. I hear several low gasps around the lab – everyone's watching.

Suddenly, the pain is easy to ignore. Instead, I feel pleasure.

This is all I ever wanted. For the Project to be genuinely interested in me. In something I've done. Something I am.

So when the wound is finished healing, I meet Rene's eyes and smile, expecting him to share my joy.

Instead, his grip on me tightens.

"Jonah. I want you to triple security. Keep that bastard out."

"Yes sir."

My heart sinks.

"Wait, Rene..."

"Neil," he continues, "start prepping for a full medical. Run every test you can think of. We need to figure out exactly what he's done to her."

He fires me a reassuring look.

"Don't be scared. We'll fix this. We'll reverse the damage and get you back to how you were supposed to be."

The world grinds to a halt around me. I wrench my arm from Rene's grip.

"I... I don't understand."

He stares, his brow furrowed.

"This... this *is* how I'm supposed to be," I blurt, "I thought this was what you wanted."

He doesn't answer – just opens and closes his mouth a few times, like he doesn't know what to say.

"It's not perfect," I tell him, "but it's something."

I step away again. He doesn't follow me.

"This was supposed to make you happy," I spit, "why aren't you happy?"

Tears fill my eyes.

"If this doesn't make me good enough, what will?"

The room remains utterly silent, eyes watching from all directions. Something hot streams down my face and I curse myself. Damnit. I'm crying. I've never cried in front of the Project, always happier being considered heartless than pathetic. I look up at Rene, who seems nothing short of mortified.

The realisation hits me like a truck.

Is it me?

The tears come faster. I get it now. It's not my body that's the problem, is it? It's me.

I'm not good enough.

Nobody speaks. Alya steps closer but I side-step her. Guilt pangs in my chest, but I brush it aside. Right now, I'm too heartbroken to worry if I've hurt her feelings.

Was Marcus right about everything? There was doubt in his eyes when I told him the Project would be happy. I recall his promises of a place to live if things went badly. Maybe he knew they wouldn't accept me. Perhaps that was his way of warning me.

I don't want to be here if I'm not wanted. Not when he's there, ready and waiting, willing to take me in.

I head for the front door, reaching out my hand for the security panel. Footsteps sound behind me.

Rene snatches my hand from the panel. I twist madly and he shifts closer, trying to yank me away from the door. I pull away with all my strength – and then I'm on my knees, my arm twisted behind my back.

The others file from the lab.

"Rene, wait..."

"Do as you're told, for once!"

He releases my arm and grabs my shoulders, shaking me hard enough to hurt. His face is filled with fury. His glasses are crooked. His hair has fallen forward.

"You're not going anywhere! We need to find out what he's done to you!"

"Let go of me!" I screech. His grip tightens.

"Neil, sedate her. It's the only way she'll co-operate."

I hear people backing away. Neil sputters.

"W-wait, Rene... are you sure that's..."

"Now!" he barks.

Fear ignites in my chest. They've never used force on me before, not even during our worst arguments. Neil's never drugged me without my consent. I writhe in Rene's grip.

This was supposed to fix everything.

I push Rene away and back off, scanning the room for an escape route. He stares at me, panic and fear clouding his normally-intelligent eyes. A split second later Jonah grabs my wrists, pulling them firmly behind my back.

I kick at him with all the strength I can muster, but Jonah's considerably larger than me. He twists my arms and pain shoots up my wrists.

"Jonah, let go! What are you *doing*?!"

"Don't make me break your arms," he breathes. I promptly stop fighting, fear filling me. I know he can do it.

Across the room, Rene stands, brushing himself down.

"Good work, Jonah."

Neil steps in front of me, one hand clutching a syringe filled with something clear. I'm not scared of needles. I'm no stranger to sedatives. I have no reason to think the Project would ever try and harm me. Even so, I'm petrified. I strain against Jonah's grip, twisting to see his face. Jonah always understands me. If I can just look him in the eye, he'll understand. He'll help me explain everything. He'll help me fix this.

But when I get a glimpse of him, his face is stony and expressionless. If he feels anything towards the situation, he doesn't show it. Instead, he looks at me as though I were a total stranger. When he sees me staring, he turns his face away.

God, if Jonah won't even look me in the eye, then I've really fucked up.

I turn back to Rene, desperation in my throat. My voice cracks.

"Rene, please. You said it yourself. Everything that's happening right now, all the attacks... it's my fault. I messed up - but I can fix it! I can make everything alright again! I just need a few more days, and then I can protect everyone! I can finally be useful to the Project. I can be good enough. Just a few more days, and..."

Sandra steps closer.

"Reya," she breathes, "please, just stop."

"Give me a chance to fix this," I plead. She watches me sadly for a moment, then looks away. Neil peels back my sleeve, pricking my arm with the needle. I don't fight him.

I turn my head.

Rene stands with his shoulders squared, looking down at me with a conflicted expression. Alya stands beside him, her eyes carefully turned away. Guilt fills her face.

The sedatives kick in and my legs promptly crumple. Jonah catches me swiftly, handling me like a small, fragile child. My head falls against his chest and I stop fighting, allowing the world to turn dark around me.

Sixteen

I wake to the sound of muttering.

Without moving, I can tell I'm lying on a metal table in the main lab. When I inhale, my nose fills with the stench of cleaning fluid. I trace my body with my mind, tracking the various aches and twinges.

I'm sore. How long have I been laying here?

It takes a decent amount of effort to open my eyes.

The lab is quiet. I turn my head to the side. Rene, Sandra and Neil stand at a nearby table, deep in conversation. They pore over charts and graphs, comparing them. My stomach tightens, but I'm not sure why. My memory is still hazy. I told them the truth – well, had the truth dragged out of me – and then...

I bolt upright, my spine aching with the effort.

"You drugged me."

They whip around, and I realise the anger from before is gone from their faces. Now, it's replaced by guilt.

I look down. The table is littered with needles, oxygen masks, and scalpels. There are lines of dried blood on my arms and stomach. My breath catches.

"You drugged me, and then you ran tests on me."

Neil steps closer, reaching out. I slap his hand away.

"*Don't* touch me. I understand you were angry, but this is too much. How could you do this?"

"It was the only way you'd let us do a full exam," Sandra starts. I let out a growl.

"And you couldn't just wait for things to calm down? You all hate Marcus because he drugged and tested on me. Isn't this exactly the same?"

My anger rises; but someone touches my arm and I spin round, ready to launch myself at whoever would dare ignore me. Then I meet Jonah's eyes and pause.

He's sitting on a stool beside the table, leaning on his elbows. I hadn't heard him move, so I can only assume he's been there the whole time, waiting for me to wake. His face isn't cold and empty, anymore. Instead, he seems calm. Contemplative. He looks at the others.

"I have to tell her."

Rene nods.

"What are you talking about?" I demand, "what do you need to tell me?"

Jonah sighs.

"The truth. About what happened with Marcus when you were younger."

"I know all about that," I snap, "he told me everything."

"Did he tell you that I helped him?"

I hesitate.

"No. He said that you took his side during the arguments. But..."

His face creases – and suddenly, Jonah looks much older.

"I wanted to tell you everything before, Reya. Years ago, even. But the Project thought it would be safer to keep you in the dark about my involvement."

Instinctively, I move away from him.

"I don't get it," I say, "the Project exiled Marcus for what he did. If you helped him, then why are you still here? Why would they let you stay?"

"Because he proved he could change," Sandra interjects. I fire her an inquisitive look and she pushes on.

"Did Marcus tell you about the time just after Rene Snr died? There was an ongoing battle for the role of Project Head, and a constant debate over whether to try and fix your body or start over."

I nod.

"Well," Jonah says, "I was on Marcus' side. I don't know a thing about genetic engineering, so I never really understood the risks of trying to fix you. I just figured it was cruel to make such hefty promises to a child and never follow through. So whenever Rene and Marcus argued, I would take Marcus' side. He would come and speak to me during the night shifts. He told me all about his theory. Some kind of miracle serum that would fix everything. He swore blind you wouldn't feel a thing, that it would leave no damage, that it would be as easy and painless as sleeping. It sounded perfect, so I backed him up every time."

His hands curl into fists, but he keeps going.

"Then, just as it seemed we had lost, he took me aside. He told me that the others planned to send you away – and they had no intention of telling us where. I thought they were going to ship you off to an orphanage somewhere, all alone. So when Marcus told me about his plan to sneak you to a Safehouse and fix you, I was all for it."

"What did you do?" I ask fearfully.

"I switched off the security systems just long enough for him to sneak you out. I disabled the tracker in his car so the others couldn't find you. And when people woke up and asked where he was, I lied about his whereabouts to buy him more time."

He drags a hand over his face and sighs, like he's pained by the memory.

"Come morning, you were still gone. The others realised you weren't in bed, and everyone panicked. They knew that you and Marcus were both gone, and they put two and two together. I'm ashamed to say it, but I kept quiet about the whole situation right up until the last second."

"Rene was the first to notice that he was acting strange," Sandra murmurs, "so he pushed him on it. It took a lot of cajoling, but once Jonah understood what was happening – the danger you were in – he told us where to find you."

"I hoped that it was all a misunderstanding," Jonah nods, "but when we arrived at Safehouse 17, I saw you covered in wires and drugged half to hell – and I knew I'd made a terrible mistake. I almost killed Marcus for lying to me and for hurting you. I realised that he had manipulated me to get what he wanted. He said you wouldn't be harmed, and he said you'd be sent away if we didn't do something. I think he would have told me anything if it meant I'd play along."

My stomach twinges and I look away.

"Yeah. I did get that impression from him."

"The Project was kind enough to let me stay after that. For several years, I wasn't allowed to be alone with you. Or alone at all, really. I had to work hard to earn back everyone's trust and prove my loyalty."

His face folds, and he squeezes my arm gently.

"All these years, I've regretted what I did that day. How I played a part in hurting you because I listened to someone who didn't have your or my best interests at heart. That's why I was so scared when you asked about him. I was worried he would fill your head with lies, just like he did to me. I know how he is. He makes you think that it's all your idea and he's just being supportive. It's sickening, but effective."

"But," I sigh, "he's been so nice to me."

"Nice and kind are two different things," he reminds me, "when we sedated you earlier, it wasn't nice. But trust me when I say it was kind. It's the kindest thing we could do for you, to check that you're okay."

I pull my knees up to my chin, deep in thought. The others watch me closely, and I wonder if they're expecting me to launch into another tantrum. Instead, I sigh.

"Why didn't you tell me this before?" I ask Jonah.

"Honestly? I was ashamed. And I didn't want you to fear me."

"Fear you?"

"Well, I am an accessory to your kidnapping."

"Yeah, but you're also Jonah."

"I made a serious mistake."

I scoff.

"You really thought that I, of all people, wouldn't know how it feels to make a mistake?"

His shoulders drop – and I wonder how long he's been waiting for me to say that. How many times he's imagined this conversation and how it would end. Did he honestly think I would reject him?

"I'm not mad that you sided with Marcus," I hiss, "I'm mad that you didn't trust me enough to tell me. I'm mad that you think I'm so hateful that I'd reject you for telling me the truth. Out of everyone here, I thought you knew me better than that."

His gaze drops, and an uneasy silence falls over the lab.

I glance at Rene. He stands several feet away, watching our conversation in silence. Our eyes meet briefly – and then he looks away.

Sandra frowns.

"Reya. We need to tell you what we've found during our examinations. Are you ready to listen?"

I stare around at the empty lab, then laugh.

"I hardly have a choice."

"You seem on edge."

"Yes, I'm on edge," I snap, "you drugged me against my will and ran tests on my unconscious body. Do you realise how unethical that is?"

"We had no choice. We had to do an immediate medical..."

"I'm not sure why you suddenly care so much about my health," I say snidely, "I routinely come home beaten to a pulp and you rarely care about it. Hell, usually you blame me for getting jumped. Even though I'm only getting jumped because I'm a freak of nature, and I'm only a freak of nature because you made me wrong."

Damnit. I can feel my anger rising, coiling in my chest like a snake ready to attack. Sandra flinches under my gaze.

"Tell me whatever you want to tell me," I say coldly, "then let me leave."

"You're not leaving Lockless House tonight. But if you sit and listen for five minutes, we'll let you go to the Dome. It's been a very long day and I think we could all use some rest."

"Then you should probably get talking," I retort.

Neil steps forward, clutching several sheets of paper in his hands. He spreads them out in front of me. I glance at them, spotting graphs and charts, and look away.

"You know I don't understand this stuff. Can you tell me in English?"

I expect someone to snap at me, or tell me to be respectful – but for some reason he just nods, scooping the paper away and firing an instructive nod at Sandra. She sighs.

"Alright. I'll try to explain it in layman's terms, since that's what we'll all understand best. Well, you understand that you and Alya started off as single cells, which then multiplied?"

"If you say so."

"Well, you were. The original clumps of cells – the zygotes – were designed to have malleable DNA. Basically, we could edit parts of your DNA while you were still developing. That's how your abilities were supposed to take form, via gene editing during the incubation process."

I nod and she continues.

"Well, the gene editing didn't work on you because of an error in our coding before your first cells were created. Although your DNA was malleable, the changes didn't stick. We could instil extra abilities into your cells, but your body would reject them, resetting to the standard human format. As you grew, we expected your DNA to no longer be malleable. That's why Alya isn't expected to age past maturity, because her cells will find a stable point and stop changing."

"I'm with you so far."

"The serum that Marcus is using has a similar effect to the gene editing used on you when you were a zygote. In other words, Marcus is trying to recreate the pre-development gene editing on you now, as an adult. You're 25 years old, which is ideal – you've reached full physical and developmental maturity, but you're also in prime physical condition. That's likely why he approached you now, because this is the opportune time to try and edit your DNA. And it's working."

At that I raise my head, confused. Did she just admit that it's working? She pushes on.

"Apparently, your DNA didn't settle the way it was supposed to. It's still malleable. That means it's still possible to instil your DNA with additional qualities, just like it was when you were still developing."

"So his theory was right."

She purses her lips.

"Not exactly. One tweak was all that Alya needed to develop new abilities and keep them for life, but your body rejected changes almost immediately. Marcus' method relies on providing you with constant treatment, which keeps your body from being able to reject the changes."

"What's wrong with that?" I ask her, "it makes sense to me."

"The human body isn't designed to undergo intense, repetitive genetic modification. That's why we did it to single cells instead of babies. A fully developed human can't survive this kind of testing for long. Not only is it painful, but it puts the organs under an immense amount of strain. And it gets worse every time you get hurt."

With that she shuffles closer, resting a hand on my arm. I don't push her away.

"When your body heals itself, it draws energy from wherever it can. The more severe the injury, and the worse your general health, the more energy is needed. If you're injured badly, it's possible that your body would deplete all energy sources to heal a wound, even if it killed you in the process."

"That doesn't make sense. Alya doesn't almost die whenever she heals."

"Alya's body doesn't deplete vital operations because it's adapted and found a solution to that issue. But this is new to your body, and it can't handle it. Right now, if you became badly injured, your healing ability would kill you long before the injury itself could."

I stare down at my hands, head spinning. I shouldn't be surprised that Marcus' plan was flawed; he's hardly a shining example of competency. But then I think about him – his gentle eyes, his kind words - and shake my head.

"He can't have known," I say, "Marcus is convinced this is working. Maybe if I explain it to him, we can tweak the tests. Figure out a way to make it permanent, and work out all the kinks."

"That won't work," she says softly, "Marcus was equally involved in your development. He knows this isn't going to stick. That it's a band-aid solution."

"No. He wouldn't just lead me on like that. What would he get out of it?"

Rene steps forward now, his lips drawn in a tight line. When he speaks his voice is gravelly, like he's trying too hard to seem authoritative.

"That, we don't know. And until we figure it out, we need to keep him away from you. Away from all of us. Your body is incredibly resilient. Once you stop running his tests, your cells should return to normal. Then we can batten down the hatches and lock everything down until we find a way to deal with him."

I stare up at him, rage and sadness mixing in my chest.

"Lock everything down. That sounds like house arrest."

"This isn't personal, Reya. We're all in danger, so nobody can leave right now. It's too dangerous."

My hands ball into fists. Before I met my friends, I was miserable. I can't do it again. I can't go back to that crippling loneliness. Sandra clicks her tongue.

"This is a lot to take in. Get a good night's sleep and when you wake up tomorrow, we'll have a good, long talk. We'll come up with a plan to keep everyone safe and get to the bottom of what's led to all this. I promise."

I nod, though I don't really agree. I don't see a plan that works for everyone. Either I leave and keep testing with Marcus, but the Project never takes me back – or I do as I'm told and risk never seeing my friends - or daylight - again.

As I stand Sandra reaches out, pressing my cell phone into my hand.

"Why would you give this back?" I ask her.

"I think it's important that we trust one another right now. You can have this back, but I want you to promise that you won't go anywhere tonight. We're all confused and angry, and there's a lot to figure out."

I turn the phone over in my hand, stomach swirling. She purses her lips.

"By the way, there's no point calling Marcus. We've politely asked him to keep his distance and blocked all contact. I hope you understand why we had to do that."

"Yeah."

She reaches out to comfort me, but I lower my gaze and she pulls her hand back.

"Get some sleep, Reya. Things will seem better tomorrow."

I slump from the room and head upstairs, ignoring the sensation of Rene's eyes boring through the back of my skull.

A half hour later, Alya knocks on my bedroom door. It's a soft tap, like she's half-hoping I don't hear her. I sit on the floor with my knees up, my back pressed against the cold, curved glass. She pushes the door open, and fires me a reproachful look.

"It's alright," I tell her, "you can come in."

She pushes the door shut behind her.

"How did you know it was me?"

"You're the only one who'd want to speak to me right now," I say, pulling my lips into a small smile. She walks over, hands folded.

"I didn't know if you'd want to see me, after what I did."

"You mean stealing my phone and giving it to Rene? It's fine."

"It's not. I feel really awful..."

"Alya," I say, "seriously, it's okay. I get it. You were worried about me, and you did what you thought was right. It's not how I wanted everything to happen, but at least it's out in the open now."

She fires me a confused look.

"You seem terribly calm, considering what happened."

"I suppose it's a relief, in a way. I thought they'd be happy if I fixed myself. Perhaps the love we used to have still existed somewhere, deep under the surface, and I could bring it out again."

I heave a long sigh.

"Now I know that's not the case, it's somewhat freeing."

"Reya..."

She sinks to the floor beside me, crossing her ankles. I notice that there are two dirty streaks down her cheeks, like she's been crying. I search inside myself, wondering if I have the urge to cry. But I don't. I can almost feel the mental walls erecting themselves, blocking me off from the Project, sealing me away entirely.

"I guess I should thank you," I say, "I was going to let Marcus kill me, if that's what it took to make the Project happy. Now, I know it wouldn't have worked."

"You really trust that man, don't you?"

"I don't know if I ever really trusted Marcus. He's either incredibly sincere, or manipulative as hell."

I let out a long sigh and bury my face in my knees.

"Can't even figure out one person. I'm just that useless."

"Will you stop that?"

Alya's voice is suddenly icy. My head snaps up. She's glaring at me, anger burning behind her usually-sweet eyes. When she speaks again, her voice is edged with irritation.

"I am sick and tired of you being down on yourself. You are *not* useless, and you are *not* a failure. You are an ordinary person and sometimes you screw up."

"But Rene and the others..."

"Love you. If they didn't, they'd have let him keep hurting you. The reason they're so angry is because they can't stand the thought of losing you."

My stomach squirms uncomfortably, and I shake my head.

"No, no, no... they think I'm a disappointment, because I turned out wrong and..."

"Has anyone ever actually told you that you're a disappointment?" she snaps.

I pause, staring at her. She stares back, holding my gaze.

"Has anyone in the Project ever said they're disappointed in how you turned out? Has anyone ever said they don't love you? Has anyone ever told you that they're not proud of you?"

I open and close my mouth a few times.

"N-no, but it goes beyond words... it's in the way they've always acted around me, and..."

"Are you sure you don't think these things about yourself, and you've convinced yourself that they think the same? Because it seems pretty clear cut from where I'm sitting. Maybe if you stopped giving up on yourself, others would, too."

It's not like Alya to be so forward. It's definitely not like Alya to hold my gaze like this, like she's trying to force a realisation into my head by brute force. Just when I feel like I'm going to burst into tears, her expression softens.

"Look, I'm sorry. I just hate to see you beat yourself up like this. Just... think about it, alright?"

I ignore the heaviness in my chest and nod.

"Good," she smiles, "get some sleep. Tomorrow, things will be clearer."

With that she stalks from the room and I watch her leave, stomach churning.

God, I hope she's right about that. About everything.

Seventeen

It's about two in the morning when I make up my mind.

I've been sitting by the window for hours, watching the city grow dark around me. I've been lost in my thoughts the entire time, trying to figure out what's really going on.

Alya's words have left me shaken. Suddenly, I'm not entirely sure what I think or why I think it. I don't know how anyone else feels, about me or anything else. Longing fills my chest, begging me to go to Rene's room. To wake him, to ask him if we can talk. To spend all night saying everything I've been too scared to say all these years.

But I don't know if he wants to speak to me. I don't know him at all, anymore.

We used to be so in sync. Back then, it never occurred to me that he might not love me. It was obvious.

Maybe it's still obvious now. Alya seems to think so.

Either way, I need space to think. So I drop Nova a message, asking to stay with her. Just for a few days, I promise. Surprisingly, she texts back immediately, agreeing.

As I pull out an old rucksack and pack my meagre possessions into it, my heart feels heavy. I don't want to leave Lockless House. They're trusting me not to sneak out tonight. But we all need space to think. If Rene and I are together, there'll be too much anger for us to really talk.

Even so, I don't want to cause a panic. So when I pull my mustard-yellow hoodie on and toss my bag over one shoulder, I know I need to tell somebody where I'm going.

Alya bolts upright as I enter her room. Once she recognises me in the darkness, her gaze drops to my bag and shoes. Her eyes narrow.

"Are you for real? You're running away?"

"No."

"This is not the way to handle this. You can't just go vanishing in the night."

"Shut up, will you?" I snap, "I'm not running away."

She pauses.

"You're not?"

"No. I'm just going to stay with Nova for a few days. I need to think."

She pushes the blankets off herself, rubbing at one eye.

"If you're not here come morning, the Project will freak out."

"Yeah," I shrug, "but if I try and leave in the daytime, they'll stop me."

"They'd stop you because it's not safe out there."

"I know. But this is important."

I tug my cell from my pocket and wave it at her.

"I'll need you to keep them from panicking. Tell them where I am, tell them I have my cell phone on me and a safe place to stay. If they want to call me or come and see me, they can. But I'll be staying away for a while."

Her head drops at that.

"You'll stay in touch, right?"

"You have my number, call me whenever. I'll always have time for my little sister."

At that I smile, and oddly, I feel it's my first genuine smile in months. Alya watches me for a long moment, then sighs.

"Fine. I think you're being ridiculous, but I get it. I'll make sure nobody panics."

231

"Thanks."

I turn toward the door, then give her a small wave.

"G'night."

She stares back at me through the darkness.

"Night."

I step into the hallway and towards the door into Lockless House. I tug on the handle; the door doesn't move. I pull again, harder this time. Nothing.

Did they lock us in?

I tap the security panel by the door, and a single word appears. LOCKDOWN.

"Are you kidding me with this, Rene?" I mutter. I touch the security pad with an open palm, hoping it'll let me communicate with the night lab – and the door pings open. Strange that they'd allow me to open the door, if the intention was to lock me inside.

I push open the door and crimson fills my vision. It takes a moment for my eyes to adjust and when they do, I realise that the silent alarm has been triggered. The hallways flash red every few seconds, leaving me momentarily disoriented. I pause, wondering if I triggered it, but everything is silent. Nobody's stirring from their beds or pounding down the hallways to see what's set the alarm off. I strain my ears. Nothing. Not even the sound of Neil's impressive snoring.

My stomach promptly knots. Something's wrong.

I creep to the top of the steps as softly as I can, listening hard.

The lights downstairs look... wrong. Most nights, the night lab is the only light source – that familiar, purple glow. But every light is on now, blinding white whenever the red lights aren't flashing. It's like the Project never went to sleep.

I get halfway down the stairs when I hear voices. Not Project voices. Strangers.

"Got the rest of them?"

"Almost Most of them have recovered from the knockout gas."

"Good. Just the freaks to go, then."

My heart hammers in my chest and I head upstairs, rushing into Alya's room and pulling the door shut behind me. She fixes me with wide eyes.

"Reya? What's wrong?"

"They broke in."

Fear fills her face.

"Who? Mortalists?"

I nod, pulling her from her bed and dragging her into the bathroom. It's a perfect mirror image of my own, each one set back a little from our bedrooms – leaving just enough space for a safe refuge in the middle. Saferoom #1.

My body moves like clockwork. The access panel beeps, recognising my handprint. We step back as the wall folds away, revealing the Saferoom door.

In our security drills, we've always been shown an example Saferoom. Blueprints, photos, the like. I've never actually stood in one before. It's somewhat colder than I expected; a metal-clad room with a large console at the far end, accompanied by a dozen small screens. Bunks line the other walls, each with a pack on top. I know without looking what's in them. Clean clothes, basic medicine, food and water. Up to a week of supplies for four people. The fluorescent lights flicker overhead and I wince. I'd go mad if I had to spend a week in here.

Alya lets out a low whimper from the doorway.

"Why are we in here?"

"Jonah's protocol," I tell her, "your safety is the Project's first priority. They won't find you in here. Even if they manage to convince the others to let them access the security system, the Saferooms aren't marked. You can wait them out as long as you need to."

"What about the others?"

"We should be able to access the security cameras from here."

I tap at the console, tensing as the Saferoom connects with every camera in Lockless House. Sweat drips down my face as I flick through them. With every new shot of the hallways and labs, I'm expecting to see bodies. I'm expecting to see someone being killed or maimed or beaten to a pulp. That's the Mortalists' usual MO.

But the hallways are empty aside from the strangers wandering through them. One shifts slightly, and the pistol in his hand catches the light. My throat tightens. Most of them wield bats or their bare hands, but a few are definitely armed.

I flick to the main lab, and Alya cries out in shock.

The Project is together. They're cuffed and kneeling, spread across the room in a long row. One or two slump forward, like they tried to fight back and received a swift blow as punishment. Others hold their heads up, trying to seem as defiant as possible. I zoom in on Rene, who seems merely unimpressed.

Mortalists pace the room, swinging their weapons. Their mouths move as they grin down at their prisoners. I wish I could hear what they're saying.

I stare at Jonah. I know Protocol. He's made an effort to drill it into me since day one. Even before Alya could walk, I knew the rules. Get her to a Saferoom. Lock it down. Call for help. Set every camera to record for evidence. Bunk down and wait it out.

But it's clear from the Mortalists' movements that they're not screwing around. I imagine they're going to come upstairs for us any minute – and then what?

I bite my lip so hard it hurts.

When they don't find us, what will they do to the others?

I crouch, prising open the hidden floor compartment. Right where Jonah always said it would be. Inside is a small armoury; for defence only, he'd insisted. I tuck a baton into my belt loop and a taser in my pocket. Lastly, I pick out a glossy black gun. The sight of it sets my heart racing, but I load it nonetheless.

I've never been trained to fire a gun. Damnit, I've never even held one before. If I try and use it at anything other than point blank range, I'll likely miss. I just pray I won't have to use it.

I stand, setting the cameras to record.

"Lock this place down," I tell Alya, "you remember how, right?"

"But the others..."

"I'll take care of it. Stay here."

She looks me up and down, and her face blanches. I fire her a reassuring look.

"It's okay. Someone already triggered the silent alarm. The police will be here in a half hour, max."

"We don't have a half hour," she whines, turning back to the screen. I frown.

"I know. But I'll try to keep them busy long enough for the cops to get here."

"You can't go out alone," she whines, "there's too many of them."

"We don't really have a choice."

"Maybe they'll get bored. Maybe if they can't find us, they'll just leave."

Our eyes snap toward the screen as one of the men strikes Jonah with the butt of his gun. They're shouting. They must have realised we're not where we should be. Jonah grins up at them, apparently realising that we must be safe. I see Rene's shoulder's relax as he comes to the same realisation.

Someone curses at the top of their lungs, raising a gun at the others. My whole body tenses.

"Look, we don't have time for a debate. I can buy us some time."

"You'll just get yourself killed!"

"We don't have many options," I tell her, heading for the door. She grabs my arm, holding me fast.

"No, no, no! You don't understand!"

Her voice cracks.

"What is wrong with you humans?! Why do always have to rush at whatever's going to kill you fastest? You're mortal, Reya. One gunshot and you're gone forever. That healing ability of yours is slow and painful; it'll be more of a hindrance than a benefit. You might know how to fight, but you can't protect yourself!"

"Well unfortunately, nobody thought to put a kevlar vest in the Saferoom, or we'd be sorted."

"Let me come with you."

I prise her hands off me, scowling.

"Don't be stupid. You're their main target. Besides, if you think I'll be ineffective, just wait until you're fighting next to me. I'd be too busy worrying about you."

"Then I won't fight. I'll just protect you."

I pause.

"What?"

"You said it yourself," she says, "on that phone call we listened to. You said that if you were immortal, you'd be a shield. You'd use your body to absorb their attacks, since they couldn't kill you."

"No... that's not what I meant. I didn't mean *you* should do that."

"But it makes sense, right? We go out together. You fight. I protect you. I watch your back, and if I see anyone about to fire a gun or come at you with a knife, I'll block it. I'll be out of action for 13 seconds, that's all. Then we can keep going. Between the two of us, we can buy them enough time, and nobody has to die."

I step away.

"Hell, no. We're not doing that."

"They shot me before, remember? I walked it off. When they shot you, you were out of action for weeks. It's a no-brainer."

"You can still feel pain!"

"Pain is transient!" she barks, "it'd be over quickly for me."

"Not a chance!"

My eyes flit back to the screen. Someone else is on the floor now, curled tightly into themselves. I recognise that position. They've just been kicked in the gut. My stomach churns.

"They'll never forgive me if I let you get hurt," I tell her. She pouts.

"If we don't work together, they won't be alive to forgive you."

My head spins. Protect Alya, let the others die. Protect the others, put Alya in danger. Even if they can't kill her, they might take her captive. I think about the death threats we've received in the post. The graphic, particularly violent ones. I can't give them a chance to follow through.

But then I imagine watching the others get executed, and my face grows hot. So much for Protocol.

"I can't believe I'm saying this," I sigh, "fine. Grab some gear, we're going."

The Saferoom door closes behind us and we tense.

"Do you hear that?" Alya asks, her voice barely above a whisper. I nod. Someone's in the Dome. I hear them ripping open Alya's pretty wardrobes and flipping the mattress on her bed. A dull thunk from behind us tells me they're doing the same to my room. They must know there's a hiding place. They just haven't checked the bathrooms yet.

I motion for Alya to move away from the door, and position myself just behind it. I slip the taser from my pocket and clutch it tightly. This thing won't have a whole lot of charge, but it's our best bet for now. Relatively quiet and - hopefully- non-lethal.

Heavy footsteps pound across the Dome, and muffled voices fill the air. I can't quite make out the words, but they're clearly directions. The footsteps come closer, and I motion for Alya to step back. She presses herself against the far wall, fear apparent in her eyes. Unlike me, she's in plain view. If someone comes in, they'll spot her in an instant.

The door opens and I slink behind it, squeezing out of sight. A hulking shadow passes over me – the kind of skinheaded thug I'm used to encountering. The man stops when he sees Alya.

"There you are."

His voice drips with excitement; the kind of excitement one feels when sizing up an especially delicious meal. Like he's preparing to devour her, and savour every last morsel. Disgust fills my chest but I fight to remain silent until he leans back, nudging the door shut.

He still hasn't spotted me.

The man takes one lumbering step towards Alya and I'm on him, pressing the taser to the base of his spine. He stiffens but I hold the device against him, ignoring the way his eyes roll.

And then I pull away, signalling for Alya to hop over his still-shaking form. She obeys and dips through the doorway behind me, locking him in with a quick scan of her hand.

"You took your time," she gasps, "I thought you weren't going to..."

"Had to get the door shut first. Come on."

We near the doorway just as someone steps inside. I don't stop to take in any detail – just grab the baton and swing it, striking them across the head as hard as I can. They crumple into a heap and Alya whimpers.

"Jesus. Are they gonna be okay?"

"Who cares?" I spit. She hesitates, then nods.

"Right. Right."

She gazes down at the person's bloodied head, swallowing hard.

"Look," I tell her, "this is your last chance. You can still go back to the Saferoom through the entrance in my bathroom. I can handle this."

She sets her jaw.

"No. I want to help."

"Then you have to get used to this," I tell her, waving at the unconscious figure. She nods.

"We should hurry."

"Right. Come on."

We hurry down the hallway. My skin tingles and when I look down, sure enough, the tiny hairs on my arms stand on end. Fear and adrenaline surge through me. I've felt this way before, though it's usually during a fight. There's a familiar dryness in my throat, accompanied by a twisting in my gut.

I'm terrified, angry, and oddly exhilarated.

I hear footsteps around the corner and pull out the taser. There's more than one set of feet – and I can only fight one at a time if we're trying to stay quiet.

"After all that, we can't find them?!"

The Mortalist's voice is shrill and impatient.

"Our intel said they'll be in hiding," the other one replies, "keep looking. They've got to come out sooner or later."

"What about the traitors downstairs?"

I grit my teeth. Traitors. I always forget they call the Project that. The thought alone makes me want to charge at them but I stay put, tightening my grip on the taser.

"This place is full of cameras, and they'll be watching. If we don't find them, we lodge a couple bullets in the traitor's brains and the freaks will come running. Then we can cuff them and head out before the cops get here."

"Seems a bit far-fetched to assume the freaks would come to save them."

"Even a poorly-trained dog will try and save its master. Besides, our intel says the older one will jump at the chance for a fight, so be ready."

Their tones indicate the end of the conversation so I move quickly, sidling up to the corner.

The first shadow I see is facing away from me; a hulking man with a red-brown ponytail. He hears me and turns. I swing at him with all my strength. The blow connects with his jaw and I feel bones crack under my knuckles, sending him reeling. I follow up with a kick to his gut, forcing him to the floor. I pull out the taser and step forward; but a low clunk gives me pause.

The woman lifts a gun, aiming it squarely at me. My stomach plummets.

The shot is so loud it leaves my ears ringing.

I hit the ground hard, Alya pinning me as the bullet whizzes overhead. She whimpers as it grazes her head - and my eyes snap open. We're on the floor, Alya sprawled atop me. Blood seeps from a fresh wound in her head, and as I push myself to my knees, I realise she's limp and lifeless. I lean forward, pulling her hair back. The wound is shallow but large, terrifying to look at but no real danger to the Tomorrow Girl.

"Alya."

Her breathing is soft and measured, but I can tell she's in pain. Some small part of me panics at the sight, but I silence it. I can hear her breathing. Pained, but it's there.

I push aside the panic in my chest and turn my fury on the woman.

I dart forward as she squeezes the trigger again, pushing her hand down – and the bullet hits her in the thigh. She shrieks and falls backwards, screeching.

I drop down next to Alya. In the few seconds it took me to handle the Mortalist, she seems to have mostly healed. She pushes up to her knees, quaking.

"How do you feel?" I ask. She looks up at me with wide eyes.

"I'm okay. It just grazed me. It looks worse than it feels."

She stares down the corridor, deep in thought.

"That shot was too low. I think... I think she was trying to shoot out your knees."

"This was a bad idea," I tell her, "you should get to a Saferoom while you still have chance."

She shakes her head and pulls her hair back, touching the freshly-healed skin.

"Look," she says, "it's gone. I'm fine."

The woman shrieks again, and Alya tenses.

"We should go. People will arrive if she keeps screaming."

I stand, eyeing the woman coldly. Strange. I don't feel any remorse for shooting her, but I can't deny that watching her writhe makes me feel a little sick.

I nod.

"We should hurry downstairs. I think I've got a plan."

Eighteen

    We hide at the top of the stairs, watching the entrance to the main lab. I can hear someone being beaten inside – threats being shouted, someone groaning, other voices pleading for them to stop. Beside me, Alya whimpers.
    "What's the plan? They know the police are coming. They won't hang around forever."
    "Let her scream," I hiss, waving a hand behind us. The woman I shot is still bellowing from the other side of the building, where we've dragged her. Alya's face fills with guilt.
    "We could have helped her."
    "She shot you."
    "But she didn't kill me."
    "If you hadn't been there," I remind her, "she would have shot me."
    She hesitates, then nods.
    "Right."
    "She won't die from that injury," I say, "at least not quickly. But it'll hurt like a bitch. If she keeps screeching like that, they'll head up to see what's going

on. Then, all we need to do is storm the main lab. I'll take out whoever's left while you activate lockdown in that sector. That'll seal them out of the main lab, and we'll be safe until the cops arrive."

"There might be a lot left in the lav, though."

"I'll handle it."

She swallows hard.

"I don't like this plan."

Neither do I. But I don't have any better ideas. The woman screams again, and my stomach twists. This is messed up, but we can't help her. All we can do is try and survive.

We hide as someone shouts in the lab, and a handful of people emerge. They talk amongst themselves, confused by what they're hearing. When the next scream rings out, they seem to decide it's one of their own and march upstairs, shouting into their walkie talkies.

"Something's happening on the East side of the building," one man says, "we're checking it out."

"Freaks were spotted nearby," someone responds, "be careful."

"They've shot someone," says yet another voice. The man curses.

"We need more people. Anyone in the area, head over there now. Find them."

We stay in the shadows until they've vanished from our sight, leaving the foyer empty. Alya clutches my arm.

"That won't keep them distracted long."

"Right. Remember the plan. Lock down the main lab on the outside only. That way we can get them out, but they won't be able to get back in easily. The security code is #DA7BL21. Got that?"

She chews her lip.

"Yeah. I think so."

"Good. Let's go."

We slip downstairs and approach the main lab, listening intently. Someone's being interrogated, but judging by the noises they're making, I don't think anything too horrific is being done to them. They seem to be sticking with a thorough beating - which is horrific, but at this point I'm just grateful that nobody's being tortured.

I glance at Alya, who nods. She knows her job. Run in, activate one-way lockdown, and untie the others. I'll take care of anything else that might come at us.

For a brief moment, my heart is in my throat. We don't know how many people are in there; it could be three, or it could be thirty. I wrack my brain, trying to remember how many people I've fought off single-handedly before. Four? Five? No more than that. Sure, these are untrained citizens, but this may end up being a numbers game. I grit my teeth. My worry must show on my face, because Alya grasps my hand, firing me a determined look. My racing heart calms a little.

Right. I may have been useless during the car chase, but this is likely to devolve into a fist fight. And I can handle a fist fight.

I pull the baton from my belt and step into the main lab, snarling.

"Alright, that's enough. Get the fuck out."

Several things happen at once.

My eyes skirt the room, finding the others still tied and kneeling.

I do a quick headcount of the strangers in the room – nine.

Alya darts past me, racing toward the security console.

Someone – a gangly man standing two feet away – points a gun at her.

In an instant I yank the gun from his hands, twist it and ram the butt into his face. His jaw breaks with a sickening crack and he falls back. I toss the gun aside, kicking him in the stomach as hard as I can in an attempt to keep him down.

I lift my head and for a split second, I make eye contact with Rene. A host of emotions play on his face, and I can tell he's fighting the urge to scold me. Of course. Protocol says I should take Alya and get to safety. I'm letting him down all over again, but this time I don't feel any remorse.

Someone barges at me and I dodge them easily, driving my knee into their ribs hard enough to send them sprawling. When he stands again I embed the taser in his spine, causing him to slump to the ground, gasping like a goldfish.

I glance at Alya, who types madly at a nearby console. She fires me a startled look and her lips part in warning.

Heavy hands fasten around my wrists and I'm flung across the room, colliding hard with the edge of the metal table. Pain fills my head as I crumple against the tiled floor, stars filling my vision.

I pull myself to my feet, shaking the spots from my eyes, and turn my attention to the Mortalist approaching me. He glances at the table and grins, clearly pleased that he was able to throw me aside. I grab my baton out and hold it out, ready to block whatever attack comes next.

Rene catches my eye again, and the rage has gone from his face. All that remains is panic.

"Alya? How are we doing?" I bark, fighting to sound somewhat authoritative. Her voice wavers.

"Done!"

As she speaks, I hear it. Metal shutters extend from the ceiling, slamming down around the room, forming a complete shell, impenetrable aside for a single, small door. Successful one-way lockdown. I flash her a grin.

"Great job. Let Jonah out, will you? I think we need his help."

She obeys immediately, racing over to him. As she fiddles with his restraints, I can hear her talking.

"It's okay," she says, "the police will be here soon, and the others can't get back in. We're safe."

Jonah nods, then turns his gaze back to the lab. I can almost see the cogs whirring in his head, as he tries to figure out the most effective way to take the invaders out once he's released. Anticipation fills my chest.

A nearby woman takes advantage of my momentary distraction, aiming a handgun in my direction. I whip around, tensing – but her comrade scoops the gun away, hissing.

"Don't! We have to take the freaks alive, remember? No guns."

He tosses the gun aside, and I eye it carefully. No guns.

They're holding back.

Hell, this'll be easier than I thought.

I tighten my grip on the baton and stand back, beckoning them forward. Come get me.

A moment later, they do.

I swing the baton at the nearest guys' head, cringing as the blow connects. Blood spatters across the pristine floor and my stomach churns. I hate this. I hate having to be this violent – in front of the Project, no less. But if the alternative is to let them die, then there really isn't an alternative.

They come at me again, and one by one I take them out. Not without injury; one twists my shoulder enough to make me yelp, and another gets a good kick at my leg, which I'm sure will bruise.

Most of these bastards are bigger than me, and logic tells me they should be winning. But they're not. Maybe it's my fighting experience. Maybe it's the adrenaline rush. Maybe they're holding back too much, and can't match my ferocity. I'm not sure, but I don't question it.

Even so, I feel myself tiring. My reaction times are getting slower. I glance at the others, hoping Alya has freed them and they're about to jump in; but no. She still wrestles with Jonah's restraints, growing more distressed by the second.

A hand grabs my arm and twists it, slamming me hard against the wall. I yank free but hands lock around my neck instead, pressing inward. My eyes snap up to face my attacker – and I pause.

Shane.

He doesn't look quite how I remember him. His nose is slightly bent following our last encounter, giving his face a lopsided look. The faux suaveness has dropped away altogether, and he looks much more like the crazed maniac I remember at our last meeting. I throw him off and step away, rolling my eyes.

"Dear god, man. We broke up months ago! It's a little creepy to let yourself into my home."

He doesn't find my joke funny. Shame, really. Instead, he sneers.

"I've been hoping I'd find you again."

Rene interjects suddenly, his voice wavering.

"Reya? Who is that?"

I glance at him.

"Do you remember my latest black eye, and the guy from the paper?"

"You mean..."

"Rene, meet Shane."

Shane steps closer, rage filling his face. I decide to push further.

"You know, I almost didn't recognise you with the wonky nose. I really did a number on you, huh?"

Anger flickers in his eyes.

"I wasn't asking much, Reya. You should have just done what I told you to do."

"I'm not very good at doing what I'm told," I retort, "just ask Rene. It's kind of my thing."

I draw my lips into a broad smile, watching as his fury grows.

"I wouldn't let you near my family before, Shane. Nothing's changed on that front."

He heaves himself at me and I step aside, tripping him. He catches himself and rounds on me – but as his nose explodes into a bloody mess for the second time, I just laugh. He falls back, screaming, and I wipe my bloody fist on my jeans.

He hurls a few choice curse words at me, but I ignore him. I fire a small smile at the others, grateful when they return it.

Someone steps up behind me, emitting a low grunt of triumph – and I grab their arm, heave them over my head and slam them against the ground. Just like with Spencer only this time, harder. Much harder. Hard enough that when I drop their limp arm to the floor, they don't move.

I look up and make eye contact with Rene. His expression has faltered. It's only now that I see a bruise blossoming on the side of his head, like they had to knock him out. I stare down the line. He's not the only one with that kind of injury. Jonah is bloodied and beaten, crimson trickling down his forehead. He watches with wide, terrified eyes – and no small amount of anger. His arms wriggle, and I realise he's trying to break through his restraints.

"I know I have a lot to explain," I tell them, "but for now, just trust me."

If they doubt me, they don't show it. They just nod, steeling themselves for a little more abuse.

And then Shane's in my face, one hand around my neck. I scowl at him. Of course he's a Mortalist. Of course he's on their side. This is what always happens and at this point, it's on me for not recognising it sooner.

I weigh him up, wondering how best to take him out.

I glance at the other Mortalists. Most seem grateful for the momentary break in the fight as they pull back, nursing their various injuries. They watch me reproachfully, as though concerned I might lash out and bite them. I fire them a toothy smile and their discomfort grows. I pull myself up to full height and get in Shane's face, until our noses are almost touching.

"You have roughly 30 seconds to get out before the cops show up. If I were you, I'd hurry."

Some do, immediately scooping up their injured comrades and running. Others don't – leaving Shane and two others. His smile widens.

"You're still outnumbered, sweetheart."

Sweetheart. Dimly, I recall the times he called me that before. When holding me in his arms, or walking with me along the riverside. The memories are suddenly sickening.

My hand drops, resting on the gun at my waist.

"Last warning."

His eyebrows raise, but he doesn't move. My hands tense.

Suddenly, the atmosphere in the room turns cold. I realise that every eye has settled on my hand, on the finger wrapped around the trigger. My stomach churns.

I want to hurt him. That way, he'll never touch any of us again. But I can't.

If I kill someone today, things will never go back to normal. The Mortalists will finally have a real reason to rally. The Project will fall apart under the controversy. And the others... I glance back at them, taking in their wide eyes. They'd never look at me the same.

I slip the gun back into my belt, lowering my head. Shane grins.

"See? It's not so hard. Now, if we're done with all the drama..."

I grab his face and pull him forward, smashing my head into his chin with all the force I can muster. He crumples immediately, knocked clean out. I step over his prone form, taking care to step on his fingers, and rub my throbbing skull.

"Shit," I mutter, "that always looks so easy in the movies."

Alya walks over to me, smiling. Her relief is apparent, and I realise that she was worried I might pull the trigger. I grab her hand and squeeze it.

"I wouldn't have done it."

"I know," she tells me, and I choose to believe her.

I turn my attention to the other men, who recoil under my glare.

"So, are you two going to get out or do I have to deal with you, too?"

One hesitates, but the other grabs his shoulder and nods.

"We're going. We're going."

"Good," I snort, turning away. I touch a hand to my head, realising that the headbutt was a poor choice. My head still hurts from the last blow, and I can feel a small cut where my skin has split from the force.

Then comes the burning.

As sweat streams from my face, Alya's expression falters.

"Reya?"

I cradle my head in both hands and she reaches out for me, eyes wide.

"Is it healing?"

I nod and try to respond, but a pathetic whimper is all that escapes my lips. The healing is nothing short of agony – ten times worse than the pain of the initial blow. I slump against a nearby table, waiting for the waves of pain to ease.

"I just... need a minute," I gasp.

I lean heavily on the table, waiting for my breathing to calm. She stands over me.

"Try and catch your breath," she says, though she's breathless herself.

Something shifts behind her. A figure drops to the ground, something glossy in hand. They point the gun in our direction.

The shot is deafening. I tense, expecting pain – but Alya snaps into action. In a split second she rips the gun from the man's hand, tosses it aside, and embeds her knee deep in his groin. His eyes bulge. When she pulls away he collapses, grabbing his crotch and howling. I grin through the pain.

"Thanks for the save."

Alya slides to the floor, clutching her bloodied stomach, and peers up at me with pained eyes.

"I don't think I like being a shield," she remarks weakly. I reach out, pulling her toward me, and prop her up against the table. Now I can feel my own breathing levelling out, I'm able to think a little more clearly.

Alya leans back, breathing hard. I spot a bloodied crater in her stomach and fight the urge to put pressure on it. Alya's body is self-regulating; it's safest to allow it to push the bullet out on its own.

"You'll be alright," I tell her, "13 seconds, remember? Do you want to count it out?"

She nods and starts counting in a whisper. Behind me, the others tense. They're worried, no doubt, but just like me they know she'll be fine. I can almost feel them monitoring her reactions, ready to plug this into their research. I swallow hard, finally levelling my own breathing enough to join in with her counting.

"Seven. Eight."

Her breathing promptly eases. I stare down at her, still counting, momentarily distracted by the sigh of her skin knitting itself back together.

"Look at that," I grin, "amazing as always."

I don't see the final Mortalist lean down and collect his comrade's gun off the floor.

"Reya!"

Jonah's voice snaps me out of it and I whip round, pushing Alya behind me. There's no need, though; he's not aiming at her. The barrel of the gun rests against the middle of my forehead. My breath catches.

"Look, just calm down," he says, "we didn't come to kill anyone. Our orders are to take the two of you alive."

247

Oddly, he seems far more rational than the others we've encountered tonight. Maybe that's how he got this far without taking a pummelling. I glare up at him, my head finally clear.

"You had better get that gun out of my goddamn face because trust me, it won't end well for you."

"Come quietly, and it'll be okay."

Behind me, Alya seems to be recovering. She straightens her back, breathing deeply, awareness flickering in her pale eyes. For a brief moment, triumph fills me – but then the other Mortalist clambers to his feet. His face is flushed red from the blow to his crotch, but he's slowly recovering. His comrade fires him a curious look.

"Do you have cuffs?"

"Yeah."

They step closer and I tense.

"Come on," says the reasonable one, "it doesn't have to be this hard."

"Do you enjoy food?" I hiss, "because if you don't get that gun out of my face, you'll become *very* familiar with a liquid diet."

He hesitates and I stare at him, weighing up our options. I could try to fight him. But Alya's not quite over the shock. She can't shield me – and certainly not from both of them, or at such close quarters. The weakness in my body seems to have faded, so at least I could hold my own. I try to figure out how much time has gone by since the alarm was triggered. Surely the cops can't be too far. I strain my ears. No sirens in the distance.

We're on our own.

The man sighs.

"Are you going to come nicely?"

"What do you think?"

"I wouldn't advise fighting me. I may get trigger-happy."

"You have orders to take us alive, right?" I spit, "I'm not scared of you."

I try to stand, surprised when he drops his aim to my legs, tightening his grip on the trigger. He grunts.

"I can disable you without killing you. Now hold still."

His buddy pulls out two pairs of cuffs while he holds the gun steady. The other man circles around me, pulling my arms back. I wrack my brain, desperate for a solution – some way to get out of this, move Alya out of the way, and protect the others. All without getting killed or having my knees shot out.

My arms tense as I prepare to grab the man behind me, hoping to fling him aside and knock his buddy's gun off course before he can fire. It's not a great plan, but it's all I've got.

It's only when a massive weight barrels into the man with the gun that I pause.

"Girls!"

Jonah sinks his knee into the man's stomach and flings him aside. As he turns, I see his arms are still tied; nylon rope is looped several times around his fists, half-cut and stained with blood from his wriggling. He fires me a frantic look.

"Get her out of the way!"

I nod, twisting my arms from the Mortalist's grip and punching him hard in the jaw. He reels back just long enough for me to scoop Alya off the floor. She stands uneasily, confused. I grab her shoulders.

"Alya. Look at me."

Her eyes blur, then clear.

"Get somewhere safe," I tell her.

"What about you?"

I glance at Jonah, and the two of us exchange short nods.

"We've got this," I grin.

As Alya races out of my line of sight – likely to untie the others – I heave the ties off Jonah's wrists. They come away in my hand and I realise he'd almost broken through them already. He rubs the cuts on his wrists and heaves a sigh.

"Jesus, you girls sure know how to cause a scene. All this worry is bad for my heart."

I smirk, and for a moment, it's like yesterday was just a dream. Like we never hurt each other. Like this is just another practice session in the gym.

"I know we're not following your protocol," I admit. He snorts.

"Fuck my protocol."

Both Mortalists stand, and Jonah steps forward. My fear promptly dissipates. If there's anyone I'd want by my side in a fist fight, it's him.

Jonah cracks his knuckles.

"Think you can handle them?" I joke.

"You've done a wonderful job, but I can handle things from here. If you could just keep this one where he is, that'd be grand. We could do with a conscious informant after all this is over."

The man closest to me panics, his eyes flitting from me to Jonah and back again. Maybe he's not frightened of me, but he wouldn't dream of messing with Jonah. I fire him a warning look and he sinks back.

Behind me, Jonah pummels the other man. The size difference is enormous, and the Mortalist doesn't really stand much chance. I watch the remaining man with cold eyes, ready to pounce if he tries to run.

Then, sirens. They start quietly at first, distant enough that I think I'm imagining it. Then, they grow louder. And louder. Until the sound consumes everything else. The Mortalist pulls out a walkie-talkie and barks into it.

"Everyone out! Out!"

I step forward but he ducks under my outstretched arm. Something clicks at my waist and he turns on me, raising my unclipped gun. I lunge at him but miss, hitting the floor hard. I push onto my elbows, staring up at the now-armed psychopath in front of me.

He points the gun – first at me, then at Jonah, then at the ground. His hands shake violently, like he's unsure what to do and bottling every opportunity. I stand, and that seems to trigger the 'flight' reaction.

He blindly fires and darts from the room, bursting through the door at a full sprint. Dimly, I realise that I should chase him down. I should re-instate the full lockdown. I should run outside and flag down the cops.

But I can't move.

My eyes are fixed on the figure sprawled on the lab floor.

Jonah is motionless, his kind eyes staring blankly at the ceiling. There's a grey sheen over them, diluting their rich colour and making it cloudy. His expression is utterly devoid of emotion.

There's a bloody crater between his eyes.

In an instant, my body turns cold.

Screams fill the room. Alya. She collapses by his side, shaking him feebly. He doesn't stir. Of course he doesn't. She fires me a terrified look, begging me to help. Pleading. She asks me to save him, to do something – anything – to bring Jonah back.

I don't hurry to her side. Nor do I respond to her pleading. I don't do much of anything, actually. I just stand there, frozen, unable to think or feel or act.

Police storm Lockless House. The Project scream for help and medics. They cry reassuring things at Alya. They beg me to snap out of it.

It's strange. I always thought that seeing someone die would break my heart. That I'd react just like Alya; screaming, crying, inconsolable. Or maybe I'd be angry, consumed by murderous rage.

But I don't feel anything. My mind is shutting down, blocking out the grief, erecting walls to protect me from the unimaginable pain. I stand frozen in a room full of screams, and allow my thoughts to cease.

Nineteen

My body has healed.

I sit in the dust of Lockless House's yard, knees pulled up to my chest. I've been here for the past two hours – from the moment the cops said I was allowed to leave. I've given them my statement four or five times, dully reciting every last detail of what happened. Every cop had fired me a confused look as I coldly described the horrors of the attack – including Jonah's murder.

Murder. God, that's a vile word.

I stare at the cop cars lined up on the other side of the fence. There was an ambulance earlier, too, but it's gone now. The medics pronounced him dead within minutes. A cursory check of the others flagged up no major injuries so they left, calling a mortician to collect the body. My throat fills with a sour taste. Body. Just his body. Not him. Everything that made him Jonah is gone.

I slap my cheeks as hard as I can. What's wrong with me? I should be angry. I should be sad. I should feel something. *Anything*. But there's nothing. It's like my emotions have locked themselves away.

Jonah would tell me that I'm in shock. He'd say it's normal. That watching someone die is traumatic, and it's completely human to shut down. But he's not here to tell me that, and I'm not sure I believe it coming from myself.

Alya's still crying. I can hear her wailing in the main lab. The main door is wide open, allowing cops to run in and out, arresting the few Mortalists who were still stupid enough to be in Lockless House when they arrived. Most fled the instant they heard sirens, but some didn't. They hurl insults at me as the cops drag them away. One or two promise to come back and do far worse next time. I don't react to them. I just stare at the gravel.

The media will go nuts over this. I can already imagine the headlines. I wonder how they'll twist it? The Mortalists are free to say whatever they like. They'll talk about how me and Alya charged through their 'peaceful protest', injuring them, threatening them. Even Shane escaped in the chaos. He was quick to cash in on a broken nose. How far will he go now that I've threatened him with a gun? I'm sure he'll have a lot to say to reporters. I bury my face again.

Soft footsteps scrape through the gravel behind me.

"I need to check your injuries."

Rene's voice is calm and steady. It doesn't sound like he's been crying. Maybe he's in shock, too. Or maybe he's just made of stronger stuff than I am. When I don't respond, he speaks more softly.

"Reya."

"I'm fine."

And I mean it. Physically, I feel okay.

I expect Rene to rage at me. To tell me that this mess is all my fault. That they wouldn't have invaded Lockless House if I hadn't antagonised them. But he doesn't. Instead he steps closer, sinking to the floor beside me.

"Let me see."

I lift my head enough for him to see my face. He reaches out, brushing a hand over the back of my head where I struck the table. His hand grazes my shoulder and lingers for a moment on the gunshot scar. I resist the urge to close my eyes. I'd forgotten how gentle Rene could be.

When he pulls back, he looks troubled.

"You seem okay, but you've been quiet."

I don't respond. He nods.

"Reality hasn't hit you yet, has it?"

"I suppose not."

I hesitate.

"Actually," I breathe, "what happens when it does? I'm going to be really angry, we both know that. What if I try and hunt the guy down?"

"Doesn't seem like the most intelligent idea," he says. I nod.

"That sounds like me. Angry and unintelligent."

"I didn't say that."

"I know. I said it."

Several minutes pass in silence, and I expect him to head inside. He probably has a million things to do right now. Gathering data, making reports. Dealing with the onslaught of media that's bound to descend on the Project any minute now. But he doesn't. He just sits beside me, ankles crossed, like he needs the peace and quiet just as much as I do.

"Did anyone figure out how they got in yet?" I ask. He nods.

"I had some trouble accessing the security system, but I know they used an approved hand print. The only people who've been in and out in the last day are Project members."

"So they got hold of someone's handprint?"

"It seems so."

He fires me a strange look.

"I'm surprised you went out last night, by the way. I thought you agreed not to leave."

"I didn't get chance to go anywhere. When I left the Dome, the alarm had already been triggered."

His face blanches, and I quickly realise why. The Mortalists didn't use just anyone's handprint to get inside Lockless House. They used mine.

Logically, it makes sense. I go out often. My handprints are more easily available than anyone else's. Even so, it makes my stomach flip. I must look as sick as I feel, because he frowns.

"Hey, now," Rene says, "this isn't your fault. If they didn't use yours, they'd have used someone else's."

I want to object and remind him that nobody else would have been so reckless. But I don't have the energy to argue.

"This is so messed up," I sigh, "Lockless House isn't safe anymore. Alya's distraught. Everyone's traumatised. The media is going to swarm the place. And Jonah..."

My throat catches and I look away. Rene clears his throat.

"It could be worse."

"How could it be worse?!"

"They had a plan," he says, "they told us before you two came downstairs. They hoped to kill us, incapacitate you and your sister, and take you both away somewhere to... finish the job."

I give an involuntary shudder. What would they have done to us? Would we have been strung up and tortured? Would they have 'killed' Alya a dozen times over, taking delight in her pain? Would they have killed me in front of her?

But then, maybe not. They seemed to hold back when fighting me.

"Hey, Rene? What exactly happened before we came down?"

"Why do you ask?"

"The Mortalists didn't want to kill us. One of them even tried to shoot out my knees to subdue me, rather than just put a bullet in my head. I was able to keep them at bay alone, for a while. So, how were they able to restrain all of you?"

He draws his lips into a tight line.

"Ah, that. The alarms triggered for unregistered people in the lobby, so we all grabbed weapons and charged out to meet them. But when we got there, the lobby was empty. There was no sign of anyone; except for these strange gas canisters on the ground. By the time I'd figured out what they were, everyone had already lost consciousness."

My stomach twists, but he carries on.

"It turns out they had come inside just to release some kind of knockout gas. When I came round, we were tied up and they'd taken our weapons. I think that gave them a sense of power."

"That makes sense," I mutter, "if they hadn't used some sneaky tactic, you guys would have easily overpowered them. They seriously could have killed you."

"Luckily," Rene says, "you and Alya were able to save us. Most of us, at least."

"Sure," I scoff, "we did a brilliant job."

"You did. If you'd followed Project protocol then the two of you may have survived, but the rest of us wouldn't have. I'll admit, when you first burst into the lab, I was furious. But... you and Alya worked well together. It was like you knew what one another was thinking."

"We've been spending a lot of time together," I say simply. He doesn't question it.

"All I'm saying is, I'm grateful for the rescue. I knew that you could fight – you wouldn't have made it this long if you couldn't – but I'd never seen you in action before. I'm impressed. You're much stronger than you look, and you can really take a punch. There were several times back there where I thought you were badly hurt, but every time you sprang back up, ready for another round. That tenacity's not something you'd get from most people. That's what saved us."

He smiles down at me, his face oddly serene.

"You're amazing, Reya."

I pause. Amazing. The word he's only ever reserved for Alya. The word he used to describe me when I was a kid, before he realised that I was mortal. My throat tightens.

"Did you just..."

"You should come inside," he says, standing, "I know it's chaos in there, but you haven't eaten for at least a day. It won't do to have you collapsing on top of everything else we're dealing with."

I stand too, suddenly nervous. He's not going to acknowledge what he just said, but I feel like I should thank him. Like I need to say something.

I reach for his sleeve, stopping him in his tracks.

"What is it?" he asks. I swallow hard.

"Rene, I just... I'm sorry."

And I am. I'm sorry for all my screwups and all the trouble I've caused him. I'm sorry for the pain he's going through, and the extra work he'll have thanks to me.

"For everything," I add, hoping he understands.

His eyes soften.

"Come inside when you're ready. I'll be back in a few minutes with some water."

I let him go, watching as his lab coat swishes behind him. He's fully dressed. He must have been working the night lab when the attack started. I can only imagine how tired he must be – and there he is, like always, holding everything together. Taking care of me when I'm on the edge of crumbling. My appreciation for him doubles.

"There you are!"

I whip around, expecting another attack – but there's no gun aimed my way, nobody trying to kill me. I search the yard wildly, but there's nobody within the fence but me. So I look to the security gate, which is still open.

There's another car parked up now. It's a sleek, mustard-yellow mustang; one that I know from experience is a stick shift. Marcus stands on the other side of the gate, flustered and slightly breathless.

"Reya, thank goodness! I was so worried," he gasps, "I came as soon as I heard about the attack."

"How did you know something had happened?"

"It's on the news. And the radio. And... pretty much everywhere. It said there had been an attack and someone had died. What happened?"

The words fall out before I can stop them.

"They killed Jonah."

Somehow, saying it makes it real. Marcus' face folds with unspoken sympathy and he shifts forward, then hesitates. Even now, he won't step into the grounds of Lockless House.

For a few seconds, I stare at him. I'd planned to cut things off after my confrontation with Rene. I'd planned to tell him that I could never see him again, and ask him to keep a respectful distance.

But even now, I feel the urge to step into his arms. I remember the times I've opened up to him – willingly and otherwise. When he found me crying in the alleyway. When I shouted at him in his apartment. Even when I sobbed in his arms.

He's the only person in the whole damn world who knows how I really feel.

"You could have saved him."

Marcus' voice is as warm as ever. My head snaps up.

"W-what?"

"If we had just brought the tests forward by a few days," he sighs, "this wouldn't have happened. You could have been immortal by now. You could have been that human shield you're always talking about. Maybe then, he wouldn't have died."

His words feel like an icicle in my chest. I hadn't thought of it that way. A few more days – a week, max – and I'd have been able to save everyone. If I hadn't given up when Rene challenged me. If I hadn't been stupid enough to get injured during the car chase, delaying our progress.

Hell, maybe if I had just turned out right in the first place. Then, Jonah might still be alive.

"I admired that man," Marcus says, "he didn't deserve to die. How could this happen?"

I open my mouth, then close it.

"I... I don't know."

"Do you think you have a place here after you stood by and watched him die?" he asks softly.

"I don't know that either."

"Can you look them in the eyes knowing what you've done?"

Something hot pricks the back of my eyes. Marcus leans closer.

"Do you still think you deserve to be here?"

The tears find their way out. I bite my lip hard enough to hurt.

"No."

"Come on," he says, tilting his head, "you can stay with me."

"But..."

"They don't want you anymore, Reya. But it's okay. I'll never turn you away."

He holds out a hand, watching me with a loving expression. I step forward – but someone wrenches me away.

Rene pushes me behind him. He glances back at me, his gaze settling on my shaking hands. Rage consumes his features.

"Reya, stay behind me."

"Hello, old friend."

Marcus shoots him a serene smile.

"It's good to see you again, after all these years."

"Leave. Now."

Rene's voice is harder and colder than I've ever heard it. His shoulders suddenly seem broad – much broader than before. It takes me a moment to realise that he's bristling for a fight, making himself appear larger. I place a hand on his arm. He's so angry he's shaking.

"Rene..."

"I said stay behind me."

"Huh," Marcus says, "you always assume the worst, don't you Rene? No wonder you and Reya clash so often. She usually has good intentions, you know."

"Don't pretend you know her."

He grins.

"But I do. See, I'm the person Reya comes to when she needs to get away from you."

Rene glances back at me. When I don't deny it, his brow furrows.

"Reya?"

"I'm not going with you."

I stare Marcus in the face, fighting to gather my composure. Of course I'm not going with him. The last thing the Project needs is for me to run away. Now, more than ever, we need to stick together.

"I know I let them down," I mutter, "but this is my home, and I'll stay as long as they'll have me."

My gaze switches to Rene, who watches me with uncertain eyes.

"I don't want to fix myself anymore," I tell him, "I just want to work on making things right."

Marcus clicks his tongue.

"But Reya, we were so close to a breakthrough."

"I'm sorry. I appreciate everything you've done for me, but I don't want it anymore. There's no point fixing myself if I hurt the Project in the process. That's not what I wanted."

"Miss Adebayo will be sorely disappointed when her funding dries up," he muses. I pause.

"You... you wouldn't."

"I'm sure it'll all work out. She'll find another way to make her dreams come true."

"No. Come on, don't take this out on Nova. She's brilliant, you know that. We can still..."

He reaches out, beckoning me forward.

"I will remove all funding from Miss Adebayo's projects with immediate effect – unless you come here, for just a moment. I'd like to speak to you without Rene's input."

Rene tenses.

"She's not stupid."

I step forward and he splutters.

"Reya!"

"I can't let him withdraw Nova's funding," I mutter, "this is her dream and I won't be responsible for ruining it."

I step around Rene and closer to Marcus, my gaze fixed on his outstretched hand. Suddenly, everything else falls away. It's just us. And then my hand is in his, and he pulls me close to his chest. One hand wraps itself in my hair. Somehow, I know that he's smirking over my shoulder at Rene.

I'm not a total idiot. I can see everything the Project warned me about. The lack of empathy, the cold, calculating intelligence. The manipulation. I think I saw it the whole time – but now it's out in the open, making my entire body quiver under his grip. This man is dangerous. Perhaps more dangerous than any Mortalist I've encountered.

"What do you need to tell me?" I ask. He leans in, brushing my hair from my ear.

"Jonah would want you to come with me, Reya. Trust me, I knew him better than anyone. He spent countless nights begging me to fix you. He risked everything to try and give you the destiny you were promised. Don't disregard his memory like this."

Jonah's ashamed face fills my head. He wouldn't have wanted this. He'd have ripped me furiously from Marcus' grip, desperate to keep us apart. He has to know that Jonah wouldn't support him. But why lie about it?

Suddenly, everything clicks.

Marcus, appearing in the alleyway minutes after an attack.

Marcus, sharing secrets that the Project would never tell me.

Marcus, empathising with my issues with Rene to drive us apart.

Convincing me to share my secrets. Preying on my fear for Alya. Worsening my feelings of guilt.

The attacks. How the Mortalists knew my every move, tracking me on foot and on wheels. How they always seemed to know what to expect from me. The new onslaught of hate mail, so unnecessarily brutal that it could only have been designed to shake me to my core.

Finally, Marcus. Scanning my handprint at the entryway to Safehouse 17, even though he already knew exactly what was inside.

"It's you."

The world falls silent around us.

"You're a Mortalist."

Marcus watches me, his expression like ice. I push on.

"You've been watching me the whole time, haven't you? Putting everyone at risk and convincing me that your serum was the only way to fix things, even though you knew it wouldn't stick. You've been working toward this for years."

I peel his fingers from mine.

"God, I'm so stupid. Of course you're one of them. It's always..."

Marcus' hand locks around my waist. I wriggle in his grip, stunned by his strength. Rene starts forward, and Marcus sighs.

"When I find out who killed Jonah, I am going to destroy them."

He rolls his eyes and in an instant, all his charm vanishes. Now, he watches me with the same sick hunger that every Mortalist possesses; only this time, he wants me, not Alya.

"This was supposed to be the last straw," he tells me, "I've been working toward this for so long. Every attack made you more skittish, angry and desperate. And that set Rene on edge, making him more likely to explode. I spent months driving you two apart. And this – the invasion of Lockless House – was supposed to be the final part. If it failed and you weren't brought to me, or if Rene survived, then he was supposed to blame you for your handprint being stolen, and for this whole mess. And that would be the final straw. You'd come to me willingly, and Rene wouldn't bother coming after you."

He squeezes the bridge of his nose.

"But that moron Jonah went and got killed by someone in my ranks. That's just screwed everything up."

"Your ranks?" Rene breathes.

"Let me clarify. I'm not one of those mindless thugs who scream about 'the virtues of humanity'. Those buffoons have always existed. All I did was pay them handsomely, build their numbers, and strike a deal with them. They follow my orders, I utilise their manpower. In return, we split the reward. They get the Tomorrow Girl."

His hands grip me hard enough to hurt.

"And I get Reya."

I wriggle in his grip but he silences me, pressing an open hand over my mouth. I shout into his palm, calling him every curse-word that comes to mind. My muffles cries must spark a reaction in Rene because suddenly he's on us, trying to peel Marcus' hand from my face. But Marcus is large, and surprisingly strong – Rene stumbles back, rolling into a heap on the ground. He sits up, coughing, and starts shouting for help. From the others. From the cops still inside Lockless House. Even from Alya.

Marcus shifts, tugging something from his pocket with a free hand. Rene leaps forward.

The gunshot echoes and my blood runs cold.

No. No, no, no.

Rene sprawls in the dirt, limbs twitching, a pool of red blossoming beneath him. I wrench myself free and dart forward – but Marcus' hands snap around me, drawing me away.

"Calm yourself, Reya. Whether he lives or dies is really the least of your concerns."

Rene writhes again, crying out, one hand clutching his bloodied stomach. His eyes roll, but I can tell he's fighting the urge to pass out. He's trying to focus on me. His mouth moves and somehow, I know he's trying to say my name.

Fear overwhelms me. I scream and strain toward him. Marcus yanks me back and I kick out, terror consuming me. I start shouting for help. Begging. Pleading.

Someone needs to stop Marcus. Someone needs to save Rene.

Why isn't anyone coming?! Can't they hear me?

Marcus snaps his arms around my neck, squeezing hard. Within seconds, dark spots fill my vision.

I twist against him, throwing out an arm.

"Rene..."

That single, slurred word is all I manage before the darkness takes over and I slump into Marcus' arms. I strain to open my eyes – to see if help is coming, to see if Rene is okay – but it doesn't work. My body isn't listening to me.

Marcus scoops me up, and then I feel nothing.

Twenty

The sterile scent of Safehouse 17 fills my nostrils. As feeling returns to my body, I realise that I'm spread out on a bare, scratchy mattress. Any exposed skin is covered with goosebumps, alerting me to the icy air. I strain to open my eyes and slowly, the world comes clear.

I'm in a small, square room with concrete walls and a single door. Nearby is a rusted bucket, a folding chair, and a stack of old boxes.

Bit by bit, my memory comes together. Lockless House being attacked. Jonah's death. A fleeting sign of reconciliation with Rene – and the sight of him collapsing into the dust.

I bolt upright, ignoring the ache in my spine. I'm wearing the same clothes I wore when Marcus took me; black leggings, grey t-shirt, and the mustard-yellow hoodie he gave me as a 'gift'. I sneer down at it, wishing I could tear it off, but the air is cold enough to make me reconsider. I check my pockets, wondering if there's anything useful inside. Nothing. He's taken it all.

I stand, my stomach burning. He took me. He hurt Rene and then he took me.

The door is locked. I wrestle with the handle for several minutes, then back up and heave my weight at the door. It creaks, straining against its frame, but holds firm. I rub my shoulder, feeling the familiar burn of my messed-up healing ability, and step back, ready to throw myself at it again.

But this time, the door clicks open.

Marcus steps inside, his face dominated by a hateful smirk.

In an instant, my chest is alight with rage. It's hard to breathe. My hands curl into fists. It takes all I have not to throw myself at him, to claw at his eyes, to scratch out his throat – but I force myself to remain still, glaring at him, matching the hatred in his eyes.

But I daren't launch myself at him, because there are two strange men standing behind him. They watch me warily, adjusting their grips on their guns. I spot the Mortalist logo on their arms and scowl.

Marcus motions for them to close the door, then his gaze settles on me.

Emotion fills me. Fear for Rene's wellbeing. Terror at what's going to happen to me. Grief at everything I've lost. And absolute, unbridled fury.

I choose the latter to act on. Fear and grief are scary and unfamiliar; but anger, I understand.

Anger, I can wield.

I growl.

"You'd better hope I don't get my hands on you."

"You're awake," he beams, "good. How's your neck feeling? I'd assumed it would heal okay."

"I'm not screwing with you," I tell him coldly, "if I get half a chance, you're dead."

"Oh, I don't doubt it. But I'm not stupid enough to give you an opportunity."

His eyes flash.

"Unlike you, I can tell when I'm walking into an obvious trap."

"Go fuck yourself."

I'm not sure why I respond this way, but I do. I open my mouth and let out a string of curse words, each more colourful than the last. Marcus chuckles.

"My, that is one hell of a vocabulary. I know Rene didn't teach you that."

He steps closer, wrapping his hands behind his back.

"But then, if you ever listened to Rene, you wouldn't be in this mess."

"You're not wrong there," I spit, "I hate to admit it, but he's usually right."

He winks.

"Don't worry, I won't tell him you said that. The last thing he needs is an ego boost."

"Looks like you have more in common than you think."

His smile widens.

"This isn't about ego. It's about so much more than that."

"Let me guess," I growl, "it's for science. No, no, for your precious legacy. Maybe for the good of all humanity. Something pointless like that. Either way, it's bull. Nothing really justifies everything you've done."

"And what *have* I done?"

I bite my lip hard.

"You kidnapped me as a kid. Then, when you didn't get your way, you stalked me for years. You attacked my family. You drove me away from the people I was supposed to trust. You tried to break me."

He tilts his head.

"Break you? Please. You were broken long before I showed up."

I pause, breathless. He pushes on.

"When I got involved with the Mortalists, I had been watching you for a while. And what I found was... intriguing, to say the least. You've spent 17 years convincing yourself that you're worthless. Your relationship with Alya was non-existent. You didn't trust easily. And Rene... wow. Let me tell you, a therapist would have an absolute field day with you two."

He's pacing now, arms folded.

"I've never known two people who want so desperately for one another to be happy and safe, yet do everything in their power to make the opposite happen. How can you love each other so much, and still push each other away? It is, in your vernacular, an utter shit show."

I lower my gaze. He's not wrong. I've never understood it myself. All I've ever wanted is to make Rene proud – and I've done everything I can to make him ashamed. It would have been so easy to please him if I'd just set my mind to it. I could have played the part well, been sweet and friendly like Alya, and maybe he would have accepted me.

Maybe he would have even loved me.

My mind bristles at the thought. No. I don't want him to love me because I play the part well. I want him to love me because he loves me. As I am, flaws and all.

I know it's not a fair thing to ask.

"Luckily," Marcus continues, "that gave me all the opportunities I needed. The wedge was already there. It wasn't hard to add a little pressure. Every time you came home bruised and beaten, he'd worry. Rene is about as clever as you when it comes to feelings. You both react with anger. Every clash forced you farther apart, so it was easy to come between you."

His smile widens.

"Of course, it helped that your sister was so desperate to be like you. That scared him even more. To see her become more confident, more outspoken. He must have been terrified to see her fighting in the main lab."

"How did you..."

"I hacked Lockless House's security months ago. I told you, they never fully disconnected this place. It was shockingly easy. Especially once I had your handprint registered, which allowed me full access."

I snarl at him, but my heart aches. Now that he's spelling it out, it makes sense.

"Why not just kill me?" I ask, suddenly defiant, "it would have been easy enough. I was alone with you plenty of times. Asleep, once or twice. Why bother involving the Project?"

"I don't want to kill you."

"Bull."

"I mean it. You're worth more to me alive. That's why I started my tests. I knew the serum wouldn't permanently fix you, but it did enough. It was just what I needed to keep you obedient. If not for your sister telling Rene, it would have gone smoothly."

"What do you mean?"

"The attack was a last minute plan," he explains, "when I saw you'd been confronted, I knew the Project wouldn't let me near you again. So I did what I had to do to finally break you away from them. It was messy, I'll give you that, but it worked. You're here, and Rene is gone."

My blood runs cold.

"G-gone?"

"Don't panic. He was alive, the last I heard. They'd called an ambulance and Neil was seeing to him."

I step back, heart hammering. Rene's alive. He's got to be. My mind can't conceive of a world without him in it.

"Speaking of the Project," Marcus smiles, "you should probably say hello."

"Huh?"

"We're in Safehouse 17, in one of the old storage rooms, converted into a makeshift cell. And that…"

He waves a hand at the camera in the corner of the room.

"Is a direct feed to Lockless House."

I stare up at the camera, ignoring the sick feeling in my stomach.

"So, what? You're going to kill me on film? That's screwed up, even for you."

He lets out a noise of mock surprise.

"Kill you? No. That wouldn't do at all."

"Keeping me here isn't going to help you get close to Alya and the others, you know."

His smile broadens.

"Of course it will. It'll simply tear them apart to watch you sit here alone, with only Mortalists to keep you alive and fed."

I step back, fear growing.

"I don't understand any of this. You were part of the Project. You helped make me. You know that I'm human."

"Of course you're human, Reya. But it hardly matters. That's not why I'm doing this."

He reaches out and I step back again, my back hitting the wall. He nudges my chin softly, encouraging me to look up at him.

"We're very similar, aren't we?" he whispers, "the Project promised us both something amazing, and we were both willing to dedicate everything to that. But then it rejected us – both of us. The Project snatched away the grand destinies we deserved, Reya."

His expression turns cold.

"The Project destroyed me. So now I'm going to destroy them."

"How?" I ask, dreading the answer.

"I'm just full of theories, you know. One of them is particularly interesting. I believe that, with the advent of you and your sister, mortality has become somewhat of a spectrum. Humans at one end, Alya at the other. And then you… somewhere in the middle."

"I'm human."

"For all intents and purposes, yes. But your DNA is malleable. It can be imbued with additional traits. In short, with the correct treatment you can slide up or down the spectrum as required. To me at least, that's all terribly exciting."

He steps even closer and my skin crawls.

"If your DNA can be changed, surely a human's can, too. Perhaps my serum is the first stage in something much greater. I believe that, if I can keep supplying serum to your system, eventually your body will accept the changes as a permanent alteration. You'd only need booster shots every so often to maintain immortality. And if that's possible, then it's only a matter of transferring that knowledge to humans."

"I don't follow."

His eyes light up as he watches me, his eyes greedily searching my face.

"Immortality, Reya. A simple dose of serum that could turn a human immortal. Imagine it. A whole world where nobody ages, nobody dies, nobody gets hurt. A few shots here and there, and everyone would live forever. It'd be a whole new world, and I'd be its founding father."

My stomach twists.

"I don't see how this plan would hurt the Project."

"The Tomorrow Project's claim to fame is the creation of a single, immortal girl," he says, "if I release a serum that can turn everyone immortal, then they will become irrelevant. Funds will dry up. Sponsors will grow bored. Why would they care about Alya when they can be just like her? The Project would crumble. They'd lose everything, including their very purpose."

And then his smile changes into something much more insidious.

"But that's all a theory. It may not work. Your body is already under strain and there's a chance you won't survive the tests. But that's okay. If my serum doesn't have the potential to change the world, it's fine. Watching you rot on camera will destroy the Project just as efficiently."

He turns tail and strides from the room, leaving me frozen against the wall. The door slams shut behind him, clanging with a certain, terrifying finality.

My anger ebbs, and in an instant it's replaced with fear. I don't want to die.

I've thought about it a million times. When cornered in an alleyway, or dancing on a rooftop, or curled up alone in a dark room. I've wondered what it's like to die. If there's a tunnel of light or pearly gates. Every time, I've laughed it off. Told myself that even if there is such a place, I'm not going to be let in. Maybe they only allow humans. More likely, I just haven't done enough to deserve my spot. I remember joking with Nova, telling her that if there's a heaven, then I'm definitely going to the other place. At the time, it hadn't felt so real.

Now, it does. I swallow hard. My throat is dry and sore. My hands are shaking. Death? I feel like I'm already halfway there. My knees quake and I sink to the floor, burying my face in my hands and praying the Project can't see me crying.

Twenty-One

Days. It's been days.

I only know this because the Mortalists bring me three meals a day, scowling the entire time. I've counted at least three days, though it could easily have been much longer. My sense of time has become warped from the rampant isolation.

I spend most of the day – at least, when Marcus isn't running tests on me - slumped in the corner of the bare mattress, eyes fixed on the camera. Though it doesn't look like it, I've been gathering information and trying to formulate an escape plan. So far, I've learned that the Mortalists have invaded Safehouse 17, lead by Marcus. I've figured out that Rene was reported alive two days ago, but badly wounded. And I've learned that they're just waiting for the Project to respond to my capture.

For the first day or so, I half-hoped the Project would stage a rescue. That they would barge in, all guns blazing, and pluck me out of here. But there hasn't been a heroic battle yet. There's no way they don't know where I am. They know. But for whatever reason, they haven't come for me.

For the millionth time, I tell myself that I shouldn't need saving. I should be able to break down this door, kick some ass, and walk out of this hellhole on my own power. But I don't. It's not that I haven't tried; I've heaved myself at the door more times than I can count. I've jumped the Mortalists who bring me food and water. I've tried to escape on the journey to the testing chair in the lab. But I never make it far.

My only saving grace is the ongoing healing. The puncture wounds in my spine fade in minutes, leaving my skin smooth and unmarred, albeit bloody.

I've stared at the consoles in the main lab countless times, wondering if I could use them. My handprint was one of the few access codes he has, and he has no reason to remove it while I'm locked up. If I could just get out then I could run Safehouse 17 like a video game, locking the Mortalists into sections, calling for help, gathering weapons. I could fight my way out.

The ferocity dulls. Fight my way out and go… where, exactly?

The Project hasn't come for me. It doesn't take a genius to figure out that Marcus brought me back to his old haunt. Rene would have figured it out in a heartbeat. The thought occurs to me that he might still not be well enough to come after me – but I shove the thought aside. No. Rene's okay. He has to be.

"Reya," Marcus says, "you really should listen when someone's talking to you."

He entered the room while I was deep in thought and now stands across from me, a patient look on his face.

"Shove it," I respond curtly.

His brow furrows and I bite back on a laugh. What started as my usual brand of sarcasm has now become a small act of defiance; some tiny way to make myself feel less helpless.

"You really are a foul-mouthed little thing, aren't you?" he asks, "I'm sure Rene would be ashamed to hear you speak like that."

"I think he'd be proud," I tell him, and I mean it. Rene may hate my behaviour, but he clearly hates Marcus more. I get the feeling that this would be the exception. Marcus sighs.

"It's been four days and my patrols haven't seen hide nor hair of the Project. They're not coming for you, you know."

When I don't respond, his smile widens.

"Don't worry. You're more than welcome to stay here."

"I'm still not calling you 'Dad'," I retort.

"We have tests to run," he tells me, "so get up before I have to call for some muscle."

"See, if you ditched the cell and the guards, I'd beat your ass into next Tuesday."

He grabs my wrist, yanking me to my feet.

"As much as I enjoy your sarcasm, we have work to do. I'm getting closer, Reya. Every day brings us nearer to creating the ultimate serum."

"Right," I say, rolling my eyes, "your vaccine for death."

"I see progress on the horizon," he tells me, "but don't worry. Sooner or later your body will self-regulate. You'll stay exactly how I want you and then, well..."

His smile widens.

"We'll have literally forever to get this right."

Briefly, the thought consumes me.

Years passing. Staying the same as I am right now, a girl frozen in time and trapped in an abandoned industrial unit. The agony of the needles has already faded to little more than a dull roar in my spine. How much longer before it feels entirely normal? I'm facing an endless, unchanging life. All in this lab. All with him standing by, watching me with that sick smile on his face.

An eternity spent alone.

I close my eyes against the thought, and he knows he's got me.

When Marcus slips from the room after another bout of tests, taking my discomfort with him, I lower my head to my chest. This is how I sleep now, but also what I do when I need to think without prying eyes watching me.

If I can get out of this room, I stand a shot at escaping. I could access a console, call for help, or grab some weapons. I try to remember how many different faces I've seen standing guard at the door, but can't. There are at least ten Mortalists I can remember clearly. Some have been especially vocal, whining and muttering amongst themselves, so I can remember them well, but I'm sure there are more. Can I fight off that many?

My chest tightens. No. But I have to try.

Sooner or later, he's going to kill me. Despite his posturing, I suspect he'll grow bored once he realises that the Project isn't going to react. If that's going to happen regardless, then I plan to give him as much trouble as possible. He wants a legacy? I'll give him one hell of a story to tell once I'm gone.

And suddenly, there it is. The fire in my stomach, the one that used to burn so brightly, has sparked back into life. I'm not going down without a fight.

Marcus tightens the nylon cords around my wrists, sighing heavily. He seems tired. Perhaps it's due to the rising tensions between him and the Mortalists. They've started to question him. More than once, I've heard him snap at them to get out so he can work. Perhaps his patience with them is wearing thin.

"Have you heard anything from the Project?" I ask him.

"No. Lockless House is on maximum lockdown and they've cancelled all public appearances. I doubt they're planning on coming for you. Luckily, you don't need them."

His lip curls and he fires me a mocking glance.

"You have me, remember?"

"Well, didn't I just win the fucking lottery," I remark.

The lab door slides open and someone shuffles up behind Marcus. He turns around, grunting in acknowledgement.

"There you are. Good to see you up and about after your... unfortunate injuries."

The man agrees, and when Marcus finally steps aside, I recognise him.

Shane stands with his shoulders back and his lips drawn in a tight line, watching Marcus like a soldier awaiting his superior's orders. His jawline and throat are bruised to hell from our last encounter, and judging by the shadows under his eyes, it's affecting his sleep.

But then his gaze drops, and our eyes meet.

He promptly pales.

"Shit."

I look around, trying to figure out what caused that reaction. But it's me he's staring at, his eyes wide and his lips twisted in disgust.

"She's still alive?!" he barks.

"Of course," Marcus says, "you knew that."

"We agreed we'd off her quickly. None of this medical bullshit."

I open my mouth to make a smartass remark, then stop myself. Shane seems shaken. I suppose I can see why. My body is wrapped in wires and tubes. Screens behind me track every heartbeat, every breath. The back of my shirt is drenched with blood from the needles. Despite my accelerated healing, I'm still breathing a little too hard. To an onlooker, the whole setup is vaguely horror-movie-esque.

Our eyes meet again, and he quickly looks away.

I can use this. The shock, the disgust. I can get him to untie me – if I can just speak to him alone.

So I draw my lips back in a smile.

"It's good to see you again, Shane."

He stares. Marcus laughs.

"Don't mind her."

"But..."

"She's harmless. You don't need to be scared."

Marcus' eyes glimmer.

"She can't hurt you. Not again, at least."

Shane flushes red.

"We had an agreement, Marcus."

"And we still do. I helped your group break into Lockless House and terrorise the Project. I know you've yet to receive your prize, but be patient. The Project is shaken. They've lost their Head of Security, and the Project Head was hospitalised. The remaining members will be too distraught to think clearly. The younger girl will be yours before you know it."

He walks away and Shane follows, fuming.

"Hold on! I don't care about your deal with the others. We had a deal. You and I."

The older man stops. Shane pushes on.

"Listen," he says, "I agreed to join the attack so I could catch Reya off guard. I've been identified by the cops and they're looking for me as an accessory to murder. I'm paying one hell of a price for your plan and in return, you promised you would kill her right away."

"I don't see why this bothers you so much," Marcus says simply.

"The bitch humiliated me. Twice. I want to see her dead."

"And you will, but not yet. I have a few more tests to run."

Shane glances back at me, and his face creases.

"This feels... wrong."

"She's alive and unharmed, as is. This shouldn't be an issue for anyone with Mortalist beliefs. Or, do you pity her? Perhaps your history with this girl is clouding your judgement."

"Excuse me," I interject, "I don't appreciate being referred to as 'this girl'. Also, does anyone care for my opinion on this?"

They ignore me. Shane snarls.

"All I'm saying is, we agreed to kill her, and that's it. Not torture."

"Torture?"

"That's what this is, right? I know you're filming it and sending it to the Project. It's a power play."

Amazingly, Marcus falls silent. He presses his lips together tightly.

He hasn't told the Mortalists what he's doing. Something clicks.

Mortalists hate us because we're not human. If they knew what Marcus was trying to do, there's no way they'd allow it. Two Tomorrow Girls is the last thing they'd want. And the immortal utopia Marcus is dreaming of? Unthinkable.

The men bicker between themselves for a few seconds, and Shane rolls his eyes theatrically before marching out. Marcus shakes his head. He sees me watching and his lip curls.

"Now then, where were we?"

His hand touches the console and my body tenses, preparing for the pain I know is coming; but this time, when I retreat into my mind, it's not out of fear.

This time, I close myself off to plan.

My opportunity comes several hours later.

I'm curled up on the filthy mattress in my cell, pretending to sleep, waiting for something – anything – to happen. A half hour goes by and I don't move. The guards outside my door relax, convinced I'm asleep, and I play along. Once they start talking, I strain to make out their words.

"Any update on when we're getting the other freak?" one asks. The other grunts.

"Not yet. Marcus seems to have lost all interest in helping us."

"We shouldn't have given him his prize before we got ours."

"I guess he's got it made," she says, "he can keep doing... whatever the hell this is, and we're still playing guard for him. For free, no less. I mean, I have a job, too. I can't spend all my time guarding his pet."

"What *is* all this, anyway? If he wanted to hurt the Project, he should just kill it."

"I don't know. He won't tell anyone what he's doing."

"Maybe we should ask Shane."

"The kid with the bruises?"

"Yeah. They had an argument earlier. Maybe he knows what's going on."

"Think anyone will notice if we go ask him?"

"Nah. It's asleep."

Another low, unhappy sound.

"...Right. Let's go."

I wait for the sound of their steps to fade and sit up. At last. I'm alone. What now?

I close my eyes and focus, dredging up every emergency access code Jonah ever taught me. If they work at Lockless House, they should work here, too, right? As long as the consoles in the lab can hear me.

"Security protocol #257CG81A. Reya Mathis."

Something beeps in the hallway. Good. The system knows that code.

"Umm... switch off the lab equipment in Safehouse 17," I mumble, "and remove all security...?"

Another beep, but nothing happens. I repeat the instruction, clearer this time, hoping it understands. Nothing. Maybe I don't have clearance. It would make sense; perhaps Rene removed my Core Project access after our argument. Or maybe the security data is too old, and the system can't recognise my adult voice. I'm not sure, but for whatever reason, it's not playing ball.

"Emergency," I recite, fighting to remember the exact words Jonah taught me, "send request for help to Lockless House. Direct the message to Rene Mathis."

Another beep, a little higher this time, like it's recording. I hedge my bets.

"Safehouse 17. Can't drop security. Only way in is through my handprint. Marcus' even crazier than you said."

I bite my lip, wondering what else I can say, but the system beeps again. I stare at the ceiling for a moment, unsure whether it worked at all. I recite the security protocol again, then follow it up with every other code I can remember. Some, I'm sure, don't mean much – they're old or expired or irrelevant – but I try them anyway.

When I toss out a code I've heard Jonah use before, the system let out a loud, robotic screech.

"SECURITY OVERRIDE: MANUAL INPUT REQUIRED."

My heart leaps.

I heave myself at the door, desperate to reach a console and get the heck out of here. But as before, the door holds firm. I back up, nursing my aching shoulder, and size up the door. I can break it down. I know I can. It'll just take time

– and probably a broken shoulder or two. I wait until the burning eases before stepping back, ready to charge it again.

But then I hear approaching footsteps and sink back onto my mattress. As the cell door opens I drop my head, hoping the Mortalist didn't hear me trying to bust out.

Shane walks into the room with shifty eyes, pulling his jacket tightly around himself. I watch through my lashes as he nears the camera in the corner, staring up at it with curious eyes. Then his gaze slides across the room, like he's searching for something in particular.

"What are you looking for?"

He jumps when I lift my head.

"You're awake."

"What are you doing?"

"None of your business," he says coldly. I tilt my head.

"Whatever it is, you don't want Marcus to know."

"No, and you'd better not tell him. The guy's a psychopath."

"Believe me, I know. You clearly don't trust him."

When Shane doesn't respond, I lean forward.

"Well?"

He ignores me again, and I click my tongue at him.

"I think I know what you're looking for. I can tell you what he's really up to."

"Shut up."

The instruction is hard and cold, edged with a not-so-subtle threat. I push harder.

"If you knew, you wouldn't be happy. That's why he's so secretive."

His head snaps up.

"I thought I told you to shut up."

I smirk.

"And I thought you liked me. People often say things they don't mean, right?"

His expression flickers, but only for a moment. He steps menacingly towards me, but I fight the instinct to shrink back. Shane isn't like Marcus. He's not ruthless, cunning, or intelligent. He's just a thug; like every other thug I've met over the years. I don't need to convince him of anything. I just need to make him hate someone other than me.

"You're just going to lie to me," he sneers.

"Excuse me? I think you'll find that I'm the most honest person here. I never looked someone in the eye and told them they mattered. Not like you and Marcus. If anyone around here can be trusted, it's me."

"You don't have a clue what he's doing."

"He's trying to fix me."

At that, Shane hesitates. His dark eyes swivel towards me, filling with confusion.

"Fix you? What the hell does that mean?"

I take a deep breath.

"I wasn't meant to be like this," I confess, "I was designed to be the Tomorrow Girl. I was meant to be immortal."

Shane pales.

"What?"

"Something went wrong when they made me. That's why they replaced me with Alya."

He watches me with a sick expression.

"You were meant to be like her?"

"Marcus is ex-Project, and he's obsessed," I tell him, "he's made some kind of serum that forces my DNA to change. My body heals almost as fast as hers, now."

His eyes light up with a fury I didn't think possible. He rounds on me, snarling.

"He's trying to make another Tomorrow Girl?!"

I nod. He slaps a hand to his head.

"Of course. When he said he was part of the Project back in the day, we should have known."

"It's not just that. He wants everyone to be like her."

His brow furrows.

"What nonsense are you spouting now?"

I buckle down, ready for his outburst.

"He wants to create a vaccine. A treatment that will make everyone immortal. That's why he's testing on me. He's trying to figure out the process so he can sell it and make a fortune."

His eyes widen, and I can almost see the cogs turning in his head. He has the same expression that I must have had back at Lockless House, wrapped in Marcus' embrace. Piecing together all the signs we willingly ignored, all the red flags we dismissed because the end result was worth it. And, just like me, his final result is rage.

Shane grabs the old wooden chair and flings it aside, smashing it to splinters. He steps closer and for a moment, I suspect I've gone too far - but he pulls back at the last moment, eyeing me carefully.

"So, what? You expect me to save you."

I swallow hard.

"I know you hate me. That's fair. But if he's allowed to continue, either he'll kill me or he'll spread immortality throughout the world like a virus. And neither of us will have a say in which path he takes. If you don't untie me, we both lose."

He glares at me.

"This isn't personal, Reya," he snarls, "it's not your fault you're a crime against nature. You didn't ask to be born a freak. I want you dead because of what you are, not who you are. As a person – if I met a person like you –"

I can't resist the question.

"If I had been human, do you think you could have grown to care about me?"

His expression wavers, and he tears his gaze from mine.

"I'll be back."

Shane slips into my cell after dark.

I snap awake as the door opens – and for the briefest of moments, I'm convinced the Project has come for me. But then I hear his heavy footsteps, and my heart sinks. Fine. I'll make do.

I sit up.

"Didn't think I'd see you again."

"Shut up," he hisses, "we don't have long before the guards get back."

I stand, pulling my hoodie on. The material has developed that awful, crunchy texture that only bloodstains can cause, but it's all I've got. I rake a hand through my hair, wondering how long it's been since I brushed it. Shane watches me with blank eyes, biting his lip like he's deep in thought.

"So," I breathe, "what changed your mind?"

His jaw tightens.

"Come on."

He pushes open the cell door.

"You'd better be able to walk, because I'm not carrying you."

I stare into the darkness and swallow hard.

"Do you have a plan?" I ask fearfully. Shane isn't the brightest bulb, and I'm not sure how much he'll know about Marcus' defences. He fires me a stern look.

"Everything's locked down tight. No way in or out without an approved handprint."

His gaze drops to my hand and I nod.

"Right. I can get us out. Just get me to a security terminal and I'll shut down all of his defences and unlock all the doors. I should have maximum clearance, with any luck, so I can keep everything unlocked for at least a day. We can walk right out without triggering any alarms."

"Good," he mutters, "and once we're out, I'll put a bullet in your head."

He strides away, but I pause.

"W-wait, what?"

"You didn't really think I'd changed my mind about you," he says, "have you forgotten everything you've done to me? You broke my nose – twice – humiliated me, threatened me with a gun. All things considered, I'm granting you a mercy by offering you a quick death."

We delve into the darkness.

"I thought you were seeing past all that," I say.

He scoffs.

"No. Look, none of us signed up for this. As far as I'm concerned, a gunshot will be more than enough to take care of you. I'm not helping that guy screw around anymore. So I'll make it quick and painless."

He glances back, wrinkling his nose at me.

"It's more than you deserve."

I give a solemn nod to keep him calm, but I'm already hatching a plan. Use Shane to get out, then escape. If it comes down to a fight with Shane, I'm confident I can handle it.

I approach the nearest security console and scan my hand. It lets out a confirmatory beep and briefly, I wonder why I still have full access. I'd have thought Marcus would remove it, if he could. But then, maybe he can't. Maybe Jonah was the only one with full, unfettered permissions and without him, there's no changing the setup.

I rest my fingers on the keyboard and realise with a start that I know what I'm doing. Somehow, all the codes Jonah taught me are still there, somewhere deep in my memory.

I disable the security bit by bit, locking it down for 24 hours. No door locks. No alarms. No scanners. Just an open building with free access – the ability to walk in and out, unbothered.

Beside me, Shane stands impatiently, his breathing low.

"Hurry up," he growls. I ignore him.

I stare at the terminal again, stomach churning. Once I move away, Shane will finish me. After all, then he'll be free to walk away without being trapped. I'll need to take him out first.

"Are you done yet?" he hisses, reaching for my arm. I spin on the spot and for a long moment we stare at one another, the lab deathly silent aside from our agitated breathing.

"Shane," I breathe, "think about this. Let's leave together, instead. Everything will be okay."

His brow furrows and he shakes his head.

"I can't let you walk out of here alive, Reya. I'm sorry."

My chest tightens.

"I'm sorry, too."

And I drive my fist into his nose.

He yelps and leaps back, cursing at the top of his lungs as blood gushes down his shirt. I jump aside.

"I'm really, really sorry," I tell him. And then I'm running, darting from the lab and into the labyrinth of hallways.

As I run, I expect to tire. But adrenaline urges me on, crackling down my legs like electricity. Dimly, I hear Shane bellow for help. Doors open around me. People call out. Someone steps in front of me and I run faster, throwing them aside.

Suddenly, I realise the alarms aren't blaring. Nobody's tracking me. The security is down, and it seems to be staying down.

Triumph fills my chest as I bolt towards the exit, mapping the lab out in my head. Another two left turns, a right, a flight of stairs – and there's an emergency exit. It should be open, with luck.

For a moment, all I hear is the pounding of my feet on the concrete floor, and the sound of my own heart pounding in my ears. I'm so close.

But then someone grabs me, twists me – and then Marcus is on me, pushing down with his entire body weight. One hand grabs my hair, yanking my head up. The other locks itself around my throat, forcing me to remain still. When he speaks, I can almost feel his lips against my ear.

"Now now, Reya. I did tell you not to misbehave."

My bindings are tighter than ever. They squeeze my wrists painfully, turning my fingertips purple.

Marcus stands in front of me, watching coldly.

"I'm impressed, Reya. Sowing dissention amongst the Mortalists like that. It was an excellent bit of manipulation. You really do take after me."

I roll my eyes.

"God, you're a psycho."

His eyes glitter.

"Yet another way you take after me."

He steps closer, reaching for my face – and I launch myself forward. It's not enough to pull myself from the chair, but I'm able to sink my teeth into his hand. Marcus yelps and pulls away, striking me hard across the mouth.

"Will you just obey me?!" he shrieks, his calm exterior momentarily cracking.

"Sorry," I retort through the pain, "I'm not very good at doing as I'm told."

I allow my lip to curl and he snorts.

"The rules have changed, Reya. You won't be retreating to your cell anymore. You will stay here, tied up, 24-7. The Mortalists won't come near you. You will either be alone, or with me. That's it."

For a brief moment, I panic.

I've always been able to fight my way out. Even when things seemed hopeless, it was always my best bet. But now? Fighting isn't an option. All I have are my words.

I've never been good with words.

"Just let me go, Marcus."

"Don't you understand?" he sighs, "you have nowhere else to go. The Project aren't coming for you, and why would they? You've been a disappointment since the beginning. They gave up on you. They *replaced* you. What makes you think they want you back?"

I close my eyes, trying to block out his words. I want to believe him. He's validating every fear I've ever had; every time I've thought that they must hate me for not being good enough. Marcus' words are all the validation I need to prove that the terrible thoughts in my head are real.

Then, I remember Alya. How she stared me down in the Dome, how she challenged me.

'Has anyone ever actually told you that you're useless?'

I close my eyes.

I don't know what to think anymore. I don't understand.

"Reya."

My head snaps up.

"Rene?"

The lab is silent for a moment, but I strain my ears, desperate to hear it again. Because that was Rene's voice. I'd know it anywhere.

Marcus' expression has changed, too. He stares up at the ceiling, grimacing.

When Rene's voice comes again, it's tinny – and I realise that he's using the emergency speakers. I stare up at the closest one, my head spinning.

"The people who invaded Lockless House were well prepared," Rene says, his voice calm.

I stare even harder, confused.

"They expected us to resist them. They expected the cops would show up. They had plans for all of that. Do you know what they didn't expect? You. Well, you and Alya."

My mouth falls open. I should probably cry out or formulate some kind of sentence, but my throat is suddenly tight. Some part of me honestly thought I'd never heard Rene's voice again.

"Keep fighting," he tells me, "and don't listen to a word that bastard tells you. Reya, you are so much stronger than you give yourself credit for. And you are so much more important than you could ever imagine."

Something hot pricks the back of my eyes. Marcus fires me a smug look, then strides over to the nearest console. I realise with a start that he's about to cut off Rene's message. A million words fill my head, a thousand things I want to tell him, but nothing comes out. Luckily, Rene keeps talking.

"Hold on, Reya. We're coming for you."

Twenty-Two

As Rene's message fades, an uncomfortable silence fills the lab. Marcus fixes me in his gaze, and I half expect him to try and twist Rene's words. To convince me that he meant something else, something worse. But he doesn't. And even if he did, it wouldn't bother me.

My chest fills with a familiar warmth, something that I haven't felt in years. It's accompanied by ferocious triumph and a vicious sense of pride. Goddamn, Rene.

So when I lift my gaze to meet Marcus', I'm grinning from ear to ear.

"They're coming for me. Do you know what that means?"

"It means..."

"It means," I interrupt, "that they're going to untie me. And when that happens, I'm going to beat your ass into the next century. Just you wait, Marcus. By the time I'm done with you, you'll wish that Jonah had beaten you to death eighteen years ago."

He stares at me for a long moment. I can't tell if he's taking my threats seriously, but there's something akin to fear shifting in his eyes. Apparently, reality is dawning on him.

The Project are coming for me. And thanks to my escape attempt, every door in Safehouse 17 will be unlocked for several more hours.

He marches from the room, his head down, and as the door closes behind him, I hear barked orders. Gather weapons. Prepare for an attack.

I listen to the chaos unfolding, slightly breathless.

Rene's message means I'm getting out of here.

Rene's message means they care about me.

I let out a small cheer, more to myself than anyone else.

Rene's message means Alya was right.

Alarms blare throughout the lab, and the world flashes red around me. I grin, lifting my head, and wait for the sound of incoming footsteps. They're on their way. I just know it.

I wait for several minutes, listening hard. I hear shouting, the occasional gunshot – and sirens. Lots and lots of sirens. I wonder how the Project managed to get the cops involved. I'm not human, so this technically isn't a hostage situation. At most it's theft, considering that I'm legally considered a business asset. Perhaps it's to do with Jonah's death. Or maybe the shooting. Or perhaps the car chase. Either way, it sounds like they've found some kind of loophole.

After a while things go quiet, and I start to get antsy. The sounds of gunfire have long since stopped, so it seems like things have ended peacefully – either that, or it's a standoff. But most Mortalists seem to be ordinary people, not crime lords or trained assassins. I doubt many of them would kill a cop over their beliefs.

After several more minutes, fear sets in. Most Mortalists wouldn't dare shoot a cop. But plenty would shoot someone from the Project. I strain at my binds again. I tug at them until my skin is rubbed raw, then watch as my skin heals.

It's happening faster than ever, now. I don't think to count the seconds – my mind is racing too fast – but it's scarily quick. I watch in silence as the skin knits itself together, stretching over the wound and leaving only flawless skin behind.

Odd. That initial feeling of exhilaration has gone. There's no joy in seeing my body heal the way it was always meant to. This may have been the original plan, but it doesn't feel right anymore. I think about the future; about the impossible, endless future Alya is facing. The same future I grew up thinking that I would have to face. I close my eyes.

    Does any part of me still want to be immortal?

    Did any part of me *ever* want to be immortal?

    This sure as hell doesn't feel like destiny.

    Just as I'm about to start freaking out, the lab door slams open.

    Footsteps fly towards me. Warm hands cup my cheeks.

    "Reya! Reya, can you hear me?"

    Rene's voice is panicked, desperate. Unlike anything I've heard from him before. Unlike his anger, his indifference, his thinly-veiled concern. He pushes my hair from my face, examining me closely. Our eyes meet and I open my mouth, then close it, unsure what to say.

    He glances at my bloodied binds and frowns.

    "Hold on, I'll get you out of there."

    I sit quietly as he removes the rope, then lower my hands into my lap. A million emotions well in my chest – fear, anger, confusion, relief. They form a blockade in my throat, making it impossible to talk. I don't know which emotion to express first.

    "Reya. Talk to me. Are you alright?"

    And he reaches out, taking my hand softly. In an instant, memories consume my thoughts.

    Rene raising me, teaching me, scolding me, worrying over me. Rene loving me.

    Instinct takes over. I heave myself into his arms, burying my face against his shoulder. His scent fills my head; cleaning solution and coffee, tinged with sweat from exertion. I tighten my grip, ignoring the way my hands quake. Several seconds pass before he returns the embrace – and when he does, I'm happier than I've been in years.

    "You're alive," I chuckle. He reaches up, stroking my hair.

    "*That's* your concern?"

    I pull back, meeting his tired eyes.

    "I can't believe you came after me."

    He looks at me like I've just grown a second head.

    "Of course we did," he says, like it's the most obvious thing in the world, "did you honestly think we'd abandon you?"

I give a weak smile.

"I guess I had my doubts."

For a moment, I take him in.

Rene wears civilian clothing. It's the first time in years I've seen him out of a lab coat or suit. His glasses are skewed. He looks like he hasn't washed his hair or shaved in days. I look down, my eyes drawn to his oddly bulky midsection. I reach out and my fingers meet something soft. Bandages. Of course. Nobody gets over a gunshot that quickly. He's injured, and he still came to get me.

Rene fires me a worried look.

"How does your body feel?"

I stand and he reaches out for me, holding my arm tightly as though he expects me to fall.

"I'm okay," I tell him. I must sound a little subdued, because his expression changes.

"Are you still healing?"

I hesitate and his grip on my arm tightens.

"Yes," I admit, "it's probably on par with Alya at this point. Though Marcus hadn't tested it yet."

"He hasn't?"

"No. I don't really want to think about it."

I glance back at the testing chair and frown. The board where my back rested is stained with brown, days-old blood. I spot my ugly yellow hoodie on a nearby chair and pull it on, more out of habit than anything. On a nearby countertop, I spot my phone and taser, and idly scoop them both into my pockets. Rene clears his throat.

"You're not okay, are you?"

"Where are the others?" I ask, ignoring his comment.

"Downstairs, with the police. They're arresting the Mortalists."

"How did you get the cops involved? This isn't a kidnapping, legally speaking."

"Well," he says, "it turns out that as far as 'business assets' go, the first artificial human is considered a pretty valuable commodity. They weren't able to help with a kidnapping, but once we told them that you were worth a few billion dollars, they changed their tune. The entire lower floors have been locked down."

"What about Marcus?"

His face falls.

"He didn't leave the Safehouse, but they haven't arrested him yet, either."

"So he's still running around."

His lips tighten into a thin line – and he reaches out, wrapping an arm around my shoulders.

"Come on. We need to get you out of here."

My stomach tightens.

"No, something's wrong. It's too easy."

I whip around, eyes skirting the lab. A trap. This has to be a trap.

"Marcus wouldn't just hide somewhere and hope he doesn't get caught," I say, "he heard your warning. He knew you were coming. He has a plan."

"If he did, he'd have done something by now."

I try to calm my racing heart, telling it that Rene's probably right, but it just pumps harder.

"We need to get out of here," I bark, "now!"

"Reya, calm down. It's okay."

He pulls a walkie talkie from the waistband of his jeans and puts it to his lips.

"Neil, I need you to come and get Reya. Something's not right."

"I'm fine!" I tell him breathlessly. He watches me with concerned eyes, only glancing down when Neil's voice burns across the line, agreeing. My fear briefly turns to anger and I step closer, gripping his sleeve.

"Please, Rene. Let's go. Before he tries something. He'll taken any opportunity to separate us and hurt whoever he can get his hands on."

"We have a van outside," he reassures me, "Neil will take you out and make sure you're okay. The rest of us will follow."

"No. No, we can't stay here..."

"Reya."

"Don't underestimate him, Rene! We can't give him a chance to hurt us."

He draws his hand back, frowning – then turns as Neil enters the lab. Just like Rene, Neil wears street clothes; a striped jumper and jeans a tad too short for his long legs.

I open my mouth but before I can speak Neil scoops me into his arms, flinging me over his shoulder with shocking ease. He mutters an apology and glances at Rene, who nods.

"Take her outside. I'm going to try to figure out what he's been doing to her."

"But..."

"The more we know about his work, the better. I'll be out soon. Hurry."

I stare at the lab door, my arms wrapped tightly around Neil's neck. I should object to this. I have to pull away and insist that Rene come with us. I have to protect him from Marcus.

But I can't. My body is momentarily out of my control. It clings to Neil for dear life, my heart racing like I've just run a marathon. There's something comforting in his warmth, and the delicacy with which he holds me. I curl tighter against him, unable to pull away.

Rene and Neil exchange a few words and we head from the room, leaving Rene alone in the lab. Neil doesn't speak as we run down the metallic hallways; his breathing is calm and even, his face carefully indifferent. It's hard to tell if he's trying to seem calm to keep me from panicking, or if he really is unbothered, but I appreciate the sudden calm.

My eyes slip shut for a moment, and it's suddenly hard to open them again. When I do, my vision is blurred and faded, like I'm seeing through my lashes. Briefly, I wonder how long it's been since I last slept. Not the hazy, uneasy sleep I've experienced since being here. Real sleep. It's been a while since I felt safe enough to really rest.

I pull my eyes open again, my blurry vision settling on a shadow in the hallway. The figure stands motionless, watching Neil's back as we run. Despite my exhaustion, I recognise them.

Marcus watches us leave in stony silence, both hands curled into fists. I blink hard, hoping to clear my vision, but when I look again he's gone, turned back towards the lab.

Towards Rene.

Something in the back of my head panics at the thought, but I can no longer focus. My eyes slip shut again, and I lean deeply into Neil's shoulder, letting sleep take me.

Twenty-Three

I wake to the sound of sirens.

Slowly, sensation returns to my body. I'm stretched out in the back of a van, someone's worn coat placed over me. I inhale deeply, my nose filling with the stench of sweat and smoke. Dimly, I remember my makeshift cell. I remember Rene charging into the lab. I remember Marcus standing in the hallway, watching Neil carry me to safety.

I sit up.

"You shouldn't be moving around."

I lift my head. Alya sits beside me in the back of the van. She looks terrible. Dirty streaks mar her pretty face, and her huge eyes seem even bigger and whiter in the darkness.

"Do..."

She hiccups.

"Do you remember me?" she whispers. I tilt my head.

"You're kind of hard to forget."

Relief floods her features and she leans closer, plucking at my sleeve.

"You fell asleep. Neil hoped it was just exhaustion, but he asked me to watch you, just in case. Do you feel okay now?"

I give myself a brief once over and nod.

"He said you weren't injured," Alya tells me, "but I know they've been hurting you."

"I'm fine," I say, "it's already healed."

Her brow furrows, but she stays silent. She tenses, as though waiting for me to launch myself at her. I reach out, planting a hand on her head and chuckling.

"Calm down, will you? It's alright."

Her lip wobbles.

"He took you."

Her voice is quiet now, barely above a whisper. Her eyes glisten.

"You were gone for so long. We saw everything on the video feed."

My heart sinks.

"The Project let you see that?"

She gives a tearful nod and I lean closer, pulling her into a half-embrace.

"I'm sorry. I didn't mean to scare you."

Her fingertips dig into my shoulder.

"Were you scared?" she squeaks.

I swallow the hard lump in my throat.

"...Yeah."

When I finally pull back, my stomach churns.

"Where are the others?" I ask.

She frowns.

"Outside. They shut the door and told me to wait for you to wake up."

I kick the door open, and my heart starts racing.

Neil and Sandra stand outside the van, their backs turned. They stare up at Safehouse 17 – which has erupted into a fiery blaze. White-hot flames fill its windows, pouring from the exits and reaching up to the heavens. Our precious Safehouse has become a burning beacon, glowing in the darkness.

I step forward, my nose filled with the stench of smoke. I see shadows racing from the few remaining doors, their heads held low to avoid the worst of the smoke. Mortalists, fleeing for their lives.

"What happened?!" I gasp.

Sandra whips round to face me, and her eyes are just like Alya's. Wide, glossy, terrified – and filled with worry.

"Reya, you're awake."

Neil glances over too, his expression softening in a way I've never seen from him before.

"Go inside," he tells me, "you need rest."

"What happened?" I ask again, firmer this time. Neil looks away but Sandra reaches for my hand, squeezing it.

"We were waiting here when Neil brought you out. We'd planned to check you over and then wait for everything to be brought under control, but then..."

"Everything started burning."

She gives a tearful nod.

"Marcus started a fire. I'm not sure how, but judging by the stench, I'd say he set fire to some of the lab's more... dangerous chemicals."

"Did everyone get out okay?" I ask.

"Most of the Project got out straight away," she nods, "they were in the lower levels with the police. When the fire broke out, they were able to evacuate."

Strange. Her words sound calm enough – but there's something in the way she shuffles, in how she bites her lip as she speaks, that makes it clear she's lying. I step past Neil, out into the open, and search the space around us. I spot some of the non-core Project members dotted around, staring at the burning building with wide eyes.

When I realise who's missing, my heart feels like it's stopped.

"Where's Rene?"

Silence. I turn around. Neil lowers his head, avoiding my gaze. Sandra's muttering with Alya, updating her on the situation. My anger grows.

"Where the fuck is Rene?!"

"He was in the lab," Neil confesses, "and we think... Marcus went after him."

"He's still in there?"

I stare back at the burning building, briefly overwhelmed by terror.

I've faced death enough times. I've seen others face it, too. Hell, I watched Jonah die right in front of me. Death isn't some unfamiliar concept in my mind. But for some reason, the thought of losing Rene – of anything happening to him – is unthinkable.

Alya steps up beside me, touching my arm.

"It's just fire. I can go in and get him out safely."

"What about Marcus?" I ask her, "you're damn tough, but you can't fight him."

She purses her lips, then fires me a smile.

"So, just like at Lockless House, right?"

"Huh?"

She gazes up at me, her pale eyes glowing gold in the firelight.

"We can do this if we work together," she says softly.

"But..."

"You're not just going to stand here while Rene is in danger," she tells me, "we both know that. So let's skip the nonsense. Let's do this together, instead."

I open my mouth to refuse, to insist that she stay here, but something stops me.

This isn't some random person offering to risk their life. It's Alya.

Who better to run into certain death with than the Tomorrow Girl herself?

"Alright, Tomorrow," I grin, "let's do this."

A hand locks around my wrist. Sandra's voice breaks as she shouts over the chaos.

"Are you crazy? Neither one of you is going in there!"

"But Sandra..."

"No!" she screams, her hands tightening on our arms, "we've almost lost both of you too many times! For once, just do as you're told and stay safe!"

"What about Rene?" I ask her. Her face creases.

"None of us want Rene to get hurt. But he signed up for this. We all did. You two are the only ones who didn't agree to any of this."

Tears stream down her cheeks. I ease her hand from my arm.

"Rene's hurt. He's in no state for a fight."

"Rene went in there to save you! You'd undermine that by going back in!"

"I'm sorry, Sandra," I tell her, "I screwed up. I get that. I'll do my best to make amends later, but right now I have to make sure nobody else dies trying to fix my mistakes."

She moves to object but Neil steps closer, fixing his gaze on Alya.

"Protect each other."

She nods, grabbing my hand – and in an instant, we're running.

We burst through the main entrance, which is miraculously still clear. Silhouettes race past, screaming at the top of their lungs, desperate to escape the flames. I spot a familiar shadow and tackle it, pinning them against the ash-smeared tiles.

Shane coughs hard, glaring up at me.

"Where is Rene?" I shout, "where is he?"

"Get the hell off me!"

"He's human and he doesn't deserve to die! Tell me where he is, Shane!" I loosen my grip.

"Please. Please, *please* tell me..."

His glare intensifies and I feel something catch in my throat.

"If you ever felt anything for me, then please. Just tell me where he is."

He pushes me away and scowls, averting his eyes.

"Top floor. With that psychopath."

"Thank you," I breathe. He doesn't respond; just speeds away. Alya leans down beside me.

"You know this place better than I do. How do we get upstairs?"

"Follow me," I tell her.

As we race upstairs, my head spins.

I don't have a plan. I can't even begin to think of one.

What if they're fighting?

What if they're trapped?

What if the fight's already over, and Rene is-

Terror sucks the air from my lungs and I slow to a stop, forcing the thought from my mind. I don't realise I'm coughing until Alya grasps my arm.

"Is it the smoke?" she asks. I nod, fighting to ignore the sudden scratchiness in my throat. Evidently, I'm not quite like Alya. I still need to breathe.

"Hurry," I say. She nods and runs ahead, leaving me to follow.

We burst into the secondary lab, and fear fills my chest.

The lab is ablaze. Broken furniture and spilled chemicals burn around a small clearing – and in the middle, bloodied but still fighting, are Rene and Marcus.

My eyes settle on Rene and for a moment, all I can do is stare. He's got a black eye and a broken shoulder, at the very least. Several teeth are missing. Untold pain fills his eyes. A quick glance at Marcus tells me that Rene is losing. Of course he's losing. You don't go from being shot in the stomach to being fighting fit in a week.

Rene slumps to the ground, overwhelmed by exhaustion, and Alya grabs my arm.

"You get Rene out of here."

"Not a chance," I snap.

"But the smoke..."

"I'm not letting him hurt you too. Save Rene first, then come back for me."

Before she can answer I hurtle at Marcus, blood pumping hotter than ever. Because he's stepping closer to Rene, tugging a gun from his pocket, his expression consumed by arrogance and victory. I consider his viewpoint for a moment, and realise how significant this is for him. He blames Rene for everything. For his failures, his weakness, his losses.

But Rene isn't to blame for his problems, just like Alya isn't to blame for mine. We both need to take responsibility.

He clicks off the safety and I plough into him, sending us both crashing to the ground.

"Reya?"

Rene's voice is terrifyingly weak. Dimly, I hear Alya explain what's going on, Rene objecting, and sternly being told to follow her. I'd love to look up and greet him, to thank him for the rescue and apologise for this whole mess; but I daren't tear my eyes from Marcus' face.

I'm crouching over him, my nose inches from his. His eyes roll as fury, confusion, and bloodlust mix into something terrifying. In spite of myself, I feel a flicker of conflict.

This man has hurt me. He's hurt the people I love. Why does fighting him feel wrong?

He grabs my arms and twists, flinging me aside with ease. I collide with a lab stool and pain jolts up my spine – but in an instant it's gone, replaced by a rush of fear and adrenaline.

He stands. His hulking figure is eerily silhouetted by the fire, his eyes glowing from the flames. I look around for Rene and Alya – but they're already gone. Good.

I turn back to Marcus, recalling all the times Rene told me to use my words rather than my fists. If we go toe to toe, I may lose on size alone. I doubt my words can sway him, but I have to try.

So I raise my hands in mock surrender, taking a deliberate step back.

"We need to get out of here, Marcus."

"You ungrateful little freak."

His voice is full of venom, sending shivers up my spine.

"I gave you everything," he spits, "you wanted to be immortal? Fine. Our goals aligned. We could have helped each other. But you had to ruin everything."

I swallow hard.

"I thought it would make them happy if I changed. But it didn't. I had it all wrong."

"They say a few nice words and you change your mind," he says, "meanwhile, I told you everything you wanted to hear. I've worked hard to win you round, and you walk away the first chance you get."

My heart sinks. Why do I feel bad? Why does this feel like some grand act of betrayal? I silence the thoughts. The Project was right. He *is* in my head.

I look up at him, at the rage in his eyes, and I wonder if I'm in his head, too.

"It sucks, right?"

He glares, but I step closer.

"I think that's why I liked you. You know what it's like to be overshadowed. To be denied something that's rightfully yours. It really, really sucks."

He doesn't respond, but I see his shoulders relax a little. I lower my hands.

"This partnership started because I felt inferior to Alya and you felt inferior to Rene. We both wanted what they had, what was promised to us. But we're not them. After everything that's happened, would either of us really be happy if we got what we wanted? Or would we just find something else to be angry about?"

I sigh, ignoring the scratchiness in my throat.

"I'm sick of being angry, and I know you are too. We're better than this. We can..."

"Oh, shut up."

He rolls his eyes theatrically.

"You still think this is about the Project Head role? I moved past that years ago."

"Then what..."

"It's about creating a grand legacy, and hurting Rene Mathis as much as possible along the way."

My heart sinks.

"What about me?"

"What *about* you?" he asks coldly.

I set my jaw, pushing my hurt feelings aside. So he didn't care about me. I can deal with that, can't I? Shane did the same thing. Countless strangers have done the same thing. That makes him no different from Shane – from the thugs I've fought a hundred times.

So when he pulls back his hand and curls it into a fist, I'm ready.

I pull up both arms, guarding my face. He hits my wrists and reels back to try again.

Sweat streams from my face as I block each blow, moving as lightly as I can in the unimaginable heat. With each movement, I can almost hear Jonah in my ear.

Suddenly, I'm back at Lockless House. Jonah paces the length of the gym, his hands curled into fists as he gives me pointers. I let slip a move learned from street fighting and he scolds me. He corrects my stance, catches my fist, and chuckles. His lips part, and I just know that he's about to tell me another story about his boxing years. For a moment, I wish I could delve deeper into the memory – but then Marcus flings me aside, and I snap back to reality.

I push up onto my elbows, confused. Even with his size advantage, I shouldn't be losing this badly.

He smirks.

"Street fighting is rather easy to memorise, Reya, and I've had plenty of opportunity to watch you."

My chest tightens. Of course. He was committed to stalking me for 18 years; why wouldn't he figure out my moves – which means I can't win this fight.

I haul myself to my feet and promptly cough. The smoke is thicker now, draping the room in a charcoal haze. It's not safe here. Briefly, I weigh up my options. I can't reason with him. I can't fight him off – at least, not before the smoke kills us both. The thought of defeat weighs heavily on my chest, but I push it aside. I can't resolve this, as much as I may want to. I have to run.

I twist on the spot, trying to locate the door – and as he lurches towards me, I pick a direction and start sprinting.

I hit a wall first, colliding with another chair, and dimly, I hear him. Half-laughing, half-coughing. There's no way he thinks we're making it out of here. Not if we keep fighting. But perhaps that's his plan. He knows the cops won't let him go after all that's happened; but at least it'll hurt the Project if we die together.

He hurtles towards me and I dart aside, taking off at full speed. Here, I have the advantage; I'm smaller than him, faster than him, and apparently handling the smoke a little better. Nevertheless he crashes after me, a hulking mass of muscles and strangled, choking roars. I find some stairs and climb them, hoping to evade him and work my way back down to the entrance. He follows, screeching some kind of threat – but the smoke catches in his throat and he doubles over, straining to gather his composure. I keep running.

My hands find the bar of a fire door and I fling it open, barrelling out onto the roof of Safehouse 17. Flames lick the sides of the building, and I realise that they're bursting from the now-shattered windows. My heart pounds. I don't know if there's a way down from here.

I shake my head, clearing it with what little fresh air I can get. My nose and throat feel thick, but at least I can breathe. I give myself a once-over; no injuries.

I strain my ears, praying that I'll hear something hopeful. Incoming sirens of a fire engine, perhaps, or maybe the Project's voices. But I'm too high up. Here, there's nothing but the stench of smoke and the deafening crackle of the flames.

I search my pockets, delving into the bloodstained remains of my mustard hoodie. I'm sure I grabbed it – yes! My hand hits something solid, and I pull out Sandra's taser. I turn it over in my hands, marvelling at the smooth plastic. I tap the button and it crackles. Perfect.

Briefly, I wonder why Marcus didn't dispose of it. He likely thought I'd never get hold of it. Perhaps he figured he was deep enough in my psyche that I wouldn't dream of using it on him.

My grip tightens on the device.

As if on cue the roof access bursts open, and a flurry of rage and strained coughs erupts onto the roof. Marcus leans heavily on the railing, choking up a lungful of ash. His entire body is stained black. The back of his lab coat glows orange, smouldering against his skin. He barely seems to notice. Instead, he turns his attention to me. His gaze drops to my hand.

I point the device at him and let out a long breath.

"You're going to tell me how to get off this roof, or I'm going to use this and leave you here."

Even as the words slip out, I know I don't mean them. I'm more than willing to hurt him to survive; but I like to think I wouldn't leave someone to burn. I adjust my grip on the taser and scowl.

Please, don't test whether I would leave you to burn.

His lips twitch – and before I can react, he launches himself at me. I kick him away with all my strength, raising the taser – but he leaps forward again and I'm forced to dodge, flinging myself aside to avoid his throttle-hungry hands.

Where has the intelligence gone? What about the charm?

He lets out a roar of anger and I leap away from him, my heart thumping frantically in my chest.

This isn't the Marcus I know. This is a man with all his culture and psychopathy stripped away. Another furious, unthinking thug. I tuck the taser into my pocket and crack my knuckles.

I know how to handle thugs.

So when he heaves himself at me again, I block his blow and step back, circling him on light toes. Jonah's voice fills my head, instructing me.

Jab. Uppercut. Block.

I'm not doing it right. I know that much. I never clicked with boxing, preferring to just punch blindly and hope for the best. But Jonah's lessons are still in there somewhere, and I hear him as clearly as if he were standing behind me, coaching me on.

Marcus staggers, confused by the sudden change – and I whip out the taser, pushing it hard against his chest. He stiffens and falls to the floor, breathing hard.

"Just... just take a minute, will you?" I snap. Sweat streams from my head, a result of exertion and the immense heat. The fire is building, catching the old wooden pallets on the rooftop and starting to spread. I glance at the roof access, but it's already been consumed.

There's no way down.

Marcus stands, but his will to fight is clearly faltering. He slumps forward, his face slick with sweat, his brow furrowed from the effort required to stay standing. His fingers still twitch from the shock.

"You little..."

"Shut up, will you?" I snap, "we're trapped up here!"

His eyes briefly widen, a flash of white in his soot-stained face, and I wonder if I've finally got through to him. I turn away, searching for an escape route – and he grabs my arms.

"-hey!"

We crash to the ground, Marcus looming over me as I twist desperately beneath him.

"We don't have time for this," I hiss, "you need to help me figure out…"

His hands tighten enough to hurt.

"There's no time, Marcus!" I screech, "if you keep this up we'll both burn!"

He twists my arms and I feel a flood of pain as the muscles tear. I growl. I curl up then kick, embedding my feet in his stomach. His hands loosen and I kick him again, but harder this time. As hard as I possibly can. Hard enough to make my thighs to burn from the effort.

He falls back. I stand, rounding on him – and freeze.

He sits up, lit up by the red glow of the flames that surround him.

For a moment, he doesn't notice the flames licking at his sleeves. He stands, grotesquely silhouetted by the fire, seemingly oblivious to the fact he's now alight. I step back, slapping my hands over my mouth.

His eyes widen, and then all I hear are screams.

Instinct compels me to look away but I fight it, watching as the orange flames consume Marcus' body. The screams cease suddenly as the fire tears at his throat, silencing him. He flails helplessly, aimlessly, like he knows there's nothing he can do to save himself. Something hot streams down my face and I tell myself it's just the smoke. That I don't feel anything for the man dying in front of me. That my heart isn't breaking a little.

And then he's gone, his body withering in the amber flames.

For a moment, I want to run over to him. To apologise, to explain that I didn't want this, that I just needed him to stop. To try and save him, even if it's impossible. To recover whatever's left of his corpse. To do something. *Anything.*

Then Jonah's face fills my mind and I force myself to turn away, leaving the flames to consume every last trace of Marcus' empty shell.

Twenty-Four

I step up to the edge of the building – one of the few spots not yet consumed by fire – and peer down. From here, there's a clear view of the area surrounding Safehouse 17. Someone actually has summoned firefighters; I can see them unreeling massive lengths of hose from their truck. What good they think that'll do, I'm not entirely sure.

The rest of the surrounding area is sparsely populated. Small groups of people stand around idly, watching the Safehouse burn. I'm too high up to recognise them. They could be Mortalists, or cops, or Project staff. Hell, they could just be random passers by who've stopped, curious as to the source of all the sirens.

I get a whiff of burning flesh and bury my nose in the sleeve of my hoodie. It doesn't help; the fabric stinks of blood and Marcus, sending my senses into overdrive.

I stand at the edge of the roof, the weight of my situation finally hitting me. I locate the mental walls that appeared when Jonah died and mimic them, blocking out the horror of Marcus' death until it seems like a scene from a movie I only half-watched. I don't have time for trauma. Not if I want to survive.

I wave my arms overhead, then hesitate. Can they even see me through the smoke? Nobody seems to notice me. But they have to have heard Marcus' screams, right? They know someone's up here.

The fire builds behind me, pushing me closer to the edge, and my heart sinks. Even if they did notice, they're not going to reach me before the flames do.

I glance over the edge again. My body's still healing – could it fix the damage if I jumped? Fear tells me no, that the exertion needed to heal would kill me if the fall didn't.

Are those my only choices? Burn to a crisp or pancake myself?

"Reya...!"

I pause, certain I just heard my name.

"Re...ya!"

There it is again. Faint, distant, like a scream heard across a football field. This time, I recognise the voice. I spin on the spot, desperate to find the source of the sound.

"Damnit, Alya," I hiss, "you'd better not have come back for me."

I stare at the roof access, which was just blocked entirely by flame – but now the doors are open, a slender shadow diving through the fire. Alya rolls to the ground, slapping madly at the scorches on her sleeves. Her eyes search the roof for me, her breathing so loud and panicked that I can hear it over the crackling of the flames.

When her gaze finally lands on me, she sighs.

"You're still alive, then," she says, her voice saccharine sweet.

I stare blankly at her. Did she really come back for me? Through the flames, past all that danger? My lips part. I want to call her an idiot for risking herself like this. But then she steps closer, and my resistance breaks.

"A-Alya...?"

She races over, gripping my arms.

"Where is he? Where's Marcus?"

My head dips, and I fire a guilty look at the flames. She follows my gaze and promptly pales.

"He... he went into the fire. D-did you...?"

"I didn't want to," I tell her, my voice cracking, "he was going to kill me if I didn't."

"Shh, it's okay. You did what you had to do."

She sounds so sure. I take a moment to ignore the fire and focus on my little sister's voice. She's always been so sheltered. This is all new for her, all scary. How can she be smiling like that? How can she be so confident when I'm falling apart?

I pull her to my chest, breathing hard. How could I have ever blamed Alya for my problems? How could I have ever resented her? She can have the word 'amazing'. It's perfect for her.

"Reya," she says, "we need to get off this roof."

I look up. The roof access has once more been consumed by flames, the hallway inside glowing red. Even if Alya were able to go back that way, I couldn't. I pull away, fighting to draw my face into a smile.

"There's no way down," I croak, "unless you want to jump."

She stares at me for a long moment, embers glowing in the air around her.

"Do... do you think you can survive the fall?" she asks in a horrified whisper. I shake my head sadly.

"I don't think so. But you can."

"I'm not leaving you."

"Listen, if I have to throw you off this roof myself, I will," I start – but she puts a hand to my mouth, silencing me. She fixes me with a stern look.

"No. We're not doing this. Nothing is gained by leaving you to burn to death. We came all this way to save you and I am *not* leaving without you."

She thinks for a moment, then nods.

"Let's fall together. I can catch you and cushion your fall. Just like I did before, with the platform."

I stare. Catch me? No way. Even if she managed to cushion my fall, the chances are I'd just hurt us both.

My mind races.

I don't want to hurt her.

But then I remember her grabbing my arm in the Saferoom.

Pain is transient.

She'll survive whatever happens, even if it hurts her. But I don't *want* to hurt her.

She squeezes my hand, then approaches the edge. She looks down and promptly pales, then turns back to face me.

"Jesus. That's one hell of a drop. I don't... I don't think I can jump off this."

I don't speak. We both know she has nothing to fear from a fall of this height. Just like how she ran through literal fire to get up here, the drop will do her minimal harm. But then she rests a hand on her chest, breathing hard, and I realise she's serious.

She can't jump.

Suddenly, everything clicks.

I can't survive the fall; she can.

She can't bring herself to step off the edge; but I can. I'm unafraid of heights. Unafraid of falling.

"Alya," I croak, "stand at the edge and face me."

She looks up, her eyes wide. I stare back, hoping she understands. Right now, I want to curl up on the floor and let the fire win. I'm tired of fighting, tired of feeling. I don't have the ability to survive the fall or the willpower to try. If I were alone up here, I'd already be burning.

But if I can do this, she'll be safe. If I can push us both over the edge, she'll be okay.

If it's for her... I can find it in myself to keep fighting.

I straighten my back, step away from the flames, and tear off my ugly yellow hoodie. I toss it into the flames, exposing the bloodied bandages around my midsection. Alya's eyes widen but she remains silent, instead standing at the edge as instructed.

The smoke thickens around me as the wind picks up, kicking my hair from my face, and for a moment, the world falls eerily silent. I look up. Beyond the flames, I can see the city. Amare sits peacefully in the distance, completely unaware of the turmoil surrounding me. It's just like sitting atop Lockless House, staring out over the cityscape. Suddenly, it all falls away.

I take a deep breath and feel my shoulders drop. All tension leaves me, the fear and panic dissolving as I walk towards Alya. She sees me coming and fear flickers in her eyes – but then she lifts her arms and opens them wide, as though welcoming me into an embrace.

I walk faster. Then, I run. I can't slow down. Can't stop.

A moment's hesitation could spell disaster.

So when I heave myself into Alya's arms, pushing us both off the edge, I'm unafraid.

Twenty-Five

I hear Alya talking. Her voice is calm against a backdrop of comfortable silence, rather than the crackle of flames from before. I reach for her, unsure how long I've been asleep, but find myself barred from my body as though by an invisible wall.

"...are they saying?"

She's as patient as ever, listening to the muffled voice in polite silence.

"None of that is true. Rene's working on dispelling the rumours."

Another pause. I realise she's on the phone.

"I get that it's not ideal."

One more pause.

"Oh."

She hesitates, letting out a low sigh.

"Neil's eased off with the sedatives. With any luck, she'll wake up soon."

More distant speech, and she lets out a grunt of agreement.

"It's Reya we're talking about. I'm sure she'll be okay. But you guys should definitely visit."

I push a little harder against the mental wall, feeling my consciousness break through.

I'm tucked into bed. Someone's dressed me in PJs and braided my hair. There's a light breeze on my face, like someone's opened a window.

Slowly, I start to put things together.

Alya saved my ass again. That must be it, because I wasn't burnt to a crisp or pancaked. My chest rises and falls gently, showing no sign of the distress it was under before. How many days has it been?

A warm hand finds mine, and Alya lowers the phone. I hear a dim beep as she hangs up, then tightens her grip.

"Nova's coming to see you later," she whispers, "won't that be nice?"

Suddenly, the patience is gone from her voice. She sounds exhausted and somewhat weepy, like the stress of the past however-many days has taken its toll on her. I fight to open my eyes, but it doesn't work.

A few minutes pass, and her hand leaves mine. Soft footsteps pad from the room.

It's at least another hour before I manage to open my eyes. When I do, they're sore, like closing them was somehow blocking out the pain. I blink several times, and my vision comes clear.

The Dome sits overhead, encasing my little half-circle bedroom. I inhale, breathing in the medicinal, sterile scent that I used to hate, but which now reminds me of home. It's accompanied by a mild stink of sweat, suggesting I've been lying here for more than just a day or two.

I try to piece together what happened. I remember the roof, and Alya's words. I remember someone screaming, too – a shadowed figure thrashing in the orange flames – and block out the memory. I don't want to think about that.

Slowly, I rebuild the walls around Marcus' death. There'll be a time to deal with that, but not now. Right now, I just need to know I'm alive. I'm home. And that's more than I deserve.

Sitting up is agony, but I manage. My body lets out a cacophony of cracks as I move. I stretch my limbs in turn, wincing as when each one clicks into position. Then, once I'm sure I can move, I search my body with both hands, rubbing my head, touching my arms. Each time I expect a torrent of pain; but nothing comes. I'm perfectly fine.

There's no medical equipment in here. No heart monitor, no ventilator. No drip wired into my arm, granting me the bare minimum I need to stay alive. I can't have been out for very long if they haven't set up life support. But there's no way I should feel this good.

The door swings open, and Neil stops in his tracks. I fire him a sheepish grin.

"Morning...? I think?"

For a moment, I wonder if he'll be mad. I go through all I've done – sneaking around, lying to everyone, betraying their trust – and shrink back, half-expecting a scolding.

But then he gives a soft smile and sinks onto the bed beside me. He pushes back my hair, checks my eyes, and rests two fingers against my neck. When he pulls back, he lets out a low, satisfied grunt.

"How do you feel?"

"Actually," I mutter, "pretty good, considering I jumped off a building. How long was I out?"

"Ten days," he replies, "Alya was able to mostly cushion your fall, but I kept you sedated for a week or so just to get you through the worst of it. Though, I doubt you needed that long."

"The worst of it? I thought my body was healing."

"No. The damage to your DNA has been repaired."

"In a few days?"

He frowns.

"We can talk about this later."

"No, I want to hear this."

"Alright," he sighs, "well, the serum that Marcus was injecting into your body did the job of affecting your DNA. The more he used it, the stronger the effects of the serum became – but keeping those effects required constant application. Once we brought you back and you were no longer receiving the serum, your DNA started to slowly revert back to its natural state."

I should probably be relieved by that, but instead my stomach tightens. If he had kept me, I'd have had to undergo that treatment for the rest of my life. The thought is sickening.

"So it just... reversed itself."

"Sort of. You might still find that accelerated healing occurs randomly due to the extent of the damage, but with luck, that'll fade over the next few months. For the most part, you're back to being your normal self."

"Normal," I chuckle, "I wonder what that's like."

To my surprise, he smiles. I stare.

"*Jesus*, Neil. Did you just smile at one of my jokes? I knew it. I'm dying, aren't I?"

"You'd better not be," he remarks, "we've all been very stressed about you these past few weeks. You should have seen Rene when we told him you'd been taken. The poor man had just woken up after emergency surgery and he somehow managed to fling a chair across his hospital room. It was chaos."

I laugh. That sounds about right.

"Hey, Neil? We've never spoken this much before."

"I'm not a talkative person," he says simply.

"But you're talking to me a lot now."

His lip curls.

"I've been known to get chatty when I'm emotional."

"Huh?"

A hand finds my head, lightly ruffling my hair. When I look up, I'm surprised to see Neil smiling.

"It's good to hear your voice again, Reya."

A blush creeps across my face, and I can't hide my smile.

"T-thanks."

"Everyone's been worried about you, you know. I had to ask people to stop coming up here, since they didn't want to leave you alone to rest."

"Alya was here earlier, I think. I heard her voice."

"Was she, now? I should have known. Lately, that girl doesn't do a single thing we ask of her. Personally, I suspect it's a trait she picked up from her older sister."

"I'm sorry."

"Don't be. It's good to see Alya standing up for herself."

"She made you bring her along to Safehouse 17. I'd say that's more than just standing up for herself."

His expression falters.

"You remember that, then. What else do you remember?"

I toy with the question, not wanting to ruin the moment. He shakes his head.

"Don't worry about that right now. I'll have Sandra give you a full psych evaluation later and we'll go from there. Right now, do you want to see the others?"

"I guess so."

"You guess?"

"I'm a little nervous," I laugh, "I got kidnapped and you guys had to save me. I'm kind of ashamed."

"It's not like you didn't save us."

He leans closer, firing me a reassuring look.

"If you and Alya hadn't appeared when you did, we may have been slaughtered by the Mortalists who invaded Lockless House. Things had gotten out of control and could have easily escalated. You saved our lives, we saved yours. There's nothing owed between any of us – except, possibly, to Alya."

"Yeah," I whisper, "she's started to get a real reputation for saving people's asses, hasn't she? I suppose that'll serve her well in future."

"We can only hope. Would you like to see her?"

I puff out my chest and nod.

"Yes, I think so."

Lockless House is quiet. As Neil and I head down the hallways, I expect someone to burst from one of the rooms, or to stroll by with a clipboard in hand. But there's nothing. Just the occasional scrape on the glossy white floor; a lingering reminder of the fight that happened here.

It's hard to believe that was over two weeks ago. Two weeks ago, Alya and I stormed these corridors, desperate to save the others. And ten days ago, they stormed Safehouse 17, desperate to save me. There's something heartwarming about that.

I run a hand through my hair, which I've untied from its braids. It falls messily down my back, but this is more comfortable. Just like the soft black jeans and grey t-shirt Neil gave me to change into. I can only assume these clothes are new, since I've never seen them before and they don't seem like anything taken from Alya's wardrobe. Either way, I feel more like myself than I have in a long time.

We pause at the top of the stairs, and he offers me a hand.

"Need help?"

"I've got it."

And I do. Despite Neil watching me like a hawk, as though prepared for a sudden collapse, I take the stairs with as much natural grace as I usually do. That is to say, not much, but enough. My body feels lighter than ever as I take the stairs, even hopping down the last few.

"You seem lively," he remarks. I nod.

"I feel great."

"Good. Come on."

He steps into the main lab, and I take a deep breath before following.

The others are hard at work, but not any kind of work I've seen before. There are no tests today, it seems; everyone stands around the metal tables, using them as desks, writing up documents and comparing with one another. Rene stands at the main table, both hands spread across a blueprint of Safehouse 17. As I watch, he lifts a plastic marker and places it in the centre, close to where they found me. Alya stands beside him, pointing to various places and speaking to him in a low voice.

Neil opens his mouth to speak, but I press my finger to my lips. I step forward, sneaking up behind Alya and covering her eyes.

"Guess who?" I taunt.

I expect her to laugh and push me away. Instead, she promptly starts bawling. I pull back and she whips around to face me. Alya's weight hits me like a truck. She hugs me so hard that I topple over, pulling us both to the lab floor. I laugh. She doesn't.

"Oh, thank god you're awake!" she wails, "I didn't fully cushion your fall, and..."

"It's fine, Alya."

Her grip tightens.

"You gotta let me go," I wheeze, "I'm happy to see you, too."

She releases me, but doesn't let go of my hand. I smile at her.

"If I remember correctly," I whisper, "you saved my life again. Thank you."

"You'd have done it for me," she replies simply. Then she stands, heaving me up with her.

Suddenly hands find me, rubbing my arms, taking my hands up in theirs.

"Reya! It's so lovely to see you up and about again!"

"Everyone was very worried about you, young lady."

"That was certainly a show back there."

I nod, trying to fight the grin on my face. This feels both strange and wonderful. They're smiling. They're happy to see me. Two weeks ago, I'd thought it impossible.

"Are you feeling okay?" Sandra asks, squeezing my hand. I nod.

"Like nothing ever happened."

She smiles again, then steps aside. In fact, they all step aside. Several seconds pass before I understand why.

Rene stands motionless at the table, watching me with curious eyes. My heart sinks. Perhaps the others won't get mad at me; but nothing will hold Rene back. I prepare myself for a tongue lashing, for a firmly-worded recap of all the vile things I've done and how I betrayed everyone. I even smile, encouraging him.

"Come on, Rene. Do your worst. I deserve it."

He steps forward and I tense; then freeze as he pulls me into the tightest embrace yet. The motion is instantly nostalgic – like something from a dream – and my head is filled with the scent of him. Cleaning solution, some deceptively expensive aftershave, and far too much coffee for one man to consume. He pulls me closer.

"You really are amazing, Reya."

Tears spring readily to my eyes but I bite back on them, returning his embrace as best I can.

"Don't be too nice to me, Rene. I might cry and trust me, that'll just make everyone uncomfortable."

He pulls back, cupping my cheek in one hand.

"I've missed you these past few days," he tells me, "this place has been dull without you running around and causing trouble."

"How many times do I need to tell you?" I joke, "I don't ever plan to cause trouble. It just happens."

To my surprise, he laughs. I stare.

"If you guys are going to keep laughing at my jokes, then I'll have to assume I died and this is some weird, hyper-realistic heaven scenario where my humour is finally appreciated."

"Oh, don't worry," he chuckles, "there'll be plenty of time for negativity. Believe me, we have a lot to hash out. But let me take a moment to be happy you're still breathing, okay?"

I grin.

"Seems fair."

I glance at the blueprints spread across the table.

"What's all this?"

"You don't need to worry about that," he says quickly, "just focus on recovering."

"That's Safehouse 17."

I circle the table, leaning over the blueprint. I feel the others tense.

"What's going on?" I ask.

Rene frowns.

311

"This is some heavy stuff, Reya. I'll tell you about it another time."

"Did I... mess something up again?"

"No. No, of course not."

He glances at Neil, who shakes his head, then back at me.

"Reya, how much do you remember?"

"Why?"

"Because..."

He chews his lip for a moment before continuing.

"The media is in a frenzy, as are the police. You have to understand how this looks to outsiders; Lockless House was attacked, a staff member was killed, and you were abducted. The next thing they know, a Project Safehouse has gone up in flames following a police raid. Nobody is quite sure what to make of this."

"Let me guess," I say, "they're twisting it. Saying I attacked them, or something."

"They're trying to. But we have plenty of evidence to the contrary. Footage from the attack here, and of you being taken by force. We even have some footage from Safehouse 17. A lot was destroyed in the fire, but the footage we saved before that made it clear you weren't a willing participant in what happened."

Strange. He's not going into detail. Not mentioning the tests Marcus ran on me. Perhaps they're hoping I don't remember.

"You guys saw everything."

It's not a question. He steps closer, placing a hand on my shoulder.

"I'm so sorry we couldn't get to you sooner. That bastard messed up all our security, and without Jonah around to fix it, we were locked out."

"Of course he messed with the security. I should've seen that coming."

"About Marcus," Sandra interjects, "the fire crew found his remains. Did you..."

I whip around, fixing her with a defiant look.

"What? Did I kill him?"

She shrinks back, and I sigh.

"I tried to talk him down, but he wouldn't listen. He had me pinned, and the fire was getting worse, so I threw him off. He hit the flames and..."

Bitterness fills my throat.

"I suppose I did kill him, didn't I?"

Sandra steps up beside me, offering me a hand.

"You seem stressed. Come with me, we'll do a psych evaluation."

"Great," I joke, "do I get a percentage when I'm done? Do I get to know how crazy I am now, compared to before? Maybe I'll reach a new personal best."

Suddenly, Marcus' voice fills my head. Deflecting with humour. Predictable. I swallow my words.

"Actually," I mutter, "yeah. I could do with a session. Let's go."

Twenty-Six

      I'm sitting on the rooftop when a cool wind blows through. It kicks up my hair, momentarily blinding me, and when it eases, Amare is still there. It sprawls out below me, unaffected by the chaos consuming my thoughts. Everything that happened to me has been reduced to a headline in papers people barely read, a casual half-conversation to be had with work colleagues.

      'Did you hear about the Tomorrow Project?' they'll say, stirring their coffee. It'll be met with a small shrug, perhaps a grunt of acknowledgement or a few exchanged words.

      To them, nothing has really changed.

      To me, everything is different now.

      I give an involuntary shudder. It's cold. Briefly, I consider heading inside and getting a jacket, but decide against it. I need to be alone for a while.

      Something beeps in my pocket and I pull out my phone, switching off the alarm. Then I reach into the other pocket, grabbing one of the bottles Sandra gave me and swallowing one of the enormous pills inside. Already, I don't remember which one this is. The anti-anxiety med? The one that's meant to prevent hallucinations? It's early morning, so it's not my sleeping pill.

I turn back to the city, thinking hard.

I think of Jonah. The carefully-built walls I've erected around the grief are still there, but the others have started to mourn. Neil told me they've set a date for the funeral. The thought makes me want to vomit. I can't stand to think about it.

And then, against my will, I think of Marcus.

I believed him when he said that he had nobody. No partner, no kids. Nowhere to call home. I suppose that's his own fault; perhaps if he hadn't dedicated his entire life to revenge, he would have had those things.

As it is, though, nobody will grieve him. The only ones who knew him were the Project, the Mortalists, and me. The Project despise him and the Mortalists clearly weren't attached to him. And me?

My chest tightens.

Dear god, I'm actually sad about him dying.

In spite of myself, I remember all the times he was good to me. When he held an umbrella over me in the rain, or pulled me into an embrace as I cried, or just remembered my goddamn birthday. I know it was all manipulation. He wanted me to grow fond of him. That way, when he finally managed to sever me from the Project, he'd be the first and only person I'd trust.

Even so, it hurts. I'd been desperate for what he had offered me – so eager to accept any amount of lies, if it meant feeling loved – that even now, my heart breaks a little that at the thought he won't lie to me ever again.

"Aren't you cold?"

Rene's voice is carried by the wind. He stands at the doorway to the roof, hands in the pockets of his lab coat. The civilian clothes are gone. He looks like himself again.

"No," I mutter, "I'm okay."

"I know you're feeling better, but you should still be careful. The last thing we want is for you to get sick after everything that's happened."

"Right."

Several seconds pass in silence and then he steps closer, dropping down on the wall beside me and letting his legs hang over the side of Lockless House. I stare, surprised, but don't say anything. I just turn back to the city, allowing myself to get lost in my thoughts again.

I've been awake for a day and a half, and the world feels so different. Like there's been some massive seismic shift, but I'm the only one who feels it. I cast my mind into the future, wondering what will happen – trials, statements, prosecutions – and it's all too much. My hands tighten into fists. If a single Sponsor stays with us after this nightmare, I'll be shocked.

Rene's said we won't be homeless if that happens. We'll have to sell Lockless House and move to a backup lab, but we'll survive. If we have to. He seems confident that with all our evidence, Sponsors should remain loyal.

Even so, I can't stand to think that I've done all this. My eyes sting suddenly and I lower my head. I don't want to cry in front of Rene. That might elicit sympathy and understanding, when that's the last thing he should feel towards me.

I look up at him.

I have so much to apologise for.

Inhaling deeply, I prepare myself. This is it. The big apology. Somehow, this apology needs to make amends for 17 years of bitterness. For all the lies, all the anger. I don't quite know what I'm going to say, but I need to try.

I meet Rene's eyes, the words hanging on my tongue.

"Rene, I..."

"I'm sorry, Reya," he responds. I stare.

"Wait, no. I was about to apologise to you."

He casts his gaze over the city, suddenly contemplative.

"Over the past few days, I've been thinking about how much I've let you down over the years. All the times you needed help, and I wasn't there. I'm so sorry."

"Don't be," I snap, "I'm the one who screwed up, and you know it. I let myself be manipulated. I let them hurt you. And I..."

My breath catches, and the grief momentarily overwhelms me.

"I let him kill Jonah."

"You didn't let that happen. Nobody could have prevented that."

"I could have stopped it long before it got to that point."

"You couldn't have known what Marcus was planning."

Rene stares up at the sky and sighs.

"Although, how were you to know? We never told you what really happened with him. We were too worried that it might spark painful memories. You had nothing but fond memories of Marcus, so of course you'd trust whatever he told you. We should have explained everything from the start."

"He did tell me everything," I say, "even the awful parts. But I still went along with it."

"Why?"

I bite my lip hard. I need to say this. Even if it hurts.

"He said he loved me."

He falls silent. I push on, ignoring the building heat in my cheeks.

"He said he wanted me to be happy, and he wanted to be my family. I knew he wasn't trustworthy. On some level, I think I knew he was up to something. But I went along with it, because it was just… nice to hear someone say those things."

"Reya…"

"Pathetic, huh?" I laugh, "I really messed up."

Another pregnant pause. Then he reaches over, touching my shoulder lightly.

"Yes, you did. But so did I."

"No, you didn't. You saved me even after I betrayed you."

His lips tighten.

"I betrayed you long before you betrayed me."

And then he leans forward. His eyes are glossy again.

"A long time ago, Reya, before you were even born, I made a mistake. A simple coding error, on a very important programme."

My stomach drops.

"That was *you*?"

He gives a tearful nod.

"I don't know if I personally did it, but I failed to see it when I reviewed the code. I was still young, inexperienced and cocky to a fault. I hadn't triple checked my work. By the time I found the error, it was too late. You already existed. I'd already seen you on our screens – this little clump of cells that would one day be a person."

He rubs his face, sighing.

"I told my father, and he made me swear not to tell you. Not yet, anyway. I think he hoped you would turn out as planned regardless of my mistake. He said there was no point in upsetting you needlessly. But then he died, and everything was chaotic for a while…"

"You wanted to send me away. That's what Marcus told me."

My stomach burns with a strange mixture of anger and defeat. He frowns.

"No. I wanted to adopt you out."

"What's the difference?"

"Why do you think your name is Reya Mathis? Why Mathis, and not anything else?"

"I don't know. I've never really thought about it."

"From the day you were born, my father and I hoped you'd turn out okay. But if you didn't, if we had to try a second time, then we didn't want you to feel abandoned. So the plan was for me to adopt you. To do the legal battle, earn your humanity, and raise you as my daughter."

I gasp, my heart pounding in my chest.

"*You* wanted to adopt me?"

"Yes," he nods, "I planned to leave the Project, and raise you like a normal child, away from prying eyes. I wanted you to live a normal life. It was the very least I could have done. But then..."

"Marcus," I say hollowly. He nods.

"After we took you back from him, he threatened to return. We knew we couldn't risk you leaving Lockless House. But still, we had to move on. We had to make a new Tomorrow Girl. So we kept both of you."

I run a hand through my hair and growl.

"Why didn't you tell me any of this?!"

"How could I?" he cries, "how could I look into the eyes of a literal child and tell her that everything I ever promised her was a lie, and she wasn't going to live forever? How could I tell a child that she was going to die someday, and it was all my fault?"

At that his tears overflow, streaming down his cheeks.

"I know it was wrong not to tell you. But it was too much, Reya. I just couldn't do it."

I open my mouth to shout at him, then hesitate. He's not lying. I can tell that much. I shake my head.

"Look, I get it," I tell him, "people make mistakes. Hell, I know that better than most. But your 25-year-old fuck-up doesn't excuse what I've done. I spent years sneaking out, ruining the Project's reputation, getting into fights and screwing up your tests."

I look over at Rene, who's sniffing deeply.

"I'm sorry that I spent the last 17 years making things hard for you. Once I realised that I could get a reaction if I pissed you off, I couldn't help myself. I kept stepping up my mistakes, over and over so that we would argue."

"But you hate it when we argue."

"No," I admit, "I *love* it when we argue. It's the only time we really talk."

"We could have talked anytime."

"No, we couldn't. Not when you felt guilty and I felt desperate. God, Marcus was right. We really are dysfunctional. If I wanted your attention so badly, I could have tried earning it instead of just trying to piss you off all the time."

"I could've been more understanding," Rene adds, "it's clear you've been going through something. And not just in these past few weeks, either, but long before that. You've been crying out for help for years, and I ignored it because I was scared of where it might lead."

I heave a long sigh, burying my face in my hands. He squeezes my shoulder.

"When Marcus took you, I was terrified. I thought about all the horrible things we'd said to each other over the years. I was scared that if he killed you, one of your last experiences would be our argument. I couldn't sleep for days, I was so worried. I couldn't stand the thought of losing you."

"Why worry about me?" I chuckle, "you're a scientist, Rene. You joined the Project to create the Tomorrow Girl, that's all. You never asked for any of this. We're a business, not a family. I'm not your daughter, and you're not my dad. Even if I really wanted..."

I choke up, surprised by the tears streaming down my face. I didn't even feel them coming.

"Reya..."

I lower my head.

"Reya," he says softly, "look at me."

I obey Rene's orders for the first time in years and he cups my chin in both hands, nudging my eyes up to meet his. He fixes me with an intense look.

"I helped make you, and I helped raise you. I worry when you're in trouble and I wish we could communicate better. As far as I'm concerned, that's a standard part of parenting."

He wipes his own tears.

"You don't have to be my daughter for me to love you."

My resistance breaks and I lean into Rene's chest. He pulls me close, and this embrace is unlike our last. That one was born of relief but this one is different. This means more. Rene strokes my hair and I fight the urge to laugh.

After everything that happened, it feels weird to be this close to him. His embrace is strange and familiar, and wonderfully safe.

"Do I have to say it back?" I choke, "I don't think I can say it without losing my mind."

"Of course you don't."

"Alright. But I do, you know. Seriously."

We sit like that for several minutes, until the tears dry on my face and I stop sniffing. When I pull away he hesitates, like he's not quite ready for the embrace to end.

"What now?" I ask. He tilts his head.

"Well, there's a lot of work to do with the media..."

"Not that. I mean, what do *we* do now?"

"What do you mean?"

I gaze at the city, lost in my thoughts. If I'm being unselfish, for once, then I should leave. Whether we've made our peace or not, I still can't make up for everything I've done. My thoughtless behaviour caused all of this. Thanks to me, everything is in turmoil. People are injured. Jonah is dead. The Project itself faces an uncertain future. I chew my lip.

"I think it would be best if I left the Project."

"What?" he gasps, "why?"

"I don't think I can fix my mistakes here. The least I can do is go somewhere far away, so I don't hurt anyone else."

"And where would you go?"

"I don't know. I guess it doesn't really matter."

"You're not going anywhere. Not unless you want to."

"Huh?"

Rene adjusts his glasses and folds his hands in his lap.

"What do *you* want, Reya?"

I blink. Nobody's ever asked me that before.

"Me?"

For a moment, my mind goes blank. What *do* I want?

"Marcus' plan was horrible," Rene explains, "but there are other theories. Unlikely theories, I'll admit, but theories nonetheless. If you still want to live forever, we can try it. We can research, and test, and try to come up with a solution. I can't make any promises – it may be impossible – but we know that your body is capable of great things, given the right tweaks. If you really want this, we can try."

My mouth is suddenly dry. He's offering to fix me. To try, at the very least. In an instant, my head is filled with images; staying here, testing with Alya, facing the world as the person I was always meant to be. A long future by my sister's side.

Suddenly, it's not so appealing.

"I want..."

I smack my lips.

"I want to get my driver's licence."

Rene stares.

"You do?"

"I want to go on trips with my friends," I smile, "I want to get a job. I want to walk down the street and have nobody give a flying fuck who Reya Mathis is."

The thought makes my chest swell. I glance at Rene and to my surprise, he's smiling too.

"You want to be human," he says softly. I nod.

"Yeah. I think I do."

"Well, that's a much easier promise to make. You'll have to allow us a few weeks, perhaps a couple of months to get everything sorted, but as soon as things have settled, we'll file the paperwork to have you legally recognised as human."

"What?" I gasp, "but you always said it was too expensive."

"It was - for something you didn't seem remotely interested in. But if this is what you want – if you really want to live a normal life – then no cost is too high."

He smiles serenely.

"But I want you to know that, even if you fly off halfway around the world, your home is always here. Do you understand?"

Suddenly, all the heaviness from earlier is gone. I look at Rene – not angry, shouting Rene, but sweet, kind Rene who saved my life – and let myself smile.

"Of course."

"Well then," he says, stretching, "I had better head downstairs. I promised I'd cook a celebratory dinner for everyone tonight. I think they've earned it after all the stress we've both put them under lately, don't you think?"

He stands and heads for the door. My chest tightens.

"Rene."

He pauses, glancing back at me.

"Hmm?"

"Can I..."

My mouth feels oddly dry, like the words are fighting to stay inside. But I have to try. I want to be one of them, and part of that is taking this risk.

"Can I join you guys for dinner?"

He blinks.

"Of course you can."

Relief floods my chest and I sigh.

"Do you... want some help cooking? You're still not fully recovered, so you should take it easy."

"Do you even know how to cook?" he asks.

"Not a clue."

"Well then," he sighs, "it's about time you learned. Come on."

My heart soars as I follow him, pulling open the roof access door.

"So," I tease, "are you the type to drink wine while you cook?"

"Alcohol is banned on Project premises, remember?"

"Everything's changing," I remind him, "and if the last few years have taught me anything, it's that drinking a beer with someone is the best way to get to know them."

He rolls his eyes, but I can see his lip curl.

"I'll consider it."

Twenty-Seven

Cameras flash from every angle, and it takes all my effort to keep smiling. The crowd is gathered around the front of Lockless House. They stand where the fence stood before we ripped it down, surrounding the small podium we built for exactly this situation.

Rene stands before them, speaking calmly into a microphone.

"...And along with these amendments, we have created a new charter to ensure that the work done by the Tomorrow Project is more open and accessible. Given the aftermath of everything that happened last year, transparency is now our number one priority."

"But Mr Mathis," someone pipes up, "what about the risk to your group?"

"Most of the Mortalists involved in the attacks have now been sentenced, thanks to the excellent work of our legal team and our tendency to record everything that happens. The movement itself seems to be dying down following these strict sentences and the influx of media coverage, but we are not going to hide away. Our work is controversial and always will be. We need to respect that and encourage our detractors to learn about us in a safe and open way."

"And the danger?"

"No longer a concern. Lockless House and its subsequent Safehouses have had a full revamp with all-new security systems, along with public codes distributed to community representatives. The high level of security we have enjoyed is now available for the public to utilise in the case of city-wide emergencies."

"Where did this change come from?" someone else barks. Rene turns around, smiling at me. I fight the urge to shrink back as our eyes meet.

"After the unfortunate demise of our previous Head of Security, Reya Mathis has taken it upon herself to read up on his notes and plans. It seems our old friend had things figured out long before the rest of us did; he left us with detailed descriptions of his imagined security systems, along with his hope that The Project would someday come out of its shell and interact on a personal level with Amare's citizens."

He glances back at me.

"Since then, Reya has been advocating for the inception of Jonah's plans and finally, we're at the stage where we can proceed. I'm sure you've all seen her talking to people. This is all in an effort to demystify the Project. We have nothing to hide."

Someone asks me to step forward and I do, fighting to keep my hands from shaking. I tell myself that I've been through worse, that fighting armed gunmen is scarier than public speaking, but my whole body quakes. I'd rather take the gunman.

Despite this I step up to the podium, adjusting the hem of the blazer Sandra implored me to wear.

"Do you care to address your recent apology about public interactions?" they ask. I inhale deeply.

"Sure. Over the past few years I've been... less than friendly with people who've approached me. It's difficult to put into words how it feels to have your humanity routinely questioned, or to be attacked because of what you are. We had no choice in whether we were made or how, so it seems unjust that me and my sister should have our lives threatened over this. Even so, I have to acknowledge that my response should have been understanding, not anger. I just fuelled the fire and for that, I'm sorry."

The crowd murmurs, but I ignore it. They're still hesitant, and I don't blame them. After all, it's me preaching peace. After all the reports of my violent antics, the juxtaposition must be somewhat jarring. I remind myself that I wasn't charged with any crimes. Even Marcus' death was ruled an accident, with the media never knowing exactly how he died.

"Speaking of fire," someone asks, "care to tell us what happened last year?"

I pause. My hands are shaking again.

God, how many times have I been asked this question? They all know I was taken, tested on, and barely escaped with my life. You'd think they'd know better than to ask about it.

"I..."

An uneasy silence falls over the crowd. They want to know. Of course they do. If things were different, I'd be curious too. My stomach squirms.

"Actually..."

Rene steps in front of me, a bright smile on his face.

"We've already answered all questions relating to that incident in our Project statement, released shortly after it occurred. You can also find plenty of information publicly available through the court system, which will go far more into depth than anything we can tell you. I'd urge you all to refer to that."

I fire a grateful look at him and slink away, falling into line beside the others, who stand and watch. Alya squeezes my hand.

"You're getting better at public speaking," she breathes. I shrug.

"I didn't grow up with it like you did. It's scary as shit."

She pauses.

"They always ask intrusive questions, don't they?"

"Ah," I grin, "they can ask whatever they like, but they'll be disappointed. My life's not all that interesting these days."

On my other side, Sandra checks her watch.

"Perhaps you should go, Reya. This may take a while and you mustn't be late."

"I'm not taking a plane or anything," I remind her, "we're just heading to the Creation Show to set up for tomorrow."

"Your friends didn't attend the show last year because of everything that happened. It wouldn't be fair to repay that consideration by being late. Have you even started to pack?"

I fire her a sheepish look.

"No..."

"Honestly. How are you going to manage on your own?"

325

"It's only a couple of days and besides, you know Nova and the guys. They're plenty responsible. They'll keep me in line."

Her smile widens.

"We can only hope."

I've spread out my belongings on the table in the main lab. There's still not much here – apparently, when I was taken the others raided my room for clues, and realised how little I owned. They've bought me a new wardrobe and some other useful basics; a phone that isn't cracked, a small laptop, and a smattering of beauty items that I don't know how to use. I've turned down their offers to buy me more. This already feels like way too much.

A soft sound brushes by my ear, and I pause.

Sometimes, when I'm alone, I still hear him. A manipulative whisper, a cruel laugh. Not enough to terrify me, but enough to make my skin crawl.

Even now, I'm not sure why I hear Marcus' voice. Maybe I'm traumatised by everything he did to me. Maybe his manipulation is still in force. Another, less comfortable thought strikes me – that I hear him because I'm the one who killed him – but I silence it. Sandra's instructions fill my head. Ignore the sound. It's just a memory. My eyes swivel to a nearby stack of clothes, and find a suitable distraction.

I'm folding a pair of jeans when Rene sidles in, eyeing my suitcase curiously.

"What?" I ask. He shakes his head.

"Aren't you taking anything colourful?"

I glance at the stack of dark, Project-branded clothes and shrug.

"I like dark colours."

"I see."

I keep packing, then pause. Rene's still standing by, watching me with intrigue. A year ago, I'd have been annoyed by his attention. I'd have snapped at him, demanding to know why he's staring and what the hell he wants. Even now the urge is there, but I bite back on it.

"What's on your mind, Rene?"

"This morning, I interviewed another couple of people for the Head of Security role."

"Any luck?"

"None. It's hard enough finding anyone willing to move into a lab full time and learn how to code such advanced systems. But once people find out what happened to the job's predecessor, they suddenly have somewhere else they need to be."

I get sick of folding clothes and promptly toss the rest into the suitcase before pulling it shut.

"We're getting along okay without a Head of Security," I remark.

"For now, we are. But things are already changing. Being more transparent with Amare also means we have to be more careful. There's a lot of work to do before we can actually remove the locks from Lockless House."

"Sounds tough."

He sighs, slips off his glasses, and pinches the bridge of his nose.

"What we really need is someone who's already familiar with our systems and protocol. Someone who's got experience dealing with Mortalists and knows basic self-defence. Ideally, someone who's already proven their loyalty to the Project."

My stomach swirls. I glance at him, and he tilts his head in my direction.

"I think you know where I'm going with this, Reya."

I do. At least, I think I do. I'm just not confident enough to say it. I must stare blankly for a moment too long because he sighs.

"Look," he mutters, "the job's yours if you want it."

My heart soars; then sinks.

"I'm just about to take off with Nova and the others for a few days," I tell him, "I can't just ditch them. After everything they've done for us in the past year, I can't let them down like that."

"I wouldn't ask you to. If you accepted my offer, we'd start on your return instead. So go and have fun. Just... think about it, okay? You already know the job, and it plays into your strengths rather well. Bear in mind that you'd also receive a salary. It could be good for you."

With that he slips from the room, a small smile on his face. I watch him go, my chest tightening with a strange combination of excitement and terror.

Twenty-Eight

Spencer fires me a cheesy grin as he sweeps the suitcase from my hands, putting it into the back of the van.

"Hey!" I say, "I'm perfectly capable of doing that myself, you know."

"Oh, I'm sure you are," he teases, "but you'd probably just throw it haphazardly in there, and we still need room for people to sit in the back."

"Maybe a van wasn't the best idea for all five of us to travel in. I can bring my car as backup, if you want. I'm sure the Project won't mind."

"Oh, you mean your shiny new jeep? You don't even have a licence to drive it yet."

"I'll get around to it someday," I shrug. He messes up my hair, then lets out a barking laugh.

"After that show on the freeway, I'm surprised the Project ever let you get behind the wheel again."

"How many times do I have to tell you, that wasn't my fault! Besides, my driving wasn't too bad considering I'd just been shot."

He pokes out his tongue. I reach for it, but he pulls it back at the last second.

"I'm convinced you work best under pressure, Plastic," he winks, "you know, like fighting off a lunatic in a burning building after being experimented on."

My face burns. I've told my friends a lot more than the public knows – even the embarrassing parts. Surprisingly, they don't see me any differently. He laughs.

"Hey, take it easy. That's a sincere compliment."

"I didn't know you could give those," I smirk.

"I don't hand out compliments to just anyone, Reya. But I'd say you earned it, considering everything you've been through."

Nova steps up on my other side, looping an arm through mine.

"He's not wrong, you know," she says, "a year ago you nearly died in a fire and now you're coming to the Creation Show! Plus you managed to land us a new sponsorship from the Project. Quite the upgrade, really."

I must seem hesitant, because she squeezes my arm.

"Hey, what's up? You seem distracted."

I bite my lip, wondering if I should lie, then think better of it.

"Rene offered me the Head of Security job."

Nova's face lights up. Spencer claps me hard on the back.

"Congrats. Seems like the perfect job for you."

"He means after the show, right?" Nova asks. I nod and her face falls.

"What? You don't want it?"

"It's not that. I think it could be fun, and it seems like something that would suit me. I'd get a salary to be a bit more independent, but I could still live with my family. It's really a win win."

"Then why are you pouting?" she teases.

"I suppose it just... it still feels like Jonah's job, you know? If anyone else does it, then it seems like they'd be taking it from him. I know that sounds really stupid, but it's just how I feel."

Nova's expression falters at the sound of Jonah's name. She never met him when he was alive, but I've told her more than enough stories. She fires me a sympathetic look, but I just smile.

"It's alright."

"You really miss him, huh?"

My chest aches.

"Yeah."

Spencer frowns.

"Didn't Jonah teach you all the security Protocol, and how to fight?"

"Yeah, he did."

"Then it kind of seems like he took you under his wing for a reason."

Nova nods.

"If Jonah were alive now," she asks, "what do you think he'd tell you to do?"

At that, I hesitate. It hurts to remember his booming laugh and tough persona – but I can do it. In an instant it's like he's standing in front of me, a too-casual presence surrounded by geniuses. I imagine him eyeing up the twin's battered van, rolling his eyes at the duct tape holding the bumper on.

I imagine asking him for advice. I imagine his response, punctuated by a grin.

"Reya?"

I look at Nova.

"I think he would tell me to go for it," I say. Her face splits into a smile.

"Well then, there's your answer."

"I guess so."

She watches me for a moment longer, then glances behind me.

"Oh. It looks like we have a leaving party."

I turn around. The doors of Lockless House are open, and Project staff pour out. I step closer, confusion building.

"What's going on?"

Alya scoops my hands up in hers. She seems much older lately, though it's only been a year. She's cut her hair to chin length, and seems to have dropped the ethereal apparel. Today she wears a pale blue shirt, and dark jeans which hug her now-grown body. It saddens me, in a way, to see her grow up so fast.

"We came to see you off," she tells me with a smile.

"You didn't need to do that. I'll only be gone a couple of days."

"Even so. You haven't been away from home this long since... well, you know. I think everyone just wants to make sure you're safe."

Sandra steps up, pressing a plastic bag into my hands.

"Here are some extra meds, just in case you lose some."

I take them gratefully. Though my body was over the whole ordeal within days, my mind is entirely different. We've been reducing the doses lately, but I still need them. Even now, the nightmares bother me. But the meds dull the memories somewhat, turning them into vague blurs rather than real, painful flashbacks.

As I tuck the bag away, Sandra fixes me with a stern look.

"Don't you dare forget to take those, Reya."

"I won't."

"And call me every night for your therapy session."

"I know," I say, "seven o'clock sharp. I won't forget."

She gives a satisfied grin.

"Oh, you should also take this."

She presses a wad of paper into my hand. I recognise it instantly.

"Do I need copies of the court papers?"

"While the case is ongoing, you should use this as your ID. Once your human status is granted, we'll get you a passport or something. For now, it's up to you if you want strangers to know who you are."

I tighten my grip on the paper, feeling it crinkle under my fingers.

"I'm not planning to tell them, if I have any choice."

She doesn't respond, just tilts her head and walks away. Rene approaches, scratching the back of his head awkwardly.

"Hey, Rene." I grin.

"Are you sure about this?"

I roll my eyes.

"I've got this, Rene. I can take care of myself."

I wonder why I keep telling everyone this. It's not like I haven't tried and failed to 'take care of myself' at least once in the past year. But I still feel the need to say it. I shrug.

"Besides, even if I screw up somehow, I'm with Nova and the guys. You know they won't let anything happen to me."

"Mortalists still exist, Reya. They're quieter now, but they haven't gone away entirely. They never will."

"I know how to deal with them," I say calmly, "don't worry so much."

"I know you can handle a fight, but you're not... let's just say, you're not a people person."

I raise an eyebrow.

"You really think I'm going to piss someone off so badly they try and kill me?"

He grimaces and I sigh.

"Well, it's not like it'd be the first time. I'll try not to make any enemies, alright?"

"Make sure you don't. Call us if anything happens, okay? We'll come running."

"Same thing here. If you need me…"

"We'll let you know immediately."

"Good. Now, we'd better head out. We only have a few hours until we need to be at the convention centre. I tried telling Spencer that I should drive and we'd get there in half the time, but apparently it's illegal to drive without a valid licence when you're trying to become human. Who'd have thought it?"

I laugh, and he returns it softly. As I turn to leave, however, he clears his throat.

"Ahem."

"Oh, right."

And I hug him, wrapping my arms tightly around his shoulders. He responds in kind, twisting one hand in my hair. I inhale his scent, which is now only too familiar – cleaning solution, fancy aftershave, and a revolting amount of coffee – and pull away.

"Take care, Rene."

He simply smiles. I reach out and ruffle Alya's hair. She follows up with a quick hug.

"Stay safe," she whispers. I chuckle.

"Shame you couldn't join us."

"We have a meeting with a new Sponsor tomorrow," she sighs, "or I'd have loved to."

"Charm the pants off them, and you can come with us next year," I tell her.

And then I'm waving, clambering into the car beside Spencer. He fires me a curious look.

"You alright? You look like you're about to cry."

"Nah," I chuckle, wiping my face, "I'm fine."

Nova pokes her head into the front seat.

"Are we good to go, or is Reya still crying like a baby?"

I give her a light shove.

"Oh, shut it. All okay back there?"

I peer into the back, where Charlie and Spencer's latest boyfriend are already buckled in, leaning on the stacked suitcases. Behind them, Nova's precious platform.

Spencer taps my shoulder.

"You're our navigator, remember? What exit do we need on the freeway?"

"Oh, right."

I pull out the enormous map Neil gave me, unfolding it as best I can, and promptly cut my finger on the edge of the page.

"Fuck."

"Don't bleed on the upholstery," Nova teases.

I wipe the blood on my jeans and tell Spencer the first leg of the journey. As the engine rumbles beneath us I tuck the map away, staring at the passenger side mirror. Watching home disappear over the horizon.

My chest aches.

"Hey, is your hand okay?" Nova asks me. I glance down at the cut, at the blood pooling on the tip of my finger, and for some reason, it pleases me.

This will take days to heal. Maybe longer, if I'm not careful with it. No 13 second rule. No close study of my refractory period. Just a papercut on a human hand.

It'd be easy to dwell on my mortality, now that it's set in stone. But honestly, that's the least of my worries. I've already wasted far too much time worrying about what I'm not. It's finally time to enjoy what I *am*, and every last filthy, funny, imperfect part of being human.

So instead I reach over, slap Spencer's hand away from the radio, and crank up the volume.